Little Pink Taxi

Marie Laval

Where heroes are like chocolate – irresistible!
www.choc-lit.com

Acknowledgements

I would like to thank my family for their support, and my lovely daughter in particular, for her patience and encouragements as I mulled over the plot for *Little Pink Taxi* in our favourite local café over too many cups of black coffee (for me) and glasses of apple juice (for her). She may not be old enough to read the story yet, but just by listening to my ramblings she helped me see things more clearly.

I would also like to thank Choc Lit for believing in *Little Pink Taxi* and my brilliant editor for her wonderful advice and suggestions.

Thank you also to the Tasting Panel who read this book and passed it for publication: Elaina J, Sigi, Jo L, Hilary B, Margaret M, Isobel J, Jenny M, Jo O, Catherine L, Rachel D, Caroline U, Elaine R and Alma H.

Merci beaucoup!

Chapter One

'I believe you're waiting for me. I'm Petersen.'

Startled by the deep voice with the hint of a French accent, Rosalie spun round, and tilted her face up to meet a pair of serious grey eyes.

'Welcome to Scotland, Monsieur Petersen.' She gave him what she hoped was her most dazzling smile, but Petersen only looked down at her and said, 'I was expecting McBride.'

Rosalie tucked the heart-shaped board on which she'd written Petersen's name in pink under her arm. 'I'm afraid Geoff was taken ill. I shall be driving you to Raventhorn.'

Petersen frowned. 'I'm sorry to hear that. I hope it's nothing serious.'

It was nothing that a cup of tea, a couple of headache tablets and a few days away from the malt whisky wouldn't cure, but Rosalie couldn't tell him that.

'A head cold, that's all. He will have recovered by this evening, I'm sure.' Her cheeks grew warm. Lying had never come easily to her, but it was even harder when a giant of a man with eyes as cool and uninviting as the winter sky stared down at her.

She pointed at his leather holdall and laptop case. 'Would you like me to carry your bags to the cab?'

Arching his eyebrows, he gave her a sardonic stare, which made her feel even smaller than her five foot one. 'No. I don't think so.'

'Ah. Very well. Shall we go then? The weather is horrendous today. At least I found a space near the terminal so we won't get too wet.' Her last words were drowned in gusts of icy wind and rain as the terminal sliding doors opened. She pulled her key fob out of her pocket and strode towards the cab. 'Here we are.'

'Is this McBride's idea of a joke?' Droplets of rain clung to Petersen's dark blond hair and the broad shoulders of his navy coat. He gestured to the bright pink metrocab on which Love Taxis was painted in large letters, then to her matching anorak.

'I hope you're not planning to take your clothes off and squirt whipping cream all over me.' Although his voice was quiet, there was a steely edge to it that made his French accent more pronounced.

She started to laugh. 'Take my clothes off, in this weather? No thank you! You don't seriously think I am one of those strip-o-grams people hire to embarrass their colleagues at birthday parties, do you?'

He didn't smile. No spark of humour lit his eyes. He'd meant what he'd said. The laughter died on her lips, and she pulled the zip of her pink anorak right up to her chin.

'You have the wrong idea about me. I'm your taxi driver, nothing else. And for the record, the only way I like my whipping cream is on a chocolate brownie or a very large ice-cream.'

Although she tried to sound blasé, her face felt like it was on fire and she stumbled over the last words. 'Now I suggest you put your bags in the boot and get in before we both get soaked. You'll have to sit in the front.' She gestured towards the boxes piled up in the back. They were filled with bottles of Geoff's favourite whisky, which she had just picked up from a distillery on the outskirts of Inverness – not that Geoff would get to sample any soon, if she had any say in the matter. He had drunk more than enough whisky the night before.

Without giving Petersen the chance to reply, she opened the door of the taxi and slid behind the wheel. How dare the unpleasant man mistake her for a strip-o-gram! She glanced in the rear-view mirror. In his conservative coat and suit, his laptop case in one hand, the leather holdall in the other, he looked every inch the stuck-up, pompous businessman as he put his bags in the boot. What could he possibly be coming to Raventhorn for?

He opened the passenger door and sat next to her, and immediately the cab felt small and crowded. Sliding the car park ticket between her teeth, Rosalie started the engine, but as she pulled the handbrake down, her hand brushed against his leg and the contact gave her such a jolt she took her foot off the accelerator pedal. The cab stalled, they jerked backwards and the whisky bottles rattled in the boxes at the back.

Flustered, she turned the key in the ignition to start the engine again. She was still in reverse gear and the taxi shot out of the parking space, narrowly missing a Mercedes coupé behind them. There was the screeching noise of tyres as the Mercedes braked, followed by loud, insistent beeping, and the cab stalled once more.

Petersen stared at her. Rosalie opened her mouth to apologise. The parking ticket dropped to the floor and landed near the gearbox. Both she and Petersen leaned forward to pick it up and banged their heads together.

'Ouch. Sorry.' She rubbed her forehead and forced a giggle even though she felt so mortified she could cry. 'I hope I didn't hurt you. People do say I'm hard-headed.'

He handed her the ticket. 'I played scrumhalf for my school rugby team and have worked in finance for the past twelve years. I am used to bumping into much harder heads than yours, Miss … ahem …'

'Heart … Rosalie Heart.'

He pointed to the gearbox. 'It's not your head I'm bothered about. It's your driving.'

'There's nothing wrong with my driving!'

He arched an eyebrow, but said nothing. Much as she hated to admit it, he had a point. Stalling the cab – twice – and narrowly avoiding a crash before even getting out of the car park didn't exactly show off her driving skills. It was all his fault, of course. If he wasn't so unpleasant, she wouldn't have got so flustered.

Swallowing her hurt pride, she started the engine again, and this time they left the airport car park without incident. Heavy rain drummed down on the roof and bounced off the bonnet. Even though they swished at full speed, the wipers couldn't clear the windscreen fast enough. It was only mid-afternoon, but already the sky was darkening and Rosalie had to focus hard on the grey ribbon of the road.

As they drove south towards Aviemore and the ominous outline of the Cairngorms, Rosalie cast sidelong glances towards her passenger, and wondered, once again, who he was and what he was coming to Raventhorn for. Geoff had never mentioned him, so he couldn't be a friend. He didn't look like one of his eccentric academic contacts either, and even less like a nature lover coming to hike in the mountains. That left business … Her chest tightened. What was Geoff up to this time? Would she have to rescue him from yet another of his far-fetched schemes? She'd better find out, and fast.

'What brings you to Raventhorn, Monsieur Petersen?'

'Your very pink taxi,' he answered, concentrating on the road ahead.

'Yes. Of course.' She took a deep breath. She would not admit defeat so quickly. 'Is it your first time in the Scottish Highlands?'

He nodded, but remained silent.

3

'And how was your flight?'

'Fine.'

She shuddered. 'Personally, being stuck in some tin machine high up in the clouds is my idea of a nightmare. I have never, and never will, travel in an aeroplane.'

This time he did turn to look at her. 'What if you had to travel long distance – to the States or Australia, for example?'

'I have no desire to go that far away, ever. Anyway, how did you meet Geoff? The only place he travelled to recently was Orkney, and I'm quite sure he has never mentioned your name before.'

'I haven't actually met him yet.'

'Really? But ...' She frowned. 'You said you worked in finance?'

Perhaps Geoff was considering investing on the stock market. The only problem was that there was no money to invest. Even paying Raventhorn's utility bills was a struggle these days.

Petersen's eyes turned even more frosty. 'I don't mean to be rude, Miss Heart, but I make it a rule never to discuss my personal affairs with bar attendants or taxi drivers.'

She tilted her chin up. 'I'm not any old taxi driver. I am a very close friend of Geoff's. In fact, you could say I'm almost family.'

He didn't reply and an uneasy silence filled the cab. Since Marc Petersen showed no inclination to talk, Rosalie switched on the radio, which was tuned to her favourite Happy Baby station, and started singing along to a catchy tune.

Marc leaned his elbow against the door. The headache that had plagued him since leaving London was getting worse, not helped by the music and the woman's awful singing. Perhaps he was suffering from an overdose of pink. He clenched his jaw and drew in an impatient breath. This trip to Scotland had been a spur of the moment decision – one he was already regretting.

The day before he'd never even heard of Raventhorn Castle, the ancestral seat of the McBride family. It had been pure chance that he'd walked into Maguire's office and spotted the file on his colleague's desk, together with photos of an imposing stone castle facing a loch, and with a forest and the ragged peaks of the Cairngorms in the background. He had studied the photos and the accompanying note from the lawyers in the firm's conveyance department with a mixture of frustration and incredulity. The past six weeks since his father's fatal helicopter crash in Hong Kong had been an endless stream of meetings with lawyers and accountants, business associates and bank managers. He had thought most of the paperwork regarding business matters was now sorted. It seemed he'd been wrong and there were still a few surprises in store. Raventhorn being one of them.

An idea had formed in his mind as he walked back to his office on the tenth floor of Petersen Holdings' London headquarters. What if he went to Scotland himself? He could do with a few days away, and he would be doing Maguire a favour at the same time. The man had mentioned a special wedding anniversary he was planning for his wife who was suffering from a chronic heart condition.

Yesterday, it had seemed like a good idea. Now, however, he had a throbbing headache and was being driven in a ridiculous pink taxi by a tone-deaf woman who didn't seem to know, or care, that she was a menace on the road.

They drove into a forest and the tall pine trees sucked in the last of the daylight.

'Corby Woods,' Rosalie Heart announced, in a loud, upbeat voice above the music. 'Not far now.'

There was no traffic. In fact, they hadn't met anyone since the last village, about five miles back. He pulled his phone out of his coat pocket, switched it on and checked for a signal. There was none.

He shoved it back into his pocket and looked up, just in time to see a woman dressed in a long, brownish cloak by the side of the road. Tears – or was it rain? – ran down her pale face. She lifted a hand in a pleading gesture as the taxi drove past.

'Stop the cab,' Marc ordered. 'I think that woman needs help.'

Rosalie Heart slowed down. 'What woman?'

'There was a woman, back there. She waved at us, she seemed upset.'

'I didn't see anyone. It must have been a tree stump.'

'I can tell the difference between a woman in a hooded cloak and a tree,' he snapped. 'Now, please do as I say and stop the cab.'

She shrugged. 'Very well. There's no need to be grumpy.'

He flung the door open and climbed out into the rain, but in the dim, blue grey light all he could see was the forest, and all he could hear was the tree branches swishing in the wind.

Oblivious to the rain running down his face and soaking his hair and coat, he walked back along the road and cut through the undergrowth towards the pine tree where the woman had been standing. A huge raven, perched on a nearby treetop, stared down at him with beady eyes. The woman, however, had gone.

Puzzled, he peered through the shadows and walked into the woods. If there was a path, he couldn't see it. He breathed in mixed scents of rain and rotting vegetation. Above him the raven flew off with a shrieking call and a loud flapping of wings.

'Monsieur Petersen? Are you all right?' Rosalie Heart called from the road. She had put her hood up so as not to get drenched.

He turned and walked back to her. 'She's gone, and yet I was sure she needed help.'

Rosalie Heart smiled. 'If it was who I think it was, she does indeed need help, but not of the kind you, or anyone of us, can give her.'

'What are you talking about?'

She sighed. 'Forget it. You won't believe me.'

'Try me.'

She took a deep breath. 'You just saw the ghost of Isobel McBride.'

He narrowed his eyes, and dug his fists into his coat pocket. His shoes were soaked and muddy. Icy water trickled down his face, his neck and the collar of his coat. He had the migraine from hell. And this small woman dressed in marshmallow pink was babbling about ghosts?

'Are you serious?' he asked, between clenched teeth.

She nodded, turned away and walked back to the cab, leaving him behind. The woman was making fun of him, that much was obvious. He followed her back to the taxi, slung the door open and sat down. His wet clothes stuck to the pink plastic seat with squelching sounds. Water dripped from his coat and trousers and pooled at his feet. The windows steamed up, and it was like being enclosed in a cosy bubble of gum.

Rosalie Heart pulled her hood off and shook her curly brown hair. As it tumbled around her shoulders he caught the scent of the rain and a deeper, fruity fragrance. She smiled again, and he couldn't help but notice she had a very attractive smile indeed. In fact, he thought, looking at her properly for the first time, she was rather pretty with her eyes a

6

warm chestnut colour, and her cheeks glowing pink from the cold.

'It's a long time since anyone reported seeing Lady Fitheach,' she remarked in a thoughtful voice as she started the engine.

'Lady Fitheach? I thought you said her name was Isobel McBride.'

'Fitheach is Scottish for raven. People call Isobel Lady Fitheach because of the raven that never leaves her side. You saw the bird, didn't you?'

There had indeed been that huge raven staring down at him from a nearby branch. He dismissed it with a shrug. 'It's a wood. There's bound to be all kinds of birds there.'

She gasped. 'So you did see it! When I tell everybody at the Stag's Head you'll be so famous you won't have to pay for a single pint for the duration of your stay.'

'There's nothing to tell. It was a rambler, that's all.'

He probably would be the talk of the local pub before long, but it wouldn't be because of Isobel McBride's ghost – or whoever had been standing by the side of that forest road.

'It was Isobel,' she insisted. 'You said she had a hooded cloak, didn't you? That's what she always wears. Actually that's *all* she ever wears. Apparently she is stark naked underneath.'

He sighed, impatient. Did the woman actually believe this nonsense? 'I don't believe in ghosts. It was a hiker, or some new age hippy … or some Isobel McBride ghost impersonator.'

She burst out laughing. 'Now you're being funny.' She glanced at him and grimaced. 'No, you're not … Anyway, I hope you don't see her again.'

'Why?'

'Men who see her more than once usually end up drowned in the loch.'

He shook his head. This had to be the silliest conversation he'd ever had. 'They probably had too much to drink.'

'Well, that too.' She reached out to switch the radio back on.

'No.' His sharp voice stopped her in her tracks. 'No music, no singing, and no more talking.'

She glanced at him in surprise. 'Don't you like music?'

'I like civilised music, not what you've been playing.'

'And what do you call *civilised* music, Monsieur Petersen? No! Let me guess. You like classical music and jazz, am I right?'

He looked surprised. 'How did you know?'

Rosalie almost replied that it was what pompous, arrogant people called civilised music, but instead she bit her lip and said nothing. Until she knew who exactly Petersen was, and what he wanted, it was wise not to antagonise him.

He reclined against the headrest and closed his eyes, making it clear he didn't wish to speak again. He wanted silence? Fine. She'd give him silence. She had better things to do than make conversation with an arrogant French businessman – or was he Scandinavian? It was hard to decide, because though he had a slight French accent, his name was unmistakably Nordic.

The rain and wind had eased by the time she turned off the main road onto the castle track. The taxi rumbled over the potholes, and splashed in deep puddles. She slowed down to a crawl to drive across the old bridge over the Filly, wondering once again if it would last the winter.

The imposing grey mass of Raventhorn Castle, with its four towers and pointed turrets, its slate roof and tall chimneys, appeared at the end of the lane. With only a few lights shining from windows on the ground floor, it looked forlorn and full of secrets and, as usual, it took Rosalie's breath away. It was the most beautiful place in the world. It was the only place she'd ever called home.

'Raventhorn,' she announced as she parked in the courtyard.

Petersen opened his eyes, and looked around.

'I'm afraid we'll have to use the kitchen entrance. We rarely use the front door.'

'Do you live here?'

'I told you, I'm practically family. I'll give you the grand tour later, if you're interested.'

His hand on the door handle, he looked at her, deadly serious.

'Of course I'm interested. I own the place.'

Chapter Two

Lorna came rushing out of the kitchen before Rosalie could ask Marc Petersen what he meant.

'At last you're back.' Lorna's eyes were red, her face blotchy. Something – or someone – had upset her, and from experience, Rosalie could guess just who that someone was.

'What has Geoff done now?' she asked.

'He crashed the Porsche on the loch road,' Lorna announced in a strangled voice. 'But don't worry, he wasn't badly hurt.'

'He went out? But he was in no fit state to drive!'

Disbelief and anger twisted Rosalie's stomach in a tight knot. Geoff had drunk himself into a stupor the night before and she'd had to pull him up the stairs and push him into bed. It had been sheer luck that she'd spotted his diary on the bedside table with the scribbled note about collecting Marc Petersen from the airport today.

'He asked for you as soon as he woke up,' Lorna said, 'and when I told him you'd left to pick up his whisky, then collect his guest from the airport, he became very agitated and said he had to catch up with you.'

Rosalie let out an impatient sigh. 'Did you say he was hurt?'

'He only suffered a few cuts and bruises. The silly man hitchhiked a lift home with a gritting lorry. He wanted to wait for you here but I insisted he went to the hospital, so Niall took him after arranging for the Porsche to be towed to the garage. They left about half an hour ago.'

'Why didn't you wait for me to take him to the hospital?'

Lorna wiped her hands on her apron. 'Geoff said you should stay and make Mr Petersen feel at home.'

'At home?' Rosalie glared at Petersen. He stared back, impenetrable, oblivious to the icy wind ruffling his dark blond hair and the icy raindrops pelting his face and coat.

'What you said before,' she started in a more hesitant voice, 'surely it's not true. You haven't—'

'Bought Raventhorn?' he finished. 'I did, or rather my father did.'

'What?' Lorna looked at them in turn, and lifted a hand to her chest. Her face turned a sickly shade of grey and she crumpled on herself.

'Lorna!' Rosalie rushed to her side but Petersen was faster. He

9

scooped Lorna into his arms before she collapsed onto the wet cobbles.

Holding the unconscious woman against him, he turned to Rosalie. 'Where shall I take her?'

'The drawing room. Follow me.'

She led the way through the kitchen and up the stone staircase that led to the ground floor, and pushed open the door to the drawing room. Petersen lay Lorna down on the battered leather sofa in front of the ornate fireplace, where a fire was lit.

Kneeling down beside the couch, Rosalie stroked Lorna's hair. How pale and frail her friend looked. Surely these white streaks were new, as were the deep lines around her mouth and the dark, hollow shadows under her eyes.

Blinking away the tears, Rosalie jumped to her feet. 'I'll get some water.' She ran down to the kitchen, her thoughts all over the place. What was wrong with Lorna? She was never ill, but she was getting older and perhaps taking care of Raventhorn, and Geoff, was taking its toll. Unless the shock of hearing Petersen's ludicrous claim about Raventhorn had caused her to faint. Yes, that must be it. Her hand was shaking so much as she carried the glass back she spilled half the water on the stairs.

By the time she made it back to the drawing room, Lorna had opened her eyes, and Petersen was helping her to sit up and pushing a cushion behind her to support her back. He moved away when Rosalie approached.

'Here, have some water.' Rosalie held the glass to Lorna's lips. 'How are you feeling now?'

'I'll be all right, don't worry.' But Lorna's voice was weak and her face still ashen.

Rosalie turned to Petersen. 'It's your fault. You gave her a shock with this nonsense about buying Raventhorn. You can't have bought Raventhorn. One, it's not for sale. Two, only a McBride can own the estate, and you're French ... or Swedish or—'

A cold smile stretched his lips. 'Half-French, half-Danish, actually, but that's irrelevant. Who says only a McBride can own this place?'

'That's the way it's always been.'

'Then I guess things just changed.'

Lorna looked at Petersen. 'You were speaking the truth, weren't you?'

He nodded.

She heaved a sigh. 'So Geoff finally did it. He sold Raventhorn.'

Rosalie recoiled in shock. 'I don't believe this. Are you saying that it's all true, and that you knew about it and never said a word to me?'

'I knew he was thinking about it.'

Rosalie shook her head. It had to be a misunderstanding, a dreadful mistake. For now, however, the priority was to take Lorna home and make sure she had a rest.

'We'll talk about it later. I'll drive you home, if you feel up to it.'

Lorna shook her head. 'I can't leave just yet. What about Mr Petersen? Supper isn't quite ready and Geoff could be at the hospital for hours yet.'

'I'll deal with dinner,' Rosalie said, 'and I'll wait here for Geoff to come home. It's Duncan's shift this evening, so I'm free.'

Lorna looked anxious. 'You're not going to cause any trouble, are you? Geoff isn't a well man, and with the accident and ...' she gestured towards Marc Petersen '... everything else, he is bound to feel a bit stressed.'

Rosalie almost stamped her foot in anger. Geoff was stressed? He should damn well be stressed if he'd been keeping a secret like selling Raventhorn from her!

'Don't worry, I shall be very gentle with him,' she lied. She turned to Petersen. 'I'll show you to your room now, unless you prefer to wait for me here.'

'Would you like some help taking your friend home?' he asked.

Although she was pleasantly surprised by his offer, her reaction was instinctive. 'No, thanks, we'll be fine. The lodge is less than a mile down the lane.'

'In that case, I'll get my bags out of the cab and work in here,' he said, walking to the door.

'Now I understand why Geoff was so moody these past few weeks,' Lorna said as soon as he'd left. 'Going ahead with the sale must have been traumatic for him.'

'Petersen has it all wrong.' Panic made Rosalie's voice rise. 'He doesn't own Raventhorn. He can't own Raventhorn. Geoff probably cooked up another of his grand schemes, which never amount to anything, or he made enquiries about raising some capital. It will all blow over, you'll see.'

Lorna pulled a doubtful face. 'I'd better cancel my holiday,' she said.

'You will do no such thing. You've been planning this break at your sister's for months. You have your train ticket, your suitcase is packed and Margaret is waiting for you. You are going even if I have to drive you to Norwich myself.'

'What about Geoff?'

'I'll look after him, and I can promise he won't get near a single drop of whisky while you're away.' She'd look after Geoff all right. She would start by asking him what all this nonsense about selling Raventhorn was about.

'What if Petersen wants to see the housekeeping accounts, conduct an inventory of the castle, or talk about the wedding bookings?' Lorna objected. 'We don't have any this side of Christmas, but he might want to look at the books.'

'I can help with that.'

She looked at Lorna and swallowed hard. She couldn't help the bitterness in her voice. 'I can't believe you kept it to yourself that Geoff wanted to sell Raventhorn. I hope there's nothing else you have omitted to tell me.'

Lorna closed her eyes, silent seconds ticked by.

'No, sweetie, of course there isn't,' she whispered at last.

It must have started raining hard again because when Petersen walked back into the drawing room with his bags, his hair was so wet it was almost dark and water dripped from his coat onto the parquet flooring.

He took off his coat, draped it over the back of a chair and loosened his tie. 'I took the boxes out of your cab and piled them up in the utility. I thought Lorna might prefer to lie down on the back seat.'

Rosalie was once again surprised by his thoughtfulness. She nodded and helped Lorna to her feet. 'Thank you. We'd better go.'

He may be in the middle of nowhere, but at least there was wifi and a mobile phone signal at the castle. He checked his voicemail, answered a few emails, and started working on his spreadsheets, but staring at the screen only made his headache worse, so he closed the lid of the laptop and reclined in his chair.

It was odd to be alone in the castle with night closing in, rain and wind beating against the windows, and flames dancing in the fireplace. He breathed in scents of wax polish and wood smoke that didn't quite cover the damp, musty smells pervading the old house. He glanced around the room.

Oak panels and dark green paper covered the walls, together with paintings of gloomy landscapes and hunting scenes. Faded green velvet drapes framed the tall windows, and a couple of frayed, faded rugs stretched over well-worn parquet flooring. The décor was a far cry from the sleek, modern apartment he owned in Paris, and the one he'd just moved into in London, where he'd relocated to take care of his father's affairs.

It didn't matter that he wasn't keen on Raventhorn's interior. He didn't intend to spend more than a week or so here, just long enough to look at the accounts and put the place up for sale. As usual, it would be surgical, efficient and successful. Like his father, he had become infamous for his cold, ruthless business ethics. Hadn't *Newsweek* run an article about the two of them a few months before, entitled, 'Slash, burn … and prosper. Are Petersen and Son the Vikings of International Finance?'

His father only boasted of his Danish roots when it suited him, and being compared to a merciless Norseman flattered his ego. There had been a time when Marc would have been proud to be tarred with the same brush. Not any more. These past few months had changed that.

His throat suddenly too tight, he got up, added a couple of logs to the fire and poked at it until flames rose again, bright and tall.

A half-full whisky decanter and sparkling crystal tumblers on a silver tray attracted his attention. He lifted the cut-glass top and breathed in. Single malt. Wasn't that supposed to cure all evils, from colds and arthritis to a broken heart and a guilty conscience? He would need more than a carafe of whisky to assuage *his* guilty conscience. He poured himself a generous measure, sipped the fiery amber liquid and walked to the window. A pair of headlights shone through the darkness. Rosalie Heart was coming back.

She had it all worked out. She wouldn't let her temper get the better of her this time. She would be charming, ply Marc Petersen with fine wine and good food and find out exactly what was going on.

Unfortunately she had to wait to confront Geoff. She had rung the hospital from Lorna's lodge, and the nurse had said that the doctors were keeping Geoff in overnight for observation, that he'd been given a sedative and was already asleep.

She ran up to the drawing room, and forgot all her good intentions the moment she saw Petersen standing in front of the fireplace, a glass of Geoff's best whisky in his hand.

'I see you made yourself at home.'

He looked at the crystal tumbler in his hand and nodded. 'I have a headache. I thought it might help. I should have waited for you. Sorry.'

Now he made her feel petty as well as rude. His cool grey eyes skimmed over her. Self-conscious, she pulled on her pink jumper to cover her hips.

'Geoff won't be coming home tonight,' she told him. 'The doctors are worried about his blood pressure, so I'm afraid you'll have to deal with me until he comes home.'

He drank a sip of whisky. 'I thought you were a taxi driver. Why should I deal with you?'

'Because Raventhorn is where I grew up and where I've lived most of my life. Because my mother was Geoff's best friend and personal secretary for years. And because I know everything there is to know about the place.'

'Yet you had no idea McBride had sold the estate.'

He was right, but she wasn't going to admit it. 'A misunderstanding, that's all.'

'Doesn't McBride employ a secretary or estate manager I could talk to?'

'Not any more. We had someone, but he left months ago. Now there's only Lorna, who takes care of all cooking and housekeeping duties, a cleaning lady who comes twice a week, and a few daily helps if we have visitors or honeymooners.'

'I see.' He put his glass on the tray. 'Why don't you give me that tour of the castle you promised earlier?'

'I don't have time now. I have to make dinner, but I can show you to

14

your room.'

The Crimson Room was the room reserved for paying guests and newly-weds, and one of the few boasting an en suite. It was also Rosalie's least favourite room. She found the four-poster bed cumbersome with its oak posts and red velvet drapes. The red wallpaper, matching curtains and counterpane made the room dark and oppressive. A walnut desk near the window, a tallboy and an old creaking wardrobe completed the décor.

The room may not be to her taste but she would cut off her tongue rather than admit it. Lorna worked hard to keep everything looking pristine with the measly housekeeping money Geoff gave her.

She switched on the light, walked to the window and pulled the curtains shut. 'The room overlooks Loch Bran. It's very picturesque and I'm sure you will enjoy the view tomorrow morning.'

She touched the antique radiator under the bow window. It was lukewarm, as usual. 'There are logs in the basket if you fancy making a fire. If not, just turn up the radiator. It's a bit temperamental but should heat up. Eventually.'

He looked around, clearly unimpressed. 'It's rather old-fashioned.'

'Old-fashioned?' she cried out, instantly forgetting that she'd always disliked the room. 'Every single piece of furniture is steeped in history. The chest of drawers and the wardrobe are Queen Anne. These oil paintings over there are originals by George Blackie Sticks and Edwin Landseer.'

'Hmm … What happened to the bed?' He pointed to the markings on the posts. 'These dents look like they were made by claws.'

She shrugged. 'There were made by knives.'

'Really? Why was that?'

Her face hot, she turned round and busied herself rearranging the cushions on the bed.

'Has there been some kind of accident?' he prompted.

Rosalie sighed. 'No … That bed is special. Most of the McBrides since the late fifteenth century, as well as countless babies from surrounding villages, were conceived here.'

'So there's a notch for every baby.' He faced her, hands pushed deep in his trouser pockets, eyebrows arched.

She cleared her throat. 'Sort of. Do you remember Isobel McBride, the woman you saw in Corby Woods tonight? Well, she had some old wizard cast a spell on the bed before her nuptials to make sure her betrothed could ...' She swallowed hard.

'Could?'

She fussed over the cushions again. 'Perform.'

'Ah.' He smiled, but it was so brief she thought she'd imagined it.

'Over the years, this bed has proved a steady source of income for the McBrides. Any man whose virility was in need of a little ... push could bring his wife here for a fee – a jar of whisky, a brace of pheasants, a good-sized salmon. Every mark on the bedposts represents a successful night.'

She rearranged the cushions for the third time. 'When he inherited the castle from his uncle, Geoff carried on with the tradition. We organise weddings here now, and people come a long way to ... ahem ... stay, in this bed.'

'I'd be curious to read how you phrase your adverts,' he said.

Was it her imagination or were his lips twitching again?

'We don't need to advertise. In fact, Geoff doesn't do any advertising. He can't stand the press, and never allows photographers on the grounds. We get most of our guests from word of mouth.'

She gasped as a thought crossed her mind. 'I hope you're not offended Lorna gave you this room. It's not at all because she thought you needed ... you know ... extra help with ...'

She closed her eyes and took a deep breath. She was making a mess of this. 'What I mean is that you were given this room because it has an en suite and the view over the loch is stunning, that's all.'

She opened her eyes and found him looking at her, deadly serious. Oh no, he *was* offended.

'The bathroom is through there,' she said quickly, pointing at the door in the corner of the room. 'You'll have to be patient with the shower, it's a little unreliable. Now, I'll let you get settled, and start on supper.'

He put his leather holdall on the bed. 'You don't have to cook anything special for me. A salad or soup and a sandwich will be more than enough.'

'It's no trouble, really. Lorna prepared everything already. All I have to do is switch the oven on.' And even *she* could manage that.

She was acutely aware of his gaze following her as she walked out and couldn't hold back a sigh of relief when she closed the door. Pressing her hands against her hot cheeks, she ran down the main staircase to the ground floor, then down the service stairs to the kitchen.

She put the potato gratin and the venison stew in the oven, then laid out slices of smoked salmon on a platter together with buttered wholemeal bread and slices of lemon. Finally she uncorked a bottle of white wine and another of red. Hopefully the food and the wine would make him amenable and help him forget her faux pas about the bed.

She piled up plates, cutlery and glasses on a tray, ready to take up to the dining room. The elegant oak-panelled room always impressed guests.

'Can we not eat here?' Petersen's voice made her jump.

'We never entertain guests in the kitchen,' she objected.

He had changed into a pair of jeans and a long-sleeved dark grey jumper that made his shoulders look even broader than his coat and suit. He must have conquered the shower because his hair was damp and she breathed in the faint scent of lemon soap as he came closer.

He sat at the table and poured some white wine out into the glasses. 'I'm not a guest, remember?'

She tightened her mouth. 'So you say.'

He held out a glass for her. She took it, her resolutions to be patient all but forgotten. 'Can you at least tell me if the sale has been completed? Did you buy the whole estate or just the castle? What about the furniture and the artwork? There are many valuable paintings, hundreds of old books in the library, and lots of personal possessions.'

Not to mention her mother's things, the memories, the laughter, and the echo of voices from the past.

'I'm sorry,' he interrupted coldly, 'I can't discuss any of McBride's business with you. It would be unprofessional.' He lifted his glass. *'Santé.'*

Her anger flared again. 'I do have a right to know what's going on. I told you before, this is where I grew up, and where I live and where—'

He pointed to the oven behind her. 'Something's burning.'

She turned and her heart sank as clouds of smoke billowed out of the glass door. 'Oh no!' She slipped her hands into oven gloves before pulling out the gratin and the stew.

17

'I might as well throw everything in the bin right now.' She shook her head in disgust at the charred food. Lorna had probably spent hours preparing tonight's meal and she'd ruined it. What's more, there went her cunning plan to soften Petersen up with good food.

'It's only a few burned potatoes,' he said, 'and I'm hungry.'

She looked up. 'Are you sure?'

'Positive. Shall we have the starter?'

They sat down and helped themselves to slices of smoked salmon. Rosalie nibbled at her food, drank a little wine and watched as he ate. The man had spoken the truth. He was hungry. He devoured most of the salmon and buttered bread in a few minutes.

'How long have you been a taxi driver?' he asked, when he had finished.

'Four years next spring.'

'That long? I wouldn't think it was the kind of job anyone would enjoy doing for any length of time, especially a young woman.'

She stiffened. 'It's a great job, the best job I've ever had, in fact – not that I've had many – and the only one I want.'

'What's with your boss's pink obsession?'

'I beg your pardon?'

He smiled. It was a real smile this time. It warmed his eyes and softened the angles of his face. 'Why does your boss insist on you dressing like a giant marshmallow and driving a pink taxi?'

She narrowed her eyes and put her glass carefully on the pine table.

'I happen to like pink very much.'

His shoulders lifted in a dismissive shrug. 'Nobody can like being around that much pink. And that name, Love Taxis, must make your life very difficult. I suspect you must get a lot of nuisance calls.'

She took hold of her fork and gripped the handle so hard her knuckles went white. 'For your information I don't have a boss. *I* run Love Taxis. The colour and the name were my idea.' Much as she hated having to explain herself, she carried on. 'I wanted to make people smile, bring a little cheer and happiness around here.'

Petersen swirled the pale gold wine in his glass. 'Pink for Rosalie, and Love for Heart. I get it.' He looked up. 'So you run the business? I'm sorry, I didn't realise. How many drivers do you have?'

'One full-time, Duncan, plus me. I hire an extra driver during the tourist season.'

'Does Duncan have to wear baby pink too?'

She shrugged. 'Of course not. Any pink will do.'

He reclined on his chair and looked at the woman in front of him. Something was niggling at him – something about Rosalie Heart's cab company.

She stood up and collected the empty platter. 'Will you try the stew and the gratin now?'

'Sure.'

She proceeded to place the two steaming hot dishes on the table, and started piling dried up meat and charred potatoes onto his plate. When it was as high as a molehill, he held his hand up.

'I think that will do. Thank you.'

'You said you were hungry and I need to get rid of the evidence. If Lorna sees the food in the bin, she'll know I burnt it and she'll be upset.'

'I promise I won't tell her.' He bit into the meat, winced, then tried the potato gratin. It was dry and topped by a layer of cheese as tough as rubber, but he soldiered on.

'I noticed you had an office in the stable block,' he said, after a few mouthfuls.

'That's right. When Geoff lent me the money to start up my business four years ago, he had the stable block renovated for me.' Rosalie smiled. 'He lets me have the stable block free of charge, both for my office and a living space upstairs.'

She chewed on her food for a minute and carried on. 'To tell the truth, I don't often use the flat. I usually stay here, in my old room. I don't really use the office either since Love Taxis' main office is in Irlwick. It's where the switchboard is, you see, and where my two part-time operators, Fiona and Fergus, work. That building belongs to the estate too. Geoff is the most generous man I've ever met. I only repay him what I can, when I can. Without him, I certainly couldn't carry on.'

'So Geoff – or rather, the Raventhorn estate – owns a share in Love Taxis?'

She shook her head. 'Not a share. The lot! I haven't managed to repay him very much so far.'

He studied her across the table. So he'd been right. Things were getting complicated.

She looked at him, narrowed her eyes. 'Why are you so interested in my cab company?'

He didn't answer but followed the play of emotions in her eyes as the truth dawned on her.

Chapter Three

'Now you've bought the estate,' she said, 'you also own Love Taxis, and you will close me down if I can't repay my loan.'

'That's right.' Of course he would close her down, whether she could repay the loan or not. That's what he was here for. To put the estate in order and sell up what could be sold for a profit. The sooner he told her, the sooner she had time to get used to the idea.

'Oh. I see.' Rosalie stood up, and crossed her arms. 'What exactly are you, Mr Petersen?'

'*Pardon?*' Her question shot straight to his heart and he spoke French without thinking. He'd asked himself that very same question far too often recently.

'I mean, what business are you in?'

He took a few moments to consider his answer. 'Buying and selling property, mainly. My father and I buy failing businesses, factories, department stores, hotels ...' Realising he was talking about his father in the present tense, he stopped and reached out for his glass.

He drank a sip of wine and carried on. 'If we can, we turn them round before selling them on. If we can't, we close them down and strip their assets.'

'To make money.'

'Of course.'

'Why Raventhorn Castle? It's not a business.'

'I wasn't party to the original deal with McBride, so I don't know what attracted my father to this place,' he conceded, 'but I guess the potential for a hotel and holiday complex could make this place very attractive to investors.'

She gasped. 'A holiday complex, here?'

He nodded.

'You said you worked with your father, so yours is a family firm.'

'It was at first. Then it grew.' *The truth was that it had grown far too big these past few years.*

'Is it a successful business?'

'It is.'

'Then why should you care about Raventhorn? Can you not forget about us for a few months, give us time to work things out?'

She looked at him. Her eyes were a deep, warm chocolate, so beguiling his mind went blank for a second.

He cleared his throat. 'It's too late for that. The sale went through last week, and, believe me, McBride got a very generous price.'

More than generous, in fact. Raventhorn had been vastly overpriced for a rundown estate, even if it included a castle, a wood and a loch, as well as a few acres of moorland – and now it seemed a pink taxi firm and a magic bed. According to the conveyance lawyers, his father had also shown unprecedented generosity in granting McBride's wish to remain on the premises until the New Year.

Rosalie got up and started pacing the floor. 'I don't just run a taxi business, you know. I help people. There are hardly any buses left around here – normal buses, not tourist ones. Thanks to my cabs, people can go to the doctor when they're sick, to the supermarket for their weekly shopping. They can meet their friends at the toddler group, at the pub or the ceilidh.'

'You make it sound like you're running a community service.'

Her face lit up. 'That's it exactly! Love Taxis is a community service. I don't even charge proper fares because most people couldn't afford them.'

'That is no way to run a business. No wonder you can't repay your loan.'

'There's more to life than balance sheets and fat bank accounts. There's helping people, belonging to a community, looking after your friends and family. If you don't understand that, then despite all your money, you and your father lead a very sad life.'

Her words swirled and echoed around him, inside him.

He looked at her and said quietly, 'My father died in a helicopter accident a few weeks ago. In fact, purchasing Raventhorn must have been one of the very last business deals he made.'

Her face drained of all colour, she lifted her hand to her mouth. 'Oh, I'm so sorry. I had no idea.'

The phone started ringing in the hall upstairs.

'I'll get that,' she said, before hurrying out of the kitchen.

He finished his glass of wine and thought about what she'd just said. He didn't know what it meant to belong. He'd been brought up by a succession of nannies, then sent to boarding school in England when he was five. After that, he had studied at a top university in the States and at one of Paris's 'Grandes Ecoles'. Even though he'd managed the Petersen office in Paris for the past twelve years and enjoyed living in the French capital, he'd never felt at home there, or anywhere else, either. He closed his eyes.

No, that wasn't totally true. There was one place where he'd once felt at home. On his grandfather's farm, on the windswept North Jutland coast of Denmark, in a past so distant it often felt as unreal as a dream.

He grabbed hold of the bottle of wine and the two glasses before going after her. It was a shame about Rosalie's taxi business but it couldn't be helped. His job wasn't to sort out the mess McBride had made of his finances, but to make a profit for Petersen and Son.

She slammed the phone down and walked into the drawing room. It was another call from an annoying call centre – at least she supposed it was, since nobody ever talked at the other end. It was happening more and more often, so often that Geoff had recently decreed they wouldn't answer the landline any longer.

She paced the floor of the drawing room, but what she really wanted to do was scream in frustration. When would she learn to think things through before opening her mouth? By insulting Petersen and his father just then, she had probably ruined any chance of saving her business. She had also been terribly insensitive. Marc Petersen's grief would still be raw, and she had unwillingly added to it with her thoughtless words.

She turned to the door when she heard his footsteps in the corridor. He placed their glasses and the bottle of wine on a small table and faced her. The reflection of the flames from the fire danced in his eyes. He didn't look angry or upset at all.

She took a deep breath and stepped towards him.

'I'm sorry for what I said earlier. It was wrong of me. I shouldn't be so judgemental of the way you run your life, or your business. And I am sorry about your father. You must be terribly sad.'

'Don't worry about it.'

Surprised by the calmness of his tone, she looked up. His face was composed, his eyes cold and devoid of any emotion.

'McBride really should have told you about the sale. He should also have made sure your taxi business was safe and all transactions conducted above board.' He paused. 'You should warn your staff about redundancies.'

She gasped. 'No, I can't tell them anything just yet!'

She moved away to stare at the flames in the fireplace. The reality of what was happening suddenly hit her. It wasn't only the locals who relied on her. She had responsibilities towards her staff too. Duncan, her driver, had two young sons to support and his wife Brenda, who worked Saturdays at the bakery in Irlwick. Her two switchboard operators needed the income she provided too. Fiona was a talented, but struggling, artist, and Fergus hardly managed to scrape a living with what she was paying him on top of his pension. His wife Marion was Raventhorn's cleaner, so they could both be out of a job soon.

How could an outsider like Petersen understand how important Love Taxis was around here? If only he could see her at work ...

She drew in a breath. Of course! There was the solution.

'Come with me tomorrow,' she said.

He shook his head, looking shocked. 'No, I don't think so.'

'Give me just one day. You can't do much here anyway since Geoff is in hospital.'

He sighed. 'Spending the day with you wouldn't influence my decision. I only take figures and accounts into consideration when I examine a business's viability.'

She put her hand on his forearm, gazed into his cool grey eyes. 'Please. I want to show you what I do, how vital my cab service is for Irlwick.'

He tensed under touch. 'Miss Heart, I don't think you understand. Your taxi firm isn't what my company is about, no matter how important you feel it is. I would never consider investing in something so ...' He frowned, seemingly lost for words.

'Small? Insignificant?' she offered. 'It may be small on paper, but it's invaluable for our town.' Her fingers squeezed his forearm. She felt his muscles tense again and heat rise from his body.

'Just one day,' she insisted, fluttering her eyelashes in a last attempt to sway him. If that didn't move him, she'd shed a tear or two.

He gave her one of his cold stares. 'Please spare me your feminine wiles, Miss Heart, and don't even think about crying. It won't work on me.'

How did he guess what she'd planned to do? So everything was lost, just like that. Her home, her business, her whole life ... Very real tears now blurred her vision and pearled at the corner of her eyes.

He drew in a breath, and shrugged. 'Oh, all right. I really don't know why I'm agreeing to this. I'll come with you for the day.'

She sighed with relief. 'Thank you. Thursdays are always busy, with the toddler group in the morning and the dance at the Four Winds Hotel in the evening. You'll be impressed when you see what we do, how we help local people, and how—'

'Don't get carried away. It won't change my mind.'

His voice had grown deeper. His eyes turned a mesmerising dark grey, the colour of Bran Loch under a stormy sky.

Just as the thought of thunder and lightning crossed her mind, the electric bulbs flickered and went off with loud popping sounds. The glow from the fire cast shivering shadows on Petersen's face and made him look rugged and untamed – a far cry from the conservative businessman she'd collected at the airport, and from the man who showed no emotion at the mention of the father he'd only just lost.

The fire crackled in the hearth, the wind howled outside and rain pounded against the windows. Petersen gazed down at her and her pulse started to race. An invisible force pulled her towards him, closer and closer until she felt she was falling.

A discreet ringtone startled her and she jerked back. As if on cue, the electricity flashed back on. He retrieved his mobile from his trouser pocket, and checked the screen. 'Sorry, I need to take this.'

He pressed the answer button. 'Good evening, Fizpatrick. I was expecting to hear from you sooner.' He walked to the window, the frown creasing his forehead getting deeper as he talked about missed deadlines, accounts and bank balances.

Her face still hot, her throat dry and her breath shaky, Rosalie walked to the fireplace, grabbed hold of the poker and prodded the logs. What on earth had just happened? Physical attraction, sudden, powerful and electrifying, that was what. The kind of physical attraction she'd never experienced before, but that could, according to her friend Alice's late night confessions, make you lose your head, your self-respect, and most of your clothing.

Disgusted with herself, she gave the log a hard jab. How could she even for one moment be attracted to Petersen? She disliked everything he stood for. He wanted Raventhorn, not because he had fallen in love with its history or its beauty, but because it would yield a profit. In the process he would put her out of business and throw Lorna out of her home without a second's hesitation. He would also put her staff out of work, and without her taxi, village life would never be the same again.

Petersen was still on the phone. He sounded angry now, but like everything about him it was a cold, flat, restrained anger. 'When we agreed the terms, you never mentioned you had doubts regarding your ability to fulfil your side of the contract. I don't care if you spent twenty years building up your company, Fitzpatrick. The fact is, it belongs to me now. You have until Saturday to sort this mess out.'

There was a pause. 'Don't waste your breath. I said Saturday. After that, I'm stepping in.'

Rosalie's blood ran cold. If she needed confirmation of Petersen's character, that was it. She put the poker back on the rack, and turned to face Petersen. 'I'm leaving now.'

She would sleep in her flat tonight. She didn't fancy the idea of being alone with Petersen in the castle.

Still frowning, he slipped his phone back into his pocket. 'Why are there no live-in staff at Raventhorn? That's unusual for a place this size.'

'We like to keep the manor to ourselves ... although we're never really on our own.'

He arched an eyebrow. 'What do you mean?'

'I don't know if I should mention this just before bedtime, but you did say you didn't believe in ghosts.'

She paused for effect, and was rewarded by the puzzled look on his face. 'You see, we have our regular night-time visitors, here at Raventhorn. There's Dughall McBride hopping about on his peg leg. He was the captain on a ship that was lost at sea sometime in the seventeenth century. There's Old Finghall, who was slain by the McGunn clan and plays his bagpipes when the mood takes him. Then there's Morag McBride who cries for the return of her man from Culloden. And Lady Isobel, of course.'

'Really? Any other ghost I should worry about?' He didn't sound scared or worried at all.

'No, that's it. Most of our residents are harmless, if a little noisy at times. All except Isobel, of course. Not only does she take men to their death in the loch, but she is also known to play tricks with the lights and the doors. Actually, I wouldn't be surprised if it was her switching the electricity on and off earlier.'

She made a show of checking her watch. 'It's late, and I bid you good night.'

He smiled, and humour sparkled in his eyes. 'So having told me that the place is riddled with ghosts, you are now abandoning me?'

'That's right. If you get too scared, you can always knock on my door. It's the blue one, across the courtyard.'

That would teach him to be mean to that poor man on the phone, and to upset her life. Between the howling wind, the creaking wardrobe in the Crimson Room and her silly ghost stories, Marc Petersen probably wouldn't sleep a wink.

'Lorna will cook your breakfast at half past seven. Our shift starts at eight thirty. I wish you sweet dreams.'

The shrill ringing of the phone interrupted her. 'Not again!' Much as she wanted to ignore it, she couldn't. It could be Lorna calling because she was feeling unwell, or the hospital with news about Geoff.

It wasn't Lorna, or the hospital.

'Rosalie, lass,' said a deep male voice at the other end of the line.

'Fergus?' Rosalie frowned. 'You sound upset. What's up?'

'I'm afraid Duncan's had a bit of bother,' her switchboard operator answered.

Rosalie's fingers gripped the phone harder. 'What kind of bother? Has he had an accident?'

'Kind of ... Don't worry, he's fine. His cab isn't, though.'

'What happened?'

'He had a pick up at the Duke's in Kingussie. When his client didn't show up, he went inside to see if he could find him. He had no luck, so he went back out, only to find that the cab's windscreen had been smashed.'

Rosalie exhaled slowly. 'All right. I'm going to the Duke's right now to talk to him.'

'There's no need. He notified the police and phoned Niall who arranged to have the cab towed back to the garage. He said he'd fix the windscreen tomorrow.'

'Where is Duncan now?'

'Brenda came to collect him. He wanted to call you but I said I'd do it, and that he should go home. He told the police about the other incidents too,' Fergus added, 'and they're on their way to talk to you.'

Guilt tightened Rosalie's chest. There had been a lot of prank calls these past few weeks. Perhaps she should have called the police before. She asked Fergus if there were any more bookings for the evening, but he said that there weren't, so she told him to lock up and go home.

'Problem?' Marc asked.

Yes, two, and you're one of them, she almost retorted. Instead she put the phone down and nodded. 'My taxi driver has had his cab's windscreen smashed.'

Petersen frowned. 'Was he injured?'

'Thankfully, no, but the police are on their way to talk to me.'

They only had to wait half an hour for the police to arrive.

The two officers didn't believe that robbery was the motive for the attack on Duncan's cab.

'He left his takings inside the car when he went into the Duke's, and it was all there when he came back. So it was probably an act of random vandalism. However,' one of the officers said, turning to Rosalie, 'we have been told that you've have a few incidents recently.'

'They weren't really incidents as such,' she protested. 'They were only prank calls. All taxi drivers get them.'

'Can you give us any details?' he insisted.

She shrugged. 'It's nothing, really … Last Sunday night, for example, I was called to Loch Morlich, but there was nobody there. Then again on Monday afternoon, I drove all the way to Laggan but the client never showed up, and later that day the same thing happened at Loch Insh Nature Reserve. It really annoyed me because I wasted over two hours driving for nothing. Yesterday evening I went to Carrbridge Trekking Centre …'

She shivered, recalling how frightened she'd been in the deserted car park. 'It was closed for the winter, and no one was waiting for me there either, so I didn't hang about.' She didn't add that the sensation of someone lurking in the shadows, watching her, had given her goosebumps. Luckily Niall had turned up in his tow truck just as she'd been about to leave. He'd been on his way back from a call-out when he'd spotted her in the empty car park. She'd been so happy to see him she'd given him a big hug before he'd insisted on escorting her back to Irlwick.

'Duncan told us he's been getting similar calls these past few weeks,' the policeman remarked. 'The calls may be unrelated to tonight's incident but you should keep a log from now on, and contact us if you are worried in any way.' He closed his notepad, slipped it back into his pocket and he and his colleague took their leave.

Rosalie watched the red tail lights of the police car disappear into the night. 'Lorna will be devastated when she finds out the taxi was vandalised. She might even want to postpone her trip to Norwich.'

There would be another, unwelcome consequence. Niall would propose again. Rosalie's shoulders sagged. Her world had been turned upside down in the space of one evening. The only place she'd ever called home now belonged to a stranger. Geoff, the man she loved like a father, had betrayed her and Lorna. And Love Taxis was as good as finished …

Chapter Four

'How is Duncan?' Niall leaned against the door of his tow truck and dug his hands into the pockets of his oil-stained work overalls.

'Shaken, and blaming himself for what happened. I spoke to him after the police had been to see me last night.'

'Do the cops have any leads on what happened to the cab?'

Rosalie shook her head. 'Not yet. There's no CCTV at the Duke's and you know how packed and noisy it is in the evenings. Nobody saw or heard anything. I still can't believe anyone smashed Duncan's cab on purpose.'

'I told you what I thought about your taxi driving a long time ago. It's not a safe occupation, especially for a girl as bonnie as you.'

'I'm not exactly a girl any more, Niall.' She sighed as a lump formed in her throat. She knew exactly what he would say next. Sure enough, he stepped closer.

'You know what I mean … and you know how I feel about you. You used to feel the same, not so long ago.'

'Niall, please. It's over. It's been over for years.'

'It could still work.'

He raised his hands to touch her cheek but she shied away. 'Don't! You have oil on your hands,' she added quickly, when hurt flashed in his blue eyes.

He looked down and sighed. 'Sorry. Any news from Geoff?'

'The doctors are keeping him in for observation. He was lucky he wasn't badly hurt.'

Niall rubbed his chin. 'The Porsche is in a bad way. It's a shame. I only serviced it recently and advertised it in a vintage cars auction in Edinburgh. Now I'm going to have to withdraw it from the catalogue.'

Surprise made Rosalie gasp. 'What? Geoff is selling the Porsche?'

Niall nodded.

'But it was always his favourite car! I thought he would never part with it.' Then again, she could not imagine that he would ever sell Raventhorn.

'Either he needs money, or he wants another car.' Niall opened the door to his truck. 'Anyway, I'd better get back. I left Kian to open the garage but I have rather a lot of work today.'

She pulled a face. 'Kian Armitage? Can you trust him with customers?'

'Why do you say that?' He frowned and looked worried all of a sudden.

'I don't know. I find him sullen, borderline unpleasant. But perhaps it's just me he's like that with. I remember his mother used to snarl at Mum and me because we lived here with Geoff, their "ancestral enemy".' She drew quotation marks in the air with her fingers. 'His dad even picked a fight with Geoff one St Andrew's night when he'd had too much to drink and shouted all kinds of horrible things at him.'

'Aye. It's the old clan rivalry between the McBrides and the Armitages. I believe there's been quite a bit of trouble between the families over the years, but it's all over now, and Kian's all right.'

'Of course he is. Forget I said anything.'

'Duncan's windscreen will be ready later this afternoon. He can come to the garage to pick the cab up.'

She stood on her tiptoes and pecked a kiss on his cheek. 'Thanks for that, and for coming here this morning to check I was all right. You're my hero. I don't know what I'd do without you.'

'No worries.' His face flushed with pleasure, he climbed into his truck and started the engine. 'By the way, who's the big guy in the kitchen with Lorna? A tourist?'

'Kind of.' She was unwilling to lie, yet reluctant to tell him the truth. Until Geoff explained why he had sold Raventhorn, nobody needed to know who Petersen was. There was something else too. It may be cowardly of her, but as long as nobody knew the truth, she could pretend nothing had changed.

She waved goodbye to Niall and went into the kitchen.

'Poor sweetie, come here,' Lorna said as soon as she walked in. She enfolded her in her arms, and Rosalie breathed in the comforting scent of her lily of the valley cologne, the same she'd worn the day Rosalie had arrived at Raventhorn, clutching her mother's hand, exhausted after a long train journey, and in awe of the beautiful castle and its dashing blond and blue-eyed laird.

Lorna released her and turned to the stove where a plate was warming up.

'Eat your breakfast now,' she said, placing the plate of crisp bacon rashers and golden pancakes on the table. 'Mr Petersen said he was going out with you today. Is that right?' Her eyes shone with curiosity.

Rosalie nodded.

'Isn't that a bit strange?'

'Perhaps he is fulfilling a childhood fantasy. Don't boys always dream about driving a police car or a fire engine?' Rosalie stirred two spoonfuls of sugar into her tea. Lorna didn't need to know that she might have to shut down Love Taxis. Not yet anyway. 'But enough about Petersen,' she said before Lorna could ask any more questions. 'You still look pale this morning. Are you sure you're feeling all right? I could take you to the doctor's later.'

'I'm fine, love. Don't worry about me.'

'Are you going to see Geoff today?'

'I have to say goodbye since I won't be here for the next three weeks.' Lorna hesitated. 'I wish you could come with me, sweetie. He wants to talk to you.'

'I fully intend to see him and ask what exactly is going on, but I'm fully booked today.' Plus today she had to convince Petersen that he should keep Love Taxis open for business.

She drained her cup of tea, finished the last bite of pancake and stood up. 'I'll wait for Petersen in the cab,' she said as she slipped her pink anorak on. It was time to make a start.

'The toddler group is called Little Angels,' Rosalie explained as Petersen returned to the passenger seat after helping a young mother fold her buggy up. She waved when Rosalie set off, but he hardly glanced her way. In fact she even wondered why she bothered to smile at him so much since he'd hardly said a word during the short journey.

'Seriously?' he asked.

She nodded.

'There is nothing angelic about the children you have had in your cab,' he said in a cool voice. 'They have done nothing but scream and yell.'

Rosalie cast him a sideways glance. 'That's because they know it's the best way to get what they want, and you must admit that it worked, even with you.'

One of the toddlers had taken a fancy to Petersen's scarf and he had let him play with it to keep him quiet.

'I suppose so.' Petersen wrapped around his neck the scarf he had managed to prize from the toddler's sticky fingers after a brief tug-of-war.

'So what's next?' he asked. 'Don't tell me we have to ferry any more screaming babies.'

'Not until half eleven. Now it's time for the Stitch and Bitch group.'

'Sorry?'

'The local knitting group or "Knit and Natter", as they are formally known,' she explained. 'They are a gathering of self-righteous women who delight in spreading malicious gossip. Elaine McBride is the self-appointed president of this small, but powerful, female gathering. She is also Geoff's cousin by marriage – and together with her son, the last of the McBrides. As such she expects to inherit Raventhorn, the ancestral seat of the McBride clan – a fact she makes sure none of us forgets, even for a second.'

Rosalie parked in front of Elaine's large detached house. Elaine immediately came out of her front door. She hooked her handbag on her arm, pulled up the collar of her cashmere coat, and smoothed her short hair with her gloved hand. She looked immaculate, as usual.

Marc got out to open the back door. 'Thank you, Mr ...' she frowned at him enquiringly.

'Petersen. Marc Petersen,' he finished with a curt nod.

Elaine sat down and tapped a finger on her watch. 'You're late again, Rosalie. I've been waiting for over five minutes.' The woman's voice was so acidic it could have melted holes in the cab's bodywork. Rosalie muttered an apology and started the engine.

'I heard about Geoff's accident,' Elaine said. 'It was bound to happen sooner or later, the way the foolish man drives. He is getting too old for that Porsche. I'll tell him to give it to Rupert next time I see him.'

Her face hot with indignation, Rosalie turned to glare at Elaine. 'How can you be so callous? Geoff is in hospital and all you're thinking about is what Rupert can get out of him.'

'Watch what you're doing, you silly girl!' Elaine screeched and pointed a finger to the windscreen just as a car changed lanes and sneaked in front of the cab. Rosalie slammed on the brakes, narrowly avoiding ramming into it.

'I see Geoff isn't the only one who drives like a lunatic,' Elaine spat.

Rosalie glanced at Marc, waiting for him to remark on her bad driving again. 'Sorry.'

She was pale and her eyes glistened with tears. She bit her lower lip but he could see it was trembling.

'There's no harm done,' he replied, suddenly reluctant to add to her distress by siding with Elaine McBride and pointing out that she should indeed watch the road instead of turning round to talk to customers. 'Where are we going now?'

'To the old church hall, at the other end of town.'

From what he had seen so far, Irlwick was a nice little place, built around a steep hill on top of which stood a ruined castle. As they had driven in from Raventhorn earlier, Rosalie had explained that it was the original McBride castle, fallen into disrepair after years of vicious wars between the McBride and the Armitage clans. 'There are a few items of furniture from those days at Raventhorn – the wardrobe and the bed in the Crimson Room, for example.'

Rosalie's cheeks had turned as pink as her anorak and he had almost groaned aloud. He'd hardly slept a wink the night before, and it hadn't been because of nightmarish images of his father's helicopter crash for once, but because of hot, vivid and erotic dreams. Every time he had managed to fall asleep he had dreamt he was making love to a woman. Who she was, he had no idea since he never saw her face, but the sensations awakened by the feel of her mouth and hands caressing him, and of her body moving under his as he took her, had been so real he'd woken up time and time again, tense with longing and frustration. In the end he'd given up trying to sleep and pulled a copy of the *Financial Times* out of his bag, hoping that it would cool him down. It hadn't. Perhaps there was some truth in her stories about the magic McBride bed after all.

When Rosalie stopped in front of the church's timber porch, he got out and opened the back door for Elaine once again.

The woman frowned. 'You're not from round here, are you?' she asked.

'Marc is from London,' Rosalie shouted from inside the cab before he could reply. 'He's training to be a cab driver so I've taken him on as my apprentice. I'll see you at twelve, Elaine. Get in, Petersen. Hurry, we don't have all day.'

He gritted his teeth but did as he was told.

'So now I'm your apprentice?' he asked as she drove on.

'It was the only explanation I could think of off the top of my head.'

'What about the truth?'

She drove around narrow, cobblestone streets for a few minutes and parked in front of a small terraced house, then turned to him. 'We can't tell anyone just yet, not until I've spoken to Geoff and he has explained what's happened.'

'There's nothing to explain. He needed money, he sold Raventhorn, that's all.'

'I'm sure there's more to it. Please. It's only until I have a chance to talk to him.'

He was about to tell her he wasn't here to play games when a ray of sunlight touched her face. He noticed for the first time the ring of warm hazel green around her chestnut coloured pupils. She parted her lips and he caught a glimpse of pearly white teeth. His pulse beat faster, his chest felt suddenly tight and he swallowed hard. Once again, the woman was having a strange effect on him.

'All right,' he conceded before taking the time to think things through. 'I'm your apprentice. For now. By the way, what's the story between you and Elaine McBride? You don't seem to like each other very much.'

Rosalie sneered. 'You're right there. Elaine always thought she was better than everybody else – my mother, in particular – and her darling son Rupert has made my life a misery since primary school. All she ever talks about is how he will one day become Raventhorn's rightful laird.'

He took a deep breath. So there were yet more complications to come. McBride's relatives were bound to feel aggrieved when they found out they wouldn't inherit Raventhorn.

Rosalie beeped the cab's horn. White muslin curtains twitched at a ground floor window in the terraced house. A few moments later an elderly woman with tightly curled mauve hair came out. Once again,

Marc jumped out to open the back passenger door.

'Good morning, Flora,' Rosalie called.

'Good mornin', Rosalie love. And who's this nice young man ye've here with ye today?' She beamed a smile at him as he helped her sit down.

Rosalie explained that Marc was a trainee cab driver, and the old woman looked at him appraisingly.

'Ye're big and strong, for sure,' she said. 'Ye'll push my trolley and carry my bags, and give Rosalie a rest, won't ye, love?'

He smiled politely, thinking that she was joking. She wasn't.

Rosalie drove to the local supermarket, and gestured for him to get a trolley and push it around the aisles while she fetched food items the old lady called out from her shopping list. They packed the bags at the till, drove back to her house where they unloaded the shopping and put everything away in her tiny kitchen, while she brewed a cup of tea so strong it was almost black and cut out slices of Battenberg cake. Flora must have been impressed by his services because she winked at him as she gave him an extra thick slice of cake.

'Don't tell me you do that every week,' he said, once they were back in the taxi.

'I do the same for most of my elderly clients,' she replied.

'But that's a complete waste of your time.'

'It's part of my job. Flora has nobody to help her and—'

'You're not a social worker, you run a taxi firm. A business. We spent almost an hour with her and the fare she paid hardly covered the petrol for the journey to the supermarket and back. Talking about fares, apart from Flora just now, I haven't seen any money change hands so far. Your meter doesn't even work.' He pointed to the meter she hardly bothered to switch on these days.

She shot him an angry glance. 'I should have known you were keeping tabs. If you must know, most of my clients have accounts.'

'Ah. And how often do they settle?'

'Every month ... or so. When times are hard, I give them a wee bit more time to pay.'

He shook his head. 'This is no way to run a business.'

She looked straight into his eyes. 'I told you, Love Taxis isn't just a business. It's—'

'A service for the community, yes, you already said.'

They were back at the community centre where they picked up the mothers and their cranky, smelly and paint-covered offspring, who left behind a dirty and mutilated teddy bear and a bubble tube topped with a one-eared plastic rabbit.

'I'll drop the toys off at their house later, if I have time,' Rosalie said as she slipped them into the glovebox.

Then it was time to collect Elaine from the knitting group and drive her home.

'You never said Duncan had some trouble last night,' Elaine complained as soon as she had made herself comfortable in the back seat.

Rosalie sighed. 'Who told you?'

'Julia Murray. It was her day off from the library and she wanted my advice on a new jumper she's knitting for Niall. She said he was very upset about the whole thing.'

Marc remembered that Niall Murray was the mechanic who had paid Rosalie a visit earlier that morning. Elaine carried on talking but he didn't pay much attention to what she was saying until she mentioned Rosalie and Niall getting married.

'Julia says it's cruel of you to keep the lad waiting. You've made his life a misery for years.'

'That's not true!' Rosalie snapped. 'Anyway, what business is it of hers, or yours?'

'We only want to see you settled,' Elaine replied. 'Niall may not be the brightest tool in the box, but he's a nice lad, he runs his own business, and let's face it, you're not likely to get a better offer, are you?'

Rosalie gripped the steering wheel so hard her fingers became white, her whole body seemed to tense up and her chin jutted forward, but she didn't answer.

'By the way,' Elaine added, 'Rupert is back from London. He wants to talk to Geoff about a new business idea.'

'I hope he isn't going to pester him for more money.'

They were back in front of Elaine's house.

'So what if he is?' Elaine said as she got out. 'Geoff helped you set up your taxi business. It's only fair he should do the same for my

Rupert. He is his heir, after all.' She shut the door and walked away without waiting for Rosalie's reply.

By late morning Marc was hungry, gasping for black coffee and getting more cross by the second. He checked his watch. Only half twelve. Why on earth had he agreed to waste a day driving around in this pink taxi?

He knew exactly why. Guilt, coupled with the pleading look in Rosalie's brown eyes, the flutter of her long eyelashes and the soft touch of her fingers on his arm. That was why.

Rosalie cast him a sidelong glance and turned off the irritating pop radio she'd been humming along to most of the morning and parked in front of a small café in the main street.

'You must be hungry. We have about an hour before the pensioners' clinic, so I'll take you for lunch. I hope you have nothing against vegetarian food.'

'The pensioners' clinic?' He repeated, gritting his teeth. *How bad could the day get?*

Rosalie nodded. 'I pick up elderly people from out of town and drive them to the surgery for their weekly check-up.' They sat down at a table covered with a red and white tablecloth. She took her anorak off. Underneath she wore another pink jumper, and that one clung to her curves like the one she had on the night before.

'I can recommend the veggie lasagne,' she said.

He said he would have some and she went to the counter to order the soup of the day and a tea for her, the lasagne and an Americano for him.

Once back with their hot drinks, she poured a generous splash of milk and emptied two sachets of sugar in her steaming mug of tea.

'Hi, Roz!' A young woman placed a bowl of soup and a lasagne dish in front of them and winked at him. 'This is my very own recipe, I hope you like it.'

Rosalie licked her spoon and put it down. 'Alice, meet Marc Petersen who is staying at Raventhorn for a few days. Marc, this is Alice, a very old friend of mine.'

'Hey, less of the old, if you don't mind.'

Alice was a pretty brunette wearing a clingy purple top and tight black jeans tucked into high boots. She flashed him a smile. 'I am delighted to meet you.'

'Marc is from London,' Rosalie explained. 'He is taking a crash course in taxi driving.'

'Not literally, I hope! We all know what a bad driver you are.' Alice laughed before turning to Rosalie. 'Seriously, Roz, how are you? Niall told me what happened to Duncan last night.'

Rosalie shrugged. 'Bad news travels fast, I see. I'm fine, but I'll be even better when the police catch the thugs who vandalised his cab. I can't stop thinking about it. He could have been badly hurt.'

'What you need is a laugh and a dance to cheer you up. I'll see you tonight, as usual. And bring your apprentice too!'

She blew Rosalie a kiss, winked at Marc, and walked back to the kitchen.

'What's happening tonight?' he asked, before tucking into his lasagne.

'It's the ceilidh at the Four Winds Hotel, which takes place every Thursday. You wouldn't like it. It's not for people like you.' She dunked a piece of bread into her soup and bit into it.

'People like me?' he asked, aware that his voice had taken on a steely edge.

'Well, you don't strike me like the kind of man who enjoys a beer or two and a dance to a fiddle. You're probably used to a more refined kind of entertainment.'

He had nothing to reply to that since she was right, and they ate in silence for a while. When it was time to pay, she got up and took her purse out of her bag – it was pink, of course.

He rose to his feet, shaking his head. 'No, I'll get it.' There was no way he would let a woman pay for him when he was about to put her both out of business and out of her home.

She opened her mouth to protest, and shrugged. 'As you wish.'

After lunch they collected four elderly people from farms and cottages out of town and drove them to the doctor's surgery. Rosalie took a bag out of the boot of the cab.

'Entertainment,' she whispered as they walked into the surgery.

Whilst she patted one lady's hand and talked about a variety of health complaints, the long-awaited refurbishment of the village hall or the blizzard that was forecast for the weekend, Marc was urged to pull a card deck out of the bag and was roped into a game of twenty-one by two elderly gentlemen who thoroughly enjoyed beating him. After the card game, they played dominoes, and before long the surgery looked more like a social club than a doctor's waiting room.

It was late afternoon and a chilly wind gathered black clouds in the sky by the time they'd dropped everybody home. Rosalie switched on the radio again and was singing along to a cheerful pop tune. Marc gritted his teeth, overwhelmed by the need for silence after a day spent listening to mindless chatter and upbeat music. He reached out and turned the radio off.

'Hey!' Rosalie hissed. 'I was listening to that.'

'How do you do it?' he asked.

'Do what?'

'Talk to people all the time.'

She cast a surprised glance at him. 'I like talking, and I like people. Don't you?'

'Not really.' Actually, now that he thought about it, he hadn't really minded the afternoon that much – surprising really. He hadn't played cards since boarding school, and it had taken his mind off the stress of the past few weeks.

'People like to talk,' Rosalie said, 'especially old folks who live alone. You must be good with people in your line of work too, otherwise how would you charm them into doing business with you?'

He arched his eyebrows. 'It has nothing to do with charm or conversation, and everything to do with hard cash. That's all the people I know are interested in.'

'I find that very sad.' She paused. 'Now can I put my music back on?'

'You call that music? I'd rather listen to an electric drill than to that screeching and panting, and I haven't even mentioned your singing yet.'

She threw him a black stare. 'Ah, yes, I forgot. You only like civilised music.'

The radio crackled and Fergus's voice came on.

'Roz, lovie, I have a pick up from Loch Armathiel car park. A woman. Her car broke down and she needs to go to Aviemore. Can you do it?'

'No problem. I'm on my way.'

She looked at Marc and said to him, 'I'll drop you off at Raventhorn

40

first.'

'What if it's another hoax?' Marc asked, remembering what she had told the policeman about being called to isolated car parks by non-existent customers.

'It can't be. You heard Fergus, it's a woman.'

'Perhaps, but I'd better come with you.'

She shrugged. 'Please yourself.'

The moon shone brightly in the darkening sky when she turned off the main road and started down a bumpy track. In the distance the shadow of a ruined castle stood on an island on the loch.

Marc scanned the empty car park. 'There's no one here.'

Rosalie switched off the engine but left the headlights on. As she opened her door to get out, a strange sense of foreboding crept over him and he put his hand on her forearm.

'Stay in the car. Lock the doors. Let me take a look.'

As soon as he stepped out, the cold wind slapped his face and sneaked through his jumper, making him shiver. He wrapped his scarf more closely around his neck and walked briskly across the empty car park to the edge of the water. Shoving his hands inside his jeans pockets he breathed in the damp, earthy scent of pine trees mixed with the loch's silty smell.

A bird of prey circled the darkening sky and let out a series of high-pitched calls. Waves crashed onto the pebbly beach with soothing, rhythmical sounds. He was about to turn back when a movement on the island nearby caught his eye. The bird of prey circled above him once again and landed on one of the ruined towers.

Then he saw her. The woman of Corby Woods. It had to be her. She stood at the top of a tower, wrapped in her long hooded cloak, her pale face glowing like a moonstone. He felt a sharp stabbing pain in his heart. He closed his eyes for a second, and when he reopened them, the pain was gone and the tower was empty.

Chapter Five

'It's another no show,' Rosalie told Fergus on the cab radio.

'I can't believe you were stood up again. Folks have no consideration these days.'

'Can you do a call back and speak to her?'

'I can't. Marion just phoned to ask me what I want for tea. Sorry.'

'Ah, well. It was worth a try. Petersen went out to investigate. We'll head off home as soon as he comes back.'

'Och, yes. I've heard about your new apprentice on the grapevine. Word has it he's a handsome fella, but a bit standoffish.'

Rosalie replied with a grunt and switched the radio off.

She peered into the darkness. Marc seemed to have been gone forever. What if he'd slipped and fallen into the water, or if he'd gone too far and couldn't find his way back to the car park? A cold fist closed around her heart. What if there was someone lying in wait, and Petersen confronted them?

She had to go out and look for him, but first she needed something she could use as some kind of weapon, to reassure herself more than to try and inflict harm on whoever might be out there. Searching the glovebox, her fingers came into contact with the plastic tube the toddler had left behind that morning. It wasn't much of a deterrent, but she felt better for holding something.

The sounds of footsteps made her look up, and her fingers closed around the bubble tube. Petersen's tall figure stood out against the moonlight as he jogged back towards the cab. Rosalie leaned to one side and unlocked the passenger door to let him in.

'Did you see her?' she asked.

He raked his fingers through his hair and stared ahead. 'No. There's no sign of anyone.'

'How infuriating. She must have managed to start her car and didn't bother to ring Fergus.'

'Unless it was another hoax call. What safety measures do you have in place to protect yourself – against drunks or muggings, for example?'

She bit her lower lip. 'I don't have any. This is a very safe area.'

'Maybe it isn't safe any longer. If anything had happened to you out here tonight, there would be no one to hear you, no one to come to your rescue.'

He took his mobile phone out of his jeans pocket, looked at her and asked, 'Shall I call the police now?'

'The police? What for? It was probably a misunderstanding. I want to go home.'

He stared at the bubble tube she was still holding. 'What was that for?'

Her cheeks hot with embarrassment, she tossed the tube onto the back seat. 'It was just in case there were indeed people who were up to no good.'

He narrowed his eyes. 'So you wanted to blow bubbles into their face before stabbing them with the rabbit's ear and finishing them off with a whack over the head?'

He sounded so annoyingly superior she was tempted to do to him just what he'd described.

'It was the only thing I could find.'

'My point exactly. You must take care of yourself, and have ways to fight back if you're ever threatened.'

'Like what? A can of pepper spray, a kitchen knife? Why not a claymore?'

Anger twisting her stomach in a hard knot she started the cab a little too fast. The tyres screeched and the cab skidded on loose pebbles as she drove out of the car park and onto the road that ran alongside the loch, offering a glorious view of the water over which the cold moon cast silvery threads and moving shadows. They drove in silence on the empty road for a couple of minutes, then met a tow truck coming from the opposite direction.

'That's Niall! He must be on a call out.' She beeped the horn, slowed down to a crawl, then braked to a stop and opened her window. Niall did the same, and stuck his head out to talk to her.

'What are you doing here? Is everything all right?' he asked.

'Everything's fine. Fancy seeing you all the way out here. I keep bumping into you, these days, don't I?'

'What's he doing with you?' Niall pointed to Marc Petersen with his chin.

'I'm taking Marc back to Raventhorn by the scenic route,' she replied.

'I see. Well then, gotta go. See you later at the Four Winds.'

Rosalie pushed the button for the window to close and drove on.

'What is this place – the forest, the loch and the ruined castle on the island?' Marc asked.

She was surprised that he should show an interest, but answered anyway. 'This is Armathiel, and used to belong to the Armitage clan. They were always fighting the McBrides. Actually, they were the ones who abducted Isobel McBride and killed her husband.'

'Ah. The mysterious Raven Lady. How old is the castle?'

'I'm not sure, probably twelfth or thirteenth century. It was abandoned after being struck by lightning. Actually it was struck three times by lightning.'

'Really?'

She nodded. 'The first time was the night Isobel died. The second time was the day after the Armitage clan rebuilt the castle. It was rebuilt again only to be struck by lightning a third time. Every time people swore they saw Isobel's ghost nearby.'

She waited for a snide remark but he remained silent. 'The Armitages finally gave up on this site and built another castle near Avielochan. This old ruin is now an osprey sanctuary, hence the bird watching huts dotted around the loch.'

'Who exactly was Isobel?'

She cast a curious glance at him. 'Are you really interested?'

He shrugged. 'Just passing the time.'

'Well, hers is a very romantic, very tragic tale. In 1469 she was promised in marriage to a powerful laird from Orkney, Harald Johansen, or Harald the Cruel as he was also known.'

'A good Viking name, like Magnus Barelegs, Sigurd the Mighty or Eric Bloodaxe.'

She looked at him again, and arched her eyebrows.

'Don't look so surprised. I am partly Danish after all, and bound to be familiar with some Viking folklore.'

'Harald was from Denmark too, but he had lands on Orkney, which at the time was still part of the kingdom of Denmark and Norway and ruled by King Christian I. He sought to form an alliance with a powerful Scottish clan, so it was agreed he would marry Isobel on his way to

Edinburgh, where he was to attend the wedding of James III with Christian's daughter Margaret. When he arrived in Irlwick for his own wedding, he was rumoured to be carrying rare and expensive gifts in a silver casket.

'He married Isobel in the old castle, the one that's now a ruin on top of the hill in Irlwick. It was love at first sight – or so the story goes –and they spent a few days there before starting their journey to Edinburgh.'

According to a manuscript Geoff had discovered, the couple spent most of their time in the four-poster bed which was now in the Crimson Room, but she wasn't about to tell Petersen that.

'Shortly after setting off for Edinburgh, Harald, his new bride and their escort were ambushed by Armitage men in Corby Woods. The Armitages were after Harald's treasure, of course. They were always stealing and plundering in those days … Harald was injured, most of his men were killed and Isobel was abducted by Finghal Armitage, who took her to his castle on the loch. It was reported that Harald went mad with rage and that the sky turned black at midday. Flocks of vengeful ravens filled the sky, the heavens opened, and it rained so hard that Loch Bran flooded and the small hunting lodge that stood near its shores was all but submerged … and it still is.

'Anyway, the water level of Loch Armathiel rose too, cutting off the old castle. From that day onward the causeway that used to link the castle to the shore has been impassable.'

'What became of Isobel and Harald?'

'Harald and the few men he had left went after Isobel. She managed to scramble to the top of the tower and cry for help.'

'She stood on that tower?' His voice was a little hoarse.

She nodded. 'Harald swam across the loch to rescue her, but he was shot down by an arrow and his body sank, never to be found again. Isobel threw herself from the top of the tower and drowned too. The resulting feud between the Armitages and the McBrides has lasted for centuries – it's still going on even now, to an extent – and whatever treasure Harald was carrying was lost forever.'

'There's still bad blood between the McBrides and the Armitages?' He sounded surprised.

'Nothing too important these days. Silly arguments, nasty comments, dirty looks in the pub. The Armitages always felt that they were wrongfully displaced and they should rule Irlwick instead of the McBrides. Over the years there were accusations of women being ravished, horses being stolen and cattle being rustled from both sides. We even had our own Romeo and Juliet drama here, back in the early nineteenth century. A McBride girl and an Armitage boy fell in love, eloped to Gretna Green but were snatched back by their respective families before they got there and forbidden to ever see each other again. The poor girl supposedly died of a broken heart shortly afterwards, the boy ran away, joined the army and was killed at the Battle of Waterloo.'

Petersen was silent so she carried on. 'Isobel's ghost has haunted the woods and the lochs for centuries. Local people claim she vowed to drown as many men as possible to avenge her murdered husband. Others that she seeks to retrieve Harald's body from the loch and will only be at peace when she finds him. Others still that she's a bird of ill omen and can foresee people's death, like one of those *fylgja* who were—'

'Guardian spirits warning people of dangers or announcing their imminent death, and who appeared in the shape of an animal or a bird,' he finished.

She had expected him to laugh or make a disparaging comment and was once again taken aback. 'You do know about Norse mythology.'

He nodded, serious. 'So do you.'

'Well, that's because Geoff has made it his life's mission to find Harald's treasure. He has collected dozens of books and parchments, and worked with researchers, academics and archaeologists. That's how he spends most of his money – Raventhorn's money, I should say.'

'What kind of treasure are we talking about?'

'Nobody knows for sure, although Geoff has this idea that it could be an ancient banner – a magic banner.'

'A banner? Surely you don't mean the Raven Banner?'

She nodded and sighed. 'That's what Geoff thinks. His books and papers are in the library, if you're interested, although I doubt you'll be able to read them since many are in ancient writing – Anglo-Saxon, old Gaelic and runes.'

Marc was quiet for the rest of the journey. Maybe she shouldn't have told him about Geoff's obsession for the lost treasure. Now he probably thought Geoff was a lunatic as well as a drunk.

They didn't speak again until she parked in the courtyard at

Raventhorn. 'Thank you for the history lesson,' he said. 'I enjoyed it.'

The hint of a smile on his lips and the soft glow lighting his eyes unsettled her. She preferred it when he was arrogant and patronising. It was a lot easier to dislike him then.

'You're welcome. By the way,' she added quickly, 'not a word to Lorna about the hoax call. I don't want to worry her.'

The kitchen was warm and filled with the fragrant scent of lamb and vegetables cooking.

'Something smells good,' Rosalie said as she took off her anorak, and hung it in the utility room. She pecked a kiss on Lorna's cheek. 'How are you today? Any more dizzy spells or—'

'I'm fine,' Lorna interrupted.

'How was Geoff?'

'Restless and complaining about the food and grumpy nurses, which I suppose is a good sign.'

Lorna took two plates out of the cupboard and laid them on the pine table. 'He's staying in hospital a while longer. The cardiologist isn't happy with his heart rate and his blood pressure is far too high.'

She slipped her hands into oven gloves and pulled a dish of shepherd's pie out of the oven. 'Do you mind if we eat in the kitchen?' she asked Marc.

'Not at all.' He pointed to his muddy jeans and shoes. 'I need to get changed. I won't be long.'

As soon as he'd left Lorna turned to Rosalie. 'Geoff was asking for you. He is anxious to tell you about Marc Petersen.'

'It's a bit late for that. I hope you gave him a good telling off for keeping us – or me, at least – in the dark about selling Raventhorn.'

She drew in an angry breath. 'However, considering that he can always twist you around his little finger, you probably fetched him a nice cup of tea and nodded at everything he said.'

Lorna gasped and turned away but not before Rosalie saw her eyes glisten with tears. Suddenly she felt like crying too. Why was she being so mean? It wasn't fair to take her anger and frustration out on her friend.

'Sorry, Lorna, I'm being horrible. None of this is your fault. It's just that it annoys me how Geoff always manages to win you over, whatever he's done.'

'I know, sweetie. And I also know how much you love him, despite everything.' Lorna served two steaming portions of shepherd's pie onto the plates and brought them over. 'Will you go to the hospital tomorrow? I think he has something important to tell you.'

'You mean he has another surprise in store for me?' Rosalie poured water into a glass.

'Please, sweetie. Do it. For me. For your mother.'

'What has Mum got to do with it?' She put the glass down, impatient once again. 'Geoff should have thought about her before he sold Raventhorn to a stranger. I mean, what am I supposed to do with all her things, all her books, her clothes and trinkets, when we leave?'

'Perhaps it's time you let go of the past,' Lorna said, a hesitant, almost apprehensive look in her eyes. 'It's been over four years since your poor mum died, yet you keep her room the way it was the day she passed away. Her clothes and shoes are still in the wardrobe, you have even left all her toiletries on the dressing table.'

'I can't believe you're saying this. You, who were Mum's best friend! I thought you would be loyal to her memory.' Outrage and hurt tightened Rosalie's chest as she carried on. 'What do you suggest I do? Clear the room, throw away her things, give her clothes to one of Elaine's charitable causes? I bet she'd have a good laugh sorting through her skirts and cardigans. She always said Mum was the most frumpy woman she knew.'

Lorna shook her head. 'No, of course not. Forget I said anything.'

Rosalie heaved a sigh. Lorna may have been insensitive about her mother's room, but there was one thing she was right about. She did need to speak to Geoff about Raventhorn, Love Taxis, and her future.

'All right. I'll go to the hospital tomorrow morning after driving you to the station.'

True to his word, Marc was back after five minutes. He wore tan chinos and a navy shirt, which made his hair lighter, and turned his eyes almost blue. He may not be classically handsome, but there was something strong and male about him that made her heartbeat quicken. She looked down and focused on her shepherd's pie.

'I'm coming with you tonight,' he decreed as he sat down to eat. 'I've never been to a Scottish ceilidh so it will be a new experience for me.'

'No way!' Rosalie slammed her knife and fork onto the table. Tonight she wanted to forget about the hoax calls, Geoff's accident, and the chaos Petersen was bringing into her life.

'Rosalie, what's got into you?' Lorna sounded shocked. 'It's only natural that Mr Petersen should want to meet people from the village. He is Raventhorn's new owner, after all.'

Lorna obviously had no idea about Petersen's plans to sell up the estate to a hotel company. Not wanting to worry her before she left for her holidays, Rosalie darted the meanest look she could manage in his direction, and spent the meal sulking as Lorna told Petersen about the different dances and steps. After a hurried cup of tea for her and black coffee for Petersen, she cleared the table and went upstairs. To her dismay Petersen followed her up the stairs and into the hall.

'When you phone the police about tonight's incident, tell them I'll be keeping an eye on you tonight.'

She spun round, crossed her arms over her chest. 'I don't need a babysitter.'

'It's not just about you,' he replied coldly. 'I am protecting my investment too. Duncan's cab was damaged last night. I want to make sure there are no other problems.' He stepped forward and towered over her. 'This isn't open to discussion. In a manner of speaking, I am your boss now, and you'll do as I say.'

She gasped. 'You're not my boss. Nobody is my boss.'

'I think that you will find that I am. Now I suggest you phone the police or I'll do it myself.'

She was so angry she was shaking when she lifted the receiver and dialled the number on the card the constable left the night before. How could she have been attracted to the man, even for a second? He didn't care about her or the business that meant so much to her. He didn't care about Lorna, Geoff or Raventhorn. The only thing he cared for was his *investment*, as he put it. He was cold and arrogant, and had a calculator instead of a heart.

Chapter Six

The Kingussie Fiddlers, Rosalie's favourite ceilidh band, were in full flow, and like every Thursday night at the Four Winds, the music was loud, the dance floor packed and the bar heaving.

'It's a nice place,' Marc remarked as they walked through the door.

Rosalie nodded, but her eyes scanned the crowd and her foot already tapped the floorboards to the fiddler's lively tune. A young couple were dancing a little too energetically and bumped into her, almost knocking her over.

'Careful!' she warned.

'Careful yourself, you silly tart,' the young man spat. It was Kian Armitage, Niall's apprentice at the garage.

Before she could say anything, Marc took hold of his arm, almost lifting him up from the floor. 'I think you need to apologise, young man.'

'Get off me.' Kian shook him loose and tilted his chin up. 'Apologise for what?'

He must have seen Marc's icy glare, because he shrugged and turned to Rosalie. 'All right, don't fret. Sorry for bumping in to you.' He glanced up at Marc again. 'And for calling you ... you know ...'

She smiled. 'Apology accepted, but in future, watch where you're going.'

'Right. Whatever.' The teenager grabbed hold of his girlfriend's hand and pulled her away.

Rosalie shook her head and leant towards Marc. 'Kian is the youngest Armitage offspring, who also happens to be Niall's apprentice.'

'I recognise the girl,' he said. 'Isn't she the doctor's receptionist?'

'Yes. I thought Stacey would know better than to hang about with Kian. He's trouble.'

Spotting Niall and Alice in the crowd, she waved. Niall's face lit up when he saw her. He yanked Alice away from the dance floor.

Rosalie felt a twinge of envy as her friend, stunning in a flirty red dress and black tights, tottered on her high heels towards her. How plain she must look in comparison, with her black top and her jeans tucked into boots. As usual, however, Niall seemed oblivious to Alice's efforts to attract his attention. When would he realise that the young woman was crazy about him, and stop fantasising about rekindling his romance with Rosalie?

'Hello again, handsome, will you buy me a drink?' Alice fluttered her eyelashes at Marc and linked arms with him. Her fingers gripped his forearm, her bright red-painted nails a sharp contrast with the conservative blue of his shirt.

'Sure. Would you like a drink too?' he asked Rosalie, but she declined.

'I didn't realise they knew each other,' Niall said as he watched the couple make their way across the dance floor. He turned to Rosalie. 'You look worried. Is there anything wrong? Did you hear from the police about Duncan's cab?'

She shook her head.

'Is it Geoff?'

'He's still in hospital for observation, but I don't think there's anything to worry about. You know him, he'll be enjoying being mollycoddled by the nurses.'

Niall narrowed his eyes and gestured towards Marc who stood head and shoulders above other patrons at the bar. 'Is it *him*?'

She bit her lip and hesitated. It would be good to confide in her friend, but the time wasn't right yet. She shook her head again. 'No, of course not! Why do you say that?'

He shrugged, looking morose. 'Any more problems or prank calls to report?'

There was no point telling him about the call at Loch Armathiel. He would only launch into another sermon about the dangers of being a woman taxi driver, then propose again.

'No. Nothing.'

He frowned. 'What were you doing on the Armathiel road earlier?'

'I told you – taking Petersen on a scenic tour,' she lied. Seeing that he was frowning again, she took his hand. 'Come on, let's dance.'

As always, the music cheered her up. She soon lost track of time as she performed the dance steps, and her heart beat to the wild rhythm of the drums. What she couldn't forget however was Marc Petersen who stood at the bar with Alice glued to his side, and whose cool grey stare followed her every move.

'What are you playing at?' Rosalie asked Alice during the interval. 'If I didn't know you better, I would think that you're flirting with the man.' They found a free table while Marc and Niall went to the bar, and Rosalie fanned her flushed cheeks with a beer mat.

Alice shrugged. 'So what if I am? Maybe it's time I got over Niall. He'll never give you up. Every time he opens his mouth it's to talk about you. I've been in love with the man since primary school and he's never even looked at me once, at least not the way he looks at you.'

She sighed and looked towards the bar where Petersen towered above everybody else. 'To tell you the truth, I wouldn't mind getting to know Marc better. He is a very attractive man and—'

'You can't!' Rosalie cried out.

'Why not?' Alice frowned, and let out a long sigh. 'Ah, I see. You want him for yourself, is that it?'

Rosalie put her hand to her heart. 'Are you crazy? I can't stand the man.'

'Why? What's wrong with him?'

'He isn't who you think he is, for a start.'

Alice burst out laughing. 'You mean he isn't really training to be a taxi driver? I could have gathered that much on my own. Did you know that his mother is a former French top model, and his father was a financial tycoon originally from Denmark? He died in a helicopter crash in Hong Kong recently. Marc had to relocate to London to take care of the business, but he usually lives in Paris.'

Rosalie let out a surprised breath. 'I am impressed. You managed to extract all this information from him in a couple of hours.'

Alice's lips stretched into a smug smile. 'When you work in a café you develop certain people skills – a bit like a hairdresser, or a spy, I suppose.' She leant forward in a conspiratorial manner. 'Come on then, tell me the truth. What's he really doing here?'

Rosalie slapped the beer mat on the table. 'Why don't you ask him, since you have such honed people skills? No, on reflection, don't ask him. I'm sorry, Alice, but I can't tell you anything just yet. All I can say is, be careful. I wouldn't want you to get hurt. Petersen is mean and ruthless, that's all you need to know for now.'

Alice sighed. 'You're acting very mysterious all of sudden. Talking about mean and ruthless men, did you know that your arch-nemesis was back in town? I bumped into him and his floozy today. I bet Elaine had a fit when she saw the girl her darling Rupert dragged back to Irlwick all the way from London.'

Rosalie sighed. 'Elaine told me he was back, but she didn't say anything about a girlfriend.'

Her phone buzzed in the pocket of her jeans. She pulled it out. Fiona had sent her a text. Duncan left for Edinburgh. His mother has had a heart attack. Gordon needs picking up from The Stag at 10:00. Can you do it?

Poor Duncan. First the attack on the cab, and now his mother ...

Rosalie glanced towards the bar. Marc was still waiting to get served. Now was her chance to sneak out and prove that she was still in charge of her own business. What's more, she couldn't let Gordon Armstrong down. One of Love Taxis' regulars, he might be a hardy eighty-year-old widower, but he lived in an isolated cottage on the edge of the Armathiel forest and would struggle to find a lift home.

She texted Fiona that she was on her way, grabbed her anorak and stood up. 'I have to go,' she told Alice. 'I'll be back before closing time to pick up Petersen and give you your usual lift home.'

'Where are you going?'

'The Stag's Head. It's darts night and Gordon Armstrong needs a lift. Duncan's mother has had a heart attack and he had to leave for Edinburgh. Please don't breathe a word to Marc. Tell him I am powdering my nose if he asks where I am.'

She almost ran out of the dance hall, bumping into Kian as she did so. As he carried a pint, some beer splashed onto his shirt. 'What the hell,' he snarled. 'Look what you've made me do!'

'Sorry, Kian.' She pulled out a few tissues from her pocket and handed them to him.

'And what do you want me to do with that, you *bampot*?' If looks could kill, she'd be flat on her back on the tartan carpet right now.

'You need to calm down, Kian. I said I was sorry, and it's not that bad. It'll dry soon.'

'You've ruined my night out now.' He carried on muttering that he'd soon ruin hers too, so she left him to his bad mood and wet shirt, and swung the front door open onto the car park.

What a lot of fuss for a bit of spilled beer ... No doubt the incident would be blown out of all proportions by Kian's parents, and revive the ever smouldering feud between the Armitages and the McBrides.

The wind had picked up and a drizzle as fine as mist left tiny pearls of moisture on her hair and face. She took a deep breath, licked her lips. Snow was on its way, she could taste it.

It wasn't a long drive to Irlwick. She put Happy Baby Radio on and started to sing along but her heart wasn't in it. Annoyed, she switched it off again, tapped her fingers on the steering wheel and let out a sigh.

She felt as guilty as a teenager climbing out of her bedroom window to sneak to a party her parents had forbidden her to go to. Marc would be angry, and she had to concede that he might have a point. Driving around at night on her own probably wasn't a good idea after what had happened to Duncan. But this was her taxi, her town, her people – and her decision!

If only there was a way to pull Love Taxis out of his clutches. She could try asking her bank manager for a loan to pay Petersen back every penny she owed and be free of him. The problem was no bank manager would ever give her a loan. She had no assets to put up as security and her accounts didn't make for very cheerful reading. The only reason she was still in business was that she didn't pay any rent, ate for free at the castle most days and only paid a fraction of Geoff's loan back every month.

A bright light filled the inside of the cab. She glanced in her rear-view mirror as the glare of high beam headlights blinded her. What was that idiot driver thinking of, having his full beam on with no care for others? The car was so close it would crash into her rear bumper should she have to brake suddenly.

She slowed down as she approached Irlwick's town centre, and was relieved to see the car behind fall further back and its headlights disappear from her rear mirror. She parked in front of the Stag's Head and got out to fetch Gordon. The old man enjoyed his whisky and would probably need a little convincing to leave.

Forty-five minutes later, she was on the road that wound its way through the forest after having dropped Gordon at home. The cab's headlights swept over the empty road and the dark, rugged landscape at every turn. She had been right about the snow. Thick flakes danced and swirled in the headlights, already coating the road with a white blanket.

'Where are you, Roz?' Fiona's voice came through the radio.

Rosalie lifted the mike to her lips. 'I've just left Gordon at home and I'm heading back to the Four Winds to catch the last dance. Any news from Duncan?'

'Yes. He called in to leave his cab at the office before setting off with Brenda and the boys for Edinburgh. He said to tell you he's sorry but he'll be away for a week at least. By the way, I've just had a very unpleasant call from a Marc Petersen who demanded to know where the hell you were – his words, not mine. I told him you were on a call. Who is this guy, Roz? He sounded as if he owned the place ... and you.'

That's because he does, Rosalie answered silently.

'He is some kind of business associate of Geoff's. I'll introduce you to him tomorrow.' She closed her eyes and sighed. She was getting deeper and deeper into lies. 'I'm taking the forest road to go back to the Four Winds. If he calls again, tell him I won't be long.'

A diffuse anxiety she couldn't explain gnawed at her as she drove. It was snowing harder, making visibility difficult. Suddenly she wasn't alone any longer. A car was coming at speed behind her, its full beam headlights dazzling in her rear mirror. Another idiot driver! Rosalie cursed and slowed right down. What was the matter with people tonight? She steered the cab to the side of the road to let the other car overtake.

The car came dangerously close and flashed his headlights, once, twice. Did he want her to stop? Maybe he was lost, or he needed help. Rosalie braked, and the car rammed into her rear bumper. She cried out in shock as her body jerked forward. She hadn't recovered from the first impact when the car crashed into the taxi's back bumper again.

This time the cab swerved across the road. The steering wheel spun in her hands, the taxi skidded, its tyres drew a half circle on the snow, and she ended up facing in the opposite direction.

Her heart thumped hard. A wave of nausea rose from her knotted stomach. The other vehicle – a black four-by-four with tinted windows – had come to a halt too and was facing her. With its engine roaring, it looked like a predator about to pounce.

All her instincts screamed at her to escape. Her fingers gripped the steering wheel. She pressed hard on the accelerator and the cab lunged forward. By sheer luck she managed to avoid the four-wheel drive and started speeding back towards Gordon's cottage and the main road.

She did not recognise the car and had no idea who the driver of the four-wheel drive was and what he wanted with her. All she knew was that he was playing some kind of sick game and she had to put as much distance as possible between herself and him. There was no time to call Fiona or the police. Her mouth dry, her chest tight, she could only clutch the wheel and focus on the road ahead.

A set of headlights soon appeared in her rear-view mirror once again. The four-wheel drive had turned round to chase after her. More powerful than the taxi, it would catch up before she even drove out of the forest.

Fear now made her shake all over. She glanced in the rear mirror. What if it crashed into her again when she was alone on the forest road? What if ... She forced a few deep breaths down. Panicking was pointless. What she needed was a place to hide – somewhere secluded and safe.

Conjuring up a mental map of the forest trails and its dirt roads, she realised she wasn't far from the bird watching huts scattered on the shore of Loch Armathiel. They stood at the end of an unmarked track that would be coming up after the next bend in the road. She could drive up to the loch, park near one of the huts and radio Fiona for help.

As soon as she spotted the gap in the fir trees that signalled the start of the track, she switched off her headlights and prepared for the sharp turn. She slowed down but didn't brake as she veered abruptly to the right so that the four-by-four wouldn't see the cab's brake tail-lights.

The tyres skidded but she managed to straighten the cab before it lurched forward on the lane. It was so dark she couldn't see anything. The cab bounced on the track, its underside scraping against stones and roots.

Suddenly a tall black shape rose in front of her. She slammed her foot on the brake but it was too late. Squeezing her eyes tightly shut, she braced herself for impact. The front of the cab hit the pine tree and the impact threw her against the steering wheel hard.

Her old Metrocab did not have airbags, but it was built like a tank and she bounced straight back as the engine coughed and died. Winded and shaken, but otherwise unhurt, she reclined against the headrest and breathed a sigh of relief. She would have aches and bruises the following day, but she wasn't injured.

She took the mike, pressed the call button. 'Fiona, it's me. Please, Fiona. I'm in trouble. Fiona, answer please.'

There was no reply, only white noise. She tried a couple more times before putting the mike down. Damn, the radio was broken, just when she needed it most. She fumbled inside her anorak pocket, pulled her mobile out but as she feared, there was no signal in the forest.

Peering at the surrounding darkness, she listened to the sounds of the night. The wind howled in the depth of the forest, rattling tree branches and making the wood creak and groan. There was something else too. An engine noise. She glimpsed twin white lights come up at speed on the road and her blood froze. The four-by-four was coming after her.

Flinging the door open, she jumped out and started running up the loch trail as fast as she could.

Where the hell was she? Marc shoved his hands into his jeans pockets and let out an impatient sigh as he scanned the empty room again.

Alice hiccupped. Lipstick smudged the side of her mouth. Her hair stuck up on the top of her head.

'Cheer up! At least we're in a nice hotel. If Rosalie doesn't come back, we can always spend the night here. It's a bit pricey but the beds are very comfortable.' Her voice turned husky, almost cajoling.

That's all he needed. A drunken woman making a pass at him.

When he didn't reply, she blew a sigh and shook her head. 'Oh well, it was worth a try. Don't look so grim, Petersen, the Fiddlers are driving back to Kingussie. We can probably hitch a lift with them. I'll have a word.'

He watched her toddle on her high heels towards the stage where members of the band were putting their gear away. The bar had closed but Niall had managed to convince the barmaid to serve him yet another beer and whisky chaser, and he nursed his drinks, his elbows propped on the counter. Marc doubted the man could stand on his own, let alone walk.

His anger hadn't abated. If anything it was even stronger now than when Alice had finally confessed Rosalie had left to pick up an elderly customer from the pub in Irlwick. How irresponsible could the woman be? She had blatantly disregarded his instructions. According to the information he'd managed to draw out of Fiona, Love Taxis' recalcitrant switchboard operator, Rosalie was now on her way back to the hotel.

However, they'd been waiting for over an hour and he couldn't help the feeling deep in the pit of his stomach that something was very wrong.

'The Fiddlers have room at the back of the van for the three of us,' Alice declared. 'They'll leave you near the old bridge, unless you want to come back to my place for a nightcap. You could teach me a bit of French … or Danish, I'm not picky.'

She lifted her hand, her index finger lingered along his jaw line. He took a step back. 'The old bridge is fine.'

One of the band members announced they were ready to leave, adding that they would have to squeeze into the back of the van among the amps and musical instruments.

'I'll get him out,' Marc said, gesturing towards Niall, who was leaning into his drink. 'Come on, you're going home, you've had enough,' he said, slipping his arm around Niall's waist.

Niall staggered and mumbled something about stuck up city boys who didn't drink like real men – a reference to the two half-pints of ale Mark had drunk during the course of the evening, no doubt. Marc steadied him and together with Alice they managed to walk him outside where snow was falling in dense, fluffy flakes.

'Will you be all right with him?' he asked Alice as he pushed Niall into the back of a battered Transit van.

'Aye, sure. I've looked after him for years. Not that he ever noticed.' She climbed into the van and plumped herself down on a tarpaulin before cradling Niall's head in her lap. She stroked his curly brown hair tenderly away from his face.

'Rosalie and Niall are my oldest friends,' she said in a slurred voice. 'They'll probably get married one of these days.'

'Is that so?' It wasn't exactly news, since Elaine McBride had mentioned it earlier, but his bad mood cranked up a notch.

He had noticed how Rosalie swirled in Niall's arms during the ceilidh, her eyes shiny with pleasure, her cheeks flushed. For some inexplicable reason, it had annoyed him. A lot.

'Niall has been in love with Rosalie for as long as I can remember,'

Alice carried on. 'They were together once, but she broke off with him, years ago. He keeps asking her to marry him, and she always turns him down, but I have the feeling she'll give in eventually and the two of them will live happily ever after.'

Alice sounded so sad he looked at her more closely. She was still stroking the young man's face as he lay there, curled up against her and snoring already. Marc shrugged. He would never understand women. Not five minutes before she had asked him back to her place and now she sat holding onto Niall as if he was the only man who mattered in the whole world.

He climbed into the van, found a space to sit and slammed the door shut. Three of the band members piled up at the front, another had squeezed in the back of the van with them, and they were off.

He was grateful for the noise from the engine and the jangling of the instruments that made any conversation impossible. After about twenty minutes, the van rattled to a stop, the driver turned round and shouted that they were at the old bridge near Raventhorn.

Marc shook hands with the musicians, bid Alice good night and got out. It was snowing heavily. He pulled the collar of his jacket up and watched the van drive away before starting along the dark track to the castle. He walked fast, lengthening his stride, not because he was cold but because he was anxious to check if Rosalie was back.

She wasn't. Or at least her cab wasn't in the courtyard. The whole stable block was in darkness. Maybe the other driver – Duncan – had dropped her off and she was already in bed? Even though it was unlikely, he knocked on the outside door to her flat. There was no answer. He walked across the courtyard, tried the door to Raventhorn's service entrance. It was locked.

Now what? He didn't have a key. He hadn't thought about asking for one, and neither Rosalie nor Lorna had offered to give him one. Even though he was reluctant to walk to Lorna's lodge and wake her up at this late hour, he could hardly stay out there all night. He pulled his phone out, and dialled the number for Love Taxis again.

'I don't know where Rosalie is,' the receptionist said. She sounded as if she was about to cry. 'She's not answering my calls. The last I heard from her she was driving on the Armathiel forest road that snakes through the Cairngorms National Park.'

'Call the police immediately,' he ordered, his bad mood now tinged with concern. 'Do you have another driver who could come to get me at Raventhorn?'

'I'm afraid not. Duncan left for Edinburgh so there's no one else. I suppose you could always take one of Geoff's cars,' Fiona suggested. 'The car keys are in the desk drawer in his study.'

'That's all very well but Raventhorn is locked and I can't get in.'

At the other end of the phone, Fiona let out a loud sigh. 'The keys are in the planter on the right hand side of the front door. Didn't Rosalie tell you?'

That was the craziest thing he had ever heard. How many people knew where to find the castle's keys and could have access to its antiques, and to McBride's cars? Considering there wasn't even a burglar alarm fitted in the place, it was a miracle Raventhorn hadn't been looted and McBride's garage emptied.

He walked to the front of the castle where he found the keys in the planter as promised. After experimenting with a couple of them, he managed to unlock the service door. He ran up to the ground floor, opened a few doors and found McBride's study in a corner of the vast, oak-panelled library.

A couple of armchairs stood in front of a fireplace, books were piled up all over the floor, papers and files littered the desk. Marc pulled the desk drawer open, rummaged among a stash of invoices and bank statements, pens and various items of stationery before finding what he was after.

Two sets of car keys, each on a ring bearing a different car manufacturer's logo. A Jag and a Range Rover. He closed his fingers around the keys to the Range Rover, then looked around for a map of the area. Fiona said that Rosalie was driving back from a hamlet at the foot of the Cairngorms, on a country road off the B970. The car probably had a satnav, but he wanted to get his bearings before setting off.

He spotted half a dozen road maps on a bookshelf, pulled out one of the Cairngorms and grabbed the keys to the Range Rover. He locked the service door again but kept the keys to the castle in his pocket. The days of leaving them in the planter were well and truly over.

For someone who kept expensive cars, McBride was sloppy with security, Marc thought as he pulled open the unlocked garage door, another converted stable block opposite Rosalie's flat and office. He flicked the electricity switch on the wall. The two cars were alongside one another. There were empty spaces where other cars must have been parked in the past, judging from tyre tracks and oil stains on the concrete flooring.

He unfolded the map on the bonnet of the Range Rover and focused on the unfamiliar names and markings to memorise the route to Armathiel forest. He then did a quick search of the car and found a torch in working order, a pair of leather gloves, and a silver flask, which upon inspection proved to be filled with whisky. There was also a pair of men's wellingtons, a shovel and a thick blanket in the boot. McBride might be negligent with security but at least he was prepared for bad weather.

Marc programmed the destination in the satnav and drove out of the garage. The Range Rover bumped over the old bridge, and the tyres bit into the thick layer of snow that covered the main road. Flurries of snowflakes stuck to the windscreen and danced in the broad beam of the headlights, making it difficult to see where he was going. If Rosalie was stranded away from the road, he probably wouldn't be able to see her.

Chapter Seven

Too scared to turn round and glance over her shoulder, Rosalie ran towards the loch. Her pursuer must have stopped near the cab because the headlights of the four-wheel-drive shone through the trees, bathing the forest in an eerie glow. The wind carried sounds too – the humming of an engine, the crunching of tyres on the dirt road.

At last she saw the huts, dark shapes in front of her. She chose the furthest one, yanked the door open and stepped inside. It was cold and smelled of damp, musty wood. She leaned against the door to catch her breath and listen to the night but all she could hear was the rush of blood in her ears and the pounding of her heart.

As her eyes got used to the darkness, she was able to make out a pile of empty sacks on one side of the hut and lighter shapes on the walls – posters about local bird species and instructions for birdwatchers. Opposite were the viewing bays and a couple of benches, which would be her only hiding place should anyone come after her. For now, she stood shivering with cold and fear in her soggy boots, alert to every sound in the forest.

Anxious minutes ticked by. At last she heard the sound of doors slamming shut and the distant roar of an engine, and then there was silence. She waited a while longer before opening the door to peer outside. It had stopped snowing. The forest was pitch black. The four-wheel-drive had left. She rubbed her hands together, blew on her fingers to warm them, and retraced her steps back to the cab, peering into the darkness, expecting any second to see shadows lunging at her.

She had almost reached the cab when footsteps sounded on the path ahead.

'Who's there?' a man asked.

She could have wept with relief. 'Petersen! Thank goodness it's you!'

He reached out. Strong hands grabbed her shoulders, pulled her closer. 'Rosalie? I saw the cab from the main road. Are you all right? What happened?'

She opened her mouth but no sound came out. His fingers dug deeper into her shoulders and he gave her a little shake as if it would make the words flow.

'I had an accident,' she blurted out. 'There was a car. It rammed into my rear bumper on the main road, and when I drove off, it came after me. I was so scared ... I drove too fast around the bend and crashed. When I tried to call Fiona, the radio was dead, so I ran and hid in one of the birdwatching huts.'

'Are you hurt?' He loosened his grip but did not let go.

'No, I'm fine.' She started trembling. 'The people in the car, they were after me. I don't know why, but they were chasing me.'

'Did you see the driver or any of the passengers? Can you give a description of the car – the number plate, perhaps?'

She shook her head. 'All I know is it was a black four-by-four. I think there were two people in the car, but there could have been more.'

'And you're sure you're not hurt?'

When she nodded, he let out a sigh. 'Then we'll get back to the road and phone the police if we can get a signal.'

'How did you find me?' she asked as they walked.

'Fiona told me where you were heading. I borrowed one of McBride's cars and found the forest road. Then, by sheer chance, I saw your taxi ...' He paused, took a deep breath. 'You weren't inside so I started up the path but McBride's torch died on me and I was left scrambling in the dark. That's when I bumped into you.'

He stopped and looked down. 'Do you have any idea how much worse this could have been? None of this would have happened if you hadn't sneaked out of the Four Winds against my instructions.'

Even though his voice was calm, his French accent was suddenly more pronounced. He was angry, very angry, and right now she couldn't blame him.

She looked down, feeling guilty and miserable. 'I'm sorry.'

He was right. It could have been much worse. Gordon Armstrong could have been in the cab ...

When they reached the main road she flipped open her mobile to check for a signal and call Fiona and the police. While she was on the phone, Marc retrieved a blanket and a flask from the Range Rover – Geoff's flask. Without a word he draped the blanket around her shoulders, opened the flask and handed it over to her as she finished her call.

The whisky burned her throat and left a fiery trail down to her stomach. As she stood there, safe at last, the events of the past few hours finally caught up with her. She buried her face in her hands and started to cry.

A primitive male instinct he didn't even know he possessed fought a brief battle with his usual reserve, and won. He stepped forward and enfolded her into his arms. He half-expected her to push him away – she had after all made no secret of the fact she viewed him as the enemy – but she nestled against him and buried her tear-streaked face in his coat.

Her body shook as she sobbed. She felt so small and helpless that he was overcome with the need to draw her closer and hold her tightly.

At last she pulled away, wiping her face with the back of her hands. 'Sorry, I'm sorry,' she hiccupped.

'No worries.' He dug his fists in his coat pocket, feeling cold and oddly redundant now she'd stepped away. 'You should sit in the Range Rover, and try to get warm.'

He held the door open, and she climbed into the car while he waited outside. He was far too restless to sit down. Ten minutes later two police four-wheel drives came to a halt by the side of the road. This time, the constable in charge – the same one who had visited Raventhorn the night before – seemed to take the incident a lot more seriously and questioned Rosalie at length, while his colleagues switched on powerful lights to take photos of the cab, scrape black paint off the bumper and check the road for clues, working fast because the snowfall was covering all traces of the incident.

By the time Rosalie had answered his questions, she was shaking with cold despite the blanket wrapped around her shoulders and her face had turned deathly pale. Enough was enough, Marc thought. She needed to go home. He went over to the constable, said they were leaving, and, ignoring Rosalie's protests, cupped her elbow in his hand and led her towards McBride's Range Rover.

'I have a few ground rules for you, and I want you to listen very carefully,' he said, once they were both seated in the car. 'For a start, you will stay at the castle tonight, and every night until I am satisfied you are safe.' He paused. 'Second, you will not take any new customers, and you will not work at night.'

She cast a fiery look in his direction. 'And how am I supposed to make a living?'

'I thought you weren't making a living. That's what you told me.' His voice sounded calm, yet he'd never felt so close to losing his temper. He relaxed his grip on the steering wheel and drew in a long breath. Losing his temper was something he never did.

'One last thing,' he added. 'You will not leave the castle keys in the planter any longer. Am I making myself clear?'

A mutinous expression pinched her face. 'Who do you think you are? It's not your place to organise my life, decide where I sleep or keep the keys of my house, or how I run my business!'

'Let me rephrase this,' he said, with as much calm as he was capable of. 'From now on you will not keep the keys to *my* house in the planter, and you will run *my* business the way I see fit ... or not at all.'

She recoiled as if he'd slapped her, then looked up, her eyes huge, dark, and filled with more tears. Cursing himself for his lack of tact when she was already in shock, he turned the key in the ignition and started to drive down the forest road.

'By the way,' she said, after a few minutes of frozen silence, 'I need you to stop at the office in Irlwick on the way back. Duncan left his cab there before going to Edinburgh, and I need it, since mine is now out of action. I have to take Lorna to the train station first thing in the morning.' She turned to him. 'If that's all right with you, of course, *boss.*'

He narrowed his eyes, gripped the steering wheel harder but didn't answer. He may not be keen on her driving back to Raventhorn when she was still shaken by her ordeal, but he did as she asked.

It was well after one in the morning by the time they finally reached the castle. Marc parked the Range Rover in the garage and suggested Rosalie did the same with the cab but she refused, insisting that it would be fine outside. He chose to let it go rather than risk another argument and upset her again.

Rosalie went straight to her room and he carried out a systematic check on every window and door on the ground floor before going up to his room. How he longed for a long, steaming hot shower ... the damn thing however only spurted out lukewarm cold water and he didn't linger.

A towel wrapped around his waist, another around his shoulders, he stood next to the antique looking radiator – thankfully hot tonight – and rubbed his hair dry. He then put a black T-shirt and jogging bottoms on, climbed into bed and switched the bedside lamp off.

Outside, the wind howled and the forest groaned. It wasn't much better inside with the wardrobe creaking and the ancient plumbing's dribbling and banging. A freezing draft blew into the room and made the curtains move. Tonight the mass of the castle around and above him felt oppressive, almost threatening, as if it was telling him he had no right to be here. It was probably picking up Rosalie's hostile feelings, if such a thing was possible.

Would he dream of his father's accident, or about the mysterious woman, he wondered as he beat the lumps out of his pillow, lay down and pulled the covers up to his chin. He closed his eyes, and waited for sleep to come.

It was still dark when Rosalie went out the following morning and brushed the snow off the bonnet and roof of her cab. She should have followed Petersen's advice and parked in the garage. Her small act of defiance now seemed silly and pointless, especially when her head hurt and her whole body felt sore and stiff – the aftermath of the accident, coupled with a sleepless night spent tossing and turning in bed.

Fergus was on morning shift and his voice came on as soon as she flicked the radio switch on and reported in.

'Hi, lass, how are you doing this morning? Pretty shaken up, I bet, after last night.'

'Who told you?'

'Fiona left a note explaining what'd happened. Have you any news from the police about the yobs who drove you off the road?'

'No and I don't think I'll get any since I couldn't give them a detailed description of the car.' She took a deep breath. 'Fergus, can you ring round and ask if another taxi firm can take over the rides we have booked for today? I'm driving Lorna to the station and then I'm off to the hospital to visit Geoff and with Duncan away ...'

'No problem. What about tomorrow?'

'I'll be back to normal tomorrow.'

'Well said, lass. You can't let a bit of bad luck stop you.'

Unfortunately if bad luck didn't stop her, Marc Petersen would, she thought gloomily.

'I'll call Ben McKay, and ask if his drivers can step in today. I'm sure they'll want to help. Geoff will be upset when he hears about your accident.'

'I won't tell him. I don't want him to worry about me, not when he's in hospital.' They had plenty to discuss anyway, including why he'd sold Raventhorn to the Petersens without telling her, why he had sworn Lorna to secrecy, and what she was going to do about Love Taxis. Then there was this mysterious confession Lorna said he wanted to make …

She gave Fergus instructions about only taking repeat customers from now on, and as a concession to Marc Petersen added that he wasn't to take any evening bookings for the rest of the week.

'It sounds sensible enough,' Fergus said.

'Please don't breathe a word about last night on the radio,' she urged. 'Lorna will probably cancel her holiday and she really needs a break.'

As she pulled up in front of the lodge, she took a deep breath, and forced a smile. She should have known she wouldn't fool Lorna, even for a second.

'What's wrong, sweetie?' her friend asked as soon as she opened the door.

Rosalie shrugged. 'Nothing, why?'

'You look awful.'

'Well, if you must know, I didn't get much sleep last night.' At least, that bit was true. 'I'll load your bags in now. I don't want us to be late.'

Lorna narrowed her eyes, suspicious. 'Are you sure you're all right?'

'Of course.'

But she felt a lot better an hour later when she helped Lorna into the train carriage and waved her goodbye. She was starting the cab when Petersen rang her mobile.

'Where are you?' he asked without preamble.

'In Aviemore. At the train station. Why?'

'I want you to phone or text me every hour. If I don't hear from you and can't get hold of you, I'll call the police. Is that clear?'

'Listen, Petersen, I'm a big girl and you're not responsible for my wellbeing. I'm on my way to Inverness hospital and may not be able to get in touch for a while.'

'This isn't open to discussion.' And he cut her off.

It took a few minutes for Rosalie's anger to subside and her heart rate to return to normal. Never had anyone made her feel so helpless before. She closed her eyes and remembered the spine-tingling sensations he had aroused the night before when he had drawn her to him to comfort her, and keep her safe. His arms had been warm and strong around her, and his chest broad and solid as she moulded herself against him. She had felt something strange and disturbing – something which wasn't safe at all.

She drew in a sharp breath and opened her eyes. No. This wasn't right. She couldn't be attracted to Petersen. She *wasn't* attracted to Petersen! The man behaved as though he owned her, the way he owned Raventhorn, and was entitled to boss her around.

However she grudgingly sent him a text from the hospital one hour later. After being told that Geoff had been moved to a single room in the Coronary Unit, she took the lift, and tried to ignore the queasy feeling rising from the pit of her stomach. The air smelled of disinfectant, medicine and sickness. Of sadness, of death.

Hospitals would forever bring back terrible memories of heartbreak, crushed hope, and despair. Images of her mother's gaunt face and hollowed eyes flashed back into her mind. She curled her fingers tightly around the strap of her handbag and forced deep breaths in.

It was different this time. Geoff wasn't as ill as her mother. He would soon get out, and be his normal, charming, infuriating self again. She had almost managed to calm down her racing heart when the lift door slid open with a pinging sound. She stepped out and walked straight into Rupert.

'Rosalie. Long time no see.' Elaine's son slapped his large hands on her shoulders and shoved her aside.

She gritted her teeth. 'Rupert. What are you doing here?'

Rupert's blue eyes narrowed, and his mouth twisted in a scowl. 'Same thing as you, I imagine. Visiting Geoff.'

'I hope you haven't been pestering him for money.'

His face turned red and he clenched his big fists by his sides. 'I'm entitled to ask him for money. I'm his cousin, whereas you're ... well, let's face it, you're a nobody.'

So the past few months he'd been away hadn't changed him one bit. He was still a lazy good-for-nothing. She ignored his last, nasty remark. She'd heard it too many times before to care.

'Geoff is not well, can you not leave him alone?'

Rupert shrugged. 'He didn't look that ill to me.' He walked into the lift, turned to face her, and the doors closed on his smirking face.

She was making her way to Geoff's room when an alarm went off. Immediately three nurses came hurrying down the corridor. One of them was pulling a trolley with medical equipment on it. They rushed inside a room at the end of the corridor.

Chapter Eight

'I'm sorry but you can't come in.'

Before the male nurse closed the door, Rosalie had time to catch a glimpse of Geoff lying in bed, an oxygen mask over his face, surrounded by medical staff and equipment.

Her legs suddenly weak, she leaned against the wall for support. Up to now she had dismissed the seriousness of Geoff's condition and found plenty of reasons for his extended stay in hospital. His blood pressure was high because the car crash had shaken him, because he liked whisky, rich foods and cigars a little too much. And of course he enjoyed being the centre of attention and having people – women especially – run around him. But what if she had got it wrong and he was seriously ill? Lorna had said he was anxious to speak to her. Perhaps he was dying, and he had sold Raventhorn to put his affairs in order.

She took a few steps to the window overlooking the car park and rested her forehead on the glass just as four floors below Rupert was coming out of the hospital. His face red, his pale blond hair dishevelled, he strode towards a black sports car, gesticulating with his hands. He appeared to be arguing with the dark-haired young woman walking next to him. Rosalie peered at her more closely. Dressed in knee-high boots, miniskirt and a short black fur coat, she had to be the girlfriend Alice had told her about.

Rosalie clenched her fists as she watched them get into the car and speed away. There weren't many people she disliked, but Geoff's cousins were definitely the exception. Elaine was a snob who'd always looked down on her mother and herself, and Rupert was a thug. She hadn't exaggerated when she'd told Marc Petersen that he had made her life a misery for as long as she could remember. Almost from the first day her mother had taken her to Irlwick Primary School, Rupert had picked on her, tripped her over in the playground, sneaked worms or dead flies in her coat pockets or her lunch box, smeared dirt or paint over her books and clothes and generally made it his mission in life to terrorise her. Elaine had dismissed the incidents as harmless pranks, and Rupert had carried on tormenting her.

At secondary school things had taken a more unpleasant turn. Rupert and his friends would make clucking sounds or sing the 'Greased Lightning' tune every time she walked past, call her a dirty *hoachin* and claim she had nits or scabies. They regularly snatched her school bag and slung it into a muddy puddle, and even slashed her coat with scissors once. Rupert was clever enough to get his friends to do his dirty work so he never got blamed for anything.

She recalled a particularly nasty incident in which he'd been involved. She was thirteen. It was winter, it was snowing and she had missed the school bus because she'd stayed too long searching for her coat in the PE changing rooms. She eventually found it crumpled on the floor in a toilet cubicle. It was ripped, wet and soiled. Swallowing her tears of anger and frustration, she had thrown it into a bin bag – she'd rather pretend she'd lost it and be punished by her mother than tell her the truth about Rupert's bullying. Wrapping her red woolly scarf around her, Rosalie had walked the three miles home, shivering in her school blazer. As she forked right towards old Raventhorn bridge three shadows had jumped in front of her.

'Isn't that Little Red Riding Hood walking home in the dark?' Rupert had exclaimed with a mocking voice. 'Watch out for the big bad wolf.' He had blocked her way.

'Leave me alone,' she had mumbled, eyeing warily his two friends who stood on either side of him.

'Or what?' he asked. 'Are you going to tell your mummy ... or your daddy? Oh, but I forgot. You don't have a daddy, do you? I bet you don't even know his name. Not surprising, really, considering what a slut your mother is.'

Her blood ran cold and she gasped. 'You're wrong. I know my father's name, I know everything about him, and one day he'll come and beat you up, you'll see!' She had clenched her fists and swallowed hard. She mustn't cry. She mustn't show him how hurt and scared she was.

Rupert had laughed, imitated by his two cronies, then had swaggered closer. Three years older than her, he was already tall and bulky at sixteen and she'd recoiled, fearful he was going to hit her. He'd stopped laughing, shoved his fists into her chest and pushed her into the snow. His eyes narrowed in hatred, he had stood over her and pressed his thick-soled shoe down on her stomach.

'You have no right to be at Raventhorn, bastard girl. It should be me living there, not you.' He pressed so hard she could hardly breathe. 'You'd better watch it because when I'm the laird, I'll do whatever I want with you and your mum, and afterwards I'll throw you both back out in the dirt where you belong.' And he'd kicked her before turning away and gesturing to his two sidekicks to follow him.

She hadn't told anyone about the incident, partly because she didn't want to cause any trouble between Geoff and Elaine, but mainly because Rupert's words had hit a raw nerve. It was true, she didn't have a father. All she knew about him was his first name – John – and she wasn't even sure it was his real name. Her mother had always met her questions with a stony silence and Rosalie had been reduced to making up stories about him. He was an American rock star, a secret agent, an explorer who had disappeared whilst searching for a treasure in the Amazonian forest.

Nothing could take away the hurt and the shame of being nobody's daughter. What made it harder too was that her mother didn't have any relatives. Rosalie had grown up without grandparents, aunties or uncles, and as talking about the past always upset her mother, Rosalie didn't ask any questions. She supposed she could count herself lucky to live at Raventhorn with Geoff and Lorna as substitute family.

'Excuse me.' A man's voice nearby made her jump.

She turned round and found herself face to face with a doctor.

'How is he?'

'Stable for now but it was a close call. I'm afraid he needs a heart bypass. I am scheduling the operation for tomorrow morning.'

A black mist closed in on her once again. So Geoff was truly ill. So ill he might very well die.

'Are you all right, miss?' the doctor asked. 'Do you need to sit down?'

'No, thanks, I'll be fine. Can I see him?'

'Only for a few minutes.'

She followed him to Geoff's room. How pale he was against the white hospital linen, and how grey his hair looked. With the drip stuck to the back of one hand, an oxygen mask on his face and the monitors wired to his body, he looked old and frail. A glimmer lit his pale blue eyes when she walked in and his fingers clutched at the sheet as if he wanted to pull them off and sit up.

'Don't move, don't even try to talk,' she warned, pulling a chair closer to the bed to sit down. 'You really are the most annoying person I know.' She tried to keep her voice light and cheerful. 'There I was, ready to have it out with you for letting the insufferable Marc Petersen into my life, and for ...' she coughed to clear her throat '... well, you know, all the other things you should have told me about, but once again you've managed to wriggle your way out of trouble.'

She took his hand and pressed it lightly. Geoff closed his eyes. His breathing deepened. He lifted a hand to pull the mask off his face.

'I have to speak to you, darling,' he whispered. 'There are things I must say ... it's important.'

She placed the mask back on his face. 'Now isn't the time for explanations. You get better first, then I'll go mad at you.'

She glanced at the heart monitor with its green dot flashing on the screen and leaned towards him. Whatever his faults, he and Lorna were the only family she had left. She blinked the tears away and smoothed his hair on his forehead.

He lifted the oxygen mask off again. 'Rupert said you'd had trouble on the road last night. Someone went after you, caused you to have an accident.'

She frowned. How had Rupert found out about the previous night's car chase already? Unwilling to alarm Geoff, she shrugged as if it was no big deal. 'It was nothing, some stupid driver, that's all.'

'He also told me about Duncan's cab getting vandalised. Please, you must be careful. Promise me.'

His face became ashen and his nostrils were pinched as he struggled for breath. 'He found us ... after all this time, he found us. He found you.'

What was Geoff talking about? Who had found her?

'Stop talking and put that mask back on,' she scolded but Geoff shook his head and became even more agitated.

'He's dangerous, that's why she left, why she had to hide. Promise me you'll be careful. Promise me ...' He had trouble breathing and his skin took on a waxy yellow shade.

Alarmed, Rosalie replaced the mask on his face once more. 'Calm down. Breathe slowly. That's it. Again.'

A nurse walked into the room, pulling a trolley of equipment behind her. 'I'm sorry but you have to leave now. We have to run more tests before the operation.'

Rosalie nodded and started to rise. She kissed Geoff's hand. 'I love you. Everything will be all right. I'll be here when you wake up.'

One last time, he tried to pull his oxygen mask off to speak but she put her hand over his to stop him. 'I'll see you tomorrow. Be good.'

She followed a nurse into a small office and was handed a pile of forms to fill in and sign since Geoff had nominated her as his next of kin. The nurse said there was no need for her to come in the morning as bypass operations usually lasted several hours. The hospital would ring her when Geoff was out of theatre.

She managed to hold back the tears until she was alone in the lift, but once she started crying, she couldn't stop. Her hand in front of her mouth to stifle her sobs she almost staggered out of the hospital, oblivious to everything and everyone around. She had no idea how long she sat in the cab, staring at the thickening layer of snow covering the windscreen.

'Are you there, Rosalie love?' Fergus's voice on the cab radio startled her.

She coughed to clear her throat. 'Yes, Fergus. What's up?'

'I'm just lettin' you know that Petersen isn't happy. He called me twice in the past twenty minutes. You were supposed to phone him, he said. You'd better do it now before he comes after you or alerts the constabulary.'

She sniffled, wiped her damp cheeks with her pink scarf. 'I completely forgot about him. I'll text him now.'

'Aye, you do that. Don't give the man a hard time. I think he's genuinely worried about you. We all are.' Fergus paused. 'You sound a wee bit upset.'

In a broken voice she told him about Geoff's heart condition and about the very real possibility of him not surviving the operation. Before starting the cab, and although she didn't like having to account to Marc Petersen for her every move, she sent him a text to say she was on her way back.

After yet another hot and restless night, Marc was ready to believe that Isobel McBride's bed was indeed enchanted. Once again it hadn't been nightmarish visions of his father's helicopter crash that kept waking him up, but dreams of the same mysterious woman as before. He could feel the texture of her skin as he pinned her under him, taste her sweetness, lose himself inside her, but every time he woke up his bed was empty and his hands closed onto crumpled sheets instead of on the warm, soft body that drove him crazy with lust. He eventually managed to fall into a slumber some time after four and got up, feeling rough and ill-tempered as daylight threw a gloomy grey into the room through the curtains.

After another tepid shower, he went down to the kitchen, his footsteps echoing in the empty house. Rosalie had already left to take Lorna to the train station and visit McBride in hospital, so he gave her a quick call to make sure she was safe. He made scrambled eggs on toast and a pot of coffee, and listened to the castle's creaking, groaning and clinking sounds as he ate at the kitchen table.

There was something he hadn't had the chance to do yet, he thought as he put his plate and mug in the sink – to explore Raventhorn, and find out where all these noises came from. He smiled. Perhaps he'd dislodge one or two ghosts on the way.

It was a strange, but not unpleasant feeling, to walk along the long corridors, wonder what treasures lay hidden behind the closed doors, and think all this was, for now at least, his. Most of the ground floor rooms looked unlived in, with furniture stacked up or covered with dust sheets, except for an imposing oak-panelled dining room, an inviting billiard room and a music room complete with a grand piano, a beautiful harp and a deflated bagpiper sitting on an old chair – ghostly Finghall's bagpipes, perhaps?

There was also the beautiful, but messy, library he'd visited briefly the night before to get a map and the keys to the Range Rover. Today he took the time to look at the books and papers scattered on the desk, next to an ashtray filled with half-smoked cigars and a tarnished silver flask. There was no need to unscrew the top to know what was inside. He'd already gathered that McBride enjoyed his whisky.

Among the books were a detailed history of the Hebrides, Orkney and Shetland, old papers about Denmark and countless original and translations of poems and sagas. Next to the desk towered a tall pile of manuscripts, all of them transcriptions of runestones. A note scribbled on the sheet stated that all of them had been found in North Jutland.

Memories flooded Marc's mind, so vivid his breath caught in his throat. Summer meadows and deep forests. Endless empty beaches and crashing waves under a sky so vast and so blue it made the soul fly.

North Jutland was where his father's family was from and where he'd spent the happiest holidays of his life. Never since had he felt happier or freer than when he left his English boarding school for the summer and spent two glorious months on his grandfather's farm, roaming the countryside, climbing ancient burial mounds, looking for runestones. And dreaming.

His grandfather had told him about the people who used to live on the land, and some of their stories and legends. Enthralled, Marc had listened to his tales of Norse gods and mythical creatures, and to stories of Viking expeditions around the world. And when one summer, he had taught Marc how to decipher some of the inscriptions on the runestones that scattered his land, he had opened up a whole, ancient and magical world.

These exciting summers had stopped abruptly when Marc reached his thirteenth birthday, and his father decided he should make more productive use of his time by attending summer schools. There had been no more holidays in Hanstholm, and he'd only seen his grandfather once more after that – in his coffin at his funeral. Eager to sever his links with his humble Danish roots, his father had then sold the farm and the land.

What he didn't know was that Marc had bought the farm back a few years ago. He hadn't returned there yet – he rented it out – but one day he would, when he wasn't so busy … or afraid to be confronted with ghosts of the past and childhood memories.

What was ironic was that his father should buy the Scottish estate of a man obsessed with the very Danish ancestors he had spent his life disowning. Not for the first time Marc wondered what he'd been thinking of. Leaving the library, he made his way upstairs. Many of the rooms on the first and second floor were closed and he didn't like to intrude, but one door was ajar. He pushed it open and stepped into an elegant bedroom – a woman's, judging by the rose blooms adorning the wallpaper, the dressing table covered with perfume bottles and the tall, narrow vase in which stood a single white lily. The bed was made. A book lay on the bedside table, with a pair of reading glasses folded neatly on top. It was almost as if its occupant had just left. Almost, because there was an echo of sadness and loss that made Marc quickly step back and close the door softly behind him.

He went up to the third floor where a spiral staircase led to the top of one of the towers. The old, rackety door at the top didn't take much effort to open, and he stepped outside, onto the battlement. Oblivious to the cold, he stood against the parapet, taking in the sweeping view of the loch that reflected the lead grey sky, the snowy forest all around and the white peaks of the Cairngorms in the distance.

The vast, unspoilt scenery called to him. Soon, he promised himself, he'd work out an itinerary and hike up to the mountains, explore their crags and glens and secret places. Perhaps there, at last, the photos of the wreckage of his father's helicopter that were etched into his brain would start to fade. What would never fade however was the guilt of knowing that the accident had probably been his fault.

He was about to turn round when a gust of wind ruffled the surface of the loch and he noticed a large shadow under the water about fifty feet from the shore. He narrowed his eyes. It was much too large to be a rock. Perhaps it was the remains of a sunken boat or a submerged islet. Then he remembered what Rosalie had told him the day before. A hunting lodge once stood on the shores of the loch, before a freak storm changed it from a small tarn into what it was now.

A freak storm caused by Harald Johansen's – Harald the Cruel's – grief and anger at having his new bride taken away from him. He had to admit that Rosalie's story suited the mood and atmosphere of the area perfectly. The image of a feminine silhouette standing in the moonlight on top of the Armitages ruined castle flashed in front of him. He shrugged. Even he was falling prey to the romanticism of the place, it seemed.

He turned round, pushed the squealing door shut and went back downstairs. He tried to call Rosalie, but her mobile was switched off, so he phoned Fergus at Love Taxis and demanded that Rosalie phoned or text him, and never mind if he sounded a little too sharp.

After another pot of black coffee, he settled down to work in the drawing room. He had hardly fired up his laptop since his arrival and he had just started to look at his emails, when he heard a car drive up the lane, followed a couple of minutes later by loud banging at the kitchen door. It must be the cleaner. Fergus had warned that his wife would call today.

A small, wiry woman ensconced in a thick anorak as bright orange as her hair stood at the kitchen door, her face unsmiling. He opened the door wide to let her in.

'You must be Marion. Good afternoon. Please come in.'

'Why isn't the key in its usual place?' the woman asked, in lieu of greeting.

When he told her it would be kept in a safe place from then on and not in the planter where anybody could find it, she pursed her lips and pushed past him in disapproving silence that lasted the whole of five minutes, the time for her to take off her fur boots and parka, slip an apron and felt slippers on. Holding a dust rag and can of polish spray, she then followed him to the drawing room where she set to find out everything she could about him.

Once again he revealed far more about himself than he ever intended. The women of Irlwick were very skilled at extracting personal information, it seemed, or perhaps he was so tired he let his guard down.

'Petersen. That's not English.' Marion stopped her energetic dusting of a massive oak dresser. Narrowing her eyes, she inspected him from head to toe.

'My father's family is from Denmark.'

'You're Danish? But, of course! Now I understand why you're here. Geoff needs your help to translate his old papers, doesn't he?'

She waved her dusting rag at him. 'Have you seen the mess he made in the library? You can't walk for fear of tripping over books and parchments but Geoff, that old fool, forbids me to move anything. I hope you're going to sort things out.'

He would be quite incapable of translating McBride's papers, since it was many years since he'd read any text in the Futhark alphabets most runestones were written in, but he didn't set Marion right. If anything, pretending to be a translator was a great cover to explain his presence at Raventhorn since Rosalie didn't want anyone to know the truth – it was certainly better than pretending to be a trainee taxi driver.

Marion frowned and a suspicious look crossed her face. 'That's funny, I could swear you've a bit of a French accent, like that chef on the telly.'

Did anything get past this woman? Half-amused, half-exasperated, Marc proceeded to explain that his mother was indeed French and that although he'd been brought up in England, he'd lived in Paris for some years.

'Really? French *and* Danish, that's glamorous!'

Marion left the room and he turned to his laptop again. His mind however kept wandering – to McBride and his fascination for Scandinavian history, to Rosalie and the thugs who had run her off the road, and to Loch Armathiel, and the tragic story of Harald and Isobel. He shook his head. He was daydreaming again, neglecting his work and putting off his phone call to Kirsty.

She must be fuming that he was here, in Scotland, when he knew that she wanted him to be in London on Saturday night. 'I have been working on a proposal,' she had told him before she left for Paris on Monday, 'a very interesting proposal that I'm sure you won't be able to resist. We'll discuss it further at the weekend.'

He didn't need to ask what she meant. Kirsty was working on a possible merger between Petersen Holdings and an American firm that his father had wholeheartedly supported. Marc, however, was not keen on the idea of relocating to the States – with or without Kirsty.

As he keyed in her number, he wondered fleetingly why he hadn't thought about her these past couple of days. She was every man's dream woman – beautiful, intelligent, sophisticated, successful – she just wasn't his dream woman. He raked his fingers through his hair and blew an annoyed breath. How ridiculous … he was thinking about the mysterious woman that haunted his dreams here at Raventhorn!

When Kirsty didn't pick up, he left a message on her voicemail and scrolled down his emails for an update from the Hong Kong police about his father's helicopter accident. He was still waiting to hear whether or not his father had been piloting the helicopter – for confirmation that their phone conversation had upset him so much he hadn't paid enough attention and crashed the craft against the side of the mountain. There was nothing from Hong Kong, so he turned his attention to Carl Fitzpatrick's file. The man was an incompetent idiot and fully deserved to go bankrupt. Yet there was no way he would let that happen, no way he would risk another man's life.

Marc reclined against the back of the chair, pinched the bridge of his nose between his thumb and forefinger and closed his eyes. Figures and business projections scrolled across his mind, and soon a risky scheme started to take shape. Yes, that might just work. It was worth a try. If Fitzpatrick was willing to follow his advice.

Satisfied, he opened his eyes and blinked in surprise when he saw how dim the room had become, in sharp contrast with the white storm raging outside. Banging noises resounded in the corridor and Marion strode in, pulling an antique looking vacuum cleaner behind her.

'That blasted boiler's stopped working again,' she grumbled. 'I don't know how many times I've told Geoff to do something about the heating, but he always says he can't afford to have it fixed. You'd better fetch some wood from the shed across the yard. It's going to get bleemin' freezing in here before long.' She plugged in the vacuum cleaner, which roared like a plane about to take off and spurted a cloud of dust.

A couple of hours later, Marc watched Marion's car skid around the bend towards the bridge. He stamped his feet on the mat to get rid of snow sticking to his shoes and walked back into the castle. Eight inches, at least, of snow now covered the ground and it was coming down hard. The wind had picked up too. It blew through the pine trees in gusts so strong the whole forest shook, moved and groaned as if it were alive.

He was greeted by the cheerful glow of the fire he'd lit in the drawing room. Next to the fireplace was a satisfyingly high pile of logs, which he hoped would last all evening. Resolving to phone a heating engineer the following day, he put a couple more logs in the grate then stood a moment, arms folded on his chest, staring at the flames, and puzzled over the mystery surrounding Love Taxis again.

Why would anyone go to so much trouble to harass a small taxi firm in the Highlands? Hoax calls were unpleasant but hardly life threatening. They were the kind of stunt a bored teenager would pull. However physical attacks and material damage, like the vandalising of Duncan's cab and the previous night's car chase, were completely different. What were the perpetrators hoping to achieve? Put Rosalie out of business, perhaps, but it wasn't as if there was a turf war between rival cab companies. Maybe he was looking at this the wrong way. Maybe this was personal and Rosalie was the intended victim. If that was the case, it seemed unlikely that whoever was threatening her had any intention of stopping anytime soon.

The most sensible thing would be to close Love Taxis – he didn't have to look at the books to know it was the most unprofitable business he'd ever owned. That would however feel like giving in to the threats, and was out of the question.

His phone rang, breaking the silence.

'What are you thinking of, letting me down at the last minute? Don't you realise what strings I had to pull to get the opera tickets and a table at Jules' for Saturday night?' Kirsty snapped at the other end of the line.

'I'm sorry. This trip to Scotland is turning out to be more complicated than I originally thought.'

She let out an exasperated groan. 'I had arranged the whole evening so that Ben Turner and his wife could be with us. Ben is vital to our New York project. Now I'm going to have to ask Maguire to come with me.'

'Don't bother Maguire. It's his anniversary tomorrow night. He's been talking about it for weeks. His wife hasn't been well and he's taking her to some country hotel for a break.'

'Well, he'll have to celebrate another day.'

He frowned. 'Turner can wait. In fact, the whole New York project can wait. Maguire's wife is very ill. There may not be another chance for him to—'

'Then she should be resting,' Kirsty cut in. 'Anyway, since when have you been a champion of your employees' family life? You don't usually care about the people who work for you. And rightly so, I might add. They get paid to work, not to socialise with their wives.'

The tone of her voice riled him, especially since she was only stating the harsh truth. He worked hard, rarely took any time off, and expected his staff to be as committed to their job.

'I don't want you to bother Maguire this weekend,' he repeated. 'I'm sure you can ask someone else from the office to accompany you or go on your own.'

She fell silent. 'All right then, since Maguire's anniversary is that important to you, I'll leave him alone. What are these complications you're talking about?'

'I'm not entirely sure but it looks like I'll have to stay up here longer than I expected.'

She laughed. 'Come on, Marc, admit it, you're enjoying being the lord of the manor, aren't you?'

'No, of course not.' There was the noise of an engine outside, followed by a door slamming. Glancing out of the window he saw Rosalie's cab in the courtyard. At last, she was back.

'I have to go. Sorry about the opera and the restaurant but I'm sure you'll be fine.'

Chapter Nine

The drive back from Inverness had been slow and treacherous, with snowdrifts building up on either side of slippery roads. It didn't help that she'd constantly peered in the rear-view mirror, dreading to see the black four-by-four that had driven her off the road the previous evening. She had gripped her steering wheel so hard her neck and shoulders now ached.

What she needed was a long soak in the bath, hot food and a rest. Talking to Petersen could wait until the morning, especially if, as she suspected, he was going to get all dictatorial again about what she could or could not do. As more snow was forecast, she parked in the garage, and went straight up to her flat.

As usual, she felt guilty the moment she walked into the cheerful living room with its sunny yellow walls, bright blue curtains and matching throws on the sofa. Geoff had spared no expense in renovating the stable block to turn it into a lovely flat for her, but it wasn't home. Nowhere except Raventhorn Castle would ever be. And yet, she reminded herself once again, she would soon have to find somewhere else to live because even this flat now belonged to Petersen.

She hung her anorak up, kicked her boots off and glanced at the pictures hanging on the walls. There were several of Raventhorn and two of her mother and herself, and these she treasured because they were the only ones she had of her since her mother was camera shy – or camera-phobic, as Alice used to say.

She opened the fridge and let out a disappointed sigh as any prospect of a warm evening meal vanished. Except for a slab of butter, a bag of wilted lettuce and a few slices of ham, the fridge was empty. She took a sniff of the ham and pulled a face before throwing it in the bin. A quick search of the cupboards produced a bag of plain crisps and half a packet of digestive biscuits. Her only hope of a decent meal was to raid Raventhorn's kitchen, but as she had no intention of talking to Petersen, she would wait until he had gone to bed.

She switched on the television, caught the end of the local news, then stepped into the bedroom to undress. She had time to take a bath before her favourite crime series started. Dropping her clothes into the laundry basket, she wrapped herself in her bathrobe and went to the bathroom to run a bath, in which she poured a generous squirt of her favourite peach bubble bath. As the bathroom steamed up, she pinned her hair up and dipped a toe in.

The water was hot, almost scalding, just the way she liked it. She was lucky to have her own boiler and heating system in the stable block and wasn't subject to the vagaries of the boiler in the house. She slipped out of her robe, climbed into the bath and closed her eyes. Right now, she didn't want to think about anything, or anyone – least of all about Marc Petersen who probably expected her to report in like a good little soldier.

He waited almost half an hour before storming out of the castle. The courtyard was empty, the garage door closed. What was the woman doing, and why hadn't she come over to see him?

Looking up, he saw some light at the windows above the Love Taxis office and shook his head, at the same time relieved and annoyed. He would give her another half an hour or so and then go over. They had things to discuss.

He was walking back to the kitchen when a high-pitched scream pierced the silence and gave him goosebumps. He ran across the courtyard, yanked the door to the stable block open. It wasn't locked. He took the stairs two by two, only to find that the door to Rosalie's flat was unlocked too. Flinging it open, he stepped into a warm, comfortable living room. The lights and the TV were on but Rosalie was nowhere to be seen.

'Rosalie?' He glanced around, barely noticing the photos of Raventhorn on the walls, and others of a woman with a little girl by her side, or the fact that there wasn't anything pink in the room, only deep blues and sunny yellows.

He called again, with more urgency, and strode into an empty bedroom. A door was shut to his right. He pushed it open and breathed in a cloud of peach scented steam. Then he saw her. She was in the bath, unconscious.

He rushed to her side, knelt down to grab her shoulders and shook her hard. Her brown eyes flew open. Her cheeks were flushed. Strands of dark mahogany hair had escaped from her loosely pinned bun at the top of her head and snaked down the slender curve of her neck. Fluffy bath foam clung to the pink tips of her full, round breasts. His mouth went dry and he was seized by an uncontrollable urge to slide his fingers down her bare shoulders and wipe the bubbles off.

Rosalie stared at him, her lips open, her chest heaving. For a few seconds neither of them moved nor spoke. At last he got a hold on himself. Letting go of her, he rose to his feet and stepped back.

She sat up and wrapped her arms around her knees.

'What are you doing in here?'

'I'm sorry. I heard a scream. I thought you were hurt.' He took another step back towards the door.

'Well, it wasn't me,' she said between clenched teeth. 'Get out.'

He remembered the television in the living room. Could he have mistaken a television programme for Rosalie's voice?

'Yes. Yes, of course,' he almost stammered, closing the door softly behind him as he left.

She wrapped herself in her robe and tried to tie the belt around her waist but her fingers were shaking too much. Letting out a shuddering breath, she put her hand to her chest. Oh, the shame of it! Would she ever be able to face him when her skin still burned with the imprint of his hands on her shoulders, and when she hadn't pushed him away or slid down into the water to hide, but sat naked and mesmerised by the hot, dangerous glow in his eyes?

She heard footsteps, and realised that he hadn't gone back to the castle but was just the other side of the bathroom door. She almost fancied she could feel the heat from his body.

'I'm going to sleep here tonight, Petersen,' she called. 'I'll see you in the morning.'

'It's not a good idea, especially since you are so careless about your own safety. Both the downstairs door and the door to your flat were unlocked. Anybody could have come in and—'

'And find me in the bath, like you did?'

There was a short silence. 'I said I was sorry. It was a misunderstanding. Listen, Rosalie, I don't want you to stay here alone. I want you to come back with me to the castle.'

There he was again, telling her what to do. She forced a deep, calming breath down. 'I'm beginning to think that you are afraid of being alone with Raventhorn's ghosts.' Would he take the bait? She held her breath and waited a few seconds.

'Don't be silly, there are no ghosts,' he retorted dryly, the way she hoped he would. 'Very well, you can stay here on your own tonight if that's what you want, but only if you promise to lock both the downstairs door and the door to your flat.'

She closed her eyes and breathed a sigh of relief. At least she wouldn't have to face him tonight.

There was another short pause. 'By the way,' he added, 'I would like to see the books and all the paperwork for Love Taxis first thing in the morning. It's about time I knew what I was dealing with.'

Her heart sank, but even though he couldn't see her, she tilted her chin up. 'No problem. You'll have the accounts in the morning. Good night!'

She breathed a sigh of relief when she heard the sound of the door closing. She had only postponed the inevitable. She would have to face him soon enough, but at least she would have time to compose herself, her cheeks would not be quite as hot and her hands would have stopped shaking.

She would use her evening to get the books ready for Petersen. He wouldn't be impressed though, especially since she had neglected them lately. A little creative accounting was in order.

She slipped into a thick flannel shirt and a pair of jeans and phoned Lorna at her sister's in Norwich. She had to let her know about Geoff's operation.

As she suspected, Lorna offered to return to Raventhorn straight away. 'There's nothing you can do. The doctors said the operation could take hours. What's more, you need a break to recharge your batteries. You'll need all your strength to help take care of Geoff when he leaves hospital.'

'Did he talk to you?' Lorna asked.

'He couldn't say much because of his oxygen mask. He did mumble a few things about some dangerous man – or was it dangerous men? – but he wasn't making much sense. Do you know what he wanted to tell me? You said it was important.'

Lorna hesitated. 'I'm not sure, sweetie.' There was a silence. 'Anyway, how are you getting on with Marc Petersen?'

'Very well.' Rosalie crossed her fingers and touched the table's wooden top. She'd never told so many lies, it could only bring bad luck.

They talked a while longer and she hung up after promising to call the following day. She settled at the dining room table with her ledgers, receipts and bank statements for the past three months, and opened the diary where she recorded all of her and Duncan's fares. If there was a time she regretted declining Niall's offer of help with her accounts, this was it.

Her heart was sinking when she pushed the books away a couple of hours later. Things were bad, very bad. She would be well over her overdraft limit after she paid Duncan's, Fiona's and Fergus's wages this month, and that was before Niall billed her for the repairs to both Duncan's cab and her own.

She could already see Marc Petersen looking down at her with his cool grey eyes as he passed judgement on the way she managed, or rather mismanaged, her taxi firm. Perhaps he was right and she wasn't cut out to run a business. She didn't charge high enough fares, gave her customers too much leeway with credit. She should work from a large town, do more airport runs, offer businessmen special deals, invest in a minibus and diversify into day trips for tourists. She would never make any money in Irlwick, and yet this was where people needed her most.

She rubbed her eyes, stifled a yawn and pushed her chair back. All she wanted now was something to eat and a cup of tea with lots of milk and sugar. She walked to the window, and lifted her curtain. Blustery gusts of wind swept fresh snow across the courtyard. All the windows at Raventhorn were dark, which meant that Petersen was asleep and she could safely sneak into the kitchen and get some food. He would never know she'd been there.

Cheered up by the prospect of Lorna's chocolate cake that she knew was in the fridge, she put on her boots, found her key to the kitchen door and wrapped herself in one of Geoff's dark green padded jackets which was far too big, but much warmer than her pink anorak, and which she often wore to go hiking. Pulling the hood down to shelter from the wind, she hurried down the stairs and across the courtyard. The security lights didn't come on. She sighed. The power must be down, once again.

The kitchen was cold – far too cold to take her coat off. She flicked the electricity switch but nothing happened. So she'd been right. The fuses had blown and the heating was down too. She didn't fancy a trip to the basement on her own right now. She'd wait until morning to fix it. That way she could show Petersen what to do if it happened again, which it no doubt would. Isobel McBride playing around with the electricity was a story Geoff had made up years before to justify not doing anything about the dismal state of the plumbing and the electricity, in the same way he used the ghostly Raven Lady as an excuse not to replace rotten window frames which let in freezing draughts and made doors slam shut. He said it gave paying guests something to remember Raventhorn by ...

She was feeling her way along the kitchen cabinets to get to the drawer where Lorna kept a torch when her sleeve caught the handle of a frying pan. It crashed to the floor with a deafening noise before she could stop it. Hoping that Petersen was sound asleep and hadn't heard the racket, she picked it up and set it on the table.

She found the torch, opened the fridge and shone the light inside, and licked her lips. Lorna's chocolate cake would go some way in helping her forget the mortifying bathroom incident and the hours spent worrying over the accounts for Love Taxis. Taking the whole cake back to the flat was tempting, but selfish, and she decided to leave some for Petersen, even if he didn't deserve it.

She balanced the torch on the table, took a knife out of the drawer and was just starting to cut the cake when a noise outside the kitchen startled her. She bumped against the table. The torch fell down and switched itself off, plunging the kitchen in darkness.

After that everything happened too fast. As she was bending down to retrieve the torch, a man's hand seized hold of her arm and twisted it behind her back, forcing her to release the knife. She extended her free hand forward, feeling for something – anything – that could serve as a weapon against her attacker. Her fingers made contact with the handle of the frying pan. She grabbed hold of it, twisted round and swung the pan in front of her. There was a loud metallic sound as it connected with her assailant's face, quickly followed by a curse in French.

Her blood froze. No. It couldn't be.

Gasping in shock, she held the pan against her chest. 'Petersen? Is that you?'

'Rosalie?' He sounded as stunned as she was.

Her heart sank. What had she done? What if he pressed charges for assault, or demanded she left Raventhorn immediately and found somewhere else to live?

She swallowed hard. 'Did I hurt you?'

'What do you think?' he grunted.

He picked up the torch and flicked it on. 'What the hell are you doing here in the middle of the night? With that coat, your hood up and that great big knife in your hand, I thought you were some psycho burglar.'

'I wanted some chocolate cake.'

He stared at her, his eyes filled with shadows, and repeated very slowly, 'You wanted some chocolate cake.'

'I'm sorry.'

He rubbed the side of his face. 'You are truly one of a kind, Rosalie Heart.' Something in his tone hinted that he didn't mean it as a compliment.

'It was your fault too! You shouldn't jump on me like that. You scared me to death. When I think I was cutting a piece of cake for you …'

His gaze travelled from her to the frying pan, then back to her, and he shook his head. Surprisingly his lips stretched into a smile and a spark of humour lit his eyes. The change was so striking it almost took her breath away.

'You should play tennis,' he said, rubbing his jaw. 'You have a terrific backhand.' Before she could respond, he carried on. 'By the way, the heating and the electricity are down. I'll call an electrician in the morning, but in the meantime do you have any idea how to fix them?'

'Grab the torch and come with me to the basement, I'll show you what to do.'

It didn't take long to sort out the electricity. The heating as usual proved a little trickier, but she tinkered with the controls and the boiler spurted back to life.

'There. All done.'

As if to prove her wrong, the lights flickered and went out again. A cold breeze blew into the basement, and the door slammed shut with such a loud bang that Rosalie shrieked, swung round, and bumped into

Petersen. His arm wrapped around her waist and he pulled her against him to stop her from falling. Her fingers instinctively gripped his jumper and she clung to him, breathing in the subtle lemony scent of his after-shave. How strong and solid he was … and how hot and tingly he made her feel all over!

'I'm all right,' she mumbled as she jerked back, confused and angry at her body's treacherous response.

'Stay here, I'll fix it again,' he said. There were a few clanking noises as he must have tripped on tools scattered on the stone flags, and a couple of muffled curses in French when he banged his head on a shelf, but a weak halo of yellow light soon danced on the walls. He removed the casing from the fuse box, flicked the small levers and light flooded the basement.

'These power cuts have nothing to do with your ghostly Isobel McBride,' he remarked, wiping cobwebs from his hair with his fingers. 'The whole place needs rewiring and renovating.'

'No, it doesn't. It has character, that's all,' she protested. 'If you wanted designer bathrooms and fancy central heating, you should have bought a modern house. Raventhorn is perfect the way it is.'

He did not reply and they made their way back upstairs.

'I only had a very uninspiring sandwich earlier on,' he said when they walked into the kitchen. 'I think there's some pasta in the fridge. Would you like to join me for a bite to eat?'

As if on cue, her stomach rumbled. A few hours earlier, she would have been mortified at the idea of sharing a meal with him. Now she was hungry and cold, and acutely aware that the cupboards in her flat were bare. And who knows, perhaps hitting him over the head with the frying pan had given him amnesia and he'd forgotten all about seeing her naked in the bath?

She nodded. 'Thank you. I'd like that. Lorna makes the best lasagne, they're even better than Alice's.'

She put a pasta dish in the microwave oven while he set the table and pulled a bottle of red wine out of the wine rack.

'I met your cleaning lady today,' he remarked, when they sat down to eat. He poured wine into her glass.

She glanced up. 'And you lived to tell the tale? Marion can talk for Scotland.'

He smiled. 'She must be the most talkative person I've ever met – apart from Alice and yourself, that is.' He leaned back in his chair. 'Marion gave me a thorough grilling. She should work for the police or MI6.'

She frowned. 'You didn't tell her why you were here, did you?'

'No. She is under the impression I'm here to help McBride translate old Danish manuscripts and I didn't put her right.' He leaned across the table. 'You can't put it off forever, you know. Petersen Holdings own Raventhorn and there's nothing you can do about it. People will have to be told eventually.'

'I want to talk to Geoff before telling anybody.' She hung her head down and sighed. 'But now I don't know when that will be.' She explained about the heart operation scheduled for the following day.

'I'm surprised you're his next of kin,' he said. 'Didn't you say Elaine and Rupert were his cousins?'

'They're not close. He knows all they were ever interested in was Raventhorn. Rupert came to the hospital this morning, but only to ask Geoff for money and gloat about my troubles.'

She proceeded to dip her spoon into the moist chocolate cake and brought it to her lips. She had a very seductive way of eating chocolate cake, slowly, savouring every mouthful and when she'd eaten the last morsel, she licked the spoon clean and passed her tongue across her lips.

Marc put his glass down, clenched his fist under the table and looked away. It didn't stop his blood pulsing and his body throbbing. He almost groaned aloud as sensations and images flashed through him – sensations of how soft she had felt as she nestled against him in the basement, and images of the creamy skin and wonderful curves he'd caught a glimpse of when she was in the bath and that she'd now hidden under her shapeless checked shirt. Once again, he wondered what was happening to the polished, controlled, disciplined man he'd striven to become all these years. It was as if Scotland's raw wilderness yanked him back to a crude and untamed version of himself.

'Has McBride ever been married?' he asked in a gruff voice.

She smiled and pushed her empty plate away. 'What would Geoff have done with a wife? He had us – Lorna, my mother and I.'

'You mean that your mother was … hmm … involved with him?'

'Oh no, things were never that way between my mother and Geoff, although I'm quite sure that, like every female over the age of five, she was a little bit in love with him.'

An unpleasant thought made him frown. He sat back in his chair, crossed his arms over his chest. 'Are you? In love with him, I mean.'

This time she stared at him in shock. 'Of course not. What a silly thing to say. Geoff is like a ... well, I suppose, he is a very dear friend, or an uncle to me.' She rose to her feet with a sigh. 'Anyway, it's late. We'd better clean up. There's no need to fill the dishwasher for just a few pots. I'll wash up if you dry.'

She handed him a tea towel, rolled up her sleeves and started clearing the plates. He helped her pile the dirty crockery by the sink and stood next to her, towel in hand.

She was close – too close. The button at the top of her shirt had come undone, giving him a tantalising glimpse of her milky white throat. Her warm, sweet and fruity scent drove him to distraction. His throat felt dry and tight, and his hands so clumsy he almost dropped several plates to the ground.

'Watch out, Petersen!' She laughed. 'I bet you don't do the dishes very often.'

'No. I don't. Sorry.'

She turned to look at him. As if she could guess what he was thinking and felt the attraction that sparked and sizzled around them, her eyes opened wide, and her pupils grew larger. A pink blush spread on her face as she parted her lips.

His fingers wrapped themselves around the damp tea towel. Damn. This was torture. It would be so easy to bend down, take, touch and taste. He'd never wanted anything more in his life. Kissing Rosalie Heart, however, was out of the question. He wasn't here to mix pleasure with business. And Raventhorn was business – only business.

He drew in a sharp breath and stepped back. His voice was cold and matter-of-fact when he spoke. 'It's time to call it a night. Leave the rest of the washing-up. I'll finish it in the morning. And don't forget to bring me the books at nine o'clock.'

Blood drained from her face, and she shrunk away from him. 'The books ... oh ... yes ... of course.'

'Would you like me to walk you back to your flat?'

She shook her head. 'There's no need. Sorry once again about your head.' She slipped her green jacket on, and opened the door, and almost ran out into the night, leaving in her place a gust of cold air and a flurry of snowflakes.

He stood alone in the kitchen, wondering what he was going to do about Raventhorn, about Rosalie Heart and her taxi business.

But most of all he was wondering what the hell was happening to him.

Chapter Ten

It was still snowing the following morning when she walked across the courtyard, clasping the ledgers against her. The plan was to leave them on the kitchen table, get the keys to the Range Rover and sneak out without bumping into Marc. But, of course, nothing went to plan these days.

'Good morning.' Marc put his coffee down and rose to his feet. He was dressed in a thick green jumper and a pair of jeans, and sported a vivid purple bruise on his cheekbone where she'd hit him with the copper pan.

'Good morning,' she mumbled back, her chest tightening with guilt and shame. She could have killed the man.

'You're early,' he remarked.

'I have things to do.' She pulled her hood down and set the ledgers on the table. 'Here are the books for Love Taxis, as requested.'

'Would you like a coffee before we start? I've just made some.'

She shook her head. 'I can't stay.'

He glanced at the window. 'There's a raging snowstorm outside. Don't tell me you're going out in your cab today.'

'Not the cab. I need the Range Rover today. In bad weather, a group of us take it in turn to visit elderly or disabled people who live out of town and make sure they're all right. We bring them essential supplies, collect their medicines or clear their drive, that kind of thing.'

She ran a finger along the spine of one of the ledgers and let out a heavy sigh. 'I did my best with the accounts but I'm sure you'll have plenty of comments about my lack of business sense and my ... what was it ... naivety – or was it stupidity – I can't remember your exact words.' She didn't even try to hide the bitterness in her voice. It probably wouldn't take more than five minutes for Marc Petersen to decide to close Love Taxis down.

She looked up. 'I need to go. Did you put the keys back in the desk in the library?'

He frowned, thoughtful. 'I'm coming with you.'

She tilted her head up in shock. 'What for?'

'I'll drive.'

'Oh I see, you don't think I can handle the Range Rover on my own. I've driven it many times before, and in worse weather than this, and I'm sure you have far more important things to do than shovel snow off someone's drive, cut wood, bring in people's groceries and ... you know ... be nice to people. You don't do nice and chats, remember?'

'I said I'd keep an eye on you, and I will, whether you like it or not. And for the record, I am capable of being nice. I'll get the keys.' Without giving her time to find fresh objections, he disappeared upstairs.

Rosalie stamped her booted foot on the floor tiles in frustration. How dare the man meddle with her life so? Now she would have to be with him all day! She poured the rest of the coffee from the cafetière into a flask, added lashings of milk and sugar, and stuffed a packet of chocolate digestives and a couple of bananas into her bag.

There was at least one good thing about Marc spending the day with her – he wouldn't be able to look at the books for Love Taxis.

Doughall McGunn gave Marc a slap on the back, his way of thanking him for clearing the drive to his cottage. The two men exchanged a few words, Marc waved goodbye and strode towards the Range Rover where Rosalie was waiting.

Snowflakes dusted his hair, his eyes were as grey as the sky and his face reddened by the cold as he flung open the door and sat behind the wheel. He glanced at the mobile in Rosalie's hand. 'Any news from the hospital?'

She nodded. 'The bypass operation was postponed. There was a problem with Geoff's blood pressure. It is now scheduled for tomorrow.'

'How is he doing?'

'The nurse said he was stable. I wanted to drive over to the hospital but he is sedated and visits won't be allowed today.' Reclining against the headrest, she tightened her grip on her phone. What if Geoff didn't get better? What if she was going to lose him, like she'd lost her mother?

'Try not to worry too much. He's in good hands.' Marc nodded encouragingly. 'So where are we going now?'

'Doughall was the last person on our list, so we're heading back to the Stag's Head for a briefing with the rest of the team.'

She stifled a yawn and closed her eyes. Her neck, back and shoulders ached, and the day wasn't over yet. They had visited twelve isolated farmhouses north of Avielochan. Marc and she had made two shopping trips into Irlwick, and driven one elderly lady to the emergency doctor's surgery, then taken her back home. They had cleared drives, and thrown shovel loads of salt to keep access lanes free. Marc had chopped wood and carried armfuls of logs into people's houses. He had even climbed on a roof to fix a television aerial. She might not like to admit it but he had worked hard and been a great help, even if he had rebuffed any attempt at small talk from the people they had visited with his usual cool, grey stares.

'Rosalie, we're here.'

She jerked awake and rubbed her eyes as Marc parked in front of the pub. She must be more tired than she'd thought to fall asleep without even noticing.

He pulled the key out of the ignition and turned to her. 'I take it you still don't want to tell anyone the truth about me.'

She nodded.

He sighed. 'I thought so. Shall we pretend I am your trainee taxi driver or do we go with the Danish translator story?'

'Whatever you prefer, I don't mind.'

'The truth will come out sooner or later, Rosalie.'

He had a point, but part of her refused to face the facts – refused to acknowledge that Raventhorn was no longer Geoff's, no longer her home.

He got out of the car and walked to her side to open her door. 'When exactly are you planning to tell people?'

'After I've spoken to Geoff. I need to understand why he sold Raventhorn.'

'He sold it because he ran out of money, that's all.'

She wasn't convinced. Things had been bad for years but Geoff always pulled Raventhorn out of trouble. There must be something else behind his very sudden, very hushed, decision to part with his beloved Raventhorn.

The Stag's Head was unusually quiet that afternoon. Other than the landlord, her friends and a couple of men with buzz cut hair and black leather coats she'd never seen before, the room was empty. Niall was getting a pint of beer at the counter.

'Hi!' Rosalie smiled, pulled her pink woolly hat off and shook her hair free before standing on her tiptoes to kiss his cheek. Slipping his arm around her waist, he pulled her to him and kissed her full on the mouth.

She pressed her lips together, put her hands flat against his chest and gave a gentle push but he clasped his fingers more tightly in the small of her back.

'What are you doing? Stop it!'

'Just saying hello to my gorgeous girl. How has your day been?'

'Busy.' She managed to disentangle herself, stepped back and bumped into Marc who stood right behind her.

The two men acknowledged each other with a curt nod. Marc rested his elbow on the polished wood counter and turned to Rosalie.

'What are you drinking?' he asked, signalling to the landlord.

'I'll get Roz's drink,' Niall cut in, taking a five-pound note out of his jeans pocket. 'Half a cider, as usual?'

She shook her head. 'Not today, thanks. I'll have a lemonade.' She glanced around. 'Is Kian not helping out today?'

'Nay, he got into a bit of a barney at home, apparently. Skidded on the snow and scratched his father's brand new car taking his girlfriend home. His dad's not happy, and got him to do some chores.'

'I can't say I'm sorry he's not here. He was very unpleasant, aggressive even, with me at the Four Winds ceilidh.'

'Was he really? I don't know. I didn't see much of him. Here.' Niall handed her a glass of lemonade.

'Get some salt and vinegar crisps and pork scratchers for us, Roz, that's a good lass!' Fergus called from the back of the pub. Love Taxis was closed to business today again and he'd been helping the rangers prioritise the calls for help from locals.

Puddles of melted snow made the wooden floor slippery and Rosalie slowed her pace as she brought her drink and the snacks to the table where Fergus and the two local rangers were sitting.

'Well, folks, I think we've done well today,' Cameron, the head ranger, declared when Niall and Marc joined them. 'We've seen almost everybody on our list. There are only a few people left to check up on.

Roger and I can take care of the area south of Kingussie and Badenoch tomorrow, but I heard there were tourists at the new ski lodges up towards Geal Charn. One of us should go up there and make sure they're all right.'

'I know where it is,' Rosalie said, 'it's off the mountain road after Armathiel forest. I'll go before it gets dark.'

'I'll come with you,' Niall said quickly.

'There's no need to trouble yourself,' Marc cut in, 'I'm here.'

'That's no trouble at all, Petersen,' Niall retorted. 'I'm just making sure my girl is safe.'

'For heaven's sake, Niall, stop this,' Rosalie hissed, her cheeks blazing hot. When was he going to understand that she wasn't his girl any longer, and would never be again?

The two men glared at each other. Niall narrowed his eyes and pointed to Marc's bruised cheekbone. 'What happened to you, Petersen? Did you fall on your face in the snow, or did you walk into a door?'

'Into a frying pan, actually.' Marc lifted his half-pint to his lips.

Niall snorted. 'By the way, how long are you here for?'

Marc raised his eyebrows. 'I'm not sure. Why?'

'I've been wondering what exactly you were doing at Raventhorn, that's all. Roz and Alice said you were on some kind of taxi training course, but Marion claims you're translating ancient Danish manuscripts for Geoff. So which is it?'

'Stop this, Niall,' Rosalie hissed. 'Marc is a business contact of Geoff's, that's all. He's been kind enough to help us today. The least you can do is be courteous.'

Ignoring her, Niall leaned towards Marc. 'Let me tell you something, Petersen. We don't care much for city boys around here, whether they're French, Danish or English, so I'm warning you. Rosalie isn't one of the posh bimbos you no doubt hang around with in London or Paris, or wherever it is you live. She's a nice girl, but she has never been away from Irlwick, and she's far too naive and kind-hearted for her own good. It's obvious she has taken a shine to you, but the thing is, she belongs here, with her friends. With me. She'll never leave. So back off.'

Rosalie's face caught fire, her heart hammered against her ribs, so loud that's all she could hear. Everybody in the pub was staring at her –

her friends, Marc, and even the two rough-looking men near the bar, and she wanted to disappear into a great big hole. Instead she rose to her feet, grabbed her anorak from the back of the chair and faced Niall.

'You have no right to talk about me like I'm a simpleton, no right to behave as if I belong to you.' Anger and humiliation made her stutter. 'We're over. We were over four years ago, and it's about time you accepted it. And one more thing. I don't fancy Marc, or anybody else for that matter, but if I did, it would be none of your business.'

Niall shrugged as if he didn't believe a word she'd said, and took a slug of beer, so she turned to Cameron whose cheeks had turned pink – with embarrassment, no doubt.

'I'll check on the tourists and let you know if there's any problem. Give me a ring if you need help with anybody else.'

Cameron's lips stretched into a smile. 'Thank you, lass.'

Trying hard not to look at anyone else in the pub, she put her woolly hat on, fastened her coat then moved in front of Marc and extended her hand. 'I'll wait for you in the car.'

He handed her the keys. 'I'll be straight out.'

She nodded and strode out.

Marc looked at Niall who sat drinking his beer as if nothing had happened, as if he hadn't just hurt and embarrassed the woman he pretended to care for.

'You claim to be Rosalie's friend,' he started, 'so act like one. She has enough to cope with at the moment without having to put up with your bruised ego and temper tantrums.'

Niall put his pint down and smirked. 'Really? I've known Roz for years. I know what she needs. I know what's good for her. And you're not it.'

Marc never paused to think. Leaning across the table, he grabbed Niall's shirt collar and lifted him off his seat. 'That may be so, but if you know what's good for *you*, then you'll not talk to her like that again.'

Niall's face flushed a deep red, his blue eyes bulged out and he made a strangled sound. Fergus sprung up and laid a pacifying hand on Marc's shoulder. 'Hold it, my lad. I think he got the message.'

Marc released Niall who slumped back onto the padded seat, rubbed his throat and started coughing.

'I'll leave you to enjoy your drink,' Marc said as he slipped his coat on. 'Gentlemen.'

Fergus and the rangers stared at him in awe and muttered goodbyes.

Once outside he took a long, deep breath of freezing cold air and looked up at the grey sky. What on earth had possessed him? He had just behaved like some Neanderthal throwback and over-reacted in a big way by grabbing Niall Murray by the throat. The relationship between Niall and Rosalie was nothing to do with him. He shouldn't care about Rosalie being upset. No, he corrected, he *didn't* care about her. She only happened to be momentarily caught in a financial transaction he was involved in, and as soon as he sold Raventhorn, she'd slip out of his life forever. And yet the urge to throttle the mechanic had been so strong his usual self-control had completely deserted him.

Behind him two men walked out of the pub. They were talking in low voices but their accent was unmistakably cockney. Surprised, Marc turned round but only glimpsed their bulky, black-clad silhouettes as they disappeared down the dimly lit street and turned the corner.

A car horn beeped nearby, startling him. Rosalie waved to him from behind the wheel of the Range Rover.

'I'm driving,' she said as soon as he opened the door.

He opened his mouth to protest that it was a bad idea but looking at the firm tilt of her chin and anger in her eyes, he bit his tongue and said nothing. The last thing she needed now was an argument about her driving skills.

They drove to the Cairngorms National Park in total silence. She didn't even put her favourite pop radio on. He guessed she was still brooding, so he didn't speak either.

Daylight was fading fast so Rosalie switched the headlights on. The road turned into a slippery track, twisting and turning as it climbed up the hills towards peaks shrouded in mist and snow clouds. On the one side a steep slope hurtled down towards a river. On the other side stood a thick forest. The car brushed against long feathery branches of Caledonian pines at every tight turn. There was no oncoming traffic, no other vehicle on the road. They were alone in a frigid white world.

They came across a sign to a holiday village and forked right.

'There are a few chalets here, but the new lodges are higher up,'

Rosalie explained after they passed several timber cottages, dark and empty. 'It's strange that anyone should be renting one at this time of year.'

The single-track road climbed in and out of the forest. A fox shot out in front of them and Rosalie slammed on the brakes. The wheels spun, the car skidded and stalled. She cursed under her breath and started the engine again.

Lights peeped through tall, dark fir trees, and he saw the holiday lodge. In the gathering dusk and with smoke billowing out of the chimney, it looked warm and welcoming. No car was parked at the front but there were tyre tracks and packed snow so it looked as if another vehicle had been there recently.

Rosalie parked and flung the car door open. 'I won't be long. I'll just ask them if they're all right and if they need anything.'

She climbed the front steps to the porch and knocked on the door. After a minute or so, the door opened and the figure of a slim, dark-haired woman stood in the doorway. Rosalie talked to her for a few moments.

His mobile pinged, signalling an incoming message. He took the phone out of his pocket, glanced at the screen. Kirsty texted that she was getting ready for her evening at the opera with the Turners and sending a selfie of her reflection in the mirror wearing a long black evening dress with the caption: 'See what you're missing?'

The sound of the lodge's front door closing made him look up. Rosalie was walking back to the car, shoulders hunched against the cold and hands in her pocket. He would reply to Kirsty later. He flung the phone onto the dashboard as Rosalie opened the door.

'They weren't very friendly,' Rosalie remarked as she slipped behind the wheel a few moments later. 'That woman practically slammed the door in my face. There was a man in the other room who shouted for her to get rid of me. How rude of him, when we came all this way to see if they needed help!'

She started the car.

'What did they say?'

'That they didn't need anyone checking up on them.' She sighed. 'Well, I suppose that's good news.'

'Was it just the two of them?'

She nodded. 'That woman, I've seen her before, with Rupert. I thought she was his girlfriend. She has a London accent, and so does the man who was shouting from the back room.'

There was something else, something she couldn't quite bring herself to say aloud. Something that had made her stomach clench and her throat constrict so much she had feared she would be unable to breathe. Some strange instinct that pushed her to turn away, run and find a place to hide.

The man's voice sounded disturbingly familiar, like the echo of a childhood nightmare. Even now, safe in the Range Rover with Marc by her side, she couldn't stop the shivers of fear crawling down her spine as she glanced towards the cabin and gasped.

A man's silhouette stood out behind the cabin's net curtains.

'Rosalie, what's wrong? You seem upset.' Marc looked puzzled.

'It's nothing. Let's go back.' But her hand shook so much she had to turn the key twice in the ignition before starting the Range Rover.

Night had fallen now and she had to focus really hard to see the road with snowflakes dancing and swirling in the headlights. She forced a smile, unwilling to show Marc her mounting apprehension. Despite what she'd claimed earlier, she didn't often drive up here when the weather was this bad. They reached the forest and the empty chalets and started on the winding mountain road overlooking the gorge with the river at the bottom.

A massive black four-by-four suddenly appeared at a twist of the road, its high beam headlights on and driving fast in the middle of the track.

'Move over to the inside, right against the bank,' Marc said, quickly assessing the situation but Rosalie had already hit the brakes hard.

'I can't!' she screamed as the Range Rover skidded on the snowy track. Marc grabbed hold of the wheel with one hand and steered towards the hillside, but it was too late, and the car plummeted over the edge.

They were going to die.

The Range Rover tumbled and bumped down the hillside. Fast. So fast everything around was a blur of white and dark – the snow, the sky, the mountain and the river at the bottom. It hit a tree and came to a crashing halt. The noise of the impact was deafening – metal crushing, glass shattering and the drumming of her heart as the steering wheel spun madly out of her grip. Her airbag deployed, almost choking her as it pressed onto her face and chest, and she couldn't breathe.

Chapter Eleven

'Rosalie, can you hear me?'

Marc's insistent voice cut through her consciousness and the cacophony of metal crushing, engine roaring, and glass smashing that still rang in her ears. Her face was squashed against something rubbery, and as she opened her mouth to breathe some foul, chemical-tasting dust filled her throat, making her cough. She jerked back and gasped for air, crying out when a sharp pain stabbed her shoulder, neck and back.

'Don't worry, it's the powder from the airbags that's making you cough,' Marc said. 'You'll feel better when we get out.'

'Get out?' Her lungs and throat were on fire, and her shoulder hurt so much she dare not move any more.

'We're stuck halfway down the mountain. We were lucky a clump of trees stopped us, but I'm not sure how long it'll hold.'

Marc peered anxiously into her face. 'You look dreadfully pale. Are you injured?'

'My shoulder and my back hurt.' She tried to move her arm but gritted her teeth as pain shot through her again. 'What about you?'

'I'm fine.' He pushed his door open and let out a muffled curse as he jumped down from the car and into the snow. Through the shattered windscreen she watched him limp around the front of the car. He tried to wrench her door open but it was stuck.

'No worries. I'll get you out from my side.' He returned to the passenger side of the car.

'Please be careful ...' But he was already pulling her out. 'Careful!' This time she cried out loud.

Marc frowned. 'Is it that bad?' he asked as he managed to manoeuvre Rosalie out of the car.

'The side of my body feels like it's on fire,' she said, through gritted teeth, 'and I can't move my arm. So, yes, it is that bad.'

'May I?' Without waiting for an answer, he touched her shoulder blade and prodded gently through her jacket. She jerked out of his reach.

'Are are trying to finish me off?'

'I think your shoulder is dislocated, but I can't do anything about it now.' He looked up towards the top of the hill, and his face hardened. 'I can't see the other car's headlights.'

'Do you think they crashed too?'

He clenched his jaw. 'No. I think they left us. Damn them … I'll call the emergency services.' He looked back inside the Range Rover, and let out a curse. 'My mobile's in pieces. What about yours?'

She patted her pocket with her left hand and retrieved her phone, but there was no signal.

'Never mind,' he said. 'We'll try later. Can you walk?'

She nodded. 'Our best bet is to head for the old holiday chalets we drove past earlier. If we follow that ridge over there and cut across the forest it shouldn't take us too long.'

The darkness and the snow covering an uneven terrain made their progress slow and difficult. Marc walked ahead, sweeping the beam of the electric torch in front of him, and Rosalie followed in his footsteps, issuing instructions now and then as to which way he should turn. Every time she stumbled on a root or a rock, or her feet sank into a pothole, pain reverberated through her body and she had to bite her lip harder and harder to stop herself from crying out. To add to her misery, her boots were soaking wet and her trousers, stiff with snow and frost, rubbed against her legs like sandpaper.

At long last, they reached the empty holiday village.

'We'll try that chalet over there,' Marc said.

'I hope the driver of the four-wheel-drive alerted the emergency services and they're on their way.'

He didn't answer and she was far too exhausted to repeat her question, so she struggled through knee-deep snow to the back of the chalet. Marc leaned against the door and gave a few hard shoves with his shoulder. The door yielded with a loud crack.

He led the way into a small dining kitchen, and flicked the light switch on. Shaking from the pain and the cold, Rosalie followed him down a narrow corridor and into a small living room. Marc drew the curtains, switched on a table lamp and turned to her.

'Let me help you take your coat off.'

'No!' She stepped back so quickly she bumped against the wall. 'I'll do it myself.' The very thought of anyone touching her shoulder made her want to be sick.

'All right. For now.' He fiddled with the controls on the small electric heater and let out a satisfied grunt when warm air started blowing into the room. 'We could do with a hot drink. I hope there's coffee or tea in the kitchen.'

While he went to check, Rosalie pulled down the zipper of her anorak and tried to wriggle out of it. Every move was torture, pain lanced into her shoulder and radiated into her back, and soon nausea made her stomach lurch.

'Here. Try that. It'll numb the pain better than a cup of tea.' Marc stood in front of her, holding out a tumbler.

She breathed in the bitter, malt scent of whisky. 'Where did you find it?'

'In a cupboard. There's also tea, coffee, a packet of crackers, and a few tins. More than enough for tonight.'

She lifted one hand to her mouth. The mere thought of food made her heave. Right now she didn't care much for whisky either.

'I want you to drink it all,' Marc insisted. 'Then I'll help take your coat off and you will lie down on the sofa.'

She eyed him with suspicion. 'What for?'

'I am going to fix your shoulder.'

'Oh no, you're not. You are not laying a finger on me, do you hear?' She pressed harder against the wall. 'I'll wait until we get to Tomintoul tomorrow. What's more, you're not a doctor.'

'If your shoulder is dislocated, then the quicker we reset it, the less chance you run of permanent injury. Don't worry, I've seen it done before.' His voice was soft and patient, as if he was talking to an anxious pet or an unreasonable child.

She looked at the glass and pulled a face. Maybe he was right and the liquor would numb the pain. She gulped some whisky down, gasping as fire trailed down her throat, all the way into the pit of her stomach.

'Have a bit more.'

After a few more sips, she felt warm, and very, very tired. The floor moved like the deck of a ship, the walls shrunk then expanded around her. She blinked, and everything became still again.

'I think I need to sit down,' she said.

He took the glass away and put it on a side table. 'Let me take your coat off first.'

She tried to move away from him. 'I told you to leave me alone.'

'I didn't think you were such a coward.'

She drew in a breath. 'How can you call me a coward? You have no idea how much this hurts.'

'Actually, I know exactly what you're going through. I dislocated my shoulder during a rugby game once. The pain was so excruciating I cried like a baby. Now stop wriggling and let me help.'

The thought of cold, controlled and steely Marc Petersen crying like a baby was so alien she stood still and stared at him. He took advantage of her surprise to peel off her coat. He let it drop onto the carpeted floor, led her to the sofa and helped her lie down. He pulled her boots off, slipped a cushion behind her head and knelt down on the floor next to her.

'Now I'm going to move your arm around until the shoulder clicks back into place.'

He didn't give her time to reply but rotated her lower arm, before pushing inwards, towards her chest. The pain was so intense she jumped straight off the sofa with a piercing cry.

'I'm sorry. Let me try again.' His voice was calm and matter-of-fact.

Rosalie squeezed her eyes shut but couldn't stop the tears from spilling out. Marc repeated the process several times until her shoulder popped back into place. The searing pain immediately vanished, to be replaced by a dull ache.

She opened her eyes. He was looking at her, so close she could see the clear grey waters of his irises and feel his breath warming her cheek.

'It's over. You were very brave.' He slid his fingers into her hair and stroked it away from her face.

'It worked,' she whispered, shivering under his touch as his fingers slid down her cheeks in a feather-light caress to wipe away her tears.

'I told you it would.' He winced as he rose to his feet, and only then did she notice the bloodstains on his trousers.

'You're hurt too.'

'It's only a cut. There's a first aid box in the kitchen cupboard. It won't take me long to sort it out, then I'll make us something to eat. In the meantime, you should keep warm and rest.'

He draped his coat over her. It was still warm and smelled of snow, of lemon and spice. Of him.

'Thank you.' Perhaps the whisky had made her drowsy, or it was the aftermath of the intense pain she'd just experienced, but all she wanted was to snuggle into his coat and close her eyes.

The room was dark when she woke. A blanket that reeked of mothballs covered her from the neck down. Disoriented, she stared at the velvety darkness and listened to sounds of pans rattling, and cupboards being opened and closed. She sat up, holding her breath and flinching when shards of pain needled her neck and shoulder. The worst of the pain may have gone, but it still hurt.

It was cold, much colder than earlier. With the blanket wrapped around her, she shuffled down the corridor towards the kitchen. Marc was standing in front of the gas cooker, stirring baked beans in a pan with a long wooden spoon. On the table were an open packet of crackers, two blue plates with matching mugs and two sets of cutlery, and three lit candles.

'Hi,' she said.

Marc turned round and smiled. 'I was just about to wake you. I hope you like baked beans. If not, I'll open a tin of tomato soup.'

'No, beans are fine. Thank you.' She extracted a cracker from the packet with her left hand and bit into it. 'Why the candles?'

'The electricity was cut off an hour ago. The power lines must have gone down in the storm. It's lucky there were a few candles and some matches to light up the gas cooker. Unfortunately, no electricity means no heating, so I piled up all the blankets I could find on the bed for you. I'll sleep on the sofa tonight.'

He pulled out a chair and helped her sit down, then took the pan off the gas ring and replaced it with the kettle. 'I'm afraid this isn't French cuisine,' he said as he pushed half the content of the pan onto her plate with the wooden spoon. The baked beans plopped down in a gooey, steaming heap.

Rosalie grabbed hold of her fork. 'It smells wonderful.' She started eating. 'And it tastes even better.'

Marc placed a cup of tea in front of her. 'There's no milk, but I found some sugar. I hope it's sweet enough for you.'

Surprised, she looked up. 'Thanks.'

He made himself a mug of instant coffee, sat down and tucked into the pile of beans on his plate. For a few minutes, the only sound in the kitchen were the scraping of cutlery against plates, the hiss of burning candles and the wind whistling in the trees outside.

When his plate was empty, Marc sat back, cradled his mug in his hands and looked at her.

'Tell me about Geoff McBride. He seems fairly unusual, eccentric even.'

She smiled. 'I suppose he is ... But most of all, he is kind and generous, and totally dedicated to Raventhorn, and to his research on Isobel and Harald.' She paused and stared at the candle's flickering flame that cast moving shadows on the walls. 'He gave my mother and me a home when we had none. He gave me a family.'

The feeling of doom, fear and pain she'd experienced earlier at the holiday lodge returned, and grew like a shadow around her, inside her, ready to engulf her. A distant echo of her mother's voice floated in her consciousness. *Quick. Hide. Don't make a sound. Don't cry. Please don't cry.*

She didn't even realise she had closed her eyes, hunched her shoulders until Marc spoke.

'What's wrong? Are you in pain?' His voice drew her back to the here and now. Her eyes flew open, and she focused on his face to dispel the dark and frightened feelings that had gathered inside her.

'No ... no, I'm fine.'

He frowned as if he didn't quite believe her, and then asked, 'How do you think Elaine and Rupert will react when they learn they won't be inheriting Raventhorn after all?'

'They'll be furious, of course. Raventhorn was the only thing they were ever interested in, which is terribly sad since they are Geoff's only family. At least Geoff has Lorna and I to love him, and he had my mother too.' Tears pricked her eyes. She wiped them away with her left hand, let out a shaky breath and looked at Marc. If her mother's death still affected her after four years, she could only imagine how badly he must be hurting, only weeks after his father's fatal accident.

She bit her lip, hesitated. 'It must be hard for you to take over your father's business after what happened.'

A muscle on the side of his mouth twitched. His fingers tightened around his mug. 'I do what needs to be done. That's all my father would have expected from me.' His voice was indifferent, and there was a total lack of emotion in his eyes.

'What about your mother? Doesn't she mind you spending time here in Scotland instead of being at her side to comfort her?'

'My mother lives in the South of France. She has no need for my presence.'

'Really?'

'My parents separated amicably over fifteen years ago, Rosalie,' he explained, 'and although upset by my father's sudden death, my mother is probably far more worried about my ability to run the company and enable her to keep the lifestyle she is accustomed to.'

'How can you say such a callous thing about your mother?'

He drank a sip of coffee. 'Because it's the truth. My parents and I were never close. There is no reason why things should be any different now.'

'I don't understand. You worked with your father. You must have been close.'

'I worked with him, I admired his drive and ambition, and the way his mind worked, but that doesn't mean we were close.' He shrugged. 'Things were always strained between us. Not surprising, I suppose, since I grew up at boarding school in England whilst my parents lived in Paris and London.'

'You went to boarding school?'

He nodded. 'From the age of five.'

'You were just a baby!'

'It's not that unusual, believe me. My boarding school was excellent. I made good friends there, and had everything I needed.'

Her heart filled with sadness. He may think he'd had everything he needed but he had missed the most important thing – a loving family. 'It must have been very lonely to be away from home for a little boy,' she remarked.

He smiled, but it was a cold smile that only made his eyes more distant. 'There was no home. Not really. Just an apartment in London, and a house in Paris, which were filled with art and antiques I wasn't allowed to touch. In any case, I didn't know any different, and I got to see my parents a few times a year, which was more than enough for the three of us, believe me.'

Now that explained a lot, she thought as she watched him drink his coffee. No wonder he was so detached, so lacking in feelings and

110

emotions. He had probably shut them out at a young age as a way of dealing with being abandoned by his parents. She may not have known her father, but she always had her mother's unconditional love. And there had been Geoff and Lorna. They had formed a family unit based on love and trust, if not blood ties.

'You have tomato sauce on your cheek.' Marc's voice drew her out of her thoughts.

Self-conscious, she lifted her hand to her cheek. 'Oh ...'

'It's on the other side.' Leaning towards her, he lifted his finger to her face and rubbed the side of her mouth. 'There's some there too.'

He ran his finger along the line of her mouth in a soft, feather-light caress that raised goosebumps all over her body. Her heart drummed faster, louder and her skin grew hotter under his touch, as shadows danced on the kitchen walls, and the flames of the candles hissed and flickered. In their golden glow Marc's eyes were a deep, dark grey, and his hair shone like burnished gold. The stubble on his face and the bruise on his cheekbone gave him a raw, dangerous, and very seductive look.

She held her breath when his finger lingered on her lips and caressed her cheek. He drew closer.

'Rosalie ...' he started, close enough for her to feel his warm breath and see the flint specks in his eyes.

'Yes?' she whispered, her voice weak and dreamy.

He frowned, broke contact, and jerked back. 'Before you go to bed,' he said, standing up and plucking a candle from the table, 'I'll fashion some kind of sling for your shoulder. Follow me.'

He started down the corridor.

What on earth had just happened? Still dazed by confusing feelings and sensations, Rosalie let out a long breath. Had she dreamt the spark, the tension, the heat between them just then? Was it her imagination or had he been about to kiss her ... and she had been about to let him?

She wrapped the blanket around her and followed him into the living room. Marc had picked his scarf up from the back of an armchair, and gestured for her to drop the blanket. Reluctantly she allowed him to tie the scarf around her neck. The contact of his fingers on her skin brought on more delicious shivers as he secured the knot and helped her slot her arm in the soft fabric.

'That should help until we can get you checked out by a doctor.'

'I don't want a doctor. I'm not even in pain any longer.'

He arched his eyebrows as if he didn't believe her. 'You still need to make sure everything is back to normal.'

He sounded so superior and patronising that she couldn't help herself, and the words were out before she could help it. 'The only way things will ever be back to normal is if you leave Raventhorn and promise never to return!'

Holding her head high despite the ache in her right side, she stomped as best she could in just her socks to the only bedroom and slammed the door shut with her free hand – a mistake since the curtains were drawn and she found herself in total darkness.

She took a few steps into the room, her left arm extended in front of her to feel for obstacles. Her fingers touched a pile of thick, fluffy blankets. She sat down on the bed and managed to remove her socks and trousers, still damp from the walk in the snow. Then slipping under the cosy blankets, she stared at the velvety darkness.

She was so annoyed with herself she could have screamed, kicked the furniture or the wall, but with her injured shoulder and one arm in the makeshift sling, she couldn't even punch the mattress.

How immature to fall for Marc Petersen's soap story. So what if he'd been left by his rich, indifferent parents in a boarding school? So what if he had never experienced a warm and loving family life? He probably wouldn't have been any different if he had. The only reason why she'd felt sorry for him was that she'd been weakened by the accident. And as Niall had said, she was too soft and naive for her own good.

What a relief that he hadn't kissed her. She closed her eyes, shifted into a more comfortable position and let the warmth from the thick blankets lull her into a doze. Guilt, however, prevented her from falling asleep. She couldn't quite forget that she had all the covers whilst Marc had none.

With a resigned sigh she got up, wrapped a blanket around her to hide her bare legs, and snatched a couple of covers off the bed before marching to the living room.

The candles had almost burned down to stumps, and it was so cold her breath steamed. Marc Petersen reclined on the couch, with his coat on and her anorak wrapped around his shoulders, and one leg stretched out on a stool in front of him. Her throat tightened. Now she felt even more guilty for not asking him if he was in any pain.

He straightened up when he saw her. 'Rosalie. Is there anything wrong?'

She shook her head. 'No, I ... well, I was wondering if you'd like these.'

She showed him the blankets. 'It doesn't seem fair that I should have them all when you're freezing in here.'

'Are you sure you won't need them?'

'Positive.'

'Then I'll take them. Thanks. You should go back to bed and get some rest. We'll leave for Tomintoul as soon as it's light. Even if we manage to get a signal and call an ambulance we still have a fair way to go.'

She shook her head. 'I don't need an ambulance. All I want is to report the accident to the police and ask Niall to tow the Range Rover back to the garage, although I'm not sure it can be repaired.'

'You'll have to phone Fergus to let him know you won't be able to drive for a while, which means that unless Duncan comes back from Edinburgh or you can find another driver at short notice, the only option is to close down Love Taxis straight away. You should let Fiona know too ...'

He heard her intake of breath, saw her stiffen her spine. And when she marched up to him he could have sworn sparks flew and electricity sizzled around her.

'I have been running my taxi business for four years, Petersen. I know what I have to do, so don't you dare talk to me in this patronising tone as if I was some stupid, incompetent, clumsy little woman!'

He held out his hands in a calming gesture. 'I was just making a few suggestions. Now, as you are clearly in pain and overwrought, I suggest you go back to bed and get some rest. Thank you for bringing me the blankets.'

He held out his hand. Without a word, she threw the blankets at him, swung round and strode out of the room. A few seconds later the bedroom door slammed so hard a couple of ornaments shook on the mantelpiece.

113

He bent down to pick the blankets up, wrapped them around his shoulders. He may have been a little insensitive just then, but Rosalie had to accept the inevitable, and in a painful and roundabout way, being injured and unable to drive would help her do just that.

Thoughts and questions about the accident swirled in his mind. Why had the four-wheel-drive failed to stop when they drove them off the road? And why had they not alerted the emergency services to rescue them but left them to their fate on the mountainside?

As soon as they were back in the civilised world, he'd go back to the chalet and confront the couple staying there. He was sure the black four-by-four had been on its way to the holiday lodge when they met on the mountain road. The road didn't lead anywhere else, and he'd seen evidence of a vehicle being parked there. He couldn't help thinking about the two rough-looking men he'd overheard talk with a cockney accent as they were leaving the pub and Rosalie's comment about the couple at the holiday lodge. She said they had a London accent too, that they seemed overly keen to get rid of her, and that she had seen the woman with Rupert McBride – the same Rupert who was desperate to get money out of his cousin and inherit Raventhorn.

A memory niggled at the back of his mind. Rosalie had seemed distracted, shaken even, after talking to the tourists at the lodge, as if something unpleasant had happened there – something she hadn't told him about.

Was there a connection between Rupert, the two men at the Stag's Head and the couple at the lodge? He took a deep breath. Could their accident tonight be related to Rosalie's crash on the forest road, since both times a black four-by-four had been involved? It was a shame he had so little to work on. The accident had happened too fast for him to read the four-wheel drive's number plate or see anything that might help identify its occupants.

Tonight had been the latest of too many incidents. He may not understand what was going on, but he knew men who could help.

There weren't many advantages to growing up in a boarding school – apart from developing a thick skin and a posh accent – but one of them was definitely making lifelong friends. Now was the time to call on his two best friends – Cédric Castel, daredevil freelance journalist, and Luc Peyrac, heir to one of Bordeaux's oldest wine growing estates who had just retired from French intelligence services. If anyone could help him figure out what was happening at Raventhorn, it was them.

He leaned back against the sofa and stared ahead. Sleeping was out of the question. He had to keep watch in case someone had spotted their vehicle or had reported them missing, and a mountain rescue team drove past, looking for them.

The candles soon burned down and he found himself in pitch darkness. The blankets Rosalie had given him hardly fended off the freezing cold, the gash on his leg throbbed more than he wanted to admit and with nothing to occupy him other than his thoughts, it was the longest, most silent night he'd ever spent.

Chapter Twelve

The following morning however proved anything but silent. From the moment she got up, Rosalie let him know exactly how she felt. Doors he hadn't known existed slammed. Walls shook. Ornaments juddered. He rose to his feet and winced as he stretched. Damn it, he was stiff. His back ached and pain shot through his leg. He needed coffee. Black. Hot. And strong.

Rosalie strode across the room, darted murderous looks in his direction before undertaking the destruction of the kitchen – or at least it sounded that way. If the woman could make that much noise with her left hand alone, how much worse would it get when she regained the use of her right arm?

He followed her into the kitchen, but stopped in the doorway in case she tried to throw a plate or a pan at his head.

'If you have quite finished making a racket,' he said in a calm voice, 'I suggest we have breakfast and leave as soon as possible.'

He pointed to the window and the low, grey clouds that held the promise of more snow. 'I am glad to see that your shoulder doesn't seem to be causing you too much pain this morning,' he added.

'Oh, yes? And how would you know?' she shot back.

She pushed a steaming cup of coffee across the table. 'I made you some coffee.'

He smiled, pleasantly surprised. She couldn't hate him that much if she'd made him coffee. 'Thank you.'

She looked at him. 'You're welcome. I hope it's to your taste.'

Something in her tone made him pause, but he shook his head. No. She wouldn't dare. Would she? He drank a gulp, coughed, and almost spat the disgusting liquid out.

He forced himself to swallow the vile concoction and slammed the cup down onto the worktop. 'Hell. What did you put in there? Rat poison?'

'I couldn't find any. What's wrong? Is it a little too strong for you?' she chuckled. 'Perhaps my hand slipped as I was pouring in the coffee granules ... unless I mistook the pepper container for sugar.'

She fluttered her eyelashes and smiled such a sweet, innocent smile that blood surged like hot lava in his veins and his body hardened. He'd never let anything or anyone get to him in this way. He prided himself on his cool, even temper and his ability to remain calm and detached in the most tense and stressful business meetings. Right now, however, he was wrestling with the basic, primitive urge to yank this woman against him, and kiss her senseless.

Rosalie had a way of bringing the worst out in him. Around her he felt distinctly uncivilised, primal even. It was as if he was fast reverting to an unknown version of himself, a man he hadn't even suspected existed.

He took a deep, long, steadying breath. 'We're leaving in ten minutes. Since you managed to create so much mess in this kitchen all on your own, I gather you'll be able to tidy up too.'

It didn't take him long to get ready and fold the blankets up. Searching through his wallet, he pulled out a business card on which he scribbled a note explaining about the door and the food and left it together with a handful of banknotes on the worktop. Then he went outside and waited for her in the crisp, cold morning. The air was so cold it stung his face and burned his lungs.

Rosalie came out a few minutes later, and started on the path out of the holiday village without a word, or even a look in his direction. He secured the door as best he could and caught up with her. They didn't talk as they hiked through snowy paths snaking in and out of the pine forest on the side of the hill. In places the snow was so deep it reached up to his knees. As morning wore on, the cold made the cut on his leg more painful. Rosalie soldiered on without even a whisper of complaint, although it must have been hard with her arm still in the makeshift sling.

It was almost lunchtime by the time they emerged out of the forest and onto a road. Rosalie immediately took her mobile out of her coat pocket. 'I have a signal,' she announced, before slipping her left arm out of the sling and keying in a number.

'Niall? It's me.' She held the phone to her ear. 'We had an accident last night on the road down from the holiday chalets … yes, it was after we checked on the tourists … I'll explain later. No, I'm all right but it was a close call and the Range Rover is stuck halfway down the mountain. I think it's a write-off.'

She frowned as she listened to the man at the other end of the phone.

'Can you come to pick us up? The roads seem fairly clear around here. I reckon we'll be in Tomintoul in about an hour. We'll wait for you at the Old Fire Station café. Yes ... don't worry. And, Niall, thank you. I mean it. I don't know what I'd do without you.'

She then keyed in another number and blew out a frustrated sigh. 'I can't believe this. This stupid phone has run out of charge. I can't now call the hospital to ask about Geoff. His operation was rescheduled for today.'

Shaking her head, she flipped the cover of the phone down and shoved it back into her pocket. 'At least Niall is coming for us. He promised to call the mountain rescue services to help tow the Range Rover back onto the road.' She glanced up at him. 'He'll phone Fergus too ... In the meantime, we'll eat something in the village. It's not too far.'

The clatter of an engine broke the silence, and they both turned to watch an old blue van appear around the bend. At last luck was with them.

Marc waved for the van to stop. It skidded as it braked and stopped at the side of the road.

'Hi, folks. What's up?' The elderly driver asked in the deep, hoarse voice of a smoker after he'd wound his window down.

Marc explained they'd had an accident and needed to reach Tomintoul.

'Sure. Hop in.' He cast Marc a puzzled glance and pointed to the bruise on his cheekbone. 'What happened to your face?'

'I walked into a frying pan,' Marc answered as he held the passenger door open for Rosalie. He slid in next to her and tried not to cough at the strong smell of woodbine cigarette smoke that permeated the van. There wasn't much space at the front, and Rosalie almost sat in his lap.

'I know it's Sunday, but is there a doctor's surgery or a chemist's open in town by any chance?' he asked, when the van rattled into motion again.

The old man arched his bushy eyebrows. 'They're shut for the weekend by now, son, but if it's medical attention you need, I can take you to my brother-in-law. He's in the trade, so to speak, and he'll sort you out.'

'I told you I didn't want to see a doctor,' Rosalie protested.

'You may not want to, but I do,' Marc replied.

She was so close her thigh pressed against his and if he moved, the side of his arm brushed against her chest. He left Rosalie to make conversation with the driver and turned towards the window and looked out at the white fields crisscrossed with half derelict stone walls, at the pine forest that stretched as far as the eye could see and the snowy Cairngorms peaks in the background. It was the wildest, the most hostile landscape he'd ever seen, but at the same time the most breathtaking.

Ten minutes later the van pulled into an untidy farmyard.

'Follow me.' The old man climbed out and slammed the door.

Marc held out his hand to help Rosalie get out but she ignored it and followed the man into a house that smelled of muddy old boots, musty raincoats, of mutton and boiled vegetables.

'I hope we're not interrupting your brother-in-law's lunch,' Marc said.

The old man turned to him, a twinkle in his eyes. 'I'm sure our George will be eternally grateful for it, and if you'd tasted my sister's cooking you'd understand why. Anyhow, it'll soon be time for his afternoon surgery, so you can be his first customers. Come with me, I'll tell him you're here.'

He pushed a creaky door open and they walked into a large, sparsely furnished room that smelled strongly of antiseptic and something else – something he wouldn't expect from a GP's surgery. Wet dogs.

'It's a little basic for a doctor's surgery, isn't it?' Marc cast a doubtful eye at the white walls, the stainless steel benches that ran all around with the black table at the centre.

Rosalie shook her head, a pitying look in her eyes. 'Don't tell me you haven't worked out what this place is.'

A small man with bright blue eyes and silver grey hair cropped short strode in before he could ask what she meant.

'Good afternoon,' he greeted them with a cheerful voice, and an even more cheerful smile. 'Toby said you'd had a wee bit of bother with your car and were in need of help. I'll see what I can do. I'm George, by the way. So, who'll be my first patient today?'

Marc and Rosalie pointed at each other and spoke at the same time.

'He is.'

119

'She is.'

Rosalie's face went pale and she edged towards the door.

'All right,' Marc sighed, 'I'll go first.' He sat on a metal chair, stretched his leg in front of him and pulled his trouser up a little to enable the doctor to examine him.

'The good news is you don't need stitches,' George declared after a couple of minutes, 'but that's a nasty gash you've got there. I hope you're up to date with your tetanus injections.'

Marc answered that he was, and explained about the accident in a few sentences while the doctor dabbed a thick antiseptic wipe all over his shin. He then rummaged through a cupboard for a dressing and pulled out a box with the photo of a horse printed on the side.

Marc blinked in surprise then relaxed into a smile. So that's what Rosalie had hinted at before. The man was no doctor. He was a vet, and he was about to strap a horse dressing to his leg.

'Now, it's your turn, lass.' George turned to Rosalie. 'What's the matter with you?'

'Nothing. Nothing at all.' Rosalie backed further towards the door.

'You seem to have hurt your arm,' the vet carried on in a soft, patient voice – the voice he must use to reassure a frightened puppy – 'or is it your shoulder?'

'I'm not letting you anywhere near my shoulder. No way.'

'Don't be childish, Rosalie,' Marc cut in, impatient, 'either you're getting it checked out here or we're going to the nearest hospital, and I don't care how much you shout or how many doors you slam.'

Rising to his feet, he told the vet about Rosalie's dislocated shoulder. When he'd finished George too insisted he examine her.

Rosalie must have realised arguing any further was futile. A sullen expression on her face, she divested herself of her coat and reluctantly perched on the examination table.

'It looks like your friend did a good job re-setting your shoulder.' George patted her hand a few minutes later.

'He's not my friend,' Rosalie muttered between her teeth.

George ignored her and turned to Marc. 'She'll be right as rain after a few days rest. Of course, she must do no strenuous activities.'

'You mean no lifting ... or driving,' Marc said.

The vet nodded. 'That's right. Our young lady mustn't drive for at least a week.'

'I hate it when people talk about me as if I wasn't there,' Rosalie snarled as she slipped her good arm into the sleeve of her coat and the vet helped her secure the scarf against her chest again.

'Driving is my job,' she added. 'People rely on me and my cab. How will they get by without me?'

George laughed. 'Of course! Now I know where I've seen you before.' He slapped his forehead with the flat of his hand. 'You're the lass who drives that pink taxi, aren't you? Well, petal, people will just have to rely on someone else for a while. You need to mend first.'

He rubbed his hands together. 'Can I offer you some refreshments before my brother-in-law drives you into the village? A cup of tea, or something to eat, perhaps?'

Leaning closer to Marc, he added. 'Although I'd steer clear of the mutton and turnip stew if I were you. I love my wife dearly, but I must say this. Her stew's a killer.'

They were in a hurry to reach Tomintoul and meet Niall, so they declined the offer and climbed into George's brother-in-law's old van once more. Half an hour later they pushed open the door of the village's former fire station, which had been converted into a café.

As soon as they walked in, they were surrounded by delicious smells of broth, warm bread and grilled bacon, of coffee and hot chocolate. A fire blazed in the stone fireplace. The dining room was full of couples and families enjoying a late Sunday lunch. Marc selected a table close to the fire. He pulled a chair out for Rosalie but she shook her head. 'Before I sit down, I'm going to ask the waitress if I can use their phone to call the hospital.'

After she explained why she desperately needed to make a phone call, the waitress led her into a small office and left her alone. She was put straight through to intensive care, where a nurse told her Geoff's operation had gone ahead as planned, that he was comfortable but heavily sedated and not allowed any visitors for the time being.

'I let him down. I promised I'd be there after his operation.' Rosalie's voice wobbled and tears pricked her eyes when she returned to the café and sat opposite Marc.

He glanced at her, pulled out a crinkled handkerchief from his coat pocket, and handed it to her without a word. She grabbed hold of it with her left hand, dabbed her eyes and blew her nose, and gave it back to him.

'Let's order some food,' he said. 'You'll feel better when you've had something to eat.'

They ordered bacon rolls and soup for him together with coffee laced with whisky, pancakes with maple syrup and tea for her, and ate in silence. They were finishing a second round of hot drinks when Niall arrived.

'At last,' Rosalie called, getting up to greet him. 'I was getting worried.'

Niall shook his head, his face grim. 'It's not me you should be worried about. It's Geoff.'

Colour drained from her face. 'What do you mean? I just spoke to the hospital and he was fine—'

'No, it's not that,' Niall interrupted. 'It's the Porsche. One of my mechanics was working on it this morning before you called and he noticed something weird.' He sighed, shook his head. 'It was no accident, Roz. The brakes were tampered with. It's a wonder Geoff got out of that crash alive.'

Chapter Thirteen

Rosalie jumped to her feet. 'What? No, that's impossible. You must be mistaken!'

Niall glared at her, a hard line forming at the side of his mouth. 'You may not think I'm good enough to be your boyfriend, but at least give me some credit when it comes to cars.'

Shocked by the anger in his tone, she put a soothing hand on his forearm. 'I'm sorry. You know better, of course ... but who would sabotage the Porsche, and why?'

Niall shrugged. 'That's for the police to find out. I called them as soon as I was sure. They have already taken the Porsche away for forensic examination.'

'How often does McBride drive the car?' Marc Petersen asked.

Rosalie hissed an annoyed sigh. What business was it of his?

'He drives it all the time,' she answered nonetheless. 'It was always his favourite car, that's why I was so surprised when Niall said he wanted to sell it.'

Her heart tightened as her mind flooded with happy memories of Geoff taking her to school or to Irlwick in the red sports car. She sat on the bucket seat when she was a child, but later he'd allowed her on the passenger seat. She would never forget the thrill of those rides in the long summer evenings, with the breeze whipping her hair around her face, the scents of the pine forest all around and the sky slowly turning to dark blue and reflecting onto the surface of the loch.

'Niall serviced it earlier this week and Geoff drove it the day before you arrived,' she added, thoughtful. 'Someone must have sneaked into the garage during the night.'

'Given the lack of security at Raventhorn,' Marc said in a sharp voice, 'and the fact everybody around here seems to know how to find the house and car keys, I'm surprised it hasn't happened before.' He paused. 'I can't help wondering about the timing, though.'

Rosalie frowned. 'The timing?'

'What if someone found out about the sale? You may have to come clean about the reason I'm here sooner than you'd planned. You'll have to tell the police at least.'

Niall frowned. 'What sale? Has Petersen bought the Porsche? What do you have to tell the police? What's going on, Roz?'

She looked at Marc with pleading eyes then turned to Niall. 'It's nothing – at least it's nothing for you to worry about. I'll tell you later, I promise. Right now all I want is to go home.'

'Fair enough, but what the hell happened to you yesterday?' Niall asked. 'I've just been to the site of the accident with the mountain rescue team and the Range Rover is definitely a write-off.'

His eyes were thunderous as he glared at Marc. 'What were you thinking, letting Rosalie drive in the snowstorm? If it'd been me in the car, I would never have let her get hurt. I knew she should have been paired up with me yesterday, not with some hopeless city wimp.'

Marc's jaw clenched. He put his cup of coffee down, slowly rose to his feet, and Rosalie's breath caught in her throat. He was a head taller and a lot bulkier than Niall, and with his face hard as stone and his eyes the colour of flint, he looked a lot scarier too.

Niall leaned forward and tightened his fists by his sides, as if poised for a fight.

Her heart pounding, she slipped in between the two men. 'Stop it, Niall, this is ridiculous. The accident wasn't Marc's fault at all. I was the one who insisted on driving.'

Much to her relief, Niall took a step back. 'Well, he shouldn't have let you have your way.'

'Nobody could have prevented the accident,' Rosalie carried on. 'We were on our way back from the holiday chalet when a huge four-by-four came straight at us, forcing me to brake and veer off the road.'

She gave Niall a tentative smile. 'Let's go home now. Please. I'm dead on my feet.'

He nodded. 'Aye. Sorry. You don't look so well, it's true.'

She didn't protest when he wrapped a protective arm around her waist and led her out of the café and into the cold. Outside, light was fading already and the temperature had dropped a few degrees. She climbed into the truck, and slid onto the seat. Marc sat next to her and once again she was squeezed against his warm, solid body.

'By the way,' Niall started, 'it's going to take me a few days to fix your cab. I need to order a newbumper and do some work on the bonnet. I'll do the work myself and wave the labour cost off.'

'Thanks, Niall. You're a pal.'

He cast her a sidelong glance. 'I only wish you'd stop this nonsense about being a taxi driver and let me take care of you. With all the upsets and the fake calls you've had lately, you should have realised by now that this job is unsuitable for a young woman. It was lucky I was around when you were stranded on your own, but I may not always be there. And I'm not even mentioning the fact you're not earning enough to scrape a living.'

There he went again. Only this time, she didn't have the strength to argue and fight. Anyway, he would have his wish before long. Because of Marc, her taxi driving days would soon be over. She was aware of Marc giving Niall a hard stare. Yet he should be glad to hear Niall echo his own words about her lack of business sense.

The sky had turned dark blue and a full moon cast a ghostly, butter-coloured glow over the frigid white landscape, outlining the shape of the mountains and making the forests even more mysterious. Inside the truck it was warm and cosy, however. Rosalie closed her eyes. She was tired, and sleep was suddenly very tempting.

The bumps on the track over the bridge shook her awake. She was shocked to realise that she was leaning against Marc Petersen's solid chest, and that he had slipped his arm around her to hold her.

She stiffened and pulled away. 'Sorry. I didn't mean to fall asleep.'

He shrugged. 'It's been a difficult couple of days.'

Niall pulled up in the courtyard. A burning pain shot through her shoulder as she straightened in her seat. She may not like it, but Marc was right. She wasn't fit to drive.

Marc flung the door open, climbed down and helped her out, and she almost stumbled into his arms.

Niall leaned towards her. 'Give me a ring if you want a lift to the hospital tomorrow. I'll drive you.'

Marc stood right behind her as she shut the door and waved Niall goodbye, so close she could feel the heat from his body. She tensed. Just how long was she going to have to endure the man's presence?

Immediately another, more worrying, thought popped into her mind. *He* was the one who was enduring her presence at Raventhorn, so how long before he decided he wanted her out of the only home she'd ever known?

'I suggest you get some rest while I make a start on the accounts for Love Taxis,' he said. 'I'll let you know my decision by morning.'

She swung round. 'You want to look at the books now?'

He shrugged. 'Why not? I have to make a start some time, and it shouldn't take me long.'

Dread squeezed a tight fist inside her. She should be there too. At least then she could give him her side of the story, explain why there were days, weeks, without any profit.

'Actually, I'd rather stay, in case there is anything you don't understand.'

He smiled his usual cold smile. 'I can assure you that I'm quite competent at analysing accounts and balance sheets.'

Resolve hardened inside her. He could say what he wanted. It was her future that was at stake. 'I don't doubt that for one second, but I want to be there. It's my right, isn't it?' She knew she sounded defensive, but she didn't care.

He arched his eyebrows. 'Of course.' He dug out his key from his coat pocket, unlocked the service door and they stepped into the kitchen.

She tried to unzip her anorak, and cursed between her teeth when a sharp pain gripped her neck and shoulder.

'Let me help.' He helped her take her coat off, taking great care not to touch her shoulder and hung it in the utility room. 'Please sit down while I get some pens and paper.'

'I'll get them.' She walked out of the kitchen before he could object. How dare he behave as if she was a guest at Raventhorn? He may own the place but she had been brought up here!

The library was in its usual state of chaos. She picked up a scroll from the floor and put it on the desk. She didn't need to read it to know it was another of Geoff's ancient manuscripts about Isobel's and Harald's tragic love story, unless it regarded Harald's estate on Orkney or in North Jutland in Denmark, where he was from originally.

Her hand stilled. North Jutland. Wasn't there where Marc said his father's family was from too? Not for the first time she found it odd that the man who had bought Raventhorn should be Danish. Who knows, perhaps Marc even had Viking blood, just like Harald? He certainly had other traits she'd always associated with the Vikings – their dark golden hair, imposing stature and cruel disposition.

Rosalie yanked the drawer open and grabbed a couple of pens and pencils. She had always struggled to understand how Isobel could have fallen in love with a man as ruthless and war-mongering as Harald Johansen. She was even rumoured to have been so scared of him that she had asked a wizard to cast a love spell onto her marriage bed. It must have worked since the newlyweds had not only spent three full days and nights in that great big bed which was now in the Crimson Room, but a bond so strong had formed between the couple that Harald had swum to his death trying to rescue his wife, and Isobel had chosen to throw herself from the Armitage's tower to join him in his watery grave. Rosalie pushed lids onto the pens and sighed. What would it feel like to love a man so much death was preferable to a life without him?

'Are you all right? You've been gone a long time,' Marc said as he walked in, startling her. As he spoke a light bulb blew up with a loud popping sound, and Rosalie dropped the pens onto the desk with a surprised squeak. She forgot about the pile of books behind her, lost her balance and fell against Marc.

'Careful.' His arms slid around her waist to steady her.

It was as if an invisible force pulled her closer. Her nose rubbed against his jumper, her fingers spread on his chest and she breathed in his hot and spicy scent.

His hands closed on the small of her back, moulding her to him. Her skin tingled, her body tightened in a flash of heat, and her heart started thudding, too hard, too loud. She looked up and met his grey eyes, so deep she felt herself fall into their turbulent waters. Seconds ticked by and stretched until time stood still. Even her heartbeat slowed down. Marc bent down, watching her all the time, and holding her captive in his serious gaze. There was only one thought in her mind. He was going to kiss her. *She wanted him to kiss her*.

Her lips parted in anticipation, her body went limp in his arms and her fingers curled in his thick, woolly jumper.

He didn't kiss her, instead he let her go, stepped back, and glanced at the chandelier. 'I really must hire an electrician. It's a wonder the place hasn't caught fire yet.'

He sounded so cool, so calm, as if nothing had happened.

But nothing *had* happened, she scolded herself. Why then did she feel lost and disappointed now she wasn't in his arms any longer?

He looked down. 'Are you all right? Is your shoulder hurting?'

She had to get a grip on herself. He mustn't suspect, even for a second, that she had once again been about to make a fool of herself.

'I am perfectly fine. You gave me a fright by sneaking up behind me, that's all, and then the light went off and ...'

'Sorry. I didn't mean to startle you. Did you get the pens and paper? Good. Then we'll make a start.'

It took a lot of self-control to lead the way out of the library when all he wanted was to pull Rosalie back into his arms and kiss the breath out of her. It was lucky he had gathered his wits before he embarrassed himself. She would most probably have slapped him. She made no secret of her feelings towards him.

What was he thinking of? Well, he wasn't thinking at all, and that was the problem. Since he'd arrived at Raventhorn he'd acted on impulses and urges, and on intense, dark desires, and that was completely unlike him. No doubt the string of sleepless nights he'd endured since his father's death were starting to wear him out.

He should be relieved that he'd stopped himself just in time, he thought as he walked out of the library, yet tantalising questions swirled into his mind. What would he have done if she'd let him kiss her? He clenched his jaw. He knew exactly what he would have done – he would have taken her upstairs, and into that great big bed in the Crimson Room, and kept her there all night.

They didn't talk as Rosalie followed him into the kitchen. He filled the kettle, flicked it on to make some tea, and took what was left of Lorna's chocolate cake out of the fridge. He cut a slice, and placed it on a dessert plate in front of Rosalie. She didn't even look at it.

'I think you should leave the accounts to me and have an early night,' he said.

She glared at him. 'So that you can shut Love Taxis down without hearing my side of the story?'

'I don't need a story. Figures usually speak for themselves. Anyway, aren't you eating? It's not like you to ignore chocolate cake.' He rubbed the bruise on his cheekbone and smiled. 'After all, you almost killed me for it.'

She shook her head and pushed the plate away. 'I'm not hungry. I want to get on with the accounts.'

He looked at her pale face, at the mauve shadows under her eyes. She needed to sleep, and he wanted to be alone to think. There were things he needed to sort out – things regarding their mountainside accident, the revelations concerning McBride's Porsche and her over-possessive boyfriend.

Something about the mechanic made him uneasy. He seemed so desperate for Rosalie to give up her taxi service and marry him, and what better way of convincing her to do that than sending her on fake errands, and scaring her half to death. He was also the one who had serviced McBride's Porsche, which meant he had had the opportunity to tamper with the brakes.

Marc sighed. Then again, perhaps he was letting his dislike for Niall Murray cloud his judgement. He had nothing to gain by tampering with McBride's sports car. But damn it, the man was a moron! He couldn't stand the way he talked down to Rosalie, as if she was unable to make her own choices. The way he called her 'his girl' and made none too subtle references to their relationship.

'I should have asked Niall in for a drink,' Rosalie said as if reading his thoughts. 'Perhaps it's time I told him what's going on. He is after all one of my oldest friends.'

'You can call him tomorrow.'

He tightened his jaw, put his mug down and rose to his feet, angry to feel so bloody annoyed all of a sudden. He was behaving like a jealous man and it was ridiculous. Of course he wasn't jealous of Niall Murray. He'd never been jealous in his life. Never been the possessive type. Never cared enough about any woman for all that nonsense, and he wasn't about to start now.

The phone rang, shrill in the silence of the castle.

Rosalie jumped out of her seat. 'I'll get it.'

She came back soon after and sat down. An elbow on the table, her chin resting on her hand, she stared into space.

'Bad news?' he asked.

She nodded. 'It was Duncan. His mother has taken a turn for the worse and he is staying in Edinburgh to look after her.' She sighed. 'I suppose I'd better call Fergus and Fiona, tell them to cancel all our bookings for next week.'

Her eyes were huge and sad. 'It seems you've won after all. With Duncan away and me unable to drive, Love Taxis is as good as finished.'

He drank his coffee, and put the empty cup down. 'There is another alternative.'

Chapter Fourteen

Fergus's voice crackled over the radio. 'Mornin', son. And how are you on this fine day?'

'Good morning, Fergus. I'm all right, thank you. And yourself?'

'My old bones are creakin' in this cold weather, but apart from that everything's tickety-boo.'

It never ceased to amaze Marc how quickly people had accepted him. Even Frosty Fiona had thawed and ventured a pleasant comment once in a while. It seemed all that mattered was that he was helping Rosalie run Love Taxis and staying at Raventhorn to look after her while Geoff was in hospital and Lorna away on holiday. Things would no doubt change the moment they found out who he really was and what he was there for. He would miss Fergus's easy camaraderie when that day came.

'Your first pick up is at eight thirty from Irlwick, Myrtle Lane to Aviemore railway station. Then it's back to Irlwick for Little Angels, followed by the Knitting Ladies and Flora's supermarket trip. And after lunch, don't forget our pensioners' GP run. Rosalie will give you the directions. Got that?'

Marc winced. Thursday. Mothers and toddlers. Screams, tantrums, bad smells, and sticky fingers ... Had it only been two weeks since the Thursday he'd encountered those crying babies from the nursery group for the first time? He loosened his green scarf in case the kid pulled it off him again and breathed in Rosalie's sweet, fruity scent that clung to it ever since she'd worn it as a sling.

'I got it. Thanks.'

'One more thing, lad.'

'What is it?' Marc smiled. He'd never been called a lad before.

'Take care on the road,' Fergus added. 'There's a weather warning for extreme cold later on.'

The passenger door opened and Rosalie sat down next to him. Her pink anorak and woolly hat instantly brightened up the dark November morning.

'Are you sure you want to drive?' she asked as a greeting. 'My shoulder is a lot better, you know, and you might want to stay at

Raventhorn this morning, since today is—'

'Thursday, which means toddlers, knitting busybodies and Flora's supermarket run,' he cut in as he started the cab and drove towards the old bridge. 'I know. Fergus already briefed me.'

He accelerated and the cab bumped over the potholes that pitted the lane. He would have them filled in as soon as the weather improved, … if he hadn't sold Raventhorn by then, of course. 'Don't worry. It is after all my second Thursday ferrying toddlers to their playgroup. I survived last week, didn't I?'

'Just about. You only just managed to keep hold of your scarf, and when the boy tried to give you a kiss, I thought you were going to be sick.'

He shuddered. 'He was very smelly, what do you expect? However, today, I'm up for it.'

And in a strange way, he was. The past ten days had disappeared in a blur of frantic activity. There had been daily visits to the hospital where a heavily sedated McBride struggled to recover from his operation, which meant both Rosalie and the police had been unable to talk to him about his accident in the Porsche.

He had driven back to the holiday lodge to confront the couple there, but it was empty, and his request to check the identity of the holidaymakers had been met by the police's polite, but firm, refusal. 'They've done nothing wrong, sir,' the constable had declared, and nothing Marc said could change his mind, even when he'd suggested that the four-wheel drive must have been going to the lodge that evening, and that it was unacceptable that the driver hadn't reported their accident to the emergency services.

Since official lines of enquiry appeared closed, it was up to Marc's friends to dig out information about McBride and his cousins. Cédric was out of the country on an assignment, but Luc had promised to get in touch with his contacts and get back to him. In the meantime, Marc had had a basic security system installed at Raventhorn and paid a hefty bonus to have the installation completed in record time. Of course, he'd had to lecture Marion and Rosalie about taking care of the house keys and not broadcasting the code for the alarm. He had also contacted a local electrician who was sorting out the heating and the hot water.

Evenings had been busy too. He had examined the accounts for

Raventhorn estate and Love Taxis, both of which made for depressing reading, and once again he wondered why his father had got involved with McBride when even a superficial audit of the books would have told him he was wasting his money.

Lastly, there had been driving the cab. Although reluctant at first, Rosalie had come round to the idea that he could help keep the business going while she recovered and Duncan was away. She grudgingly sat next to him to order him about every day. But however short-tempered she was with him, she never showed anything but kindness and good humour to her clients. Much to his surprise he found he liked listening to her chattering about sweet nothings. Most of all, he enjoyed seeing her smile. And she smiled a lot, at least to her friends and customers, if not to him.

Yes, he thought as he negotiated the road through Corby Woods, his life had changed beyond recognition, and he wasn't sure whether the fact he was actually enjoying it was a good thing or not. He hadn't told Kirsty about driving Rosalie's taxi – yet – but had explained his extended stay at Raventhorn by the amount of paperwork he had to go through. She'd snapped at him on the phone a few times, but couldn't really complain too much since he still managed to get the work done on his most pressing files.

Rosalie switched on the radio and a loud, catchy dance tune filled the inside of the car. She turned to him, cocked her head to one side and grinned mischievously. 'This is just what we need. Nice, happy music to cheer us up.'

She probably expected him to tell her to turn the music down or change radio stations. He didn't. He had grown accustomed to Happy Baby Radio's upbeat songs and over enthusiastic disc jockeys – so accustomed in fact that he'd caught himself drumming his fingers on the steering wheel to the beat of a tune or two.

The station run went smoothly. The toddler group less so. This time he lost his scarf in the tug-of-war with the two-year-old he had defeated before.

'I'm so sorry, I don't understand why he likes your scarf so much when he has plenty of his own,' said the boy's apologetic mother as he unloaded the buggy from the boot and unfolded it on the pavement for her. Marc had assured the blushing young woman that he really didn't mind, and to prove he didn't bear any grudges he had even accepted a moist, sticky kiss on the cheek from the boy.

'I know!' Rosalie looked at him with a twinkle in her eyes as soon as he started the cab again. 'I'll ask one of Elaine's ladies to knit you a new scarf. I hope you have nothing against pink.'

'Pink?' he grunted as the beginnings of a headache needled the back of his eyes.

Rosalie smiled. 'You have to wear pink if you drive a Love Taxis cab. It's the staff uniform.'

He refrained from saying that as the new boss he could change the staff uniform to grey or black if he wanted to, and that there most probably wouldn't be a Love Taxis soon anyway, but she seemed happy this morning, and he wanted very much to see her smile, so he said nothing. Rosalie's smile faded quickly when Elaine got into the cab a little later.

'Rupert needs to call at Raventhorn for some papers he left behind when he and Geoff had that silly misunderstanding last summer,' Elaine said.

Rosalie arched her eyebrows. 'What papers?'

'He didn't say. He still has his keys so if you give me the code for that new alarm you have had installed, he'll be able to let himself in later today.'

Sensing Rosalie's hesitation, Marc answered. 'I'm afraid that won't be possible.'

Elaine drew in a sharp breath and he saw in the rear-view mirror that two bright red spots had appeared on her cheeks. 'And what business is it of yours, may I ask? You're only Rosalie's trainee.'

He glanced at Rosalie. She shook her head, the familiar plea softening her brown eyes. No one was to know he was Raventhorn's new owner yet. Very well, he would indulge her a while longer.

'The system is difficult to operate,' he said. 'I wouldn't want your son to inadvertently trigger the alarm and alert the police.'

Elaine's mouth tightened in a thin line and her eyes hardened.

'I wonder what Geoff would say if he knew his own cousin wasn't allowed to go in and out of Raventhorn as he pleases. The place will be his to inherit after all – and perhaps sooner than you think with Geoff being so ill.' Without waiting for her change, or for Marc to help her get out, she flung the door open and slammed it behind her.

'How I hate that woman!' Rosalie's cheeks were almost as pink as her anorak. 'No wonder she drove her husband to an early grave and brought her son up to become an arrogant thug. She spoiled him rotten, gave him the notion he was destined to be Raventhorn's future laird and was far superior to everybody else around here.'

'What misunderstanding was she talking about?'

'There was no misunderstanding. Four years ago, at about the same time I started Love Taxis after ...' she swallowed hard '... after my mother died, Geoff relented to Elaine's pestering and hired Rupert as his estate manager. He was too preoccupied by his research to give Raventhorn his full attention, and I was busy setting up Love Taxis so I couldn't help as much as I used to. Rupert was a disaster. He would turn up late, disappear for hours on end, and he bossed us around, and was horrible to Lorna and Marion.'

Her voice became indignant. 'He even used to sneak out and drive off in Geoff's vintage cars. I know for a fact he took some paintings and artefacts and sold them off. In short, he behaved as if he already owned the place and we were his servants.'

She took a deep breath. 'I never understood why Geoff tolerated him for so long, but he finally came to his senses last summer. They had a massive row and he sent him away.'

She took off her hat, and combed her fingers through her brown curls. Her fruity scent filled the inside of the cab, hitting his senses. For a few seconds he was transported back to the night he found her in the bath. The memory of her lovely nakedness was so potent his throat went dry. His body hardened, his blood caught fire, and his heart started thudding. He closed his eyes, gripped the wheel and took a deep breath.

Behind them a couple of cars blasted their horn.

'What's the matter, Petersen? You look a little tense. Are you not feeling well?' She leant closer, put her hand on his forearm, her thigh brushed against his.

He gripped the wheel harder, clenched his jaw. 'I'm fine.'

'Then you'd better get a move on or we'll cause a jam.'

'Sure.' He took a deep breath, forced himself to focus on the road, and drove on. 'So what happened after the argument?'

'Rupert scuttled off to London. I don't know what he did there but

135

now he's back and up to no good. He had the nerve to visit Geoff in hospital before his operation, and left Geoff in a very agitated state.' She frowned, as if remembering something. 'So agitated he was almost delirious. He kept talking about a dangerous man, about a woman hiding and keeping secrets. He didn't make any sense at all.'

She tapped her index finger against the dashboard clock. 'Anyway, let's hurry or we'll be late for Flo's supermarket run.'

It was after eleven when they returned to the old lady's terraced house to put her shopping away, eat a slice or two of Battenberg cake and drink a cup of tea so strong it made his heart rate shoot up.

After a few more fares they stopped at Alice's for a coffee and a late lunch.

'Hello, there.' Alice gave Rosalie a hug, flashed Marc a smile and led them to a table near the window.

The café was almost empty but warm smells of herbs, soup and freshly baked bread filled the air. A moody Scottish ballad played in the background, in perfect harmony with the grey skies outside. Marc took his jacket off and sat down.

'I'll have my usual,' Rosalie said before making her way to the ladies' at the back of the café.

Alice handed Marc a menu. 'I hear your training is going well. Is the boss going to give you a permanent job?'

'The boss?' He must have looked blank, because she rolled her eyes to the ceiling.

'Rosalie, silly. It was real lucky for her you were here, although I know a certain mechanic who wasn't pleased when he heard you'd be doing all the driving for a while. In fact, Niall was furious. Still is, I think.'

'He'll get over it. I'm only standing in for Rosalie until she is able to drive again.'

'Try telling him that.' Her eyes filled with sadness. 'He wanted to be the one helping her out, as usual.'

Once again, the mention of Niall left an unpleasant sensation at the pit of his stomach. 'You said they were engaged once.'

'That's right. For a few months, but that was over four years ago, after Rosalie's mum died. Rosalie broke it off when she set up Love Taxis.'

'May I ask how Rosalie's mother died?'

'She had a stroke whilst out on a walk. By the time she was found, it was too late to save her. She was in intensive care for weeks but never recovered.' Alice stared at a point in the distance. 'It was so very sad. Poor Rosalie was heartbroken, and Geoff too – he was a wreck and spent days in a drunken stupor. He was even too distraught to attend the funeral service.'

'What about Rosalie's family – her father? Did he not come to the funeral?'

Alice shrugged. 'Rosalie doesn't even know who he is. Her mum wasn't from round here, but from London – or at least somewhere down south. She didn't like to talk about her family or what she did before coming to Raventhorn.'

He frowned. 'So Rosalie doesn't have any relatives?'

Alice shook her head. 'Not that I know of. She always said that her mum, Geoff and Lorna were the only family she had – the only family she wanted.' She shrugged. 'Anyway, Love Taxis was Rosalie's salvation. She put her heart and soul into it. You should have seen how proud she was the day she drove her pink taxi for the first time! It may not be the most profitable business in Scotland but she kept it going. In fact she was featured in the *Inverness Courier* in the spring. "Girl in Pink drives Love Taxis," was the headline!'

She shook her head. 'I never understood why Geoff was so angry at Roz when he should have been so proud of her. I thought he was going to have a fit when he read her interview and saw Sophie's photo in the Gazette.'

'Sophie's photo?'

'Rosalie told the reporters she set up Love Taxis in honour of her mum, and that it was her way of remembering her.'

'Why is that?'

Alice smiled. 'Because helping others was what Sophie liked to do. She was a kind, loving and generous woman. Rosalie is a lot like her. The only difference between them was that Rosalie loves bright colours whereas her mother only wore dull, boring clothes – it was almost as if she wanted to blend into the background and not be noticed, which of course was impossible because she was a strikingly beautiful woman. She could have been a model … if she'd enjoyed being photographed, that is. She was always finding an excuse to disappear when someone was taking photos.'

'I saw a few pictures of her in Rosalie's flat.'

'I think they're the only ones she ever agreed to have done, and only because Geoff took them. Roz would be lost without her taxi business, and without Raventhorn, of course.' She chuckled. 'And Irlwick would be equally lost without her. The toddler group would probably have to shut down, and so would other local services like the old people clinic, the library ... even my café would suffer. You wouldn't believe how many people use Love Taxis, especially since the bus service was cut down. Rosalie could make so much more money if she charged proper fares, but she won't hear of it, of course!'

Guilt stabbed at him but he made himself dismiss it. He wasn't responsible for Rosalie's happiness, or for the future of Irlwick's small community.

'Hey! Why do you two look so glum?' Rosalie's cheerful voice made them both jump. 'Have you run out of my favourite chocolate brownies and are too scared to tell me?'

Alice laughed. 'Of course not. Don't worry. I have made a fresh batch so you can eat as many as you fancy and the whipping cream is on the house.' She took her pad and biro out of her apron pocket, turned to Marc. 'So what are you having for lunch?'

He ordered a cheese and onion pie and a coffee, and tried not to stare as Rosalie took her pink anorak off to reveal yet another of her deliciously clingy pink jumpers.

As soon as Alice brought their orders over, Rosalie reached out for a bread roll, but instead of eating, she toyed with it until she'd reduced it to a pile of crumbs. 'Have you by any chance taken a decision about Love Taxis?' She paused. 'I know you've been busy with Raventhorn but I saw you looking at the books again last night ... I know they aren't great, well to tell the truth, they are dismal, but I have thought of a way of improving our service, and making it more profitable.' She looked at him, her eyes full of hope, and he found himself lost for words.

Damn it. He'd never been indecisive in his whole life. Right now he had no idea what to do about the small taxi business that should have been closed down long ago. The only thing he was sure of was that he couldn't bear to see Rosalie upset, and even less be the one responsible for it.

'I haven't made any decision one way or another yet,' he answered in a gruff voice.

Her face lit up. 'You mean there's still a chance you'll keep it going?'

'I only said that I hadn't made up my mind.'

He was suddenly aware of a middle-aged woman staring at him from a table at the opposite end of the café. 'Do you know that lady over there? She seems very interested in you – in us.'

Rosalie turned round and waved. 'That's Julia Murray – Niall's older sister. She's our local librarian, and one of Elaine's knitters.'

The woman waved back at Rosalie, but he noticed that she tightened her lips together in a thin, disapproving line before gathering her coat and bag.

Rosalie put her cup of tea down, a frown creasing her forehead. 'The woman hates me. No doubt she's now on the way to the garage to tell Niall she saw us having lunch together. Then Niall will call and I'll have to explain myself.'

He frowned at the mention of the mechanic, his mood suddenly turning as dark as his coffee. Muffled, soulful musical notes of a bagpipe tune resounded from his coat pocket. It took him a few seconds to realise it was the ringtone of his new mobile.

Rosalie laughed as he took the phone out. '*Braveheart*? That's a little sentimental for you, isn't it?'

He pulled a face. 'The shop assistant didn't give me a choice. He said it was their most popular ringtone here in Scotland and set it up for me.'

He hadn't wanted to rebuff the young lad at the time but now promised himself to change the ringtone back to the discreet and innocuous one he had before. He looked at the number flashing on the display screen and cursed under his breath. He really wasn't in the mood to put up with Fitzpatrick's empty promises and pathetic excuses.

His grey eyes were hard, his face stony and his voice sharp as he lifted the phone to his ear and took the call.

'Fitzpatrick, what can I do for you?'

There was a pause as Marc listened and frowned. 'This isn't how things work, Fitzpatrick, and you know it. You should have followed my instructions through. Now it's too late and we're doing things my way.'

Rosalie's throat tightened. How cold and inflexible he sounded. And she, who'd foolishly believed he had mellowed over the past few days, become more approachable, more friendly, was far too naive. Marc Petersen was a businessman. The only thing he cared about was his bank balance, and the only reason he was driving her taxi was to protect his investment. It wasn't *Braveheart* he should have chosen as a ringtone, but *Cold, Cold Heart*!

She looked at him and swallowed hard. The winter daylight pouring into the café made his eyes a lighter grey, and his hair a burnished blond, and emphasised his strong profile and broad shoulders. She remembered what it had felt like to rest her cheek against his chest and feel his arms around her waist, and experienced the usual yearning that made her heart ache for him. How she despised herself for the silly crush she seemed to have developed and that had spiralled out of control.

She rose to her feet, snatched her anorak from the back of her chair and marched to the counter where Alice was busy rearranging her cake display.

'What's up? Didn't you like the brownie? It's a new recipe but I've only had positive comments so far.'

'The brownie was great,' Rosalie grumbled.

'Is it your shoulder?'

'No, I can hardly feel it any longer.' The time had come to take her friend into her confidence and tell her the truth about Marc. 'It's Petersen,' she started in a whisper.

Alice's eyes widened. 'I knew it! You're madly in love with him, aren't you? I can see the way you blush every time he looks at you. So tell me, have you slept with him yet or are you still thinking about it?'

'Have you lost your mind?' Rosalie hissed, feeling her cheeks burn. She hated that her friend could see through her. 'All I want is to get rid of him, pretend he was never here and for things to go back to the way they were before he arrived.' That, at least, was only a partial lie.

'I don't understand why you dislike him so much. You must admit he's done a good job standing in for you since last week. People are raving about him. They like him.' Alice winked. 'Especially the ladies.'

'I wonder why. He's a cold fish. A snob. Never makes small talk. Rarely smiles or laughs at people's jokes. Doesn't even like my Happy Baby Radio. The man claims only classical music or modern jazz are civilised enough for him. If I didn't do all the chatting, the cab would be as gloomy as a morgue.'

That wasn't completely true. Marc had changed over the past week, enough to smile or join in a conversation with a customer, even share the odd joke. She had even seen him tap the beat of a few pop songs when he was driving.

Her friend smiled. 'He may be the silent and brooding type but that only makes him more attractive. At least you must admit he's rather handsome with his soulful grey eyes ... and his French accent is so very sexy.'

'Handsome? I never noticed,' Rosalie lied, turning to look at Petersen who was still talking on the phone. 'As for his French accent, he only turns it on when he's annoyed with me, and that would be most of the time since he finds me stupid and irritating. Listen, I said I owed you the truth. I'm sorry I didn't tell you before but the thing is, Petersen is a businessman, a property developer. Geoff sold Raventhorn to him and the only reason he's here is to complete an inventory and sell the estate's assets – and that includes Love Taxis.'

Her voice quivered, unwanted tears filled her eyes, and blurred her vision. Alice stared at her open-mouthed. She put down the plate piled high with her homemade scones and leaned over the counter.

'What did you just say?'

'Raventhorn now belongs to Petersen.'

Alice shook her head in dismay. 'Geoff sold Raventhorn? But why?'

'I don't know. I haven't been able to talk to him, with the accident and his heart operation ... I suppose he needed money.'

'What was he thinking of? You grew up there, it's your home. And what about Lorna who has spent years looking after the place, and after him?'

'Yep.' Rosalie's voice broke and Alice gave her hand a squeeze.

'You know you can always stay at my place and work here if you need a job. Although I'd rather you kept out of the kitchen.'

Rosalie's breath hitched in her throat. 'Thank you.'

'You must tell Niall,' Alice added. 'He'll want to help. Although he'll no doubt propose again when he finds out you're jobless and homeless.'

'No,' Rosalie said. 'Nobody is to know just yet, and I won't be marrying anyone, let alone Niall. It's about time he accepted it.'

'You know what he's like. He'll never let you go.'

Rosalie closed the gap between them and gave her a tight hug. She was well aware of her friend's feelings for Niall – Alice had never made any secret of them – and it made her sad and angry that Niall carried on chasing after the memory of their brief romance instead of opening his eyes to see the beautiful, warm and caring young woman who had loved him for years.

'You should tell him how you feel,' she said.

Alice shrugged. 'It's you he wants, you he's always wanted.' She stepped back. 'So what will happen now?'

'I'm trying to convince Petersen to keep Love Taxis running, but I don't think he's interested. As for Raventhorn, he said he might turn it into a hotel.'

'It'll be a blow to Rupert and his darling mother.'

'I suppose I should tell them. It's only fair they know.'

'You don't owe them anything, Roz. They're both greedy and mean and were always horrible to you and your mum.' She glanced away and whispered, 'Petersen is heading our way. I take it I'm not to breathe a word of what you just told me.'

Rosalie nodded. 'That's right. Pretend you don't know anything.' Swinging round, she found herself almost against Marc Petersen's chest.

'Ready for the doctor surgery run?' she asked in a tight voice.

'Can't wait.' His face sombre, he nodded and pulled the cab keys out of his pocket as well as a handful of banknotes that he left on the counter.

He walked out into the frigid cold afternoon without even waiting for her. Outside the sky was filled with low, pale grey clouds and Rosalie squinted against the glaring white light that reflected onto the snow-covered pavements, the roofs of houses and the distant hills.

'It looks like the ice storm is heading our way,' she remarked.

Marc walked to the front of the cab and pulled out the piece of paper that stuck out from under the wipers. He frowned as he read it, then slipped it into his pocket.

'What is it?'

'Nothing important. Don't worry about it.'

But for some reason she felt that she had every reason to worry.

Chapter Fifteen

By the time they drove the last of the pensioners home, the temperature had dropped to below freezing. A sheet of ice covered the road, forcing Marc to drive at crawling speed, and an arctic wind blew through the pine trees, which groaned and moved like living beings.

'They're gritting the road,' Marc said after they passed a truck with orange lights flickering in the night. 'At least the weather will keep your friend Rupert away from Raventhorn tonight.'

'I wouldn't count on it. Rupert is nothing if not determined. I'm sure he is desperate to assert his claim on Raventhorn and make sure you know he is Geoff's heir. In fact, I'm surprised he has stayed away for so long.'

She leaned back against the headrest, closed her eyes and let out a weary sigh. A confrontation with Rupert would ruin the rest of the day. Against all expectations, it had turned out to be an enjoyable afternoon, and the mood inside the doctor's surgery had been buoyant as Marc led a disputed game of cards. He may think talking to people was a waste of his precious time, but once again got on surprisingly well with everybody there, especially Angus McLean, who in a rare accolade had given him four bottles of his homebrewed pine needle beer after they drove him home – and it was well known that Angus didn't part willingly with his precious ale.

'He said it was just what I needed to keep me going,' Marc had said as he put the plastic bag with the bottles on the back seat. 'He also suggested you drank some. He found you a little pale. He seems to think his beer has medicinal properties.'

She pulled a face. 'Hmm. Well, one could say it does.'

He cast her a doubtful glance. 'Really?'

'That's right. It's full of ... ahem ... vitamins.' She had no intention of enlightening Marc about the beer's alleged aphrodisiac properties. It had been embarrassing enough to see Angus wink and give him a clap on the back as he handed him the bottles.

'Angus used to work at The Glen, a brewery that shut down about six years ago,' she carried on quickly before Marc could probe any further. 'He has dreamt ever since of setting up his own microbrewery

144

with his son and some of the staff who were made redundant when The Glen closed. He organised a beer festival last year, and even got Fiona to design labels for the bottles, but nothing came out of it. I guess he doesn't have enough business experience to go ahead with his plans.'

'It's a shame. Microbreweries and real ale are rather trendy these days,' Marc said as he slowed down to negotiate a bend in the slippery conditions.

She turned to him. 'I know! Why don't you talk to him about it?'

'I'm not here to offer business advice,' he answered coolly.

'Of course you're not.' She couldn't help but feel disappointed. 'How silly of me to suggest you might want to help Angus. After all, you said it yourself – your job is to shut down businesses, and once you've destroyed someone's dream, you move on to your next victim.'

His fingers tightened on the steering wheel and he glanced at her, shadows darkening his grey eyes. 'Victim? That's a bit strong.'

He sounded hurt. Already regretting her outburst, she swallowed hard and crossed her arms across her chest.

'What was all that about with the receptionist at the surgery?' he asked after a few minutes.

'Kian's girlfriend? I'm not sure. I was only trying to be friendly. Niall said Kian had an accident with his father's car when driving home after the ceilidh. I don't know why Stacey got so flustered when I asked how she was and how badly Kian had damaged the car. It was as if she was embarrassed and didn't want anyone to know about it.'

Suddenly, Marc slammed on the brakes, and the cab swerved and came to an abrupt halt. 'There she is again,' he muttered under his breath.

Rosalie peered into the night and the dark forest at the side of the road. 'Who? What?'

'That Raven woman. Whoever she is.'

'Isobel? Are you sure?'

But Marc had already jumped out and run into the woods and Rosalie's words echoed in the empty cab. What did he think he was playing at, running into the night to chase after Lady Fitheach? It was dark, the snow was deep, an arctic gale was blowing and he didn't know Corby Woods. She would have to go after him. Sighing, she zipped her anorak up, pulled her hat down and ventured outside.

'Petersen, come back!' The wind howling through the woods and the sound of pine tree branches swishing around her drowned her voice. Her feet sank into deep, frozen snow at every step, but she carried on in the direction he'd disappeared into. Within seconds her face and hands tingled with cold, and before long she couldn't feel them any more.

At last she glimpsed his silhouette between the trees, and headed his way. 'Did you see anything?' she asked when she was close enough.

He shook his head. 'She vanished before I could get to her.'

'I could have told you as much and saved us both getting cold and wet. Since when do ghosts let themselves get caught?'

He looked at her as if she'd just said the most stupid thing he'd ever heard. 'There is no ghost. Ghosts don't exist. Anyway why did you come out? You should have stayed in the cab.'

'And leave you on your own? You might have got lost. You could have tripped and got hurt.'

His jaw tightened. 'What do you take me for?'

He strode back to the road, his face so grim she thought it better not to argue even if she struggled to keep up. Once they were both back inside the cab, he slammed his door and turned to her.

'Let's get one thing straight.' His French accent sounded a lot stronger.

Rosalie's throat tightened. He was annoyed. Very annoyed.

'Contrary to what you and your pal Niall seem to believe, I am neither some fancy city boy nor a helpless fool of a tourist, and I certainly don't need to be rescued from the woods by a girl in pink. Got that?'

He leaned towards her. The glow of the taxi's overhead light cast threatening shadows on his face and turned his eyes almost black.

She nodded.

'Good.' He pulled away and started the engine and drove off.

'So you think you saw Isobel again,' she said to break the tense silence after a few minutes. 'That's twice you've seen her.'

'Three times, actually,' he replied. 'I saw her on top of the tower at Loch Armathiel.'

'You never said.'

'It didn't seem important at the time.'

Rosalie coughed to clear her throat. 'Three times, that's not good. I don't want to worry you but—'

'I know, you told me what happened to men who see her several times. The thing is, I don't believe in ghosts. This is no spectre of doom, Rosalie, but someone playing tricks on us.'

She tutted. 'This is completely ridiculous.'

He turned to her and arched his eyebrows. 'Any more ridiculous than a vengeful ghost and her faithful crow?'

'It's a raven, actually. Anyway, who would play tricks on us?'

'Someone involved in the hoax calls and the attacks on yourself and your cab.' Marc turned off the main road, drove over the bridge and into the courtyard at Raventhorn where a black sports car waited with its engine on. Even though the security lights were on, the car's dark windows prevented them from seeing who was inside.

Not that it mattered. Rosalie knew exactly who was waiting for them. She sighed. 'I told you it would take more than a freezing gale to keep Rupert away.'

'Nice car,' Marc remarked as Rupert climbed out of it.

'I wonder how he can afford it,' Rosalie muttered under her breath.

Marc grabbed hold of the carrier bag on the back seat. The beer bottles clanked as he walked towards Rupert, who stood head tilted back, spine stiff and legs slightly apart as if bracing himself for a confrontation.

Marc extended his hand. 'Pleased to meet you. I'm Marc Petersen.'

Rupert made no move to shake Marc's hand but stared at him, his lip curled in a sneer. 'Ah, yes. The infamous Marc Petersen. Rosalie's new driver, and the talk of the town.' He turned to Rosalie. 'Can we go in? I've been waiting for ages.'

'You shouldn't have bothered,' she said as she made her way to the kitchen door, clenching her key in her hand so hard the dents bit into her flesh. 'Why are you here?'

'Didn't my mother tell you I was after some papers?'

'You'll be lucky if you find anything. The library is a mess, as usual.' Rosalie unlocked the door, walked into the kitchen and started punching the alarm code in.

Rupert whistled between his teeth. 'That's a swanky security system you have here. It must have cost Geoff a packet to have it fitted, and yet he claimed he was broke when I visited him in hospital before his operation. Give me the code, so I won't have to bother you next time I come back.'

'We'll talk about it inside.' Marc pushed the door shut behind him. He put the carrier bag on the kitchen table and pulled the four beer bottles out. They all had a distinctive blue and green tartan label with a sprig of pine at the centre and 'Angus's Ale' printed in fancy gold lettering.

Rupert pointed at the bottles. 'Don't tell me that old devil Angus McLean sold you some of his homebrew! I bet he said it would make you as randy as a stag during rutting season and was better than Viagra.'

'Viagra?' Marc stared at Rosalie who immediately looked down and busied herself with the zip of her anorak.

Rupert McBride laughed. 'It looks like you're in for a treat tonight, Rosalie.'

She let out a shocked gasp and her face turned bright red.

Marc set the last bottle on the table and looked at McBride. 'What exactly is your point?'

Rupert must have heard the cold warning in his voice. He swallowed so hard his Adam's apple bobbed up and down a few times. 'Nothing. Nothing at all. I was only making conversation.'

'Well, I wish you didn't. You're talking rubbish as usual.' Rosalie gestured towards the stairs. 'Come on, then. If you want to find your papers, we'd better make a start.'

'You don't need to come with me,' Rupert protested. 'I'll be fine on my own.'

'It's no trouble,' Marc said. He couldn't explain why but he was uneasy about leaving McBride's cousin alone in the library.

The place was indeed a mess, but he had grown to like it that way. It was odd that he, who favoured minimalist interiors both for his London and Paris apartments, and who knew exactly where every single item he possessed was to be found, didn't mind towering stacks of books and a desk littered with papers, maps and folders here at Raventhorn.

Rupert whistled between his teeth and turned to Rosalie. 'What a shambles. You know what you need, don't you?'

'What?'

'Me, of course. I could spend a few days reorganising everything and won't even charge you a penny for it.'

'How good of you to offer.' Rosalie's voice dripped with sarcasm.

'No, I mean it. I worked here so I know Geoff's filing system ... I see he's still crazy about all that Viking stuff. I forgot what he told me this alphabet was called.'

'Actually there are two alphabets – Elder Futhark and Young Futhark,' Marc said.

He felt Rosalie's puzzled gaze on him and smiled, feeling a little smug.

Rupert shrugged. 'Whatever ... I can't believe these old papers hold the key to the location of Harald's treasure.'

Rosalie shook her head. 'Geoff never said it was a treasure, at least not in the sense you imply.'

'Of course it's a treasure. Harald was going to a royal wedding. He must have carried a casket filled with coins or jewellery, precious gems or artefacts.' He gestured to the pile of papers again and looked at Marc. 'Marion said you were translating them.'

'That's right,' Marc lied. He had only flicked through McBride's papers late at night when he'd had enough of working on accounts and balance sheets. Despite what he'd claimed, he would be quite unable to decipher much without doing some serious work. Yet he felt it was important to pretend he could.

He didn't trust Rupert McBride. He didn't like his bullish attitude, but above all he didn't like the way his small, shifty and bloodshot eyes stared at Rosalie and followed her every move like a predator about to pounce on his prey.

'I still have quite a bit of work to do,' he stated in a cautious voice, 'but you're right, the documents contain clues about Harald's treasure.'

Once again, he was aware of Rosalie staring at him in surprise.

'Now,' he carried on, 'what exactly are you looking for? I don't want to be rude but Rosalie and I have had a long day.'

Rupert pulled a face. 'I'm after some personal documents ... and a diary I left behind when I resigned. The diary has a dark blue cover, and is about this big.' He made a gesture with his hands and looked at Rosalie with an anxious look in his pale blue eyes. 'You haven't seen it, have you?'

Rosalie curled her fists on her hips and tilted her face up to look at him. 'No, I have not. And you didn't resign. Geoff sacked you.'

'It was a misunderstanding. Geoff told me so himself when I visited him in hospital.'

'I very much doubt it! You upset him very much that day.'

A cloud seemed to pass over McBride's face. 'Really? What did he say?'

'He was worried about something, someone ... a woman. Talking about women, I met your girlfriend at the holiday lodge.'

McBride frowned. 'What girlfriend? I don't know who you're talking about.'

'Dark-haired girl, pretty, a bit brash, London accent,' Rosalie insisted. 'I saw you with her in the hospital car park.'

'Ah ... well. What about her?'

McBride sounded so defensive Marc looked at him more closely.

'Nothing. I thought it was a bit strange that she should be staying in such an isolated place, especially when the weather was that bad. She and her friend could have been cut off.'

McBride's cheeks flushed. 'Her friend?'

'There was a man with her. He was in another room. I heard him. He sounded ... angry.' She shuddered and turned to Marc. 'I'm tired. I'm going to my flat now. I'll see you in the morning.'

Before Marc could insist that she stay at Raventhorn another night, she walked to the door.

'She was always highly strung.' One side of Rupert's mouth lifted into a sneer and his eyes narrowed to slits as he watched her leave. 'Shame about that temper of hers. Takes after her mother ...' Rupert shook his head. 'Sophie Heart was a very attractive, but strong-willed, woman, like Rosalie. Always fancied her – well, both of them, really.' He licked his lips and made a loud smacking sound.

Overcome with the gut-wrenching urge to punch him in the face, Marc clenched his fists and drew in a deep, long breath. 'That's enough, McBride,' he growled. 'I won't have anyone talking that way about Rosalie.'

The man chuckled. It was a slow, slimy laugh that grated on Marc's nerves. 'Fancy her yourself, do you? Can't say I blame you.'

Marc forced another breath down, and made himself uncurl his fists. He had to calm down. He really was turning into a Neanderthal, at least where Rosalie was concerned. 'Get what you came here for and leave.'

He sat on a battered leather armchair and picked up a folder overflowing with papers and manuscripts. He didn't believe Rupert's story for a minute. The man had come to snoop around, but what was he after – his cousin's will, or the location of Harald's treasure, even if it only existed in Geoff McBride's imagination?

Marc flicked through the papers. There were dozens of photos and transcriptions of runestones from all over Scandinavia as well as Orkney – presumably because this was where Harald had his estate. As he painstakingly deciphered a few lines, his grandfather's tales started to come back. It was as if his memories were buried under a layer of dry sand a cool North Sea breeze was blowing away – the same cool, gusty breeze that swept across the long beaches and sand dunes he used to roam during his Jutland summer holidays.

A muttered curse at the other end of the room broke his concentration. He lifted his eyes from the papers. Rupert McBride was rummaging through the desk drawers, a bundle of what looked like bank statements in his hand.

Frowning, he rose to his feet. 'These are your cousin's.'

Rupert's face reddened. He shoved the sheets of paper back in the drawer and slammed it shut with an impatient sigh. 'Well, that was a bloody waste of time.' There was the hint of desperation in his voice.

The two men walked down to the kitchen where Rupert glanced at the alarm. 'I'll have to come back, and it would make sense if you gave me the code. I don't see why you should know the code when I don't. You're only an employee whereas this place is as good as mine.'

Marc gave him a cool stare. 'So you keep saying.'

Rupert stood staring at him, waiting to be told the alarm code.

Marc ignored his request. 'By the way,' he said, 'would you mind giving me the name of your friends – the ones who were staying at the lodge?'

McBride stiffened. 'Why?'

'Rosalie and I had a serious accident on the mountain road – an accident caused by the driver of a black four-by-four who I believe was visiting the lodge. He didn't stop to help us when our car went off the road. He didn't even report the accident. We could have died that day.'

'That had nothing to do with my friends.'

'I'd like to check with them anyway. They might know who the driver was.'

'They're not in Irlwick any more. I have to go now. Goodnight.'

Marc hardly had time to step aside as McBride, suddenly in a great hurry to leave, flung the door open and rushed out towards his car.

Chapter Sixteen

Marc watched McBride's sports car speed away, so fast it skidded on the bend of the lane. The man was hiding something, and hopefully Luc or Cédric would find out what it was.

After picking up a bottle of Angus's beer, he went up to the library to collect a couple of books and a folder filled with papers, and took them to the drawing room.

He lit a fire, and uncorked one of Angus's pine needle ales with a popping sound, like a bottle of champagne. The smell emanating from the bottle, however, was so bitter it made his eyes water. 'It's an old Highlands recipe,' Angus had explained, 'and just what you need as a pick-me-up, my lad, you'll see.' He had leaned closer and winked. 'It won't do Roz any harm to drink a wee drop either.'

Marc smiled. So Angus believed his ale could increase his libido ... As if he needed help in that respect! Being near Rosalie day in, day out was enough to give any man raised blood pressure, not to mention the dreams that plagued him every night as he tossed and turned in that big bed in the Crimson Room. At times he could almost believe that Isobel's bed was indeed enchanted.

He lifted the bottle to his lips and drank a swig of beer. Although the taste was sharp, it wasn't as unpalatable as he'd feared. In fact, he thought after a few more sips, it was rather nice. With the heavy green curtains drawn against the night, and the soothing, almost hypnotic crackling of the flames dancing high in the fireplace, a pleasant torpor soon crept inside him. Stifling a yawn, he relaxed on the sofa. So much for the beer's special powers. It was more likely to make him fall asleep than give him any lustful urges.

He sighed, and closed his eyes. What was he going to do about Love Taxis? The businessman in him knew exactly that he should already have shut it down. Of course he understood why Rosalie was so keen to keep it going – it was her project. He also had to admit that she more than compensated her lack of business acumen with her warmth, kindness and enthusiasm. It was plain to see how much people loved and respected her. With one smile she lit up a cold, grey morning, made a lonely old woman feel cherished and cared for, and reassured an exhausted, insecure young mother. From a more pragmatic point of view, there was definitely a need for affordable transport in the area as he had seen very few buses in and around Irlwick since he'd been there.

Perhaps he could turn Love Taxis into a social enterprise project and set up a non-profit bus company. He might be able to find ways of subsidising it, with company money and public grants. He could even turn it into a clever marketing ploy to promote the Petersen brand as humane and people-friendly.

Humane? With his and his father's track record? He let out a derisive sigh, as once again his past rose up before him and the memory of what had happened to Van Bernd flooded his mind. Whatever he did, he would never atone for that tragic mistake.

The idea of half a dozen pink minibuses with the name Love Bus painted on the side and drivers wearing pink uniforms brought a smile back to his face though. It wasn't a bad idea. Not a bad idea at all. He grabbed a pen and a pad, scribbled a few notes and figures down and started working.

One hour later, he nodded with satisfaction as he looked at the spreadsheet on his screen and the notes on his pad. There was more research to carry out, but he already had a rough business proposal. He would put it to Rosalie the following day and ask for her thoughts and suggestions.

Rosalie … What was she doing right now? His pulse beat harder and heat flashed inside him as once again, images of her naked loveliness and the sensations of holding her in his arms swirled back to torment him.

Enough! This was turning into a seriously disturbing obsession.

He finished the beer and grabbed one of McBride's books at random and opened it and recoiled. Two pairs of dark, beady eyes stared at him from the brittle, yellowed page.

A raven.

He started reading the text aloud. It had been a long time since he'd spoken any Danish and his voice sounded odd at first, but after stumbling on the first few sentences, the words started flowing and before long he was totally absorbed in the tale of Odin, the Raven God, who sent his two pet ravens to fly over the world every morning. Marc remembered how important ravens were in Norse mythology and how often they were depicted on shields, banners, helmets, and runestones.

There were many runestones on his grandfather's land – his land now, even if he rented it out – but most of them were broken, buried and long forgotten. One however had stood near the gateway to the Petersen farm, a proud reminder of the family's more glorious past. Even though it was worn, one could still see the ravens carved on its surface – a dozen small birds flying around a much larger one, its fierce claws on display and wings wide open. An old photo of it had even featured in the *Newsweek* article about his father and himself.

Ravens seemed to be everywhere here too. In the name the McBrides had chosen for their new castle – Raventhorn. In Isobel McBride's nickname – Lady Fitheach, the Raven Lady. In the improbable tale that Harald, her murdered husband, was carrying a mythical Viking Raven banner from his Orkney estate to the wedding of his King's daughter. Even in the name of the woods surrounding the castle – Corby Woods, or Raven Woods.

He closed the book with a sigh. Enough with fairy tales. It was time to go back to the real world. He rose to his feet, and pulled his mobile out of his jeans pocket. It wasn't too late to call Kirsty. She was after all a workaholic like him, and they had things to discuss – a new office in the States if the proposed merger went ahead being one of them.

A small piece of paper stuck to his phone. It was the message that he'd retrieved from under the cab's wipers at lunchtime – the message he hadn't wanted to show Rosalie.

I AM WATCHING YOU.

The words were written in capital letters and in black marker pen. The sheet of paper was thin and white, and with its jagged edges appeared to have been torn from a notebook. Apart from that, there was no clue as to who had written it.

Anger tightened inside him. He may have vowed to keep Rosalie safe, but the note showed that he had failed miserably. Someone was still out there, making threats, and he still had no idea who that might be.

He scrunched the paper into a ball and threw it in the waste-paper basket just as the lights flickered and went out. Damn. The electrician had assured him that he'd checked the wiring and dealt with the worst issues at Raventhorn. There was obviously quite a bit of work still to be carried out.

He was about to make his way down to the kitchen when an eerie screech pierced the silence of the night. His blood froze. What the hell was that? It didn't sound like Rosalie's voice. Or any woman's voice. He wasn't even sure it was human. Perhaps there was an injured animal – a fox or a deer – out there.

He walked to the window and pulled open the curtains to peer outside but couldn't see anything.

Then he heard it again. Urgent, insistent.

His heart drumming hard, he rushed down the service stairs to the kitchen, and flung the door open. There wasn't anyone out there, human or animal. He glanced towards the loch shimmering under frigid moon rays and muttered a curse. Someone was in the water ... Without stopping to take his coat, he started to run.

As he got nearer, he could see who it was. A woman with long, dark curly hair. Rosalie! He'd never run so fast in his life, and pebbles clanged underfoot as he sprinted across the shore to the edge of the water.

'Rosalie!' he called, his voice hoarse and urgent.

Her face gleamed in the moonlight as she looked at him, then slid under the surface of the water. Seized with panic, he marched into the frozen loch, gritting his teeth against the cold. He had to get to her before she drowned. Perhaps it was already too late ... There wasn't even a ripple on the surface of the loch. It was as if she'd never been there.

'Rosalie,' he shouted again, his voice echoing in the dead of the night. Lunging forward, he started swimming, and when he thought he'd reached the spot where she had gone under, he gulped down a lungful of air and dived.

He could see nothing. Nothing but blackness. His eyes stung, his lungs burned, but he dived further down. He had to find her, save her. He couldn't let her drown. When his lungs felt like they were bursting, he kicked his legs and swam back up to the surface. He took a deep, long breath and got ready to dive back down despite the terrible cold that bit into his body.

'Petersen! Marc! What are you playing at?' A woman shouted from the shore. 'Are you out of your mind? Come back here, right now!'

He blinked the water out of his eyes. A white shape stood on the shore. Had the cold got to his brain and he was hallucinating, or was one of Raventhorn's ghosts standing in front of him?

'I said to come back. I have no intention of getting into that freezing loch to fish you out, do you hear?' The voice was high-pitched and slightly hysterical.

It was no ghost. It was Rosalie. But if she stood in front of him, who then was in the water? He glanced around him. The loch was empty. Its smooth surface reflected the moon and the stars. Had he imagined the woman? Had he drunk too much ale, or had some kind of dream?

He tried to swim but his arms and legs were too cold, too heavy, almost numb, and he gulped another mouthful of silty water. His muscles were seizing up. Now wasn't the time to puzzle about the mysterious figure he thought he'd seen. He had to get out.

The shore wasn't that far. He had to make it. He gave a few desperate kicks, his arms jerked into a clumsy breaststroke, and after what felt like an eternity he felt the pebbly ground under his feet at last. He reached out for a dead tree that stuck out of the water.

As he scrambled to his feet, a raven perched on a rock close by and let out the same blood-curdling cry he'd heard before. It glared at him, its small, shiny eyes reflecting the moonlight, then flapped its wings and flew off.

'Come here, you big *eejit*.' Despite what she'd just said, Rosalie didn't hesitate for a second. She walked into the water, slid her hands under Marc's arms and dragged him out of the loch and onto the beach.

The hem of her flannelette pyjamas was soaking wet, and so were the boots she'd hastily slipped on when she'd happened to glance out of the window of her flat and seen Marc run out of the kitchen towards the loch without even a coat. Something must be wrong, she thought, and she'd gone after him. Just in time, it seemed.

Now he was safe, anger took the edge off her fear.

'What did you think you were doing?' She curled her hands on her hips and tilted her face up to look at him. 'If you fancied a bath there are plenty of tubs at Raventhorn, there's no need to risk drowning in Loch Bran or catching pneumonia.'

He coughed, and struggled to pull himself upwards. His hair, his clothes dripped water onto the pebbly beach. His chest heaved as he drew in a few harsh breaths. He was shaking all over, his face grey in the silvery moonlight and his eyes dark and glazed, as if he was dreaming.

The truth dawned on her. *Isobel.* She'd never really believed any of the stories about Lady Fitheach. Until now.

'It was her, wasn't it?' she whispered. 'She was there, she tried to kill you.'

He shrugged her off and stood up to his full height. 'I don't know what you're talking about.'

He was lying. It didn't matter. What mattered was to get him back inside and into the warm. She started to unfasten her coat. 'Quick, put that on, you need it more than me.'

He shook his head. 'No. You keep it. I'll be all right. How did you know I was here?' he asked, his teeth chattering, as they hurried back to the castle.

'I saw you run out of the house and followed your trail. Then you were in the loch.' There were no words strong enough to express the icy fear that had gripped her when she'd seen his head bob in and out of the water and his arms beat the surface of the loch.

She forced a smile. 'I know you have Viking blood in your veins, but surely the loch is too cold at this time of year, even for you.' She paused and asked in a softer voice. 'So, if it wasn't Isobel, what happened?'

'I have no idea. One minute I was having a beer, the next the electricity went off, I heard something and went out to investigate. And then I thought I saw ...' He shook his head. 'It doesn't matter.'

They were in the courtyard, outside the kitchen now. He pointed at the rectangle of light reflecting onto the snow where he'd left the kitchen door open. 'That's strange ... the power is back on.'

His lips had turned blue and his hands shook so badly it took him several attempts to pull his drenched shoes off. The man was freezing. It would be a miracle if he didn't slip into hypothermic shock.

'You need a hot shower.' Rosalie kicked off her wet boots, threw her coat on the back of a chair and led the way up the stairs and to the first floor. The cold, wet hem of her flannelette pyjamas slapped her legs when she moved and her feet felt like blocks of ice.

'Can you show me how that blasted shower works?' Marc asked

when they reached the first floor. 'I don't think I can face any more cold water tonight. Or ever.' His lips stretched into a tentative smile.

Her heart did a flip and started pounding hard. Suddenly all she wanted was to comb his wet hair back from his forehead, wrap her arms around him and snuggle up to him to make sure he was warm. He might act as if it was no big deal but he'd had a narrow escape tonight. Men had drowned in Loch Bran before. Big, strong men like him.

'Sure. Get undressed.'

While he sat down on a chair to take his wet socks off, she went into the en suite and turned the shower control on.

'It's ready,' she shouted when steaming hot water spluttered out of the showerhead.

The door creaked open. 'How do you it? I've been here a fortnight and still can't work it out,' he said from behind her.

'That's because you have to turn the dial very slowly until you hear a click.' She turned to face him and the words died on her lips.

He stood tall, strong and naked apart from the towel he held around his waist. Steam rose from the shower cubicle, drowning the en suite in heat and white mist, and the lack of air made her lightheaded – unless it was the man who stood only a few feet from her and whose broad shoulders filled the doorway.

'I'll leave you to it, then,' she stammered, her cheeks burning and her heart racing.

He stepped aside but she bumped against the doorframe in a clumsy attempt to get out without touching him. Shutting the door behind her, she hurried to her old room where she cast her wet clothes off and rubbed her legs dry. She tried not to think about the man showering a few paces away. The man who had come to mean so much in the space of a couple of weeks.

She rummaged through her wardrobe for another pair of flannelette pyjamas, a green woolly cardigan, and slipped a pair of thick brown socks on her cold feet. She was about to step out of the room when she caught a glimpse of herself in the wardrobe mirror, and stopped in her tracks. No, it wouldn't do at all. No woman should ever wear these sort of nightclothes around a man, except perhaps her granddad.

She stepped closer to the mirror. Her hair was wild, her skin red and blotchy from the cold. Her gaze travelled downwards and she sighed.

That she was plain was nothing new, but these past few years she had also become a lot curvier and her old pyjama and cardigan did nothing to flatter her figure.

The thought of Marc Petersen seeing her shabby flannelette pyjamas was suddenly unbearable. She pulled the wardrobe doors open again. There must be something else she could wear. Didn't she buy a peach satin nightdress and dressing gown in the sales once?

There it was, folded in tissue paper at the back of the shelf. She stripped off again, except for the socks, and slipped the nightdress on, enjoying the feel of the silky fabric as it glided on her bare skin and swished down to her feet.

After adjusting the straps so that the tight bodice of the nightdress covered her breasts, she wrapped herself in the matching dressing gown and checked her reflection in the mirror once again. Yes, it was better, much better. She combed her hair with her fingers, and winced. Now she needed to get rid of the muddy smell of the loch. She was reaching out for an old perfume bottle when her hand froze.

What did she think she was doing? Did she really hope that Marc would take one look at her in her slinky peach nightclothes and ravish her there and then? She heaved a shaky sigh and closed her eyes. That was exactly what she was hoping for – yearning for.

How silly of her to get so smitten, so infatuated … It wasn't only his deep grey eyes, his strong shoulders or his rare smiles that sent her whole being into disarray – it was the way he was. The way he climbed out of the cab to help people get in and out. The way today he'd crouched down to be at eye level with the toddler who'd almost strangled him to get his scarf and let him give him a sloppy kiss on the cheek. And later he had lent Flora his arm and debated on the merits of value crackers as they walked down the supermarket aisles.

She knew she shouldn't feel that way. It was dangerous, and pointless. Let's face it, she was not the kind of woman he would ever be interested in. He had come to sell Raventhorn's assets, and when he was done he would leave, never to return.

She closed her fist and pressed it against her heart as if it could make the yearning go away. Why couldn't she just be happy with Niall's steady, loyal affection? Why did she have to be attracted to the most unsuitable man alive, and have these impossible dreams? It was pathetic, and it had to stop.

With a last look at her reflection, she snatched the green cardigan from the bed and slipped it around her shoulders before going down to the kitchen.

Marc was sliding a tray covered with frozen potato wedges into the oven when she walked in. She was relieved to see that his face was no longer grey and he seemed to be no longer shaking.

He looked up and smiled. 'Dinner should be ready in about fifteen minutes.'

'Thanks, but I'm not hungry.' As she moved away from the door, the sleeve of her cardigan snagged on the handle and the cardigan fell to the floor.

Marc bent down to pick it up. His gaze travelled from her unruly hair to her feet and he smiled. 'Nice socks. They look very ... warm,' he said as he handed her the cardigan.

She almost groaned aloud. He hadn't even noticed her sexy nightclothes!

'There's some of Marion's chocolate cake left. It's not as good as Lorna's but I'm sure you'll enjoy it.' He smiled again, humour sparkling in his eyes.

So not only had he not even noticed her lovely nightclothes, but he called her a glutton too! With a strangled cry, she swirled round and flew down the corridor and back up the stairs, clutching the edges of her cardigan tightly over her chest. She might as well put her ugly flannelette pyjamas back on. She wasn't even halfway up the stairs when he caught up with her.

'Rosalie, wait.'

She ignored him and climbed a couple more steps. The touch of his fingers on her shoulder made her gasp.

'What's the matter with you?'

She repressed a sob. 'Nothing. Leave me alone.'

'Was it something I said?'

She turned to face him. He stood on the step below hers, so their eyes were almost level, for once. His were filled with shadows.

The words were out before she could think. 'No, of course it wasn't. I mean, why should I be upset if you only ever notice what I'm wearing to compare me to a giant marshmallow, complain that pink gives you

161

headaches or comment on my ugly old socks? Why should I be upset if you think all I'm interested in is stuffing myself with chocolate cake ...' *And she should stop before she made a complete fool of herself.* Shame rose inside her like nausea. She pressed her hands to her burning cheeks and closed her eyes.

'I didn't mean to upset you.' His voice was deep and unusually soft, like the night when he'd fixed her shoulder in the holiday cottage. 'I'm glad you like cake,' he carried on. 'In fact, I love watching you eat cake. I find it incredibly attractive.'

This was the most ridiculous thing she'd ever heard. She opened her eyes, expecting to see him smile. He was serious.

'If that's your idea of a compliment, I can't say I'm impressed,' she said in a shaky voice. 'I thought French men were the kings of romance.'

'I'm only half-French, remember? I doubt my Viking ancestors used poetry to woo their women. As for your clothing ...' His voice deepened. 'Socks or no socks, I would have to be blind not to notice what you're wearing tonight.'

He lifted a finger to her cheek and very slowly followed the wet trail a tear had made to the side of her mouth. It was only the lightest touch, but her lips parted, her breath hitched in her throat and her body sizzled, tightened and ached all at once.

His hand fell to his side. The heat in his eyes was as potent as a caress as they skimmed down her body, and she responded as surely as if he was touching her. A liquid, molten ache spread inside her. Goosebumps pricked her skin all over. This time, surely, he was going to take her in his arms, kiss her ...

He pulled away, took a step down the stairs. 'Let's get back to the kitchen. There's something I want to talk to you about.'

Chapter Seventeen

He ached to touch her but he clenched his fists by his sides instead, as he turned round and went back to the kitchen. He had to step away before it was too late, before he gave in to the urge to pull her into his arms, pin her against the wall and kiss her until he was lost.

He had no idea if she followed him or not. What he did know, however, is if he wanted to catch his breath and give his body a chance to cool down, he had to keep busy. He opened the oven and grabbed a tea towel to take the tray of wedges out. They were nowhere near ready yet, so he shoved the tray back in. He had lost his appetite anyway.

Rosalie walked into the kitchen, lifted her coat from the back of the chair without saying a word, and bent down to grab her wet boots.

'Where are you going? I told you we needed to talk,' he said as he opened the fridge, grabbed some ham and cheese and put them on the table. They would do while they waited for the potatoes to be ready.

She cast a thunderous look in his direction. 'I can't think what we have to talk about.'

'I'll explain in a minute. For now, sit down and have something to eat.'

'I told you. I'm not hungry.'

The atmosphere in the kitchen was decidedly frosty as she sat down.

She narrowed her eyes and crossed her arms on her chest. He tried not to stare at the delightful décolleté barely concealed under her ugly green cardigan.

'So what did you want to talk to me about?' she asked, tilting her chin.

'Love Taxis.'

The phone ringing interrupted him.

A look of alarm on her face, Rosalie jumped to her feet.

'Who could it be at this time? I hope it's not bad news from the hospital.' She rushed up the stairs, the hem of her peach satin dressing gown flying after her.

Sighing, he turned the oven off and went after her.

'Yes, of course, I'll call him. Please hold on.'

163

Rosalie put the phone down on the console table and turned when she heard his footsteps behind her.

'Is it the hospital?' he asked.

She shook her head. She had been so scared of getting bad news about Geoff that it had been a relief to hear the impatient woman's voice demanding to speak to Marc.

'No, it's for you,' she replied, handing the telephone to him. 'A Miss Kirsty Marsh.'

His face hardened and he said as he grabbed hold of the phone, 'This won't take long. Please wait for me in the drawing room. We still need to talk.'

Even though all she wanted was to be alone, she did as he asked. The moment of truth had arrived. He was about to deliver his verdict about Love Taxis, tell her he was closing her down, and ask her to speak to Fergus, Fiona and Duncan about redundancies.

She closed her eyes and swallowed hard. If only she could find new arguments to convince him, but she'd said everything already. What's more, she could hardly look him in the eye after tonight's mortifying incident – yet another instance when she'd misread his intentions. Shame heated her face. She believed he wanted to kiss her, thought she'd seen heat and desire in his eyes. How could she have been so mistaken?

She heard him talking on the phone as she walked to the drawing room.

'No, Rosalie isn't the maid. She lives here. Yes, with me. I told you, it's complicated. Is there a problem? My mobile? Sorry, you're right, I haven't checked it for the past couple of hours or so. To tell you the truth, I can't even remember where I left the damned thing.'

There was a pause. 'What? When did that happen? Four days ago? Why didn't you phone me or email me earlier? Poor Maguire. He must be devastated. I'll be there to represent the firm. Of course, I have to. More to the point, I want to. You can do what you want, it's your choice ... I'll come back to Scotland after the funeral. I haven't made much progress with the inventory here. I've been busy ... Doing what? Driving a taxi, if you must know, and no, this isn't a joke.'

Feeling suddenly guilty for eavesdropping on his conversation, Rosalie pushed the door open and walked into the drawing room. Fire

164

smouldered in the fireplace, Geoff's papers and books were scattered all over the floor, and a bottle of beer stood on the coffee table. She lifted it up. It was empty. Angus would be proud. It looked like his homebrewed ale had made a new convert.

She poked at the embers and placed a couple of logs on the grate to start the fire again, then sat on the sofa and flicked through one of the manuscripts. A few minutes later the door creaked and Marc strode in. He stood facing the fire for a moment, hands shoved deep in his jeans pockets, before turning to face her. He looked so sombre she did not dare speak.

'I have to go back to London,' he said. 'Will you take me to the airport tomorrow morning?'

A fist squeezed her heart but she forced a smile. 'Of course. Shouldn't you check the times of the flights first?'

'There's no need. I arranged for the company jet to come for me. They'll be there at noon. Is that all right with you?'

'Should be. You know our bookings schedule as well as I do by now, since you've been doing all the driving.' She almost added that she was surprised he trusted her to drive, but the quiet sadness in his eyes stopped her.

'That phone call ... Was it bad news?'

He nodded. 'One of my employees, Maguire ... His wife died a few days ago.'

'Oh. I'm sorry.'

'The thing was, it was their anniversary a couple of weeks ago. He'd arranged a surprise for her. It was partly the reason I'm here. It should have been him who came to Raventhorn.'

He turned to stare into the flames again and added in a quiet voice, 'The funeral is the day after tomorrow.'

'What was her name?'

His lips stretched into a thin, bitter smile. 'You know what? I can't even remember. The man has worked for me for the past five years and I can't recall the name of his wife. What does that say about me?'

She rose to her feet, and went to him. 'It's because you're in shock. What really matters is that you'll be there for him, and you'll support him.'

He took a deep breath and smiled. 'I don't think I've ever met anyone as nice as you, Rosalie Heart. You are truly one of a kind.'

She forced a laugh. 'You said that the night I bashed you on the head with Lorna's copper pan, but I don't think you meant it in a good way then.'

He didn't reply, but there was something unfathomable in his eyes – something soft and tender that made her soul fly. But no! It was impossible. She was reading too much into it, once again.

'You said you wanted to talk to me. Is it about Love Taxis?'

He nodded.

'You're closing me down, aren't you?'

'I am, but—'

'I knew it.' She swallowed hard. 'I was hoping you would see beyond the poor accounting and the bank overdraft. Obviously, I was asking too much. Your priorities are to yourself and your company, not to the people around here.'

'Rosalie, let me speak.'

'There's no point. I have no intention of listening as you dissect my inability to manage my business and give me perfectly sensible reasons to shut me down.'

'Will you hear me out?' He sounded impatient now – impatient to list her inadequacies, her failings, no doubt.

'What for? So you can treat me the way you treat that poor man on the phone, the one you threaten with ruin because he didn't follow your instructions?'

He frowned. 'It's you I want to talk about, not Fitzpatrick.'

She crossed her arms and tilted her chin up. 'Go on then, I'm listening. I know what you think already. All I'm good for is eating chocolate cake, wearing silly pink clothes, and boring people stiff with my chatting and my bad singing! And now …' she stammered and this time she didn't even try to stop the tears from falling, 'now you're taking away the only thing I have ever managed to achieve. Love Taxis was my idea. I knew I had no talent for business but I tried.'

Through a veil of tears she saw him shake his head and smile. How dare he smile when he was destroying everything she loved? All the emotional upheaval of the past week suddenly caught up with her, swept her up in a tidal wave of grief and anger.

'I have to go.' She turned away and made for the door.

She didn't get very far. Two strong arms snatched her back.

'Calm down and listen.' He spun her round until his arms encircled her waist and she was trapped against his chest.

'Let go of me.' She struggled to break free but he was too strong.

'Not before you listen to me. I'm trying to explain that although I must shut down Love Taxis because it's not viable as a business, I have come to agree with you about the need for more public transport around here. I want to start a new venture – a minibus company – and ask you to help run it.'

His words took a few seconds to penetrate her brain. Her body stilled, she lifted her face towards him and met his cool, grey stare.

'A bus company?'

'A social enterprise, a non-profit venture if you like. I don't believe any private hire firm would be profitable around here.' He was still holding her tight, and his warmth was seeping through her nightclothes, and making her dizzy all over again.

'I do, however, believe I can find enough capital and public grants to start something.' He gazed down at her. 'Will you stop crying now?'

She smiled. He wasn't selfish and cold-hearted, after all. He had listened. He cared about the people of Irlwick. On an impulse, she rose on her tiptoes and kissed his cheek.

'Thank you.' There was so much more she wanted to say. That she loved him, for a start. She loved him so much. She'd known it, fought it, for long enough. Now she had to accept it.

He held her more tightly. Something shifted in his eyes, his face became tense. 'Rosalie … I want to kiss you.'

'Oh.' Her heart stopped then started again with a bump. Mesmerised by the heat in his eyes, the closeness of his mouth, she felt quite unable to speak. He slipped his hand onto the back of her neck and drew her to him. For the briefest of moments their breath mingled, then his lips touched hers.

With a groan he wrapped his arm around her waist and moulded her to him as if she was made of hot, soft and yielding clay. His mouth caressed and teased, light as a feather, until she parted her lips, and then he kissed her hard and deep.

Her heart drummed hard as his hands glided along the curve of her back in a slow, fiery caress. Her satin dressing gown rustled as he drew her closer, and her breasts felt full and heavy as they rubbed against his hard body in an arousing caress that caused her to whimper and arch against him. Her fingers gripped his shoulders, laced at the back of his neck. Closer, she wanted to be closer. It was like being thrown at the centre of a whirlwind. Never before had her body felt so alive. Never before had she been filled with this burning need to be touched, kissed, and taken.

The silk and velvet of female skin. Its sweet, warm, intoxicating scent. A man could lose himself in so much softness. His fingers pushed Rosalie's dressing gown over her shoulders and he bent down to kiss her jaw line, the side of her throat and the hollow at its base where her pulse beat, fast, erratic.

She threw her head back and her breasts pushed upwards, straining against the nightdress's bodice. He wanted to touch, taste and savour, get drunk on the taste of her. There was only one force driving him – primal and overwhelming. Strip her down and expose her body to his gaze, his hands, his mouth. Then lay her under him and thrust deep inside her. The heat of feeling and need swelling, pulsing inside him threatened to annihilate any conscious thought he might have.

He heard her moan softly and looked down. Her eyes were unfocused – dark pools of warm, liquid chocolate. Her lips were red and swollen, the skin of her cheeks and throat flushed a delicious pink. Her fingers stroked the back of his neck in a light, insistent caress that made his body harder. Could it be that, despite everything that stood between them, she wanted him as much as he wanted her?

Hope soared inside him, only to be immediately crushed. She might want him right now, but it still didn't mean he had the right to take her. He didn't do relationships. He had nothing to give a woman, especially one as special, kind and genuine as Rosalie – nothing but a few moments of heat and pleasure. Rosalie deserved better.

He tore his mouth away with a ragged breath, took a step back.

'Wait,' he said in a rough whisper. 'I can't make any promises. I can't stay with you. My life, my work are a long way away from here …'

She shook her head. 'I don't want your promises, I only want your kisses.'

He smiled. 'That sounds suspiciously like one of your Happy Baby Radio tunes.' He bent lower, closing the space between them. 'All I can give you is the here and now.'

She put her index finger on his lips. 'That too sounds like a song.'

'I'm serious, Rosalie.'

'So am I.'

'Are you sure?'

For an answer she stood on her tiptoes, brushed her lips to his, traced the outline of his mouth with the tip of her tongue.

He kissed her again, revelling in the taste of her mouth, aroused by her soft, lush, female body. He felt like he was burning with a fever, and it had nothing to do with the flames dancing in the fireplace behind him.

'I want to take you to my room and make love to you.'

He waited the space of a few pounding heartbeats, felt her shiver in his arms.

She let out a low chuckle. 'Then what are you waiting for?'

He took her hand and led her up the stairs to the first floor and the Crimson Room, pausing every few steps to kiss her lips, her eyelids or the tender skin of her throat. When they finally reached the first floor, he pushed the door to his room open with his shoulder and strode across the wooden floorboards. The bedside lamp was on and cast a dim, warm glow onto the bed, leaving the rest of the room shrouded in thick shadows.

He slid one hand against her cheek, the other around her waist and drew her close. He could have taken her anywhere in Raventhorn – on the drawing room sofa or the rug in front of the fire, on the stairs or standing against the wall in the corridor, but for some inexplicable reason it was in the massive four-poster bed he wanted to make love to her.

As he kissed her mouth again, and again, there was no clear thought in his mind, only a chaos of sensations and needs, of colours and scents. He wanted more. He wanted everything. And he wanted it now. He tumbled her onto the bed, covered her with his body, and started nuzzling the side of her neck, trailing kisses down to her shoulder and back to her earlobe until she writhed and sighed and whimpered under him. The sounds of satin and skin rustling against the ruby red counterpane inflamed his senses further.

His fingers felt thick and clumsy as he untied her belt and pushed the dressing gown off her shoulders. With a sharp tug, he pulled the bodice of her nightdress down and his hard, eager mouth closed onto her breast. She tangled her fingers in his hair to draw him closer while he kissed and teased and suckled one tender pink tip, then the other, into hard buds.

He pulled up the hem of her nightdress until it bunched up around her waist and then he stroked the silky skin inside her thigh, and when he touched her at last he caught her moan in his mouth. Drunk on the smell and the feel of her, he deepened his kiss. His fingers caressed, applied pressure, took. Nothing mattered but her and the feel of her body trembling under him. Her hands clutched at the bedcover, her breathing was short and shallow, and her heart thudded against his chest. And when she arched against his hand and cried out, he felt like the strongest, the wealthiest, the most powerful man on earth.

Suddenly touching her wasn't enough. He wanted to be inside her. He lifted himself off the bed, stood up to peel his jumper off and take his jeans off. He couldn't take his eyes off her as she lay on the bed, eyes closed, a half smile on her lips, and her body almost naked, soft, flushed, open. An offering. For him alone.

Naked at last, he lay next to her on the bed and his hands found the lush curves of her breasts, her hips and stomach. Bending down, he kissed her lips softly, teasing and nipping, until she moaned and her fingers tickled once again the back of his neck, slid down his spine then up again to knot into his hair. Every one of her caresses was a sweet torment; every one of her kisses drove him wild.

In the small corner of his subconscious that was still dimly aware of reality, of her, himself and their surroundings, he felt her body tremble and was experienced enough to recognise it was probably because she was shy, or a little scared.

In another lifetime he would have forced himself to slow down, gentle his touch, wait until he was sure she was ready. Tonight, in that great massive bed which looked like an island in a sea of shadows, something wild and hot and primitive drove him.

He thrust away the last glimmer of awareness and rolled on top of her, bent down and kissed her mouth again whilst his hands roamed, hard and impatient now over her body. He pushed a knee between her legs to spread them wider apart, grabbed hold of her wrists and pinned her arms above her head.

'I want you.'

She opened her eyes. Her lips were red, her cheeks flushed a deep pink. Her brown curls tangled on the red counterpane, since in his haste he hadn't even pulled the covers down. At that moment his heart knew exactly who she was.

She was the mysterious woman he'd dreamt of every night since he'd arrived at Raventhorn. The woman who made him feel whole. The one who touched his soul.

He pushed deep inside her, slowly at first then harder and faster, and together they moved and soared inside that dark and delicious place where time and space ceased to exist.

She sobbed his name once, then once more. She tensed, threw her head back against the pillow. He took hold of her hands, pinned them on the bed and interlaced his fingers with hers and followed her.

Chapter Eighteen

She curled up against him and buried her face in the crook of his neck, as if she was suddenly too shy to look at him. He had no idea of the time. They had made love twice, and already his body stirred at the feel and intoxicating scent of her skin. Guilt suddenly stabbed at his chest and he cursed himself silently. In his brutal, all-consuming need to make her his, he hadn't spared her injured shoulder a thought and had probably been too rough. If truth be told, he had been quite incapable of thinking at all.

'I didn't hurt you, did I?' he asked, anxious now.

She snuggled closer. Her breath tickled his chest. 'Not at all.'

'I think I might have got a little carried away.'

She looked up. 'At least now you understand why this old bed is so popular.'

It took a second to understand what she meant. He rolled on top of her, lifted her hands and pinned them on the pillow by either side of her head.

'You mean you don't think I could make love to you anywhere else but here?'

She laughed. 'Probably not as well. This is a magic bed after all.'

He smiled, lowered his face to hers until their lips almost touched. 'This is a challenge I can't ignore. I must prove you wrong, starting right now.'

'You seem very sure of yourself.'

Rolling off her, he got up, picked her dressing gown from the floor and handed it to her. 'Come with me.'

She sat up, stifled a yawn and shook her hair. It fell in a mass of tangles on her shoulders, tantalising close to her breasts, conjuring images of him playing with the silken strands to stroke her and awaken her desire once more.

'Where to?' she asked.

'The drawing room.' He retrieved his clothes from a corner of the room and slipped them on.

'I was only joking, you know,' she said.

'I wasn't. Anyway,' he added. 'We could both do with a drink, and I want to check on the fire.'

'Don't worry, neither Dughall McBride nor Old Finghall will let anything bad happen to Raventhorn.'

He frowned. 'Who?'

Then he remembered the names. They were Raventhorn's house ghosts. Dughall, Finghall, a howling woman he'd forgotten the name of. And Isobel, of course. A shiver of unease crept down his spine. He didn't want to think about Isobel, or whoever pretended to be her. Only a few hours ago he'd known without a doubt it was all a scam and someone was out there posing as the Raven Lady. Now he wasn't so sure, and it annoyed the hell out of him.

He could easily dismiss the silhouettes he'd seen at the side of the road in Corby Woods or at the top of the ruined castle for trick of shadows and light, but he'd been sure he'd seen a woman in the loch – so sure he hadn't hesitated to walk into freezing water. *It was only a dream – some hallucination brought about by stress, not enough sleep, and Angus's strong ale. Not to mention moon shadows on the water.*

Rosalie was looking at him. 'Don't look so cross.' She sounded worried.

He stroked her cheek with his index finger. 'I'm not cross.' *At least not with her, never with her*, he finished silently. 'Come on, let's go down and check on that fire.'

'I need my nightdress,' she said, looking around the bed.

'Your dressing gown will do just fine.' His hands tingled with the urge to touch her again. The way he was feeling right now, she would probably end up naked in his arms the moment they reached the drawing room – if they made it down there at all. This was ludicrous. He hadn't lusted after a woman this much since he was a teenager.

She covered up and pointed to the post. 'Aren't you going to carve your mark? It's tradition, you know.'

'Not just yet … I'll wait until I have a few.'

Once downstairs, Rosalie insisted on making hot drinks whilst he tended to the fire. He put several logs in the grate and poked at the embers until sparks flew and flames rose once more in the chimney.

She came back carrying a tray with a teapot, two mugs and a plate of chocolate biscuits she put down on the side table near the sofa.

'We're having tea. It's too late for coffee, and I don't think you need another of Angus's special ales.' She chuckled and poured them both a drink, then grabbed hold of a biscuit and bit into it.

'I see you've been busy reading some of Geoff's research papers,' she said, pushing some of McBride's books off the sofa to make space to sit down.

Marc lowered himself and sat at her feet. He reached out for his mug of tea, stretched his leg in front of him – the one he had hurt in the accident – and winced. It had been healing nicely but his swim in the freezing loch hadn't done his wound any good. He drank a sip of tea, looked around the drawing room and let out a contented sigh.

Tonight, Raventhorn was a warm, welcoming cocoon. It felt like home, he thought, surprised. Leaving in the morning would be hard, and not only because he dreaded the emotional turmoil he would find Maguire in. He had no inclination to deal with office business or Kirsty's imperious demands for his time and commitment to a New York project he did not support – to a company he no longer wanted to be part of. With a pang he realised he would gladly give up the life he was accustomed to and stay here, to drive the cab, listen to Rosalie talk and sing to her Happy Baby Radio, and make love to her all night …

Rosalie cast a quick glance at his profile as he stared at the fire. His hair stuck up at the front, and his hands curled around his steaming cup of tea – the very same hands that had earlier roamed over her body, and possessed her so thoroughly the very memory made her pulse beat harder and heat burn her cheeks. How wanton of her to give herself so completely to a man she'd only known for a few weeks, a man so different from her in every respect. A man she knew would leave in a few hours.

Her throat tightened. He had done the decent thing and warned her that there could be no relationship between them, that his life was far away from Raventhorn, and she had accepted his terms. Thinking about what might happen in one day, or one week, was pointless. She only wanted the here, and the now – or at least that's what she'd claimed. The problem was that she had lied.

Her throat tightened. She discarded her half-eaten biscuit on the plate, swallowed some hot tea, and put her mug down before pulling one of the manuscripts onto her knees.

Her finger ran along the lines of fine, spidery writing that covered it. The paper was yellow and brittle, the ink had faded to a pale blue. This was probably a very old, very precious manuscript, yet Geoff now kept them in careless piles in the library. After her mother's death, he had refused to hire anybody to catalogue his books. She had tried to help for a few weeks, but when she set up Love Taxis the library had descended into chaos.

She pointed to the rune-covered pages. 'So you can't really translate any of this?'

He shook his head. 'I can only decipher a few lines, I'm afraid.'

'Yet you told Rupert you were close to finding the location of Harald's treasure.'

'I lied. I don't trust him. He seemed far more interested in McBride's bank statements than in those personal papers and diary he claims to have lost.'

'He looked through Geoff's bank statements? Oh, I hate that man! I wish he'd stayed in London with his girlfriend, whoever she is.' Unease and dread wrapped around her heart as she remembered the young woman at the holiday lodge and the man who'd shouted from the back room. The man whose cold, angry voice she couldn't forget. In fact, she'd heard it in a nightmare so vivid a few nights ago she'd woken up in tears, her heart pounding with fear and calling for her mother like a little girl.

She shrugged to dispel the unpleasant feeling and looked down at the runes again. The ancient writing looked beautiful, mysterious, magical ... and completely incomprehensible!

'How did you learn? Geoff tried to teach me but he was never the most patient of men, and I wasn't a good student.'

'There were runestones scattered on my grandfather's land and neighbouring farms. I used to copy the inscriptions in a notebook and my grandfather helped me make sense of some of them.'

'What was he like, your grandfather?'

He stared at the fire. 'He was quiet, reserved, hard-working. My father and he weren't close, probably because they were so different. My father wanted to conquer the world. My grandfather was content with his farm.'

'Yet you said you used to spend your holidays there, so your father must have wanted you to get to know him.'

'True, but when I was thirteen he decided I should attend summer school and focus on exams. I often wondered if he was afraid I was growing too fond of life on the farm.'

'Would you have liked to become a farmer?'

The idea of Marc managing a farm would have seemed ludicrous only a week before. Now she looked at his rugged profile sculpted against the light of the fire, his broad shoulders stretching the fabric of his T-shirt and his strong hands, and she wasn't so sure.

He turned to her. 'I don't know. Probably not. My grandfather wasn't just a farmer. He was also a self-taught scholar, and with him I learnt a lot about the Norse people, their history and culture. He used to read to me in the evenings – poetry, mythological tales or the sagas.'

He smiled. 'I have to confess that more often than not, he would send me to sleep, especially after I'd been playing in the sand dunes all day.'

He pointed to the papers on her lap and narrowed his eyes as he focused on the signs. 'If I'm not mistaken, these are runes from the Elder Futhark alphabet. McBride probably told you that there were twenty-four of them, and that each one had a name with a specific meaning, chosen to represent the sound of the rune itself. Let me see … This one, for example,' he pointed to a sign shaped like a giant X, 'sounds like a "g" and meant "gift". And that one, from what I can remember, is "m" for "man", and these funny lozenge shapes represent the sound "n" and the god "Ingwaz".

He paused and read the manuscript more closely. 'It looks like McBride translated most of the inscriptions already, like this one about *"a mighty warrior who travelled to foreign lands, bringing fame and fortune to his family."* There were similar stones on my grandfather's farm that commemorated kinsmen who had travelled to faraway lands.'

He looked at the papers again. 'Here McBride has translated another inscription, this time about a warrior called Kolli who too died on foreign land. This is intriguing. It says that after Kolli fell on the battlefield his soul came back to his homeland in the shape of a great raven.'

He frowned and added in a thoughtful voice, 'So it seems we're back to ravens.'

'Wait a minute. You just reminded me of something I've read.' Rosalie flicked through the bundle of pages on her knees. 'There's something else about souls here. Listen. "*Is Harald's soul wandering? He is the raven at Isobel's side.*"'

'Let me see.' He narrowed his eyes to read the document. 'This is nonsense, of course. There is no Isobel, no ghostly raven, and Harald's soul is certainly not flying around Raventhorn like a bird of ill omen.'

She bit her lower lip, unwilling to remind him about the legend that said that men who saw Isobel several times ended up drowning in the loch, and how close he had come to doing just that himself tonight. Instead she gathered the papers and piled them up on the sofa.

'I'm sure Geoff will explain everything when he feels better.'

'We'll have a lot more to discuss than ravens, runestones or Harald's wandering soul, believe me,' he said.

She forced a smile. 'Yes, I suppose you will. Although you may not think much about Geoff's research, many of his academic contacts agree about Harald being the bearer of precious gifts to the royal wedding. There is an account of him travelling from Orkney with a silver chest containing presents.'

He cocked an eyebrow. 'Including the famous Raven Banner, I suppose?'

She nodded. 'At least that's what Geoff believes. You know how important raven banners were, don't you?'

'Viking warlords believed they had magic powers and brought luck in battle.'

'That's right. A very old poem claimed that the banner was woven from men's entrails by Valkyries using a loom made of dead warriors' body parts.'

She pulled a face. 'Another, less gruesome, story stated that it was made of pure white silk and a raven would appear on it during the battle and flap its wings to announce victory, but if it stayed still it meant that the army would be defeated. The most famous warlords had one. King Harald Hadrada had one, as did Sigurd the Stout, who was the first earl of Orkney. According to the sagas, it was Sigurd's own mother, a sorceress, who had made it. When she gave it to him she claimed it would bring victory to the man riding behind it but death to the man carrying it.'

'Yes, I know the story. He had to carry it into battle one day and got himself killed.' Marc smiled. 'I didn't realise you knew so much about this.'

'That's because I grew up with Geoff's stories.'

'Why does he believe Harald had a raven banner?'

She leafed through the pile of documents and pulled a photo out. 'Because of this.'

'It looks like an ancient burial mound.'

'It's Maeshowe, on Orkney, on what used to be Harald's land. It is a Neolithic tomb but it was broken into by various groups of Norse or Viking groups in later times and some of them left graffiti in rune – very interesting graffiti as far as Geoff is concerned, even if they have been the cause of heated arguments with his academic friends over the past few years.'

He arched his eyebrows. 'In what way?'

'The rune graffiti indicate that Maeshowe was broken into several times, the first time to be used as a burial chamber for a Viking warlord in the early days of Norse settlement in Orkney. One inscription is about a "fated banner" – another word for a raven banner – that was found there, a treasure, and right next to it are carvings of ravens very similar to a shield believed to have belonged to Harald. We actually have the shield in the tower upstairs. Geoff thinks the treasure was removed by ancestors of Harald's and that he was taking it, or what was left of it, as a mark of respect and allegiance.'

'Hmm. I can understand why he would take precious objects but an old banner ...'

'That one was special. Some of the graffiti at Maeshowe were carved by the sons of King Ragnar Lodbrok. Geoff believes that the banner belonged to him.'

This time Marc laughed. 'Wait a minute. Are you talking about *the* King Ragnar? The very same who killed an enormous serpent to rescue a fair maiden, raided England and France and in the end was thrown into a pit of snakes? He was a legend, a mythical figure, not a real man.'

Rosalie shook her head. 'Not at all. Geoff believes he was based on a real character, who also had a raven banner. In fact, according to Geoff and a few of his contacts, Ragnar's nickname, which is usually translated as "hairy breeches" because of the shaggy coat he put on to fight the serpent, can also be interpreted as "fated banner".'

'Like the inscription in the burial chamber ... So McBride thinks that Harald had in his possession the banner of legendary King Ragnar?'

She nodded. 'And he believes that Harald's honour, and the fate of his very bloodline, was linked to the preservation of the raven banner.'

'So that when he lost the banner, he was cursed and lost his honour.'

'Yes,' Rosalie agreed. 'That's it, exactly. Geoff is convinced that Harald and his men managed to hide the chest before they were attacked by the Armitage clan. It is clear from Geoff's notes ...' she gestured towards the paper on which Geoff had scribbled '... that he believes Harald is under some kind of curse, or spell, until he can retrieve the banner.'

A sudden gust of wind down the chimney made the flames hiss and rise high. They both turned to look at it. Rosalie shivered as a fanciful thought crossed her mind. Was that Isobel's way of letting them know she was right?

'A nice fantasy,' Marc snapped, his face stony and his eyes dark as slate. 'I wish McBride put as much energy and imagination into the management of Raventhorn. I don't know why we're wasting time discussing this fairy tale when we only have a few hours left together.'

Tomorrow he would leave and she would be alone. Even though her chest tightened, she managed to keep her voice calm and detached.

'How long will you be away for?'

'A week, maybe more. I'll take the opportunity of being in London to sort out some urgent business. I may even make a quick trip to Paris.'

She smiled, bravely.

He looked at her. 'You must be careful while I'm away. There may not have been any more prank calls this past week or so, but I still don't want you to drive at night or take any new customers. I don't think you should be alone at Raventhorn either. Perhaps you could ask Alice to stay here with you in the evenings.'

He was right. It would be far too sad and lonely for her to be alone here at Raventhorn. 'I'll ask Alice if to come over.'

'Good.'

'You be careful too,' she said then. 'I really don't like the idea of you flying, especially in this weather.'

He smiled. 'It's strange, that phobia of yours, and completely

179

irrational. Flying is very safe, a lot safer than driving.'

'That's what people say, but I can't imagine myself on an aeroplane, ever.' She shuddered. 'In fact, I often have this nightmare where I'm on a plane. Suddenly it starts shaking and making a terrible noise, and it dives through the clouds towards the ground and everybody starts screaming and—'

He stood up. 'Shh ... Don't think about it. It's only a dream. I have taken lots of planes and nothing like that has ever happened. Now, it's time I took you up on your challenge.'

She didn't need to ask what he meant. The smouldering look in his eyes was enough for her to understand. She swallowed hard. 'Now? Here?'

'That's right.' He took her hands and pulled her to her feet, then bent down to nuzzle the side of her neck whilst tugging at the belt of her robe. The silky fabric slipped off her shoulders and fell to her feet like a peach cloud. She now stood naked in front of him.

'If there are any ghosts lurking around,' he said in a hoarse voice as he trailed kisses along her throat, 'I suggest they return to their broom cupboard, their tower or wherever they usually hide right now.'

Chapter Nineteen

She shouldn't be feeling this good on less than three hours sleep.

Heaving a contented sigh, she snuggled closer to Marc. It had been late, very late, when they had made it back upstairs, stumbled into bed and fallen asleep. Her body might be a little sore and her head foggy, but it felt like she was floating on a heavenly cloud, and it was all thanks to the man next to her.

'What time is it?' Marc's voice was rough and sleepy.

She craned her neck to read the alarm clock dial on the bedside table. 'Just after seven. I must call Fiona. She's on the early shift at the switchboard today.'

'Don't forget to tell her you're driving me to the airport,' he said, bursting her lovely, warm and dreamy bubble.

'Oh ... yes, of course.'

He pulled her on top of him and fastened his arms around her waist. His hands stroked her back. His chin, rough with stubble, rubbed against the top of her head. She listened to his strong and steady heartbeat. Never had she felt so whole, so protected, so loved, even if that was just an illusion.

'I'm going to miss driving your cab and listening to your customers. I'm even going to miss listening to you singing to your Happy Baby Radio.'

She curled her fist and gave his chest a pretend punch. 'Liar! You don't like chatting to people, you don't like smelly toddlers. You find pushing a supermarket trolley a waste of time, and you hate my Happy Baby Radio – that's what you said the day you arrived.'

His arms tightened around her waist and he kissed the tip of her nose. 'Maybe I was wrong. You enlightened me, in more ways than one. Not to mention saved my life last night, and for that I'll be forever grateful.'

Her throat tightened. It wasn't his gratitude she wanted. It was his love. 'Well, then, I must call Fiona or she'll worry.'

'And we wouldn't want to worry Frosty Fiona, would we?'

He let go of her and she scrambled to her feet to retrieve her robe and cover up quickly. She felt keenly aware of her body's imperfections this morning.

'She's not that bad,' she objected as she made her way towards the en suite. 'She can be a little grumpy from time to time, but deep down she really is a very nice girl and a very talented artist. She designs the menus and posters for Alice's café and a few other businesses. She actually came up with the logo for Love Taxis. I'm sure she'll have lots of great ideas for the new minibus company. I can't wait to tell her and Fergus the good news.'

'No. I don't want you to say anything to anyone.' His voice snapped, cool and sharp.

She turned round, surprised. 'Why ever not?'

'I'd rather have my business plan worked out and the funding in place before you involve other people.'

She shrugged. 'All right. I won't say a word, if that's what you want.'

He pulled the sheets down, got up and walked towards her, gloriously naked. Holding her breath, she took a step back.

'Monsieur Petersen,' she said, forcing a note of playfulness in to her voice even though her chest was so tight it hurt, 'you might deny that Isobel's magic bed has anything to do with it but I think it has worked wonders for your … hmm … stamina.'

He came closer. And closer. Her back pushed against the door to the shower room but it wasn't the feel of the cold wood against her skin that made her shiver. It was the hot and dangerous glow in Marc's eyes.

'I think I should put that bed's magic powers to the test one last time, don't you?' He slipped one hand under her hair to the back of her neck, the other around her waist to draw her to him and bent down. Her heart sang a happy tune and she couldn't help smiling as his lips touched hers. He may not love her but right now, he wanted her, and she would have to be happy with that.

A few hours later, she was negotiating the busy Inverness traffic through a blur of tears. Marc had left. Dressed in the crisp white shirt and the navy suit and coat he'd worn the day he'd arrived, he had once again looked cool and businesslike – a far cry from the passionate man who had driven her cab, and shared a game of cards or dominos with her elderly customers. From the man who had made love to her time and time again.

His last words at the airport resonated inside her. 'Call the police immediately if you're worried about anything. Then call me.' He had slipped a business card into her hand. 'I can't remember where I left my new mobile last night, so you'll have to try the numbers to the London office. There's no point ringing my flat, I'm never there.'

He had made her promise again to ask Alice to come over to Raventhorn in the evenings, and in return she had urged him to be careful on the plane.

'I have no need to be careful. I'm not doing anything but sitting down and reading my reports. It's the pilot who'll do all the work and I trust him to do a good job,' he had answered with a brief smile.

She almost retorted that she'd never trust any pilot enough to climb into a plane, but remembered just in time that Marc's father had died in a helicopter crash only a few weeks before, and bit the words back.

So she had rested her head against his shoulder, breathing in the fresh sharp citrus fragrance of his aftershave and his own, deeper scent, as if to imprint them into her memory.

'I'll be back in a few days,' he had said as he put his hands on either side of her face and pulled her gently to him before giving her a long, searing kiss that left her breathless. And then he had got out of the cab and disappeared through the terminal's sliding doors.

She took advantage of stopping at a red traffic light to dab her wet cheeks with a soggy tissue.

The radio crackled. 'Hi, Roz, I've just taken over from Fiona. She told me Petersen's left for London. Is that right?'

She grabbed hold of the mike. 'Hmm, yes. He had to go to a funeral.'

'So he won't be away too long?'

'A few days.' She sniffed back the tears.

'Are you all right, lass?' asked Fergus.

'Of course, I'm all right. Why wouldn't I be?'

'Well, it's just that the man hasn't left your side for over two weeks now. I reckon you may feel a wee bit lonely without him. Anyhow,' he carried on quickly, 'I have a few bookings. I've checked the numbers. They're all legit.'

'Go on. Give me the details.' At least work would stop her from feeling sorry for herself.

Fergus listed names, times and pick up locations.

She was busy the rest of the day and by the time she dropped her last client at Aviemore train station, it was well after seven and she was starving. She drove up Irlwick's main street, found a parking space and climbed out of the cab. She hadn't had time to phone Alice and ask her for a bed for a few nights, but the café was open until eight most evenings, and her friend rarely had visitors to her flat, so it shouldn't be a problem.

She licked her lips in anticipation of a cup of sweet, hot and milky tea, a bowl of soup and a chocolate brownie, and couldn't repress a moan of disappointment when she arrived in front of the café and saw it shut and the blinds drawn. Worse still, the windows of Alice's first floor flat were dark too. Rosalie buzzed the intercom and stomped her feet on the pavement to stave off the cold. There was no answer.

Her boots made slurping sounds in the wet snow as she walked back to the cab. That would teach her to take people for granted. She should have phoned ahead instead of turning up unannounced. Now it seemed she would have to stay at Raventhorn on her own after all, and for the first time the prospect depressed her.

Perhaps she could call at Fergus and Marion's house. They'd put her up for the night, except that Marion was probably watching her favourite soap after a long day's cleaning, and Fergus would be doing his model making or his crosswords, and it wasn't fair to impose on them. No, she'd have to toughen up, be a big girl, and go home alone.

As she drove out of Irlwick, the flashing neon sign of a Chinese takeaway caught her eye. She slammed on the brakes and slid the car in a parking spot at the side of the road. She should have thought of it before. Niall loved Chinese food. She'd get a selection of his favourite dishes and stop at his house for a couple of hours.

Thirty minutes later, she was ringing the bell of Niall's bungalow, a bulging carrier bag in her hand.

It wasn't Niall who opened the door but his sister Julia.

'Ah. It's you.' Julia's voice was as sour as her long, narrow face.

'Hi, Julia,' Rosalie started in a forced cheerful voice even if she felt equally unhappy to see her. 'Is Niall in?'

Julia crossed her hands on her chest. 'No. He went out with Alice.'

'Really? Where did they go?' Rosalie couldn't help the pang of disappointment that her friends should have gone out without inviting her.

Julia narrowed her eyes. 'A party in Nethy Bridge. What did you want?'

Rosalie lifted the carrier bag. 'I thought I could share a Chinese with Niall, but I guess I'll have to eat it on my own.'

'What about your fancy businessman – Petersen? Is he not with you?'

'Marc? Oh no, he went back to London earlier today.'

Julia let out a snort. 'I see. So now he's left, you come running back to Niall. Well, I have something to say to you, Rosalie Heart. I've had enough of seeing my brother suffer because of your fickle ways. You've taken him for a fool long enough.'

Taken aback by the animosity in Julia's voice, Rosalie gasped. 'I didn't ... I never treated Niall badly.'

'You've kept him on a tight leash for years,' Julia retorted. 'You took advantage of his good nature to get your car repairs on the cheap, you called him when you had nobody to go dancing with, and all the time you thought you were better than him. He would have done anything for you, even closed his garage for a week to drive your cab, but no, you chose that foreigner – that Petersen – and cavorted with him all over town. I told Niall tonight that enough was enough, that he should forget about you and try and enjoy himself with someone else for once! So he called Alice and they went out.'

Stunned and dismayed by Julia's tirade, Rosalie could only shake her head. 'You're not being fair, Julia ... but I won't waste my breath arguing with you. I'll go home now. Goodnight.'

She started to turn round when something Julia said came back to her mind. 'Hang on a minute. What did say just then, about Marc Petersen being a businessman? How did you know? Did Alice say anything?'

Julia shrugged. 'Alice? No. Why would she? I recognised him, that's all. When I saw him in the café yesterday, I knew his face was familiar but I couldn't quite place him. It's only when I went back to the library that I remembered where I'd seen him before. Wait here, I'll show you what I mean.'

She turned on her heels and disappeared inside the house, only to come back a couple of minutes later, clutching an edition of *Newsweek* magazine. 'There, what do you think of that?' She shoved the magazine into Rosalie's free hand.

Rosalie stared at the cover. It showed Marc dressed in a smoking suit and an older man who looked so much like him he could only be his father. *'Slash, burn ... and prosper,'* the headline read. *'Are Petersen and Son the Vikings of International Finance?'* The article was dated from the summer, before Marc's father's fatal accident.

'It makes for interesting reading,' Julia added. 'Geoff thought so too.'

Startled, Rosalie looked up. 'Geoff saw this?'

'Aye, he did. You know how he loves spending hours searching through the archives, using the computer and chatting with me about his research,' Julia answered, looking smug.

'When did he see that magazine?'

'It was back in July. I had just put it on display when it caught his eye. He flicked through it, found the double page with the article on Petersen and spent almost ten minutes muttering to himself before leaving with it. I had to run after him to get it back. He looked weird, he hardly heard me. Naturally I was curious to read what he'd been so upset about. Well, there's one thing I can tell you for sure. These Petersens –father and son – they sound like real nasty individuals.'

She suddenly stared at Rosalie, her eyes shining with curiosity. 'So what's Marc Petersen doing in Irlwick? It's all a lie, isn't it, that he's learning to drive a cab?'

Suddenly all Rosalie wanted was to be alone and read the magazine. 'That's none of your business. Thank you for the magazine. I'll bring it back tomorrow.'

And before Julia could object, she turned on her heels and walked down the path back to the cab. Sliding behind the wheel, she put the magazine and the carrier bag with the Chinese takeaway on the passenger seat and started the engine.

It didn't take long to drive back to Raventhorn. The roads were empty, and it had stopped snowing. The castle stood, dark and ominous against a very dark, cloudy night sky. The security lights came on. An owl hooted as she got out and fished for the keys to the kitchen door inside her anorak pocket. She punched the alarm code in, opened the door and flicked the light on. Heavy silence closed in like a thick cloak around her. Feeling lonely and miserable, she slipped her anorak off, put the takeaway cartons in the microwave oven and filled the kettle to make some tea.

Was it only last night that Marc had made love to her? That he had held her, kissed her, made her feel alive and cherished? Tonight the castle felt cold and sad, and as hollow as her heart.

She dished out some fried rice onto a plate, made some tea and sat down, the magazine open on the table in front of her. She looked at the photos first. There were a number of them, of Marc's father, of his mother Cécile, who the journalist said now lived in the South of France and still modelled occasionally, and of Marc and Kirsty Marsh – the same Kirsty Marsh who had called him last night.

Rosalie's heart missed a beat. The woman was stunning. Her honey blond hair cut in a smooth bob framed a beautiful face, her elegant dark blue dress emphasised her perfect figure. And to make matters worse, Marc had his arm wrapped around her slim waist and looked as if he never wanted to let go.

Of course … Kirsty must be Marc's girlfriend. That was why he had warned her the night before that he didn't want a relationship, that he could only give her the here and now. Rosalie was even surprised he'd found her attractive enough to make love to her.

Feeling suddenly sick, she pushed her fried rice away and made herself focus on the article. Julia was right. It did make for interesting reading. The reporter retraced the story of how Marc's father had earned his fortune and risen from a humble beginning as a salesman in agricultural machinery in Denmark to make the *Sunday Times'* rich list for the past twenty-five years. It was basically what Marc had said. His father bought failing companies, closed them down and sold their assets to the highest bidder. Sometimes he restarted them, hired new staff, injected a lot of cash then sold them off for a huge profit. No matter how many jobs were lost, how many families or communities were thrown into dire financial circumstances, he never negotiated, never changed his mind, never altered his course of action.

His son Marc, the reporter wrote, was, like him, an astute businessman who kept his eyes firmly set on the company's balance sheet. After successfully managing and expanding Petersen's Paris office for several years there were now plans for him to relocate to New York together with Kirsty Marsh, one of the firm's bright new stars.

The reporter speculated that the move may be seen as a damage limitation exercise following the suicide of Patrick Van Bernd, an industrialist from Northern France. Van Bernd's luxury chocolate production and distribution outfit had been bought up by the Paris branch of Petersen and Son. It had been forced to shut down – only to re-open under a new brand name and with a completely new set of staff a few weeks later and to become one of Petersen's success stories. Van Bernd had asked, and been refused, the right to return to his former company as executive manager. He had suffered a severe mental breakdown, his family had disintegrated – his teenage daughter had been killed in a drink driving accident, his wife taken an overdose of sleeping tablets shortly after. The evening after his wife's funeral, Van Bernd had driven his Jaguar to a local beauty spot and shot himself.

'Oh my God.' Rosalie pressed her fist to her mouth.

Kirsty Marsh was quoted as saying that the world of business was indeed a harsh place and that not everybody was cut out for it. Under no circumstances could Sigmund and Marc Petersen be held responsible for Peter Van Bernd's decision to end his life. Van Bernd had played, and lost, and there was nothing more to say. She also said that Marc had acknowledged not letting Van Bernd return to work had been an error of judgement on his part but did not admit any responsibility in the tragedy.

A knot curled and tightened inside her, her mouth went dry. A man was dead, a whole family destroyed, and Marc talked of error of judgement? What kind of cold, ruthless man had she fallen in love with? Her breath came out fast and shallow, and she felt so dizzy she feared she might faint.

In her haste to grab hold of her cup of tea and sip some of the hot drink to calm herself down, she almost missed the short fixture about Marc's family and the old sepia photos of the North Jutland farm where his ancestors had lived and worked for centuries.

She blinked, put the cup down and lifted the magazine closer to her eyes. 'I don't believe this.'

In the far corner of the photo of a very tall man dressed in a dark suit, holding a wide-brimmed hat, was a standing stone depicting a series of runic inscriptions around what appeared to be the carving of a large raven surrounded by a dozen smaller ones.

Pushing her chair back, she jumped to her feet and searched the kitchen cabinets for the magnifying glass she knew Lorna kept to read her old recipe books. Surely she was mistaken. There were hundreds of carvings of ravens on standing stones in Denmark, what were the odds that the Petersen stone had the same design as Harald's shield?

She took the magnifying glass from the cabinet and held her breath as she pressed it against the photo. There was no mistake. It looked exactly the same. No wonder Geoff had walked away from the library in a daze. He must have thought this was the breakthrough he'd been waiting for all these years. At last he could trace Harald back to where he came from – Hantsholm in North Jutland.

And even more accurately, the farm of Marc Petersen's ancestors.

The magnifying glass slipped from her fingers onto the table. Did it mean that Marc was a descendant of Harald's? Suddenly Geoff's decision to sell Raventhorn to the Petersens took on an entirely new meaning. Perhaps it wasn't so much because Geoff needed money that he'd approached Marc and his father, but because he wanted to reunite them with their family history. Perhaps he believed they could help him find Harald's treasure at last.

If only Geoff would wake up and she could talk to him!

She looked at Marc's photo again. If he and his father hadn't slain and murdered men in battle like Harald had, they had driven men to despair and destroyed families in their relentless pursuit for wealth. Shaking her head in disgust, she threw the magazine on the table and walked out of the kitchen and went up to the drawing room, where she drew the curtains and made a fire. How cold she felt – how numb, lonely, and lost.

A soft, melancholic tune behind her startled her. It was the ringtone from Marc's new phone, which she quickly located, jammed between the cushions of the sofa. She pulled it out, flipped the cover open and saw a text from Carl FitzPatrick.

Need to meet at your Paris office asap. Please.

She recalled Marc's cold voice as he spoke to the man. It was clear that he was another of his business victims – a man desperate enough to beg. Disgusted, she threw the phone so hard it bounced off the leather sofa and landed near the waste-paper bin. Just how many people had Marc and his father driven to despair before profiteering from the company they had set up and had been unlucky enough to lose? She would phone the office number Marc had given her and relay FitzPatrick's message in the morning.

As she picked the phone up, she spotted the writing on a piece of paper in the bin. She pulled it out. **I'M WATCHING YOU.**

She gasped in shock, and glanced around, almost expecting to see a threatening figure step out of the shadows. Then she remembered the note Marc had peeled off the windscreen after their lunch at Alice's café. He hadn't said anything, because he probably didn't want to worry her.

So, once again, someone was trying to intimidate her.

Well, whoever they were, she wouldn't give them the satisfaction of seeing her running scared. She wouldn't abandon Raventhorn, and she certainly wasn't going to give up Love Taxis. She would carry on as normal. She scrunched the note into a ball and threw it into the fire.

Chapter Twenty

'It's been almost two weeks since his bypass operation. Shouldn't he be awake by now?'

Still holding Geoff's hand, Rosalie turned to the nurse.

'His body is in shock, you must give him time,' the nurse replied, whilst checking the wires connecting Geoff to several machines that beeped and flashed by the bedside.

What if time didn't make any difference? What if Geoff never got any better? What if he was going to die, just like her mother? Rosalie swallowed hard and looked at the man she had loved like a father for as long as she could remember. His face was sallow and thin, with deep grooves at the sides of his mouth. A drip kept him fed and hydrated, but the operation had taken its toll. He looked like the ghost of the vibrant man he had once been.

'Keep on talking to him. Even when they're asleep, hearing the voice of a loved one can do patients a world of good.' The nurse gave her an encouraging smile before leaving the room, the rubber soles of her white shoes squeaking on the lino flooring.

Rosalie squeezed Geoff's hand again and bent down to kiss it.

'You'll get through this,' she said in a choked voice. 'You have to. You may be the most annoying man I've ever known, but I miss you.'

She didn't know how much he heard or understood, but once she started talking the words kept tumbling out. 'The police still haven't found any clue regarding the Porsche. I still can't believe anyone tampered with the brakes and caused you to crash, but then again many things have happened since that I didn't think possible. You selling Raventhorn, for a start.' *And me falling in love with the most unsuitable man alive.*

The room was silent except for the medical equipment whirring and beeping softly. It was warm too. Her body weary and her head fuzzy from exhaustion, she slumped back in the chair and closed her eyes.

She had been far too restless to sleep the night before. After reading the article about Marc and his father once again, she had retrieved a bunch of keys from the study and climbed the stairs to the second floor gallery where Geoff kept the artefacts generations of McBrides had

191

collected over the centuries. It was one of the few rooms that were always locked.

It had been a while since she'd ventured into the turret she used to call the treasure room when she was a child. The wooden door squealed as she pushed it open. Switching on the light, she'd breathed in the dusty smell that permeated the place. Tall glass cabinets lined the walls, filled with a collection of random objects – combs and hairbrushes, claymores and dirks, belt buckles, diaries and old recipe books, amulets and a few items of jewellery that hadn't been sold off to pay for fuel or tax bills.

Geoff's prized possession glinted dully from behind the glass – Harald's shield, which had been found on the shore of Loch Armathiel after the Dane swam to Isobel's rescue. The raven engraved at the centre stared straight at her. It was the same design as on the runestone on the Petersen's Danish farm.

Rosalie opened her eyes and leaned closer to Geoff. 'Julia Murray gave me a copy of the magazine with the article about Petersen,' she said. 'I saw the photo of the runestone on their family farm. The raven looks exactly like Harald's shield, doesn't it? Is that why you sold Petersen the estate – because you thought there was a connection between his family and Harald?'

She waited a few moments but there was no reaction.

'Talking about Petersen,' she added, 'something very strange happened a couple of nights ago.'

She told Geoff about Marc swimming into the loch in some kind of trance and how she'd helped him get out. 'He denied it but I'm sure it had something to do with Isobel.' She sighed, and pushed away the memories of what had happened after they had returned to the manor house. 'I never really believed in your ghost stories, but Marc said he's seen her before, even if he thinks it's only somebody playing tricks. Now I'm not so sure, and I can't help thinking that he was lucky … very lucky.'

She paused, and stroked Geoff's cold hand. 'By the way, Rupert came to Raventhorn the other night, supposedly to retrieve some documents he said he left behind, together with a diary too … I think he's up to something.'

This time Geoff's fingers trembled under hers. Rosalie leapt to her feet and leaned over the bed. Geoff's eyelids twitched a few times, as if he wanted to open his eyes but was too weak.

'Geoff? What is it?'

His hand slid sideways on the covers – a small, jerky movement only, but a movement nonetheless. Frantic, she looked at the window and the nurses' station outside the intensive care room and gestured to one of the nurses.

'What's the matter, love?' The woman glanced at her, then at Geoff, as she hurried inside.

Rosalie pointed to the bed. 'He moved!'

The nurse proceeded to check the readings on the machines. She then pulled a pen out of her pocket, slipped Geoff's file out of the folder at the foot of his bed and scribbled some notes on a chart.

'His readings are normal, but his heart rate is slightly raised.'

'Maybe he's in pain, or he wants something.'

The woman replaced the chart in the folder.

'I don't think there's anything to worry about – it's probably good news, in fact. I'll call the consultant so he can assess him straight away. You should go down to the cafeteria and get yourself something to eat.'

It was almost lunchtime and the restaurant was full. Rosalie bought a pot of tea and an egg mayonnaise sandwich, and sat down at a small table near a window.

She poured the tea, added some milk and stirred in a spoonful of sugar, and unwrapped the sandwich and bit into it. She put it down with a grimace. It tasted as unappetising as it looked. She pulled her mobile out of her handbag and switched it on to check for messages. There were two texts from Fiona about bookings for the afternoon. That was all.

What did she expect? Marc must be too busy to get in touch today. She'd phoned his secretary in London to pass on Carl Fitzpatrick's text, but Marc was at the funeral of his friend's wife today. Then he would have meetings to attend and people to see – among them, no doubt, the clever and beautiful Kirsty.

Did she really want to talk to him anyway? Reading the article in *Newsweek* had been the painful confirmation of everything she had thought of him when they'd first met. He belonged to another world, he had opposite values and priorities. He didn't care who he hurt.

And yet, the memory of his touch and kisses filled her with a yearning so strong it was almost unbearable, and she couldn't stop thinking about the way he looked at her, the way he made love to her in the Crimson Room's bed, as if she belonged to him and their hearts and souls were entwined forever.

She lifted her cup to her lips and winced. She'd waited too long and now the tea was lukewarm. She forced it down anyway, and stared out of the window at the low, grey, snow-laden clouds filling the sky and dimming the daylight. She put her tray away, and went back up to Geoff's room.

The elevator pinged as it shook to a halt on the tenth floor and she walked down the long corridor, breathing in smells of medication and disinfectant. A different nurse was on duty at the desk. She asked her what the consultant had said about Geoff.

The woman smiled. 'Everything is following its course, Miss Heart, but he's going to run more tests, so don't stay too long.'

Rosalie spent a few minutes at Geoff's bedside, chatting about the weather, and Lorna's visit to her sister, and hoping to trigger another reaction from him, but he did not move again.

'I have to go,' she said, before kissing his cheek. 'Fiona booked a couple of rides for me this afternoon. I'll come back tomorrow. And, Geoff, don't worry, you'll soon get better,' she whispered, more to reassure herself than him.

As she left the hospital, she picked up a couple who wanted to go to Inverness town centre, and after that she was busy all afternoon. As night fell, and despite Happy Baby Radio playing her favourite tunes and Fergus's cheerful banter over the cab radio, she felt increasingly dispirited.

'Are you sure you want to work tonight, lass? It's St Andrew's night,' Fergus asked after she dropped her last customer at Aviemore golf club.

It was St Andrew's night, and she'd completely forgotten! In previous years, she had always spent the evening with Lorna, Geoff, Alice and Niall at the Four Winds' ceilidh. There would be no celebration for her this year, and if Niall and Alice were going to the dance, they hadn't invited her.

'I'm not sure it's such a good idea, lass,' Fergus said. 'Petersen wasn't keen on you working at night and specifically instructed me not to take any bookings in the evenings.'

She hissed an annoyed breath. 'Well, he's not here, is he, and I need to keep busy. What do you have for me?'

It seemed most of Irlwick was out enjoying themselves at the Duke's or the Stag's Head or attending the ceilidh at the Four Winds Hotel that evening. Couples, groups of friends and families piled up in the back of the cab, laughing and chatting excitedly whilst she forced a smile and listened to their accounts of a great night out.

Finally it was time to pick up her last clients of the evening at the Four Winds. It was late and there were only a few cars left in the car park. She drove to the front and checked the time. She was ten minutes early, so she switched off the engine, and reclined against the headrest and watched the last of the partygoers leave.

A group of young men and women came out of the hotel and walked towards a large black four-wheel drive parked under a lamp post. She recognised Kian Armitage and Stacey, his girlfriend, and an older couple – Kian's parents. Kian clicked the key fob, opened the door to the car, and got in, followed by Stacey and his parents.

Rosalie sat up and wound her window down to get a better view of the car. Her mouth went dry. Her heart beat faster. With its tinted windows and radiator grid, it looked disturbingly familiar. She shook her head. No, she was mistaken. It couldn't be the car that had chased after her on the forest road. There were so many black four-wheel drives around, and most looked the same. What's more she was so scared that night she hadn't taken a good look and would be quite unable to identify it.

'Sorry we're late!' A man's jovial voice boomed outside the cab.

She forced a smile, looked at her next clients, and unlocked the back door. 'Not at all. Hop in!'

It was well past one in the morning when she told Fergus to lock up and go home, and she finally drove back to Raventhorn, and parked in the snowy courtyard in front of the castle. She was so tired her fingers shook as she unlocked the kitchen door and keyed in the code for the alarm. She stepped into the empty kitchen, pulled her pink hat off and unzipped her anorak, but instead of switching the lights on, she stood still and forlorn in the dark.

All the emotions she had managed to keep at bay rose in a tidal wave of sorrow and despair, and once she started crying, she couldn't stop. She cried over Geoff, over the loss of her home, over Marc and the wretched love she felt for him despite everything, and the mother she missed so much.

Every time she thought there were no more tears to cry and the edge of her despair had dulled, fresh grief welled inside her. She cried until her chest and throat hurt, until she was hollow inside and her whole being had melted into nothingness, until all she could see before her was misery and hopelessness.

At long last she dragged her feet out of the kitchen and up the stairs, and climbed to the first floor. She walked along the corridor and pushed the door to her mother's bedroom open.

Breathing the familiar scent, which the passing of time hadn't totally erased, she switched on a side lamp and sat at her mother's dressing table. Her fingers lingered over the perfume bottles, over the small make-up set that she knew consisted of powder, mascara and a tube of pale pink lipstick, and her mother's jewellery box. Everything was exactly as her mother had left it that last summer evening, before she went out for her fateful walk. If she regularly dusted the room and put fresh flowers in a vase, Rosalie hadn't moved anything, not even the book her mother had been reading the day she died. It was still on the bedside table, with her mother's reading glasses neatly folded on top.

Perhaps Lorna was right and it was time she sorted her mother's things. Perhaps clearing the room wouldn't be an act of betrayal after all. For the first time in four years, she realised that it didn't matter if her mother's wardrobe stood empty at last, or if the top of her dressing table was bare. She would never forget the sound of her voice or the feel of her loving embrace.

She would make a start right now. Seized by a sudden burst of energy, she went back to the kitchen to get a roll of black bin liners, and started emptying the wardrobe, methodically sorting out the clothing in different piles – some for her to keep, others to send to the charity shop, and those that were too worn to be given away and could only be recycled. She paused every so often to bury her face in a jumper or a scarf to breathe in the sweet, floral scent her mother favoured.

Soon piles of clothing towered on the bed and bulging bags lined the floor. Rosalie looked at the dark-coloured cardigans, baggy jumpers and long skirts that her mother had worn day in, day out. How strange such a beautiful woman had cared so little about her appearance, and had sought all her life to hide her gorgeous figure and blend into the background.

When the wardrobe was empty, Rosalie turned her attention to the dressing table. The jewellery she would keep, the perfume too, but the make-up was out of date. She threw away the brushes and hair accessories as well. When the tabletop was bare, she pulled open the small drawers at the top of the dressing table.

Immediately her heart tightened as she recognised the cards, paintings or ornaments she had made at school over the years for successive mother's days, Christmas or Easter celebrations. It looked like her mother had kept every single thing she'd ever made. She was always sad that her mother had no photos or mementos of her own parents – both long dead in a house fire, she had said. She didn't even have any photos of Rosalie as a baby, and had nothing to remind her of her life before Raventhorn.

At the bottom of one drawer, she found a heart-shaped box painted in garish pink and red she had made for Valentine's Day. She remembered exactly the day she'd given it to her mother. She must have been ten, and felt sad that unlike most of her friends at school, her mother had no husband or sweetheart to give her flowers or a card on Valentine's Day. Lorna had taken her to Irlwick's only craft shop to buy pink paint, sequins and feathers to decorate the box. Her mother had cried when she'd given it to her. She had hugged Rosalie tightly, kissed her forehead and promised she'd always keep it. The paint was chipped now, most of the sequins had fallen off and the feathers were ragged and stuck together.

Rosalie lifted the lid carefully. Inside were more things she'd made, colourful beads and necklaces, a tiny paper doll with yellow wool for hair. A piece of paper was folded at the bottom. Pushing aside the other trinkets, Rosalie pulled it out, unfolded it. It was a photo of a young woman in a graduation gown, with her long brown hair loose on her shoulders and a little cap perched on her head. It was her mother, but as she'd never seen her before. She looked young, happy, and carefree. Next to her was a couple – the man in a dark grey suit and the woman in a smart summer dress. The family resemblance was so striking it had to be her mother's parents. Rosalie's grandparents.

Rosalie turned the photo over. At the back was a handwritten inscription. 'Graduation day, East London Poly, July 1987.'

Rosalie glared at it.

Her mother had lied. Why?

She had claimed she had no memento of her parents and had always been vague about the place where she grew up. She hadn't even mentioned ever going to university!

Lorna might know. Rosalie would phone her at her sister's in Norwich in the morning. For now she closed her fingers around the photo and got up. She would finish clearing out her mother's things later.

Chapter Twenty-One

'Your secretary said you were putting our New York project on hold because of Raventhorn. Is that right?' Kirsty's voice on the telephone was so sharp Marc winced.

'Yes.'

She let out an impatient sigh. 'But why? At the dinner you missed at La Table de Jules, I told Ben Turner we were interested in merging some of our operations with his firm and he was very positive. This is a chance we can't afford to miss.'

Marc looked around the café, gestured to the garçon and ordered an espresso and a bottle of mineral water. He'd order a bite to eat later when his friend Cédric arrived. 'Perhaps, but I think you should have waited until I actually gave you the go ahead before making plans.'

'What on earth is going on, Marc?' she asked, her voice more mellow this time. 'I remind you that we are colleagues – and friends too, I hope. You've been very secretive these past few weeks. You've hardly told me what you've been doing in Scotland, or why you wanted to leave for Paris last night immediately after the funeral. I was hoping we would have a drink and discuss … you know … things.'

Marc had been only too aware of Kirsty's plans for the evening, and even if his secretary hadn't passed on Rosalie's message about Fitzpatrick wanting to meet in Paris, he would have made excuses not to return to London with her. Hell, his father was to blame for giving her the wrong idea, and leading her to believe that she'd be welcome into the Petersen empire, both as director *and* a daughter-in-law. Marc's efforts to keep their relationship businesslike had failed miserably.

At the same time he knew keeping her in the dark was unfair.

'If you must know,' he conceded, 'Raventhorn is turning out to be a rather tricky investment and I needed to stay there a while to oversee things.'

Kirsty laughed. 'I don't understand why you're so preoccupied with that pile of old stones when you could delegate the whole thing to one of our office juniors. It's not as if it's going to bring the company a vast amount of money or publicity … or as if you want to keep it, is it?'

He closed his eyes briefly. Keeping Raventhorn was something that had crossed his mind several times these past few days. He had dismissed the idea as ridiculous, but it kept coming back, persistent and strangely seductive.

'No, of course I don't want to keep it,' he replied reluctantly.

If he didn't want to discuss Raventhorn with Kirsty just yet, he had to let her in on his plans for Love Taxis. At least she could set things in motion while he was in Paris.

'Actually,' he started, 'there is something I'd like you to look at.' He explained about his idea of setting up a subsidised bus company.

'Could you get someone to make the preliminary enquiries and sort out the financing? I'll deal with the details when I return in a few days.'

Kirsty burst out laughing. 'You're having me on, right? You're wasting your time – and mine – setting up a charitable bus company in the sticks to help a bunch of old ladies and a handful of mothers and toddlers?'

He smiled. 'That's right.'

'Petersen Holdings has never done anything like this before. Let me remind you that we're a business, not a charity.'

His smile faded. 'I don't need reminding.'

There was a short silence, before Kirsty spoke again. 'Is it because of your father? Have you grown attached to the place because buying it was one of the last things he ever did?'

'No, it's not.' And yet, he thought, perhaps there was some truth in what Kirsty was saying. Perhaps he needed to understand what had attracted his father to the Scottish estate.

'Then has it got anything to do with this woman – Rosalie Heart?'

He waited a few heartbeats before answering. Rosalie. He could see her in front of him, feel her warmth, her kindness. The way she had given herself to him.

'Yes, it does have a lot to do with Rosalie,' he said quietly.

There was another short silence.

'I see.' Her tone became sharp and businesslike. 'Very well. I will make enquiries into your little project, if that's what you want. I'm not sure what your father had in mind when he purchased Raventhorn, but I bet it wasn't running a charity bus company.'

'Thank you. I appreciate your help.'

'When are you coming back to London?'

'I'm not sure. In two or three days. I have a few things to sort out in the office here first.' He said goodbye, put the phone he'd just bought back into his pocket.

The waiter brought his drinks over and he thanked him with a curt nod. He drank his espresso, absorbing the bustling atmosphere of Le Caillou, the café at the end of his street where he and his friends usually met when they were in Paris.

'I'm late. Sorry.'

Cédric stood in front of him, dressed as usual in his black leather jacket and matching leather trousers tucked into motorcycling boots, a black helmet under his arm.

Marc smiled. 'You're always late.'

'True.' Cédric sat down.

'What are you drinking?'

'Same as you.' Cédric rubbed his facial stubble. 'I need at least a litre of coffee after the week I've had.'

Marc signalled to the garçon to bring two more espressos to their table and looked at his friend more closely. He hadn't seen him for a couple of months, and Cédric did indeed look exhausted.

'Too many late nights at the club?' he asked. Cédric was a talented saxophone player and had gigs at a popular Parisian nightclub when he wasn't chasing a scoop in a remote and dangerous part of the world.

His friend sighed wearily. 'I wish.'

Marc frowned. 'Any problems?'

'You could say that. I've just spent a week with the Italian coastguards boarding ships full of half-starved people who had given everything they had, and more, to gangs of traffickers for the privilege of crossing the Mediterranean on a rusty, crowded ship. It's been hard.' He stared at a distant point, his fingers clenched into fists on the tabletop. 'Real hard.'

He shuddered and looked at Marc. 'What about you? How are you bearing up? Have the Chinese authorities been in touch regarding the investigation into your father's accident?'

'Not yet. I'm waiting to hear from the lawyers, but the enquiry is coming to an end and I'll soon be able to organise the funeral.'

'I'm sorry, mate. Let me know if I can help in any way.'

Marc nodded.

'I have some information for you,' Cédric said then. 'I got in touch with my contact in London after getting your message and she unearthed quite a bit of info on McBride and a few other characters.'

The garçon brought their order over. Cédric drank his red hot coffee in one gulp, put his empty cup down, closed his eyes and started in a low voice. 'I'll start with Geoff McBride,' he said. It was as if he was reading a file in front of him – except that his eyes were closed and there was nothing on the table to read.

Marc smiled, amused to see that his friend hadn't lost his photographic memory. As children growing up at the boarding school, Luc and Marc has often relied on his visual memory to get them through batches of tricky history or Latin tests. Cédric also had the uncanny ability to pick up languages or replicate any piece of music on the sax or the piano after hearing it only once. 'There's not much to it, all I do is listen and mimic,' he would often say with a dismissive shrug when people praised him. His friend never boasted about his talents or abilities, and was as modest as ever, even now he had become an award-winning investigative journalist.

'Sixty-two years old, bachelor, no children,' Cédric started. 'Geoff inherited from his uncle Malcolm McBride just over thirty years ago. Collector of vintage cars – although he appears to have sold all but one in the past few months. Published a dozen or so papers on the history of Norse settlements in Scotland, seems well-regarded in certain academic circles – enough at least to be invited to deliver lectures at a conference organised by the Centre for Nordic Studies in Orkney several times. Seems to have become a bit of a recluse and hasn't published anything for the past five years.'

Marc frowned. Could it be because his assistant – Rosalie's mother – had died and his research had taken a more erratic, and eccentric, turn as he focused on Isobel and Harald?

'At the same time, his estate and financial affairs have been in steady decline,' Cédric carried on. 'The estate was mortgaged and re-mortgaged, there were also a couple of very large bank loans … But, of course, you would know all about that, wouldn't you?'

Marc nodded. 'The estate is indeed riddled with debts and McBride won't have much left once he's settled them all. Anything else?'

So far Cédric hadn't told him anything he didn't already know.

As if he had sensed his disappointment, his friend smiled and leant across the table. 'Actually, there are a few interesting characters linked to Geoff McBride. I'll start with Rosalie Heart – or rather, her mother, Sophie, who used to work for the man as some kind of secretary cum librarian.'

Anxiety made Marc's pulse race faster. 'Sophie Heart? What about her? She died four years ago. A stroke when she was out walking, from what I've been told.'

'My London contact did an advanced search of the criminal records database, and it so happens that Sophie had a rather interesting career as a glamour model and a criminal record dating from the late eighties.'

Marc almost jumped out of his seat. 'What?'

'And so does the sister of McBride's housekeeper.'

'Lorna's sister? Really?'

Cédric nodded. 'Yup. Both Lorna's sister – Margaret Dunford, or Chichi, as she was known as in her modelling days – and Sophie Heart were arrested for a series of petty thefts dating back from the late eighties – 1988 – to be exact. Both worked for the same sleazy London photographer, and, interestingly, Sophie also spent time in a women's refuge in Birmingham.'

Sophie Heart, a glamour model, a convicted thief, and most probably the victim of violence and abuse? Marc could hardly comprehend what his friend was telling him.

'Lorna's sister lives in Norwich now,' Marc said. 'That's where Lorna is right now, on holiday ... Did your contact find out anything else about Sophie, her family, Rosalie's father?'

Cédric nodded. 'She did. Sophie grew up in Bermondsey, the only child of Mike and Angela Heart. She graduated from East London Poly with a degree in Art and Design in 1987, but didn't seem to have had much success as an artist. She got a job as a waitress in a pub, did a bit of modelling for catalogues and worked as a hostess for conferences and conventions. That's when she started moving into the shady world of glamour modelling and having problems with the police. My contact found records of her sharing a flat with a certain Jake Tyler. She gave up modelling after having a baby girl in January 1989. Rosalie.'

'So this Jake Tyler is Rosalie's father?'

Cédric shrugged. 'Who knows? There's no name listed for the father on her birth certificate. Sophie moved back to her parents with her daughter in the spring of 1992.' He paused, poured some mineral water into a glass and drank.

'What happened after that?'

'Mike and Angela Heart died in a house fire a couple of months later. The police suspected arson but no one was ever convicted for it. Sophie was staying at a friend's with three-year-old Rosalie that night or both would probably have died too. Jake Tyler was arrested but released without charge. Soon after her parents' funeral, Sophie took her daughter to live at the Birmingham refuge. They stayed there a few months. After that, they seem to have vanished. They must have moved around until Sophie took up a position at Raventhorn where Lorna, her friend's sister, worked.'

'And Jake Tyler?'

'He has been in and out of jail ever since. His latest conviction was for aggravated burglary and grievous bodily harm in 2010.'

'Did your contact find anything on Rupert McBride?'

Cédric smiled. 'Now, there's an interesting fellow. He has debts coming out of his ears after several failed ventures – the latest with a very dodgy London vintage cars auctioneer who happens to be Jake Tyler's brother, and who's just been sent down for fraud.'

'Thanks, Cédric. I'm really grateful for all this.'

Cédric leant over the table. 'You must take care, Marc. The people Rupert McBride is mixed up with aren't *enfants de coeur*. They are thugs, criminals. There are also rumours about Jake Tyler being involved with Russian criminals, in particular one Anatoly Bazanov who has been on Europol's radar for years, and believe me these men don't mess about. They kill first, and ask questions later.'

'Don't worry, I'll be careful. It's Rosalie I'm worried about. I can't let anything happen to her.'

Cédric's lips stretched into a smile. 'Is there anything you want to tell me?'

'No, it's not what you think. I mean, I'm only trying to help her out and …'

He took a deep breath, raked his fingers in his hair before leaning back against the padded banquette seat. Who was he trying to fool? He hadn't been able to get Rosalie out of his mind. All he longed for was to return to Raventhorn, make sure she was all right, but most of all, he wanted to see her, touch her, make love to her in that great big bed in the Crimson Room. And just about everywhere else in the castle.

'Only trying to help her out, of course.' Cédric smiled again. 'Go on, mate, tell me about this lady who has thawed your frozen heart.'

Frowning, Marc turned his spoon in the cup of coffee. 'You make me sound like a bloody snowman,' he grumbled.

'An iceman would be more accurate. For as long as I've known you, you never let anyone get close. It was like you had vowed never to feel any emotions and you stuck to your pledge, no matter what. For some reason, you tolerated Luc and myself, but you kept anyone else at arm's length, your parents especially. I always felt a bit sorry for them. Every time they came to visit at Grange's, which I grant you wasn't often, you looked so bored, so blasé – it was as if you couldn't wait for them to leave.'

Guilt tightened Marc's throat. He swallowed. Had he really been so hard, so unapproachable, so damned stubborn? Cédric made it sound like he had sought to punish his parents for leaving him at boarding school.

'So, come on,' Cédric said, breaking his dark mood, 'what is Rosalie like?'

Marc drew in breath. 'She lives in an old castle full of ghosts. She runs, very badly, a cab firm she called Love Taxis. She loves pink. She can't sing. She smiles a lot, and talks even more.'

He realised he was smiling as an image of Rosalie floated in his mind.

Cédric whistled between his teeth. 'That's a hell of a woman. No wonder you're hooked.'

'Hooked? I just told you. It's just—'

This time Cédric laughed. 'What's the point in denying it, mate? I always knew you were a romantic under that cold fish exterior of yours.'

The meeting with Carl Fitzpatrick took place at nine o'clock sharp the following morning in Marc's office. Fitzpatrick had agreed to all his terms. More than agreed, in fact. The man literally leapt out of his seat to shake his hand and sign the new contract Marc had prepared, which wasn't surprising, given the fact that Marc was saving his skin and giving him a very generous deal in the process.

Nothing would ever erase the guilt of Van Bernd's death, but at least he would do his very best not to let another similar tragedy happen if it was in his power to do so.

The rest of the day had been spent in business meetings and phone calls. Eager to despatch all urgent issues so that he could return to Scotland the following day, Marc ate his lunch at his desk and worked non-stop until after seven. He tried to phone Rosalie at Raventhorn a couple of times during the day, but she was out so he left messages and decided to phone Love Taxis for news. Fergus reassured him that everything was fine. Rosalie was busy, but there had been no further incident to report. He promised to tell Rosalie that Marc had called and even volunteered his home telephone number, should Marc need to reach him outside office hours, and Marc had to be content with that, for now at least.

He could have taken the metro home but he fancied the long walk back to his apartment near the Champ de Mars. He loved walking in Paris, especially at night. Tonight the Champs-Elysées, crowded as usual, looked magical as their two thousand trees glittered with Christmas lights. Aromas of *steak-frites*, draft beer, crêpes or roasted chestnuts wafted in his path from kiosks and *brasseries*, making his mouth water.

It was well after eight when he finally keyed in the security code to release the heavy wooden front door of his building. He didn't want to wait for the lift so he started climbing up to his loft apartment on the top floor. Tucking the takeaway bag of Tunisian chicken couscous he'd purchased from the small restaurant at the end of his street, he dug into his coat pocket for his keys.

'You've been working late.' Kirsty's voice at the top of the stairs startled him.

She was sitting on the last step, her back leaning against the wall and a small leather case at her feet.

Frowning, he offered his free hand to help her up.

'This is a surprise. What are you doing here?'

Kirsty pouted. 'I decided to pay you an impromptu visit. We have things to discuss, and with you being so preoccupied with a certain Scottish castle I thought I'd better take my chance and meet you here before you disappeared again.'

Her fingers stroked the back of his hand. Her nails were long and painted a dark purple to complement her purple cashmere coat and trouser suit, no doubt. The colour was striking against her straight blond hair and flawless skin, and made her blue eyes bluer, sharper, harder.

'It's been ages since we spent time together. Saturday didn't count with the funeral and that awful reception at Maguire's afterwards. I had no idea you wanted to stay until the end. I couldn't wait to leave, it really was too dreary.'

Marc freed his hand from her grasp. 'The man just lost his wife, Kirsty. She was a daughter, a sister, a cousin. Can you blame him or his family for grieving?'

'No, of course not.' She gestured towards his keys. 'Aren't you going to open the door? I brought some paperwork for you to look at.'

Although there was nothing he wanted to do less than to let Kirsty into his flat, it would be the height of boorishness to send her away when she had travelled from London to see him.

'All right, I suppose you'd better come in.' He unlocked his door, flicked the light switch on.

'Make yourself at home. I hope you like Tunisian chicken,' he said as he shrugged his coat off and made his way to the kitchen. He poured the contents of the bag into a serving dish and rattled inside a drawer for some cutlery.

'I'll pass, thanks. I had a salad on the Eurostar.' She took her coat off and draped it on the back of his leather sofa.

'In that case, you don't mind if I tuck in, do you? I'm famished.'

'No, go ahead. I wouldn't mind a glass of wine, though.'

He poured out two glasses of Château Peyrac and handed her one, then brought the dish of food to the dining table.

'You must have the best view in the whole of Paris,' she said as she stood at one of the tall windows overlooking the Eiffel Tower, all lit up against the winter night sky. Whilst he ate, she poured herself another glass of wine and talked about great locations for Paris properties, and how she'd always wanted to have a base there.

'You're so lucky,' she remarked, looking at him above the rim of her wine glass. 'You have amazing flats in Paris and London. With your background – your French and Danish parents, and your private education in an exclusive boarding school in England – you can blend in anywhere and be at home wherever you choose.'

'It would be more accurate to say that I'm never really at home anywhere.' A fact that had never truly bothered him until recently.

He got up and took his empty plate into the kitchen. 'I'll make us some coffee.'

'I'd rather have another glass of this excellent wine.' She pointed to her empty glass.

He frowned. 'Didn't you say you had paperwork for us to go over?'

She let out a low chuckle. 'Don't worry, we'll get down to business soon enough.'

When he came back with the coffee and another bottle of wine, he noticed that she had taken her blazer off, and that her high heeled shoes lay discarded on the rug. Curled up on the sofa, she looked at him, smiled and patted the cushion at her side.

'Why don't you sit down and relax? You look dreadfully tired. Let me give you a massage.'

He put the tray down and chose to sit in the armchair opposite.

'I'm all right, thanks.'

Kirsty's disappointed pout didn't escape him. Her thin white blouse gaped open as she leaned forward to take hold of her glass of wine and he couldn't help but wonder if she'd undone a button or two when he was in the kitchen.

'So where are these papers you are so eager for me to go over?'

She tightened her lips, gestured towards her small case. 'In there. I'll get them in a minute.'

She sipped her wine in silence. 'By the way, I took a look at that proposal of yours to run a subsidised bus service in … Irlwick.' She pulled a face. 'Well, let me tell you it's a total waste of time and money. I thought Raventhorn was earmarked for redevelopment as a hotel, and as usual any asset should be sold off to maximise profits. If that taxi firm isn't making any money, we should close it down straight away.'

Marc forced down a few deep breaths to quell his mounting impatience. 'You don't have to understand, or approve, what I'm trying to do.'

'It's my responsibility to be aware of potential problems or investments that could have a negative impact on the company,' she retorted.

'Surely we can afford to invest a little capital in a scheme which would benefit Raventhorn and the local community.'

He rose to his feet and walked to the window.

'Who do you think you are all of a sudden?' she snapped. 'Sir Galahad crusading to save poor peasants? Since when do you care about people and local communities?'

'Since Van Bernd,' he replied in a low voice. He looked at the moonless night against which the sparkling Eiffel Tower cut a striking, elegant and magical silhouette.

Kirsty's hand slid down his back. Surprised, he tensed and turned round. He hadn't heard her stand up and walk up to him, no doubt because she was barefoot.

'I know the business with Van Bernd affected you,' she said. 'It affected us all.'

He wanted to say she was lying. She didn't care. She'd even gone as far as misquoting him to the press and to pretend he believed the whole thing had been some kind of mistake on his part. He had been livid when he had read the article in *Newsweek*.

'What happened to Van Bernd and his family wasn't your fault.' Her fingers brushed his shirtsleeve in an unwelcome caress.

He took a step back. 'It was my fault, and I vowed to do everything I could to never have it happen again.'

He looked down. Kirsty was a very clever, very beautiful woman. Yet she had a fundamental flaw. She lacked kindness, compassion, and warmth.

In a swift move, she closed the gap between them again, and before he could react, pressed her body against him and hooked her arms around his neck. 'Why don't you let me help you forget the whole thing?' she murmured as her lips trailed against the side of his throat.

He stiffened, lifted his hands up and unlocked her fingers. Holding her wrists, he brought her arms down by her sides. 'Please don't do that.'

Confusion and hurt flickered in her blue eyes, quickly replaced by anger. 'Why not? We are bound to end up together sooner or later and you know it. We're alike, you and I. We're both high achievers. We both want the same things from life – success, money. So why waste time?'

'You are wrong. On all counts.'

She glared at him, then shrugged. 'So what is she like, this Rosalie Heart? She must be quite wonderful for you to leave behind all your business sense.'

Marc looked at the Eiffel Tower's sparkling arrow of light and smiled. 'She is.' He paused. 'I'm sorry, Kirsty. Sorry if I misled you in thinking I wanted us to become ... you know ... lovers. It was never my intention.'

Her cheeks flushed, her eyes hard, she snorted. 'And what about our plans? The merger with Turner? Our move to New York? How does that fit in with your bus company and country bumpkin Rosalie?'

The phone ringing came as a relief in what had become a very awkward conversation, but he was so distracted by Kirsty standing close behind him that he didn't understand straight away what the voice at the other end was telling him.

A couple of minutes later, he put the phone down, then turned to face Kirsty.

'That was Jonathan Field, the Hong Kong lawyer dealing with the enquiry into my father's death.'

Kirsty arched her eyebrows. 'At this time? It must be six in the morning over there.'

'He starts early. He said there was a message from the coroner's office on the answerphone. They want to see me before closing the case. I will be flying out in the morning.' He took a deep breath. 'Now I think I'd better take you to your hotel. It's late. Where are you staying?'

'I haven't book anywhere. I thought I could stay here.'

'No. It's not a good idea. There's a nice hotel at the end of the street. I'll give them a ring, see if they have a vacancy. Leave me your paperwork. I'll look at it later.'

Chapter Twenty-Two

Her mobile's insistent ringing drilled through her foggy brain. What time was it, and why were there crumbs prickling her cheek? She must have fallen asleep at the kitchen table after snacking on tinned soup and buttered toast for lunch. Again. She sat upright with a moan, and her eyes still closed, reached out for the phone with one hand whilst brushing the crumbs off her cheek with the other.

'Aye, Fiona.' It sounded more like a grunt than a greeting.

'Oh dear, what's wrong with you?' Fiona laughed at the other end. 'Grab a pen and a pad, Roz, I have a few bookings for you, starting with an airport pickup at three thirty.'

'I'll have to hire another driver if Duncan stays in Edinburgh any longer,' Rosalie said with a weary sigh. She had worked from dawn to late at night every single day since Marc had left. She really shouldn't complain. At least business was good, and working kept her away from empty, gloomy Raventhorn and her equally gloomy thoughts.

'Who am I picking up at the airport?'

'A woman called Kirsty Marsh, who oddly said she was coming to Raventhorn. Who is she, Roz? You never mentioned her.'

Rosalie's throat tightened. 'Kirsty Marsh? Are you sure?'

'Positive. Do you know her?'

'Well, not personally. She is one of Marc's colleagues.' And most certainly his girlfriend, she finished silently, remembering the magazine photo.

'I wonder what she wants.'

'No idea.'

Fiona gave her details of several more bookings and hung up.

Rosalie glanced at the clock and jumped to her feet. She'd better hurry or she'd be late. She grabbed her hat and anorak and hurried out.

Questions swirled in her mind as she drove to Inverness airport. Why was Kirsty coming here? Was Marc sending her to set up the bus company because he was too busy to return? Perhaps he wasn't busy at all, but he'd rather not come back and sending Kirsty in his place was his way of letting her know that their night together didn't mean anything, that it had been another 'error of judgement' on his part.

This may be why he hadn't spoken to her since leaving Raventhorn. She had phoned his office twice and both times his secretary had said he was in business meetings and would call her back. Unfortunately, she had been out driving when he had called, and she'd listened to his cold, slightly distant voice on the answerphone saying that he trusted she was all right and everything was in order at Raventhorn, and urging her to phone or text should she be worried about anything. Fergus had told her that he'd phoned Love Taxis too, and said that he was looking forward to coming back ... But he hadn't come back, and now Kirsty Marsh was here.

Rosalie parked near the terminal and looked at her reflection in the rear mirror. With a resigned sigh, she wiped the smudged mascara from under her eyes, combed her hair back with her fingers, dislodging a few more greasy crumbs from her brown curls, and pulled her fluffy pink hat down.

Then digging out her heart-shaped board from the door's side pocket, she scribbled Kirsty's name with her purple felt pen and ran into the arrivals hall, just in time to hear the announcement that the London flight had landed.

Kirsty was the last of the two dozen passengers to stride into the hall, pulling a sleek, black designer case behind her. Tall and slim, wearing high-heeled boots and a long, expensive looking dark purple coat, and with her sleek blond hair swinging around her face, she was even more striking in the flesh than in the magazine photo. She stopped in the middle of the arrival hall, and her icy blue eyes surveyed the crowd.

Self-conscious, Rosalie pulled her jumper down to cover her bottom with one hand, and waved her board with the other. The woman saw her, nodded but did not move an inch. Rosalie plastered a forced smile on her face and walked over.

'Good afternoon. I am—'

Kirsty pointed at the board. 'Rosalie Heart, of course,' she interrupted. 'You look exactly like Marc described. All pink, from head to toe.' Her eyes swept over Rosalie and a fleeting smile lifted the corners of her mouth. Somehow it didn't sound like a compliment.

Kirsty indicated her case. 'Please be careful when you pull it.'

Rosalie bit her tongue to repress the urge to tell the woman she could pull her own case. Instead she grabbed hold of the handle and led the way to the exit. The sliding doors opened onto flurries of wet snow.

'Oh … That must be your taxi over there,' Kirsty said, pointing at her cab. 'Now I understand what Marc meant when he said it was quite … hmm … unique.'

That didn't sound very flattering either. A lump rose in Rosalie's throat. So Marc had been poking fun at her outfits, at her taxi … What else had he shared with Kirsty? The fact she liked silly pop music or ate too much chocolate cake? Surely not the fact she had made love to him with the unrestrained enthusiasm of a lovesick puppy. He wouldn't do that if he and Kirsty were lovers.

Well, she'd soon find out. Kirsty Marsh didn't seem the kind of woman who would spare her feelings. Rosalie focused on getting the cab doors opened and Kirsty's designer case safely into the boot.

'I've never been to Scotland before,' the young woman remarked from the backseat as they set off, 'but Marc warned me. He said it was bleak, very bleak. Between you and me, I think he was glad to have an excuse to leave.'

Another painful stab in the region of the heart. Rosalie glanced in the rear-view mirror. 'I thought he returned to London to go to a funeral.'

'Is that what he told you?' Kirsty sighed. 'Well, it is true that we had to go to that ghastly funeral, but we didn't stay a minute longer than necessary.'

Rosalie couldn't help herself. 'You make it sound as if Marc didn't care, yet I know he was upset about the passing of his colleague's wife.'

Kirsty laughed. 'Upset? Marc? I don't think so. He is the most unemotional man I know. We left the funeral as soon as it was polite to do so and flew to Paris. That's where we've just spent the past two days. Two very nice days, actually, though we didn't see much of Paris.' She drew in a long, whimsical breath.

'Paris is magical at this time of year and Marc has the most beautiful view of the Eiffel Tower and the Champ de Mars from his apartment, especially at night.'

'Ah.' Rosalie tried to focus on the road.

'Anyway,' Kirsty resumed speaking, 'Marc asked me to take care of Raventhorn but I have to say I'm confused. I don't understand why he allowed you to carry on with your little taxi business when it's obvious it should be shut down immediately.'

Rosalie turned sharply round. 'I thought I would be able to carry on until the bus company is set up.'

A loud klaxon made her look back at the road, just in time to slam on the brakes and avoid crashing into a white van.

'The bus company? Yes ... Marc did toy with the idea for a while. He asked me to look into it but I'm afraid we decided it wasn't viable.'

Rosalie glared at her passenger in the rear-view mirror. Kirsty's blue eyes glared right back. 'I don't understand. He promised.'

'Marc would never commit himself until he had all the facts. I am quite sure he told you he'd look at the figures and projections before making a business proposal.'

Rosalie swallowed hard. It was true that Marc hadn't really committed himself. He hadn't even wanted her to tell Fiona and Fergus about it.

'So if you're not here to help set up the bus company, what are you here for?'

In the back mirror she saw Kirsty smile. 'Isn't it obvious? I'm here to do what Marc should have done before he got ... hmm ... distracted. I mean to start the procedure of liquidation of Raventhorn assets, strip the place down and sell it off.'

Rosalie gasped. 'But that's not possible! Marc would have phoned, he would have warned me.'

'He's had other things on his mind. He's had to set off for Hong Kong this morning.'

'Where is she now?'

Alice gave the counter another energetic scrub.

It was closing time. The café was empty. The chairs were stacked up on the tables and the cakes and pies safely stored in the fridge.

'At Raventhorn. I was working all afternoon, so I had to leave her.'

'I hope you told her about every single one of Raventhorn's ghosts – that should give her a good fright!'

'I didn't think about it.' Rosalie swallowed the painkillers Alice had pushed into her hand, then massaged her forehead with her fingers to relieve the headache that had settled there the moment she'd shown

Kirsty into Raventhorn. The ache that clawed and tore at her chest every time she breathed, however, wouldn't be so easy to soothe. Once again, she realised what a fool she had been where Marc was concerned. He had lied about wanting to help the people of Irlwick. He had lied about setting up a bus company. He had no intention of coming back after his trip to Hong Kong. Kirsty didn't need to say so. Her very presence in Raventhorn was enough.

'She is probably poking her nose everywhere, checking her inventory as we speak and ticking off the paintings, artwork and furniture from her list to be sold off at auctions or sent to private collectors.'

'She can't do that!'

'She can. Marc sent her.' She swallowed hard and whispered. 'He won't come back, Alice. I'll never see him again.'

Alice's hand stilled. She looked at her, and bit her lower lip. 'Oh my. There's more to it than just Raventhorn or Love Taxis, isn't there? You slept with him, didn't you, and now you're in love with him.'

Rosalie pressed her hand against her mouth to stifle her anguished sob. 'I slept with him all right but I'm not in love with him. How could I love a man who lies, who is cold and calculating, and whose only concern is with making money?' She shook her head. 'It goes against everything I believe in.'

Alice put her tea towel down. 'Why don't you phone him and ask him what he's playing at? He can't go back on his promises, that's just not right. And he can't treat you like this.'

Rosalie shrugged, and flinched at the twinge of pain in her shoulder. It ached tonight, probably because of all the driving she'd done these past few days, and because of the tension and the lack of sleep.

'He is travelling to Hong Kong as we speak, and then he'll have his father's funeral to organise. The thing is, he never made any promises about Raventhorn,' she confessed. 'I naively assumed that he meant for Geoff, Lorna and I to carry on living there, at least for the foreseeable future.'

'Well, at least he could come back to explain that he changed his mind. He owes you that much. How can he sleep with you then cast you aside as if it didn't matter?'

'You don't understand. He warned me he didn't want to get

involved.' She propped her elbows on the counter, buried her face in her hands. This time she didn't even try to hold back the tears. 'I've been stupid. It's all my fault,' she managed between two hiccups.

'Oh, love, come here.' Alice walked around the counter and enfolded her in her arms. Rosalie leaned against her. Her friend smelled of pine cleaning spray, of hot chocolate and tomato soup. She didn't say a word but patted her back as Rosalie wept.

'Are you sure you'll be all right to drive?' she asked a while later as Rosalie wiped her eyes on the sleeve of her pink jumper. 'I could come with you, keep you company tonight.' She scrunched her face into a fierce scowl and curled her fists on her hips. 'I'd like to see that woman try to give you a hard time. I'll put her in her place.'

Rosalie shook her head. 'That's very kind of you but you need to be up early to open up tomorrow morning, and I know how you don't like being up late during the week – except on ceilidh night, that is. I've taken too much of your time as it is.'

Alice bit her lip. 'Actually, there was something I wanted to tell you. I don't quite know how to say it. It's about Niall ...' She took a deep breath. 'The thing is, we've been seeing quite a bit of each other this past week – going out, I mean, and ... you know ...'

Rosalie wiped away her tears and gave her friend a wide smile. 'So at last he has opened his eyes and realised what a beautiful, smart and fun girl has been right under his nose all this time?'

Alice's lips stretched into a timid smile. 'We're not there yet, but I hope that maybe, one day, he could see me as a proper girlfriend, rather than the boring, dependable Alice he's known all his life. You wouldn't mind if that happened?'

'Mind? Why would I? You're the best thing that could ever happen to him.'

'Julia said you came round the other night and didn't look very happy when she told you we were together.'

'Julia is a troublemaker and she hates me. If I was a bit down that day, it had nothing to do with you two going out. I had been to the hospital to see Geoff. I was worried, and sad, and confused about Marc. You're my best friend, so I am happy if you're happy. I mean it.'

Alice let out a long breath. 'I'm so relieved! I was dreading telling you. Now come into the kitchen with me. I'll give you some leftover broth and a few brownies for tonight. You need all your strength to stand up to that Kirsty Marsh and I bet you've nothing in your fridge.'

Just over half an hour later, Rosalie parked the cab in the garage, and took out the two plastic containers Alice had given her. Crying had left her drained and she ached all over as she locked the garage door then walked across the courtyard. She would have preferred to go up to her flat and spend the evening alone, but there was no way she would leave Kirsty Marsh alone at Raventhorn.

She was opening the kitchen door when she saw headlights in the distance. A car had stopped on the lane on the other side of the old bridge.

Clutching the plastic containers against her chest, she peered into the night, but the car was too far away for her to see what make, shape and colour it was. What if it was Rupert coming back to search through the library again, or the driver of the four-wheel drive who had chased after her on the forest road? The police had failed to find out their identity, or the identity of the thugs who had smashed Duncan's windscreen.

The lights flickered and disappeared, and Corby Woods became dark once again. Still uneasy, Rosalie hurried inside. She put the food containers on the kitchen table and climbed the stairs to the ground floor.

She found Kirsty in front of a slim laptop in the drawing room, a plaid shawl wrapped around her shoulders.

'About time you came back,' the young woman complained. 'Is there no heating in this dreadful place? I swear I'm about to freeze to death.'

'The heating has just been fixed, but this is an old castle and I suppose you're just not used to it.' Rosalie looked at Kirsty's mobile phone. 'Have you had any news from Marc?' The words were out before she could help it.

Kirsty nodded. 'He just messaged me. The Hong Kong authorities have closed the enquiry into his father's death, and he can now make arrangements for the funeral.'

'How sad for him to be alone at a time like this,' Rosalie remarked.

Kirsty arched an eyebrow and said in a cold voice, 'Yes, it is sad indeed.' But she didn't sound sad at all. 'Why don't you sort the heating out then get us something to eat?' she asked.

Rosalie's cheeks became hot but she forced a calming breath down. She may hate the woman's tone, or the assumption that she was to wait on her, but she didn't want to antagonise her. There was too much at stake. As Marc's representative, the woman could turn her out of Raventhorn that very same evening if she wanted to.

'By the way,' Kirsty added as Rosalie was leaving the drawing room, 'I had a look around and saw some of Marc's things in the room with the four-poster bed. I'll sleep in there too.'

This time Rosalie had to lean against the wall for support. She had changed the bedding and tidied up since Marc had left, but the thought of Kirsty sleeping in the very bed where Marc had made love to her only a few nights before made her want to be sick.

There was nothing however she could do, or say.

'Suit yourself. I'll sort out something to eat now,' she whispered, before turning on her heels and walking out.

Chapter Twenty-Three

'You found what?' Lorna asked in a low voice.

At last Lorna and her sister were back from their mini-break to Suffolk and Rosalie was able to ask her about the photo she had found in her mother's room.

'A graduation photo of Mum and a couple who I'm sure are her parents – my grandparents, aren't they? It's dated 1987,' Rosalie repeated, a little impatiently. She meant to have answers to her questions.

'It is strange that Mum always maintained she had no photo left of her family when she kept one in her trinket box all these years. Do you know why she did that?'

There was a long silence.

'Lorna, are you still there? Can you hear me?'

'Yes, sweetie.' Lorna sounded hesitant. 'I know the photo you mean.'

'Really? And you never told me, even when I asked you about Mum's family?'

'It wasn't my place, sweetie. I promised your mother not to say anything.'

Rosalie's fingers squeezed the phone receiver more tightly and she swallowed hard. The feeling of betrayal and hurt was almost too hard to bear. Her mother had chosen to confide in a friend about her family, rather than in her own daughter. Why? Had Rosalie been such a hopeless daughter? Had she meant nothing?

'At least you can tell me if these people were my grandparents.'

'Yes, they were.'

'Are there any other relatives I don't know about? Maybe I could contact them, visit them.' She heard the uncertainty, the almost childish hope in her voice.

Lorna didn't answer. 'I don't think so, love.'

'Why did Mum never talk about her parents? Did they argue and throw her out? Were they horrible people? They look very nice in the photo.'

'All I can say is that she had her reasons. Very good reasons.'

Rosalie tutted, annoyed now. 'What's the big secret, Lorna? I think I have the right to know.'

'You do, but it's difficult, and I'd rather not say anything over the phone. In fact, that's what Geoff wanted to talk to you about before his operation.'

'So he also knows all about my mother's family? Of course! And what else do you two know? Do you have my father's name too, his address even?'

Lorna gasped. 'Rosalie, please. I don't want to talk about it, not now, not on the phone.' She sounded as though she was about to burst into tears.

Even if it was clear there was something in her mother's past she'd never even suspected, Rosalie was reluctant to upset Lorna further.

'All right.' She sighed, resigned. 'I'll wait until you come back or until Geoff is better.'

'Perhaps I will cut my holiday short and come home after all,' Lorna said. 'You must be lonely at Raventhorn now Marc Petersen has left. I know you said you had plenty of work to keep you busy, but I worry you won't look after yourself properly.'

'I'm not lonely at all,' Rosalie lied. She had said nothing to Lorna about Kirsty Marsh's unwelcome arrival yesterday. 'I meet Alice and Niall most nights and we … hmm … go to the Stag's Head or the Four Winds.'

They talked a while longer about what Lorna had been doing and the other excursions Lorna's sister had planned for that day and the following few days. As soon as she put the phone down, Rosalie stared at the photo of her mother and grandparents. Why the secrets, why the mystery, and why did Lorna and Geoff know more about her relatives than she did?

Perhaps she could carry out her own research. After all that's what the internet was for. She would use Geoff's old computer in the library. Kirsty was busy in the drawing room and with any luck she would leave her alone for a while. The woman was infuriating with her constant demands and complaints. Would Rosalie fetch a scarf from her room or some paper from the study? Would she get some fresh fruit, bottled mineral water or a fashion magazine from the shop in Irlwick? Could she turn the heating up … or down, switch more lights on because the weather here was *so* gloomy, or make a cup of coffee or pour another glass of wine?

Actually, Rosalie thought with a wry smile, given the ease with which Kirsty had knocked back glasses of wine the previous evening, it was surprising she'd managed to complete any work at all. Maybe she should bring up a few more bottles from the cellar …

She switched on the computer in the library. Where to start? She looked at her mother's graduation photo – her mother's beaming face, her parents' proud smiles. Sophie had always been interested in art and history, in music and literature, but how could Rosalie find out what she had actually graduated in?

She typed the name of the polytechnic – now a university – but didn't get very far, even on the alumni page. She decided to key in her mother's name into the search engine. Nothing relevant came up. It looked as though she would indeed have to wait for Lorna or Geoff to talk to her. Disappointed, she clicked on the images section and started scrolling down the screen. Together with the many pictures of hearts she had expected, there were photos of girls and women, dozens of them – Sophie Heart must be a popular name. She scrolled right down the screen, and was about to give up when she spotted a black and white photo with a familiar face on. It was the photo Geoff had taken of her mother and herself, the one that hung on the wall in her flat.

Frowning, she leaned closer to the screen. How did it end up on the internet? A couple of rows below was a photo of herself standing next to a pink cab. Curious, she clicked on it and the link took her to the website of a London magazine and an article about young entrepreneurs. Of course, now she remembered!

When the *Inverness Courier* had featured an article about Love Taxis back in May, she had told the reporter about her mother being her inspiration, and had given him a copy of her mother's photo for the front page. Rosalie had been delighted when the story had then been picked up by a couple of newspapers in Glasgow and Edinburgh. Any mention in the press was publicity, and publicity could only be good. Couldn't it?

Geoff however had flown into a rage. Had she gone mad to tell the press about her mother, to let them have Sophie's photo? He had shouted and ranted so much Rosalie had driven off in her pink cab in tears. When a few weeks later, a London magazine about young entrepreneurs had contacted her to write a piece about Love Taxis, she had been glad of the free publicity but hadn't dared mention it to either Geoff or Lorna for fear of causing more arguments.

She went back to her search, and this time caught a glimpse of the cover of a rather old-fashioned and very tacky glamour magazine. That was strange. The woman looked just like … Her finger froze in the air, her heart skipped a beat, her mouth gaped open in shock.

It couldn't be, surely she was mistaken!

Marc squinted against the bright sunlight as he lifted the blind ready for landing at Hong Kong International Airport on Lantau Island. He rubbed his unshaven chin and glanced around the Airbus 380 business cabin. After a twelve-hour flight from Paris, he wasn't the only passenger to look tired and dishevelled. He'd debated earlier whether to take advantage of the facilities to freshen up, but he wasn't meeting anyone at the airport so showering and shaving could wait until he reached his hotel.

He looked down. Today the South China Sea was the colour of lapis lazuli. Islands of all sizes dotted the surface of the water, some tiny and covered with lush forests, others a jungle of tower blocks. The plane flew over Hong Kong's main island, compact and overcrowded with skyscrapers that rose straight from the foot of the mountains, and he watched the late morning traffic snake along the Tsing Ma suspension bridge.

Not long to go now. He reclined against his seat and closed his eyes, waiting for the impact of the aircraft tyres on the landing strip, trying to hold back the thoughts and feelings that had churned inside him ever since he'd got the message that the investigation into his father's helicopter crash was closed at last, and that the Hong Kong coroner had given the authorisation to cremate and repatriate his father's body.

Two hours later he checked into the Four Seasons Hotel, and took the lift to his room on the thirty-fifth floor. As he slid his card into the electronic door lock, he couldn't help thinking about the last time he'd been there. His father had asked him to give a presentation at an important meeting. They had clinched the deal, then celebrated at Caprice, the hotel's French restaurant. How different he felt today.

He dropped his bag down onto the thick dark red carpet and walked straight to the floor-to-ceiling window overlooking Victoria Harbour. He'd always liked the view, with the ships crossing the bay, the tower blocks reaching for the sky, and the emerald green mountains in the background. Today, however, all he could think about was his meeting with the Hong Kong police and the coroner later that afternoon and the depressing prospect of his flight back to Paris with his father's ashes the following day.

After a shower, a shave and a belated lunch, he sat at the desk to do what he should have done before. Phone his mother. It would be mid-morning in France, so he might have a chance to speak to her before she went out shopping or for lunch with her friends.

'Ah, it's you *chéri*, you just caught me on my way out.' His mother always spoke to him in the same hurried and impatient tone of voice that made him feel like he was an unwelcome interruption in her busy schedule.

'You sound a little preoccupied,' she added with unusual insight after he returned her greeting. 'Is there anything the matter?'

In a few short sentences, he explained why he was in Hong Kong. His parents may be divorced, but Céline had been the first person he'd called when he got the news about the helicopter crash, and she was once again the first he informed of his plans.

'I didn't think it would be appropriate to hold a grand funeral with Dad's friends and business contacts and make a big show of it in London or Paris,' he said. 'I didn't think you'd want to travel all the way here either.' He paused to give her time to protest. When she didn't, he carried on. 'So it will be just me at the crematorium tomorrow ... I thought I'd let you know.'

His mother sighed at the other end of the phone. Her voice sounded sad when she next spoke. 'He was such a formidable man, wasn't he? It's hard to imagine that he won't be travelling to the four corners of the world any more, to plan and plot to make his company bigger, better, stronger.'

She paused. 'I think you're right about the funeral, *mon chéri*. I think that's exactly what he would have wanted. Actually, I've been thinking a lot about your father these past few weeks and I think there is something else he would have wanted.'

'What is it?'

223

She sighed again. 'To return to the place where he grew up.'

Marc frowned. 'You mean my grandfather's farm?'

'Yes, that's exactly what I mean.'

Marc frowned. 'But he never mentioned the place, or North Jutland. He didn't even talk about his father.'

'That's because he felt guilty. He knew he'd hurt and betrayed him, and he never forgave himself for it.'

'You're wrong.' Marc stiffened. Tension made his shoulders ache. His hand gripped the phone harder. His mother was mistaken. His father was and had always been self-centred, and totally focused on business. He'd never been sentimental or prone to soul-searching.

'Marc, listen to me,' his mother interrupted. 'Sigmund always wanted to make amends with his father, that's why he sent you to the farm every summer. He also wanted you to know where you – and he – came from and feel a connection with the past and the family.'

'Then why did he never stay with me? Come to think of it, why did you never spend holidays there either?'

'Because you were always so happy there and we would only have spoilt your fun. I know you loved your grandfather, but the truth is he could be a very harsh man. He never hid his contempt for my job as a model or his disappointment about your father's decision to make his own way in the world instead of following in his footsteps. He loved having you there, but he didn't want us.'

Marc had always thought his parents never spent holidays with him because they had far better things to do than stay on a windswept farm. What his mother said now put a completely new slant on his memories, on his perception of the past and his childhood, and of his parents.

'Why did father stop me from going to the farm when I was thirteen if he knew I loved it so much there?' he asked, his throat tightening. 'Those holidays on the farm were the only time when I could be free, when I didn't have to study, compete, be the best.'

His mother sighed. 'They had an argument. Your grandfather wanted you to live with him all year round. He wanted to teach you about the land and the farm so you'd be ready to take over. Your father refused, and your grandfather gave him an ultimatum. He said that if you didn't come and live with him, then he didn't want to see you any more. Your father pleaded with him to let you come for the holidays, but there was nothing he could do to change his mind. They never spoke again.'

Marc was speechless. Everything he thought he knew about that time blown into a thousand pieces.

She paused. 'I'm sorry. Perhaps I should have told you this before.'

'Yes, perhaps.' He closed his eyes a moment. So he'd had it all wrong. He'd had the people in his life all wrong.

'Then again,' he said, 'we never really talked, did we?'

There was another silence. 'Sadly that's true. Now, *chéri*, I do have to dash out, but will you think about what I said?'

'Yes. Of course.' He had a lot of thinking to do, and not just about his parents and the past.

'And Marc,' his mother added, and from the tone of her voice he could tell she was smiling now, 'please come and see me soon. Christmas is wonderful on the Riviera. You'd love it. And more to the point, I would love to spend some time with you. Good luck for tomorrow. I'll be thinking about you.'

It wasn't luck he needed. It was courage.

'Thanks,' he said anyway. 'I'll be in touch, and I'll try and come to see you soon.' As he put the phone down, he realised that he'd meant it, for once.

He walked to the window and stared at the bay, and the ever-changing light glimmering on the surface of the sea, until it was time to leave for his meeting with the coroner at the High Court.

Chapter Twenty-Four

'Where are you, Lorna?' Rosalie almost shouted as she left the message on the answerphone. 'Call me back as soon as you get this. It's important. It's about Mum. I found something I don't understand, something horrible, and I really need to talk to you about it.'

Why did Lorna have to be out, again? She slammed the receiver down, and put a hand over her heart. She should calm down, and think, but her mind was a turmoil of thoughts and questions, and she felt like she was about to be sick.

'What's going on?' Kirsty stared at her from the doorway to the library and shook her head in an impatient gesture. Her sleek, blond hair fell back in place, framing her perfectly beautiful face. She had accessorised her skinny black jeans and a plain black tunic with a beautiful gold pendant and matching gold ring, and she looked incredibly chic and glamorous.

'Nothing,' Rosalie mumbled, her hand still shaking as she brushed her curls away from her face. 'I have things on my mind.'

Kirsty shrugged. 'I suppose I might as well finish work for the day. Not that I have made much progress. I don't know what Marc's father was thinking of when he bought this place. Marc will be lucky if he recoups half of the money the company paid for Raventhorn, never mind make a profit. Even Marc's American contacts have gone cold about the idea of turning the castle into a hotel. I called them all and no one is prepared to commit to an investment now. I am wasting my time.'

'So you'll be leaving soon, then?' Rosalie asked, although right now she had other, much more worrying things on her mind than Kirsty Marsh or Raventhorn.

'It looks that way. I'm thinking of hiring a house clearance firm, put the castle up for auction and be done with it.'

'You can't do that! They'll take away all the paintings and the furniture and pay you a pittance for them.'

Kirsty snorted. 'I don't think we'll get much anyway. Talking of furniture, I'm not spending another night in that horrid crimson bedroom. There's a cold draft blowing through the window. The wardrobe creaks, the bed curtains twitch, and don't even mention the door to the bathroom which slams shut on its own in the middle of the night. I hardly slept a wink. Poor Marc, no wonder he looked so exhausted after a couple of weeks. I had a look around this morning and I decided to move my things into the nice pink and white bedroom down the corridor.'

Rosalie felt the blood drain from her face. 'No, you can't sleep in there. You can have my room, or any other room, but not that one.'

Kirsty arched her eyebrows. 'And why on earth not? It's empty, isn't it?'

'It's my mother's room.' The mother she had loved and trusted, the mother who'd always been there for her, strong, supportive and truthful –the mother who had lied and hidden her past from her all her life.

The enormity of what she'd just found out finally dawned on her.

'Is she coming back any time soon?' Kirsty looked puzzled.

Rosalie stiffened and replied in a harsh voice. 'She won't be back. Ever.'

'Oh. I see. I'm sorry.' Kirsty nodded, her eyes softened and for the first time she looked almost kind.

'Listen, I need a break from this place tonight. I'm not cut out for spooky old castles. I need to see lights and people, to listen to music. Is there anywhere around here where I could have a decent meal?'

'The Four Winds Hotel has a nice restaurant,' Rosalie replied.

'A hotel, did you say?'

Rosalie nodded. 'It's a four star hotel.'

'You're a lifesaver,' Kirsty said with a relieved sigh. 'I've had enough of draughty rooms and creaky wardrobes. I'm off to pack. I'll stay at the hotel tonight and until Marc arrives.'

Rosalie's heart lurched, her throat went dry. 'Oh. So you have heard from him.'

Kirsty pursed her lips. 'He emailed to say he should be back in London by the end of the week and will probably make his way up here.'

Rosalie turned away and pretended to stack up some old telephone directories in a neat pile so that Kirsty wouldn't see the blush that heated her face. Marc was coming back!

'It's such a shame about his father,' Kirsty carried on. 'We're all still in shock about his death. He was an extraordinary man – the archetype of the powerful businessman, driven, cool-headed, completely dedicated to making his company bigger, stronger, and more successful. Marc is very much like him.'

Driven, cool-headed, dedicated to making money, Rosalie thought. Yes, that summed up Marc all right. And yet in the weeks he'd spent with her, she had seen another man. A strong, warm, if reserved, man. A man she could fall in love with. She'd probably imagined him, made him all up.

'And his mother is wonderful and so much fun!' Kirsty added. 'I've met her a few times and we had great fun shopping together.'

'You know the family well, then?' Rosalie couldn't help the bitter sting of jealousy in her voice.

Kirsty nodded, smiled and stretched her arm in front of her to admire the gold ring on her finger. An awful thought struck Rosalie. What if this was no mere accessory, but an engagement ring?

'Let's say that I have become very close both to Marc and his parents since starting work at the company. Marc and I are moving to New York to open a new office – a dream come true, both professionally and personally, for both of us.'

She started to walk away but suddenly turned round.

'By the way, you might want to put the burglar alarm on before we leave. There were a couple of rough-looking men hanging about at the front of the castle earlier today. I thought they might be checking the place out and was about to call the police when your demented cleaning lady arrived. They hopped back into their big four-wheel drive and drove off.'

'A four-by-four, you said?'

'Yes, a big black one.'

She forced herself to remain calm. 'What did the men look like?'

Kirsty shrugged. 'I don't know. Tall and burly, with buzz cut hair. They were dressed in black coats – leather, I think. Like I said, they looked a bit rough.'

'Did you see their number plate, or the make of the car, by any chance?'

Kirsty let out a sharp laugh. 'My eyesight isn't that good. Your cleaning lady might have spotted something, though. Give her a ring … although I wouldn't give much credence to anything that woman says.

She's a complete lunatic, you know. Not only was she incredibly rude to me, asking me all kinds of questions, and telling me stupid stories about the ghosts that supposedly haunt this place, but she also claimed that Marc worked as a translator for McBride, and that he'd been doubling up as your apprentice cab driver! She even claimed she didn't know anything about McBride selling Raventhorn to Marc's father, and had the cheek to call me a liar when I insisted it was true!'

'You told her about it?' Rosalie opened her eyes wide in shock. If Marion knew, the whole of Irlwick would know about it by the following morning, if not earlier.

Kirsty shrugged. 'Yes, of course. It wasn't a secret, was it? I'll go and pack now.'

As soon as Kirsty had gone upstairs, Rosalie dialled Marion's home number. She started by asking her about the two men Kirsty had seen near the castle.

'I didn't see much of them, love,' Marion said. 'They were just big men dressed in black. They left as soon as I arrived. Is there anything wrong?'

'I'm not sure. I don't like the idea of people hanging about when I'm here alone.'

'What about that snooty blonde – the one with the designer clothes and the posh accent – is she not staying with you?'

'Kirsty Marsh? She was but she doesn't like it here. I'm taking her to the Four Winds tonight.'

Marion tutted loudly. 'In that case, you should come and stay with us. I don't like the idea of you being on your own.' She paused. 'By the way, what's this nonsense about Geoff selling Raventhorn to that nice young man Geoff hired as a translator – the one who drove your cab when you were poorly?'

'That's nothing. Don't worry about it, Marion. Kirsty got things wrong, that's all.'

Rosalie fanned her heated cheeks with a piece of paper. Marion may not be able to see how red and hot her face had become but her shaky, hesitant voice was a giveaway and she'd be lucky if the woman believed a word she said.

'Hmm. I thought so. I mean, it's not as if Geoff would ever sell Raventhorn. It's his home, his life. Besides, where would you and Lorna go? No, I told my sister at the supermarket tonight that it was all a lot of nonsense.' She paused. 'The thing is, Elaine was doing her shopping and overheard me. She went as pale as a ghost and made me repeat word by word what that blonde woman had said. Then—'

'Then what?' Rosalie whispered.

'She marched out of the shop, leaving her trolley behind. I wouldn't be surprised if she decided to pay you a visit to talk about it.'

Rosalie dreaded the thought of such a visit – especially if Elaine had Rupert in tow. What could she tell her? Until she could speak to Geoff she knew no more about the situation that Elaine now did.

'One last thing,' Marion said, sounding indignant all over again. 'That blonde woman also claimed she and Marc were ... you know ... together and as good as engaged. Fergus said this couldn't be true, that it was obvious the man was besotted with you, so don't worry too much about it.'

Rosalie's throat tightened and tears pricked her eyes. 'I won't,' she answered in a small voice, and put the phone down.

She had to get Kirsty to the Four Winds Hotel as soon as possible. If Elaine and Rupert came round now and found Raventhorn empty, they'd leave her alone, for tonight at least.

'I'll be glad to be away from here,' Kirsty said when they set off half an hour later. 'I don't understand how you can be happy to live in that creepy castle.'

Rosalie sighed as she drove over the old bridge. 'It's where I grew up, where I've always wanted to live,' she said. Once on the main road, she called Fiona on the cab radio to let her know she could close up for the evening.

'I'm driving to the hospital to check on Geoff so I won't be working,' she explained.

'You might want to keep well away from Raventhorn afterwards,' Fiona remarked. 'I've just had a visit from Rude Rupert who demanded I told him everything I knew about Marc Petersen. When I said I didn't know very much about him, apart from the fact he is gorgeous, he threw a tantrum, shouted that he was going to get some answers from you one way or another and slammed the door behind him so hard my bones are still shaking! What's going on, Roz, and what is he so angry about?'

'I don't know.' So Elaine had alerted her son, of course, and now

Rupert was on the warpath. Fiona was right. She would have to be careful tonight when she came back from the hospital.

Chapter Twenty-Five

The nurse stepped out from behind her desk. 'I have news for you, Miss Heart,' she said. 'Mr McBride is conscious at last.'

Rosalie stared at her in shock. 'Oh ...' She held her breath, bracing herself for bad news. She had been warned Geoff could be brain damaged or paralysed when he came out of his coma.

The nurse smiled. 'Don't look so worried. The doctor was very happy with his progress. Of course, Mr McBride is weak and disoriented, but that's only to be expected. You can pop in and say hello for a short while. He'll be glad to see you. In fact, he's been asking for you ever since he woke up.'

It was as if a great weight was lifted off Rosalie's chest and she could breathe again – hope again. Geoff would recover, he would leave the hospital and go back to being his old self, minus the whisky and cigars. She'd make sure of that.

She followed the nurse into the room where Geoff was propped up against several pillows, his eyes closed. His face appeared pale and thin, but most of the machines that had been bleeping and flashing constantly around him these past few weeks had been removed.

'I'll leave you for now,' the nurse said in a quiet voice, 'but remember you can only stay for a few minutes. He must rest.'

Rosalie nodded and approached the bed.

'Hello, pretty,' Geoff whispered without opening his eyes.

'Oh, Geoff, I'm so happy to hear you at last.' Repressing a sob, she grabbed hold of his right hand and squeezed hard.

'Ouch, watch it, girl. That's no way to treat an invalid.' He opened his eyes. The corners of his mouth lifted in a tentative smile.

She brought his hand to her lips and kissed it, then pressed it against her cheek, by now wet with tears. 'How are you feeling?'

'Alive. Barely. What about you? Is everything all right?' He looked at her anxiously.

'I'm all right, don't worry,' she said quickly as she sat on the edge of the bed, reluctant to let go of his hand. 'I don't want to be cross with you – not just yet – but you have a lot of explaining to do.'

He sighed. 'I know. Go on then, fire.'

She sighed. Now she could ask him the questions that had been burning her lips for the past few weeks, she didn't know where to start.

'I want to know why you sold Raventhorn without telling me,' she blurted out. 'Lorna and I had a nasty shock when Petersen announced he was the new owner. In fact, I thought he was lying at first.'

Geoff sighed. 'It was cowardly of me to keep quiet about it. I wanted to tell you, but the longer I waited, the more difficult it became. As soon as I realised you were picking up Petersen from the airport, I rushed after you but then I had that stupid accident and I've been stuck in here ever since.'

'It was no stupid accident. The Porsche's brake lines were cut. Someone meant for you to crash. The police are investigating.'

Geoff gasped. 'Really? I thought I had been driving too fast.' He frowned. 'Have the police found anything?'

'Not yet. Do you have any idea who could have done it?'

'I'm not sure. I'll have to think.' Maybe it was the harsh tone in his voice, or the way he narrowed his eyes to look away, but it sounded as if he already knew the answer.

'Who was it, Geoff?'

He closed his eyes briefly and drew in a long breath. 'I have no proof. It would be wrong of me to point the finger at anyone just yet.' He opened his eyes. 'About Raventhorn, I am so sorry, but I had to sell. I had no choice.'

'You've had money problems before and you always bounced back. We could have organised more weddings or even conferences, we could have—'

'There was no other way this time, but I'm confident that with Petersen, Raventhorn is in good hands.'

Rosalie bit her lip. Now wasn't the time to tell him Marc and his girlfriend were planning to auction off the castle and all its treasures.

'Why did you choose Petersen? Is it because of the runestone on their family farm – the one with the same raven design as the one on Harald's shield?'

His eyes widened in surprise. 'You know about that? I suppose Marc Petersen told you. I've been in touch with his father by email for months. He was very interested in finding Harald's treasure. It was terrible that he died in that helicopter crash. I hope his son will show the same interest.'

Red-hot anger flashed through Rosalie. Letting go of Geoff's hand, she jumped up from the bed and walked to the centre of the room. 'Harald and his treasure, again! That's all you ever think about, all you ever care about. When are you going to give up and acknowledge it doesn't exist?'

He flinched and his face became even paler as his fingers gripped the sheet. Immediately alarm and remorse drowned her anger and she rushed back to his side. 'What's wrong? Do you want me to call the nurse?'

He shook his head. 'No need. I'll be fine in a minute.' He took several deep breaths. 'You are wrong, Rosalie. I care about you and Lorna a lot more than I ever cared about Raventhorn or Harald.'

He took a moment before he continued.

'If I'm truthful, I cared about your mother even more. Every day without her has been a torment. It broke my heart when she died, as much as it broke yours.'

The pain in his eyes was so intense Rosalie took his hand again. 'I know you loved her too. I'm sorry.' She hesitated, torn between the need to find out if he knew about her mother's secret past life and the desire to shelter him. The need to learn the truth won.

'Actually, there's something else. It's about Mum. I don't quite know how to say this, but I found something – something too shocking for words, something that changes everything I thought I knew about her.'

She bent her head, and swallowed hard.

'Go on.'

'First I found a photo of Mum and her parents when I was clearing out her room. I asked Lorna but she didn't want to talk about it, so I did an internet search and found more photos – horrible glamour photos dating back to the late 1980s.'

She shuddered as she recalled how crude some of the images had been. 'At first I thought I was mistaken. I mean, Mum would never have posed for such trashy magazines, would she? She had no interest in fashion or make-up, she hated having her photo taken. Then I looked more closely, and saw that it was Mum all right.'

She paused. 'I just can't believe she'd pose for those kind of photos. It's disgusting.'

'Poor Rosalie. I'm sorry you had to find out like that.' Geoff's voice was a harsh whisper. His blue eyes stared at her fixedly. 'I should have spoken to you earlier. Once again, I was a coward.'

Rosalie gasped. 'So it was really her? I was hoping I had got it wrong somehow.' She swallowed hard. 'And you knew. Why didn't you tell me?'

The door squeaked open behind her and it was the nurse's voice that answered. 'I'm afraid I have to ask you to leave and let Mr McBride have some rest now.' She walked in, pulling a trolley with medical supplies on.

'Just a few more minutes,' Rosalie implored, 'it's important.'

'So is sleep,' the nurse replied, a little more forceful now.

'Please, Matron.' Geoff gestured for the nurse to come to his side. 'I promise I'll do everything you say, take all your pills and drink every drop of your concoctions without a word of complaint.'

He gave her what he must have hoped was his most charming smile. It seemed to work. The nurse sighed. 'All right, you can have five more minutes.'

As soon as she'd left, Rosalie crossed her arms on her chest and glared at Geoff. 'Why did you not tell me before? Why did Mum never speak about her parents, about her past?' She swallowed hard. The last question was the hardest. 'Why did she not trust me with the truth?'

Geoff closed his eyes briefly. When he reopened them, they glistened with tears. 'Because she was ashamed, Rosalie. She was terribly ashamed.'

Rosalie shrugged. 'I know the photos are vile, and I can't believe Mum got mixed up in anything like that, but I would have understood, I wouldn't have judged her.'

His blue eyes stared at her. 'You did judge her when you found out though, didn't you? Anyway, it wasn't only the magazines. Your mother suffered terribly for the mistakes she made when she was young. They cost her a lot – her family, her self-respect, her safety. She lived in a constant terror that you, or someone else, would find out about her and that the man she escaped from all those years ago would come after her –and after you.'

'Who are you talking about? What man?' Sudden understanding made her eyes grow wide. 'My father!'

Geoff nodded.

'Who is he? Where is he?'

'His name is Jake Tyler and, as far as I know, he's in jail in Winchester.'

A lump formed in her throat. 'He's in prison? What did he do?'

'This time, he beat a woman up and robbed a grocery store, but I believe he's been in and out of prison for a string of offences over the years.'

She took a deep breath. 'You said he beat a woman up. Did he hurt Mum too?'

Geoff nodded. 'Many times. And he forced her to pose for those magazines. But there's more.' His mouth twisted in a grimace. 'Your mother believed that he set fire to your grandparents' house to punish her for leaving him. They both died in the fire. The police couldn't prove anything against Tyler at the time, so your mother decided to run away. All she ever wanted was to protect you from him.'

Rosalie's stomach contracted in a tight knot. There did not seem to be enough air in the room to breathe suddenly. Her childhood dreams had just crumbled in a sordid mess at her feet. Her father wasn't a rock star, a spy or a courageous explorer. He was a brute, a woman beater, a convicted felon – a murderer, perhaps.

'Why would he come after us?' she asked in a hoarse whisper.

'Because your mother took something from him when she left – a diary that could incriminate him and his associates in serious crimes. For years your mother lived in terror of him finding her – and you. Despite all our precautions, he did find you. I have no idea how. That's what I was trying to warn you about that day before my operation.'

So that was why her mother always refused to be photographed, and shied away from any publicity and stayed in her room whenever there were visitors to Raventhorn. Sophie's frumpy style now made sense. She didn't want to draw attention to herself, didn't want to risk being recognised.

And what had Rosalie done? She had talked about her to reporters; she'd even given them her photo to copy. Anyone carrying out a basic internet search like the one she'd done would have been able to trace her to Raventhorn. If Jake Tyler had found her, then she was probably the one to blame.

'I thought you said *he* was in prison.' There was no way she would ever acknowledge this man as her father.

'Men like him are dangerous, even from behind bars. They have no shortage of friends or accomplices to carry out their dirty work.'

'Why didn't Mum give the diary to the police?'

'She was scared, love. She didn't want to testify in court and risk his revenge. She just wanted to disappear and try to give you a normal childhood – as normal as it could be, under the circumstances.'

'You could have given the diary to the police yourself after she died.'

'I suppose so, but I wanted to protect you as well.'

Rosalie took a deep breath, pressed her fingers to her forehead. Her thoughts were all over the place. There was something she was trying to remember. Something about the diary, a vague memory she just couldn't pin down right now. Never mind. She'd think about it later.

She looked at Geoff again. 'You said Tyler found me. How can you be so sure?'

'A few months ago, I received an anonymous letter demanding a large sum of money in exchange for your mother's past to be kept a secret. An old photo of your mother was attached.' He swallowed hard. 'Well, you've seen some of the photos. I don't need to tell you any more.'

Rosalie clenched her fists. 'How do you know it was from him?'

Geoff sighed. 'I don't. I assumed it was from him.'

'Did you pay up?'

He nodded. 'I didn't want your mother's past life to be dragged up into the open and become the talk of Irlwick. I didn't want you to be ashamed of her.'

His hard blue stare stopped her from protesting. 'I should have known paying up that first time wouldn't be the end of the matter. A few weeks later, I got another letter, then another, and every time the amount of money the blackmailers asked for was higher.'

'Why didn't you go to the police? They could have stopped this.'

'Perhaps, but there would have been a scandal, and everybody would have known about your mum. I tried to catch who was behind the blackmail and lay in wait at the different places where I was asked to leave the money – usually car parks in the national park – but they were very clever, or lucky. I never saw them.'

'You sold your classic cars to be able to pay up, didn't you?'

Geoff nodded. 'They were my only source of ready cash. You know as well as I do how little there is in my bank account. Rupert was still working for me then. He had contacts in London, and he helped me sell the cars.'

She stepped closer to him, took his hand and gave it a little squeeze. 'Oh, Geoff. You took Rupert into your confidence, when you should have told me the full story.'

He shrugged. 'I didn't want you to worry. I must say that Rupert surprised me at the time. He wasn't his usual brattish self. He didn't ask me why I was selling the cars, didn't even demand a commission for arranging the transactions. He genuinely helped. Then the blackmailers made more specific threats against you, and I realised I needed to take more drastic action to keep you safe.'

'So you decided to sell Raventhorn.'

'That way I could pay all my debts and give you enough money to disappear and make a new start somewhere where you would be safe.'

'You should have known I would never leave you or Lorna.' Tears pricked Rosalie's eyes.

He sighed. 'I wasn't thinking straight. I put Raventhorn up for sale. I had to be discreet. I didn't want Rupert to find out. You know how obsessed he is with inheriting the place and being the laird. Anyway, one day last August I caught him sneaking out with the Landseer painting from the Crimson Room.'

'That's why you sacked him.'

He nodded. 'I should have done it a long time before.'

He closed his eyes and took a moment to catch his breath.

'He kicked up a fuss, of course, and said he was in big trouble. He had some gambling debts, and needed some cash. Call me soft or stupid but I didn't want him to upset his mother, so I gave him some money and he left. By that time I was getting desperate to sell Raventhorn, but no one was interested in a decrepit castle with acres of forest, a loch and a few live-in ghosts. I didn't know what to do, who to turn to, until I read an article about Sigmund Petersen and saw the photo of the runestone on his father's farm. I knew then that I'd found the link I'd been looking for all these years between Harald and his homeland. I went over to North Jutland—'

Rosalie frowned. 'I don't remember you travelling to Denmark.'

'I told you I was going to Orkney. I didn't want anyone to know about Petersen. Anyway, I found the old farm and the runestone, researched Petersen's genealogy in local parish records and the national archives in Copenhagen and found there was indeed a connection – albeit a tenuous one – with Harald Johansen's lineage. I then contacted Sigmund Petersen and offered to sell him Raventhorn. He was my best chance. Not only was he rich but as a distant relation of Harald's, I hoped he would be interested.'

He paused, turned to Rosalie and smiled. 'He was.'

'What about Lorna?'

'She understood my reasons. You see, Lorna was a friend of your mother's even before you came to live at Raventhorn. They met through her sister. It was Lorna who told your mother to come to Raventhorn.'

Geoff took hold of her hand. 'Now, listen, Rosalie, you understand that you must be very careful. When he came to see me at the hospital, before my operation, Rupert mentioned a couple of nasty incidents you and Duncan had been involved in. Has anything else happened since?'

'No, nothing,' she lied. He was too frail to tell him the truth about her troubles.

Geoff blew a relieved breath. 'That's good. Listen, I have Tyler's diary and other papers of your mother's in a blue metal box on the work unit in the garage. The key is in the cupboard, Sellotaped to the underside of the bottom shelf. Give everything to the police. They'll deal with Tyler.'

She nodded. 'There's one thing I don't understand. If it was Tyler blackmailing you, then why didn't he just ask for his diary back?'

'Who knows? He is a criminal after all. He probably wanted to get as much as he could from me first, then he would have come for the diary.' He relaxed against the pillows, closed his eyes. As if on cue, the nurse marched back into the room. 'This time, that's enough. Mr McBride, you will take your medication and go to sleep.'

There wasn't a trace of a smile on her face when she turned to Rosalie. 'And you will leave. He really must rest.'

Rosalie nodded. The nurse was right. Geoff looked drained and exhausted. 'Yes, of course.'

She cast one last glance in his direction. He looked so frail, so vulnerable, so old. For years he had done everything in his power to protect her and her mother. Now it was her turn to keep him safe. She would find that brute Jake Tyler – the man she could never think of as her father – and the men he employed from his prison cell to blackmail Geoff, and she would show him that she wasn't afraid.

She clenched her fists. Yes, she would show him.

The drive back to Raventhorn seemed interminable. The roads were dark and almost empty once she left Inverness behind. Motorists had obviously heeded the weather warnings for snow and gone home early. Fat snowflakes danced and swirled in the headlights, and she had to focus hard on the road when all she wanted to do was think about Geoff's revelations about her mother … and father.

When she arrived at Raventhorn, she went straight into the garage and stood in front of the tool shelf. Among the screwdrivers, pincers, rolls of duct tape, half-open cans of car polish and rugs smelling of paint and turpentine, old driving gloves and spare parts covered in oil were several metal tool boxes, all reminders of the classic cars Geoff had lovingly restored and tended to for years.

She reached out for the blue box and placed it on the worktop before walking over to the cupboard, getting down on her knees and searching for the key, which Geoff had said was Sellotaped to the shelf. He really had taken a lot of precautions to make sure her mother's papers were secure, she thought as she pulled off the tape and caught the small key in the palm of her hand.

She slipped it into her anorak pocket and tucked the box under her arm. She wanted to be in Raventhorn to open it, not in that cold, smelly garage. A dark and silent Raventhorn greeted her. Shivering with cold and nerves, she went up to the drawing room, and sat down on the rug with the box in front of her. The key was so tiny and her fingers shook so much it took several clumsy attempts to unlock the box. Holding her breath, she lifted the lid up and peered inside.

There wasn't much – a few official documents and faded photos, an old passport, and a small diary bound in dark blue leather. That was all her mother had salvaged of her past after running away.

Half an hour later, she sat back on her heels, tears streaming down her face as her mother smiled at her from a faded photograph. Sophie looked so young, so happy and vibrant. So beautiful too. It must have been hard for her to deliberately sabotage her looks and make herself dull so that she could blend into the background. Erasing her looks and her past had been the price of her and her daughter's safety.

From what Rosalie had managed to piece together from the various documents and certificates, her mother had grown up in South London, the only child of Mike and Angela Heart. She had studied art, English literature and history at her local college before attending East London Poly and graduating with a degree in art and design.

Rosalie touched the battered blue cover of her mother's old passport. Tucked inside were a handful of photos of a baby girl – herself, presumably – and the couple from the graduation photo. Her grandparents.

She would make sure these photos were displayed as they should have been all these years. They would never be locked into that blue box ever again, and forgotten.

Her fingers toyed with the diary. She flicked through the pages covered in tight scribbles – dates, names, addresses. She leaned closer. How odd. Some of the names looked Russian. One in particular kept cropping up: Bazanov, Anatoly Bazanov. Was he, and the other Russians, associates of Tyler, or were they his victims?

Just touching the thing made her want to be sick. She didn't want to have anything to do with Jake Tyler, the thug who had destroyed her mother and her family. She would give it to the police the following morning.

The whirring of a car engine followed by the screeching of tyres on the courtyard's cobbles ripped through the silence. A car door slammed, and seconds later a hard fist pummelled the kitchen door.

'Rosalie, open up. I know you're in there,' Rupert shouted from outside. 'I'm warning you. If you don't open this door right now, I'll kick it in.'

He would be capable of doing it too! Rosalie looked around in a panic. She gathered the photos and documents, shoved them all back into the blue box, slapped the cover shut and turned the key in the lock. She slid the box under the large oak dresser, threw the key into one of the drawers and ran down to the kitchen where Rupert's bulky silhouette was clearly visible through the door's frosted glass panel.

Chapter Twenty-Six

'About time.'

Rupert strode into the kitchen and pushed her out of the way.

'What do you want?' she asked, even though she knew exactly why he was there.

'I want some answers, and I want what's mine.'

He was so close she could smell the beer on his breath, saw the blood vessels in his eyes and felt the anger that always seemed to sizzle around him like an electric current. She stiffened her spine and forced a deep breath down.

'I don't know what you're talking about. I was about to make a cup of tea. I'll make you one too. Or maybe I should make you some black coffee. From the booze fumes you're giving off, I gather you need to sober up.'

He grabbed her arm and his fingers closed around her wrist. 'Don't go all superior on me. You know exactly what I'm talking about.' He pushed her until her back caught the edge of the table. He shoved harder until she was reclining on the table and he was almost on top of her.

'What are you doing? Let go of me.' This time her voice held a trace of panic, her breathing came out too fast and her heart beat so hard it hurt.

He smirked. 'I know Geoff sold Raventhorn to that Petersen guy. There's no point in denying it. I went to see Marion earlier. She told me that the woman who works for Petersen – Kirsty Marsh – was now staying at the Four Winds, so I drove there to talk to her. She confirmed it.'

He leaned further forward, got hold of her left wrist and pinned both her hands to the table by her sides. His legs encased hers like a cage, his breath touched her face like a cloud of warm, noxious mist.

'Geoff said Raventhorn was mine, but he sold it. So now I want my money. If I can't have this place, at least I can have the money from the sale.'

'Money? I don't have any money.' She tried to laugh but only managed a squeak.

He leaned closer, and slammed her hands onto the table. 'You're lying. Geoff thought he could con me out of the money like he conned me out of this place. Well, he can't. I bet he gave you most of it, didn't he? He always liked you best – you and your slag of a mother.'

Rosalie swallowed hard. Rupert's eyes were glazed, his face flushed beetroot, his breathing hard. He looked beyond listening, beyond reasoning, yet she had to try.

'Listen, Rupert, you may not believe it but it's the truth. He didn't tell me he was selling up. I had no idea Petersen had bought Raventhorn until the day he arrived. I swear Geoff hasn't given me any money. I can show you my bank statements if you want, and you'll see there's hardly anything in my account.'

'Then I'll look at Geoff's bank statements. He must have the money somewhere.'

'I don't even know which bank or building society he put the proceeds of the sale into,' she said.

He stared at her as if trying to determine if she was lying or not. She must have put in a good performance because he finally nodded.

'Then I guess we'll just have to find out, won't we? So here's what we'll do. We're going to get his bank details, and then we'll think of a way of transferring the funds into my account.'

The man was deluded, he wasn't thinking straight! There was no way he could do that, and even if there was, she would never help him steal Geoff's money. She was however desperate to be freed from under his weight – desperate enough to promise anything.

'All right. I'll see what I can do. Will you let me go?'

She held her breath, uncomfortably aware of his body pressing against her, of the hot glint in his eyes, the white spittle at the corner of his mouth, and his raspy breathing. For a moment she thought he wasn't going to move, but at last he straightened up and she slid away from him.

'Forget tea,' he said, 'I'll have some of that whisky Geoff always keeps handy.'

'Sure.' She opened the cupboard to get the bottle of liquor down. She started to pour some into a tumbler but Rupert snatched the bottle away.

'I don't need a glass.' He drank a few swallows straight from the bottle, wiped his mouth with the back of his hand and swayed against the kitchen worktop. 'We'll start in the library. I know he keeps his bank statements there.' He gestured to the door with the bottle. 'Let's go.'

Once in the library, he started flicking through the piles of books and folders towering on Geoff's desk and littering the floor while she pretended to search the shelves. He wouldn't find any bank statements in the library because she had moved them after his last visit, but she intended to stall him for as long as possible. The man was delusional, and unhinged. How could he not understand that even if he got hold of Geoff's bank details, he would not be able to transfer the funds into his own account without Geoff's authorisation?

'Damn!' He slammed his hand on the desk. 'I'm sick of this. Where can these bloody statements have disappeared to?' He glanced around. 'They were here last time I came.' He glared at her. 'Do you have any idea where they could be? And that diary I already asked you about? Are you sure you've never seen it? I told you what it looks like. It's small, dark blue.'

She felt the blood drain from her face. Rupert had just described Tyler's diary. But no. It was impossible! How could he know about it?

She shook her head. 'I don't know.' She hoped he hadn't heard the hesitation in her voice.

He narrowed his eyes and walked towards her.

'Yes, you do.' He grabbed hold of her arms and shook her so hard a shard of pain shot through her injured shoulder and she let out a cry. 'Answer me. Where are they?'

She pressed her lips together. He shook her again, harder. This time the pain was so intense her breath caught in her throat, lights sparked in front of her eyes and a wave of nausea made her heave.

'Tell me, you stupid bitch,' he growled.

Still she did not speak.

'Then you leave me no choice.' Rupert said. 'I'll call my friends. They'll know how to make you talk.' He pushed her away and searched through his jeans pocket for his phone. Looking at the screen, he scrolled down a list of numbers, pressed a key and put the phone to his ear.

This was her chance to escape – her chance to run to the kitchen, get her keys, and drive to the police station. But as she made a dash for the door her foot caught one of the books Rupert had thrown to the floor and she fell face forward. The last thing she saw was a flash of light as her head hit the corner of the desk. The last thing she felt was an explosion of pain in her skull. Then there was nothing.

Marc woke up with a start, his heart pounding, his body covered with sweat. Something was wrong. He glanced around his hotel room but didn't see anything amiss, so he tried to ignore the uneasy feeling in his gut. It was probably due to a bad dream brought about by his meetings with the coroner and the prospect of his father's funeral later today.

The investigators' report was clear and unequivocal. The accident had been due to poor weather conditions. No technical fault or human error was to blame. His father hadn't been piloting the helicopter. Therefore the argument they'd had just before he took to the air had not caused the crash, and he could stop tormenting himself with guilt. His telling his father that he wasn't sure he wanted to keep on working for him hadn't upset him so much he had not concentrated on piloting the craft and crashed into the mountain.

After coming back to his hotel room, he'd stayed up late, drinking cognac, revisiting the past and thinking about what his mother had told him. His soul-searching had made him feel quite sick and disgusted with himself.

He had wronged his parents. Misjudged them. He'd always thought they were so wrapped up in each other and in his father's business that there was no place for him in their life. In reality, *he* had been the stubborn and cold-hearted one. How often had he pleaded schoolwork, a rugby tournament or a school trip to avoid going home at weekends or cut short a half-term holiday? He had behaved like a spoilt brat, and had rebuffed any attempt they'd made to be closer, whilst placing his grandfather on a pedestal.

Cédric was right. He'd been hard on his parents. He'd been an ass. It was too late to mend his relationship with his father, but he could still work things out with his mother, or at least he could try.

Now he stared at the digital clock next to the bed indicating it was just after seven, and poured himself a glass of water. He lay back in bed again, threw the covers down, beat his pillows with a hard fist, closed his eyes. And sighed.

It was no good. That uneasy feeling wouldn't go away. Unable to go back to sleep, he got up, drew the curtains and stood in front of the window to watch dawn touch the sky with greys, blues and pale yellows as the sun rose slowly behind the tall buildings that lined Victoria Harbour.

He checked his watch. Hong Kong was seven hours ahead of England. It was just after midnight in Irlwick. Never mind. He just had to speak to Rosalie and check that she was all right. He keyed in Raventhorn's number, and let the phone ring, but no one picked up and the answerphone clicked on. He tried again, then rang Rosalie's mobile phone, only to reach her voicemail.

Where was she, and why hadn't she phoned him since passing on Fitzpatrick's message? His London secretary said Rosalie hadn't called once, even after he'd left messages on the answerphone at Raventhorn and called Fergus at Love Taxis.

He tried the office at Love Taxis, but there was a message announcing that it was closed until seven the following morning. Could he ring Fergus at home? The old man wouldn't thank him if he woke him up, especially if he'd just got into bed after putting in a late shift on the switchboard. Torn between his need to know that Rosalie was safe and well and the voice of reason that told him he was overreacting, he paced the floor until he felt he was going out of his mind.

Since sleep was out of the question, he slipped into his sports gear, grabbed a towel and made his way to the hotel gym.

An intensive workout only softened the edges of his anxiety. As soon as he was back in his room, showered and dressed in a crisp white shirt and black suit, fear slammed right back into him. He rang Raventhorn and Rosalie's mobile again, but it was the middle of the night over there, so, of course, the answerphones clicked on. However if Rosalie was at home, she would pick up the phone, he was sure of it.

He still hadn't managed to get through to Rosalie when it was time to leave for his father's service. He had declined the limousine the funeral director had offered and asked the hotel to book a taxi to take him to Diamond Hill instead.

The funeral service lasted exactly fifteen minutes – standard procedure in Hong Kong, he'd been warned. Feeling empty, drained, and utterly alone, he signed all the relevant paperwork, then loosening the knot of his black tie and slipping his jacket off, he wandered through a nearby park for a while.

It was after lunch by the time the taxi took him back to the Four Seasons. He calculated that it would be six am in Scotland, which was early, but not unreasonably so. When he still got no answer from Rosalie, he dialled Fergus's home number.

'Aye. Who is it?' Fergus sounded sleepy.

Marc apologised for waking him up, and explained that he was in Hong Kong and had been trying to contact Rosalie but couldn't get through.

'She must be asleep,' Fergus replied. 'The poor lass has worked flat out these past few days. With Duncan still in Edinburgh she's had to cover two shifts. Pity your lady friend isn't at Raventhorn any more,' Fergus added, 'she might have answered the phone.'

'What lady friend?' Marc asked, puzzled.

'Kirsty something or other. She told my Marion a lot of rubbish about you and sparked quite a bit of trouble with that no-good cousin of Geoff's – Rupert.'

Marc's throat tightened. What was Kirsty doing at Raventhorn? He'd only instructed her to start the preliminary paperwork for the bus company. There was no need for her to travel to Irlwick just for that.

'She claims you bought Raventhorn and are going to sell it,' Fergus explained in a puzzled voice, 'and that not content with putting Roz, Lorna and Geoff out of their home and auctioning all the furniture, you also plan to close Love Taxis down and put our Roz out of business as well.' He coughed to clear his throat. 'She said something else too.'

'What was that?' Marc asked, dread tightening his chest.

'That you and her were as good as engaged and flying off to live in America together soon.'

Marc took a deep breath. 'That's rubbish.' At least that last claim was rubbish. The rest was the truth.

'I do hope so, lad,' Fergus said in a serious voice, 'because we've grown to like having you around here. Anyway, I can tell you're worried about Roz, so I'll go to Raventhorn as soon as I've had a cup of tea and I've cleared my drive. It's been snowing hard all night and it might take me a wee while to get there.'

Fergus promised to call from Raventhorn as soon as he arrived.

Marc gave him heartfelt thanks and put the phone down. His anxious wait resumed. It might be an hour or so before Fergus rang back. To keep busy, he ordered lunch, enquired about flights to Denmark from both Hong Kong and London, and dialled Kirsty's mobile. He couldn't care less about waking her up. She owed him an explanation. Unfortunately the call went straight to voicemail. He hung up with a frustrated sigh.

He didn't have long to wait for Fergus to call back.

'It's odd,' the old man said. 'Rosalie's cab is in the courtyard, but she's not here. Perhaps she's staying at Alice's.'

'Call Alice and ask her if she knows where Rosalie is. If she doesn't, then call the police. I'll come as soon as I can. And by the way, Kirsty was right on one point only. My father did buy Raventhorn. For everything else I need you to trust me. Now, please, call the police and report Rosalie missing.'

His nerves were so taut that his hand was shaking as he dialled Luc's number. Rosalie was missing. She may be in danger. His only hope was that his friend would know what to do.

Chapter Twenty-Seven

Marc pulled up the handbrake and leaned back against the headrest of his hired Range Rover with a frustrated sigh. He might as well switch off the engine. The A9 was at a standstill. He was stuck in a queue of cars and lorries, and wasn't going anywhere any time soon. He'd been driving for over an hour since picking up the car at Inverness Airport and hadn't even reached Tomatin yet. What should have been a straight forward one hour road trip to Irlwick had turned into a nightmare journey because of a snow blizzard engulfing the whole of Scotland.

In front of him flickered a long line of red lights from the cars and trucks. He was jet-lagged, cold and hungry. Above all, he was worried sick about Rosalie and frustrated by the police's lack of interest in her disappearance. According to them, Rosalie hadn't been missing for long enough, there was no reason to suspect she was in any danger, and the emergency services were too stretched with the ongoing blizzards to spare any of their staff.

Marc glanced at the phone he'd thrown on the passenger seat after his last call to Luc. His friend may have left the French Intelligence Service but he still had useful contacts and together with Cédric, he had been digging up information for Marc.

As if on cue, the phone rang.

'Where are you now?' Luc asked in his usual brisk manner.

'Only ten miles from the airport. I'm stuck in a massive traffic jam.'

'Damn.' Luc paused. 'I have news and it's not good. Jake Tyler was released on parole three weeks ago. I have an address for him – a flat in Croydon registered under the name of Richard Tyler, his brother, currently in jail for fraud – and where his daughter Cheryl is supposed to be living too. The thing is, when my agent checked earlier today, there was nobody home, and according to neighbours, Cheryl and Tyler have been away on and off these past few weeks.'

Marc sighed. 'I don't like this, Luc. I can't help thinking that Tyler is involved in what has been going on at Raventhorn. From the information Cédric gave me, the man is a nasty piece of work.'

'He was still in jail when the hoax calls began, and since his release he has attended all his scheduled meetings with his probation officer in

London.'

'He could have instructed his associates to make the calls, smash the cab's windscreen or go after Rosalie in the forest. Now I understand why they didn't report the accident on the mountain road. Even if they didn't cause it on purpose, it wouldn't look good for Tyler's probation if the police discovered Tyler outside his parole licence area. It also explains why they left the holiday lodge straight away. They were scared the police would start asking questions.'

'I found out a few more interesting facts about Tyler,' Luc said. 'Although there was never enough evidence to prosecute him, he was suspected of organising and taking part in several robberies and racketeering, not to mention involvement with a Russian gang headed by Anatoly Bazanov, a mobster who has managed to evade arrest for years. Tyler is a nasty piece of work indeed.'

Marc's throat tightened. 'Cédric did mention that when I saw him in Paris. And now Rosalie is missing and the police won't do anything to help. They even suggested she might have gone Christmas shopping in Glasgow or Edinburgh! I asked them to interview Elaine and Rupert McBride but they said there was no reason to do so.'

The cars in front of Marc started crawling forward. 'Hang on,' he said. 'It looks like we're moving at last. I'll call you back.'

It took a further hour to reach the services outside Aviemore, where he bought a large black coffee and a ham sandwich, and another to get to Irlwick. The small town looked empty in the blustery snowstorm as he drove through. He had to slalom around a couple of jack-knifed lorries and half a dozen abandoned cars on the road through Corby Woods, and finally he turned off the main road and onto the bumpy lane leading to Raventhorn. At last he was home.

Chapter Twenty-Eight

The man's voice grated through her consciousness. It was a cold, slightly raspy voice, filled with barely suppressed anger and the threat of violence. Rosalie remembered it, and just like when she was little, it triggered one panicked thought inside her.

Leave. Escape. Now.

She opened her eyes to pitch darkness, felt the soft mattress and a cotton duvet beneath her and knew she was on a bed. She wasn't tied up, but someone had removed her boots. As her eyes got used to the darkness, she started distinguishing shapes. A window with the curtains drawn. A wardrobe, a dressing table. The room smelled of plastic, of new furniture and cleaning products. No sound came from outside, other than from the wind lashing at the window.

She must be in a holiday let, possibly even in the same lodge she'd visited before with Marc. Gritting her teeth against the pain, she sat up and slid her legs sideways so her feet touched the floor. Every move made her head spin and her shoulder throb with pain, and brought tears to her eyes. Slowly she rose to her feet and, her legs wobbly, tiptoed towards the door.

The men now seemed to be arguing, then the one whose voice made her skin crawl with cold shivers spoke. 'If Cheryl and Joe don't find that blasted diary, I'll have to go back down there myself.'

The diary. Rosalie's blood froze. If that's what *he* was after, then she knew exactly who *he* was – but Geoff had said *he* was in prison.

'Damn,' he snarled. 'Things haven't worked out the way I'd planned. That idiot Rupert is hopeless. When I ordered him to dispatch McBride to a better world so that he would inherit that bloody castle and could then tear it apart, he wasn't even capable of doing a proper job of cutting the brake lines of the Porsche.'

Rosalie pressed a hand to her mouth to stifle a gasp. So it was Rupert who'd sabotaged the Porsche! On Jake Tyler's orders.

There was the sound of a match being struck, and the smell of cigarette smoke drifted through the bedroom door.

'And last night he botched things up again and knocked the girl out, so we had to bring her here and Cheryl had to give her some sedative to keep her quiet all day until we figure out what to do. What a bloody mess.'

So she'd been drugged … No wonder she felt weak and sick.

'I suppose we can always cut our losses,' the other man suggested, 'go back to London pronto before the probation officer pays you a visit, and make a few bob selling whatever Cheryl and Joe manage to grab from the castle. They took the inventory of valuables Rupert drew up when he was working for McBride. That will help them. Rupert is a liability indeed, but he can be fixed. As for the diary, perhaps the woman never had it, or she lost it. It's been a long time.'

'Hmm. She had it all right. I know she did. And she would have kept it as leverage against me, in case I ever found her again. No, I can't let it hang over me. You know what would happen if the Russians found out about it. I must get my hands on it.'

'What about the girl? She may know where it is.'

The girl. Rosalie held her breath. They were talking about her. Well, she wouldn't wait in the dark for them to come and get her. She may have wanted to run away before, but now she would show *him* she wasn't afraid.

She pushed the door open and stepped into the living room.

'What about me?' she asked, trying hard to ignore the burning pain in her shoulder, her throbbing headache and the fear that, despite her earlier resolution, made her heart beat too fast.

Both men swung round to stare at her. One of them, a short, bulky man with dark cropped hair and ruddy cheeks, sprang to his feet. It was one of the men she had seen at the Stag's Head the day of the accident on the mountainside.

The other man drew on his cigarette and narrowed his eyes to consider her as she walked towards him.

So here he was, at last. Jack Tyler. Her father.

'Well, well. It looks like sleeping beauty is awake at last.' He leaned back against the back of his armchair and blew a cloud of smoke that hid his blue eyes and his pale, handsome face for a few seconds.

'Are you not even going to ask who I am, princess?'

'I know who you are.'

He rose to his feet, and she was able to take a good look at him for the first time. He was tall and lean. He had deep grooves on either side of his mouth, a straight nose and very clear blue eyes. Despite the grey streaks in his dark hair, it was difficult to guess his age. He could just as easily be in his early forties as in his late fifties. What was obvious, however, was the icy threat radiating from his person.

He flicked the butt of his cigarette on to the floor and put it out with the heel of his boot, not caring that he'd burnt a hole in the beige carpet, then he looked up and smiled. It transformed his whole demeanour from ruthless to charming. It was odd and disturbing and she watched with a mixture of fascination and revulsion.

'You'd better take a seat, princess,' he said, gesturing to the armchair vacated by his friend. 'We have a lot of catching up to do – the best part of twenty-five years, to be exact. How did you work out who I was?'

'You were in the lodge with that girl the evening I came, weren't you? It was your voice I recognised – your voice I must have heard countless times shouting at Mum when I was little, before she left you.'

His jaw clenched but he said nothing.

'I have nothing to say to you. You disgust me.' She forced herself to remain still as he stepped forward, even though fear tightened her insides and all she wanted to do was to run away. There was nowhere to run to, anyway. He stopped smiling.

'I asked you to sit down.'

'Do as he says.' The other man took her arm and pushed her into an armchair. 'Sit down,' he growled.

Rosalie cried out in pain.

'Leave us alone, Sam. Go have a smoke outside, or take a walk. My girl and I have things to talk about.' Jake Tyler sat opposite her, and lit another cigarette and inhaled deeply. 'You don't look much like me.'

'I'll take that as a compliment, shall I?'

He arched his eyebrows, then smiled again. 'I looked for you everywhere, do you know that? I'll never know how *she* managed to elude me all these years. She's the only one who ever ran away from me. The only one.'

He was talking about her mother with so much spite and hatred, it made Rosalie go cold. 'She even died before I could get to her, and deal with her, the bitch.'

Rosalie felt the insult like a slap to the face. Suddenly the fear was gone. There was only loathing. Ignoring the pain in her shoulder, she leaned forward too.

'My mum was the bravest, the kindest, the most wonderful woman who ever lived. What she ever saw in a man like you, I'll never know. You're nothing but a thug and a criminal. Don't even try to play the long-lost father sentimental rubbish because I really don't care.'

Surprise flickered in his blue eyes. He whistled between clenched teeth. 'And I thought you were just a dumb girl in pink. I guess I was wrong. Nobody talks to me like that. You've got guts, girl.' He drew on his cigarette. 'Aren't you even going to ask me how I found you?'

'It was the article about Love Taxis, wasn't it?'

He nodded. 'It was indeed.'

No wonder Geoff had got so mad at her when he'd found out.

'I was in the nick then. I can't tell you how happy I was to finally find out what had happened to you and your mother.'

Rosalie swallowed hard. She was this man's daughter. She had his blood, his genes. 'How could my mother fall in love with a man like you, how could she throw away her relationship with her family, her career, her hopes for the future, just to be with you? It makes me sick.'

A twitch appeared at the side of his face. 'Careful, princess, I may be willing to tolerate a bit of tongue-lashing from you, but don't push your luck. Anyway, how's your head, and your shoulder? That idiot Rupert hurt you pretty bad. He'll pay for that, don't you worry. Nobody touches my girl.'

'Your girl?' She shuddered. 'I'm not your girl, I was never your girl,' she said between clenched teeth. 'The only father I ever had is Geoff, the man you have been blackmailing for months.'

He smiled. 'What touching words ... Would you like anything to drink or to eat?' he asked. 'We had to give you something to keep you asleep all day and you've been out cold for hours. I bet you're hungry.'

She rose to her feet, flinching as pain lanced her neck, shoulder and back. 'I want my boots and my coat and I want to go home.'

He slid his cigarette between his lips and got up too. 'That, my dear, is out of the question. I haven't finished with you yet. You see, your mother took something from me all those years ago, something very valuable, and I want it back.'

Chapter Twenty-Nine

The lights were on at Raventhorn. All of them, or so it seemed from the end of the drive. Relief washed over him. Rosalie was back, safe and sound.

Almost immediately a worrying thought made him stop the car at the side of the lane and switch the engine off. Rosalie would never leave the lights on in every single room like that. Something wasn't right.

He got out and walked the rest of the way, pausing near the stable block, and making sure he stayed out of the glare of the security lights.

A black four-wheel drive was parked in the courtyard. Its boot and back seat were piled high with boxes filled with paintings and ornaments. But that wasn't all. Rupert McBride's sports car was stationed near the garage, next to Rosalie's taxi.

A man walked out of the kitchen, carrying a cardboard box full of crockery. 'Are you sure these are worth anything, Cheryl?' he shouted. 'It looks like a pile of junk to me.'

'Jake said to grab anything that was on that list Rupert gave us,' a woman's voice answered from inside the house.

Jake. She must mean Tyler. Marc balled his fists by his sides. So he'd been right. The man was there, or close by. But where was Rosalie?

'I think we have enough. Jake's waiting for us and, as you know, he's not the patient type.'

The man put the box inside the car and straightened up, and Marc recognised him from the Stag's Head the day of the snowstorm.

'Get a move on, will you? We need to leave. And don't forget the silverware.' The man shouted as he opened the driver's door.

Marc's heartbeat quickened. Looking around he saw a pile of wooden sticks discarded on the ground. He picked the largest, heaviest one up before stepping out of the shadows and walking into the courtyard.

'You're not going anywhere until you tell me where Rosalie is.'

The man swung round and stared at him in surprise. 'What the—'

'Step away from the car,' Marc ordered. 'So, where is she?'

The man frowned but remained silent.

Marc clenched his fist around the stick. He'd never been spoiling for a fight so much in his life. 'I asked you a question.'

The man shrugged. 'Relax. She's with Tyler. Knowing him, I'm sure he has a more lucrative career in mind for her than driving that cab. Something like modelling, for example. She may not be much to look at in boots and anorak but I bet she looks tasty naked.' He laughed, a throaty, sleazy laugh.

Marc tensed as red-hot rage surged through him. Before he realised what he was doing he threw his weapon to the ground, grabbed the man by the collar of his jacket and pushed him against the bonnet of the car. 'Shut up.'

The man grunted, slackened under his grip and raised his hands in a gesture of surrender. 'All right, calm down. I was only joking.'

'Where are they?' Marc asked again, taking a step back.

Just then his mobile rang. Perhaps it was Luc with important news. He looked down, patted his coat pocket, and wasn't ready when the man suddenly lunged at him with such force that he lost his balance, slipped and fell back with a hard thump. His head hit the cobbles, his phone flew from his hand and landed a few meters away in the snow. Damn. How stupid of him not to have seen that coming.

'There, take that too!' The man growled as he kicked his side, his shoulder, and went for his head, but Marc managed to grab his ankle and pulled him down.

Rolling on top of the thug, he straddled him and smashed his fist into his face. He was about to hit him again when the tiny part of him still capable of rational thought whispered that knocking his adversary out when he needed information would be pretty stupid.

Breathing hard, he grabbed the man's jacket and lifted his face up until their noses almost touched.

'Tell me where she is!'

'What's going on, Joe?' Cheryl shrieked behind him. Glancing over the thug's shoulder he saw that she had a holdall in one hand and a couple of silver candlesticks in the other.

Ignoring her, Marc looked down at the man again. 'Damn it. I'm losing patience here.'

There was the sound of hurried footsteps. The man's pupils dilated as he stared at something behind Marc. Marc turned round but it was too late. He didn't have time to get out of the way as Rupert

McBride brought a candlestick down onto his head. The pain was so intense he saw a bright flash of light, then spiralled into darkness.

An hour had passed in tense silence as Tyler smoked and stared at Rosalie. His henchman, Sam, came back in a couple of times to complain he was freezing to death, but Tyler sent him out again to keep watch. She gathered they were waiting for their associates to come back from Raventhorn. She had no idea what would happen to her then, although it was obvious Tyler had no intention of releasing her.

Ignoring the pain that stabbed her shoulder every time she moved, she leaned forward and said in a low voice. 'What if I told you I can get what you want?'

He put his glass down on the armrest. 'And how do you know what I want?'

She took a deep breath. 'I know my mum took a diary from you, and that you want it back.'

Tyler narrowed his eyes. 'Do you, now?'

She nodded. 'I know where it is. I'll give it to you if it means I get rid of you and your friends, and never see, or hear from you again.'

He narrowed his eyes, drew on his cigarette, and studied her for a moment. 'How do I know I can trust you?'

'You don't.'

Silence anxiously dragged on. Would he take the bait or would he see right through her?

The door to the living room opened and the man called Sam burst into the room. 'Joe and Cheryl are back, and Rupert is with them.'

Tyler grabbed his coat and slipped it on. 'Tell them to come in. You're staying here while the girl and I drive to Raventhorn.'

He threw her anorak and boots in her direction. 'Put them on and hurry.'

It was a struggle to get dressed but she managed and followed him outside.

He was talking to Cheryl and another man who had bruises all over his face and one eyelid badly swollen. Rupert stood apart, hands deep in the pocket of his anorak. He sneered at her, but didn't speak.

'Looks like things got messy at Raventhorn,' Tyler said. 'Your boyfriend caused a bit of a commotion.'

Rosalie's heart did a somersault. 'Marc? Marc is there?'

Tyler turned to his associate. 'Where did you leave him?'

'In the courtyard,' the other man replied.

'Then it'll look as if he interrupted a burglary – which in a way he did.' Tyler's lips stretched into a thin smile.

He gestured towards Rosalie. 'Get in the car.'

Struggling to understand, she asked, 'Where is Marc? What did you do to him?'

Tyler pointed at Rupert. 'Your friend here bashed his head in with a candlestick. The man's dead.'

It felt like her heart stopped, and she swayed against the side of the car. No, that wasn't true. Marc couldn't be dead. He just couldn't!

Tyler was now talking to Rupert. 'You know what that means, don't you? You have to disappear or you'll get arrested and charged with murder. I don't want you anywhere near me.'

Rupert snorted. 'I didn't mean to kill him, I swear. He was punching Joe. I didn't think ...'

'That's your problem, isn't it?' Tyler retorted. 'You never think.' He shook his head. 'What about your car? Is it still at Raventhorn?'

'No. I drove it back home. Joe followed me with Cheryl in the four-by-four and gave me a lift.'

'You can stay here for now,' Tyler said. 'We'll drop you somewhere in town when we set off back to London.'

Rupert shook his head. 'Nobody will know it was me who did it. I was wearing gloves, so my prints won't be on the candlestick. Anyway, I can't leave Irlwick at the drop of a hat. There's my mother, and Cheryl.' He stepped closer to the young woman and put his hand on her shoulder.

'What about me?' The woman snarled as she shook him off and edged away from him.

'You said we would be together. You said you wanted to live here with me.'

She let out a short, hard laugh. 'I said a lot of things, Rupert. You don't get it, do you?'

'Get what?'

'You were set up, mate. I was only with you because you were useful to my uncle Jake. Didn't you think it was a bit of a coincidence that we met just before McBride needed to sell his cars and my dad happened to run a vintage cars auction mart?'

'But I was the one who chatted you up in that club in Inverness after I spilled my drink all over you. I made you laugh, I thought you liked me ...'

Cheryl snorted. 'If you believe that, then I am a better actress and you're a bigger fool than I thought.'

'But why? Was it all about Geoff's cars?'

'Nah. Uncle Jake needed you to watch over McBride and help him sell his nice cars so that he had plenty of cash. He also needed you to list the valuables at Raventhorn and sneak away what you could, and keep searching the place for his diary.'

Rupert looked crestfallen. 'I did all that. I did it for you – for us –not for him.'

She shrugged and turned to Jake Tyler. 'Enough talking. I'm going in. I'm bloody freezing. I'll see you when you get back.'

She went in, followed by Rupert who was still pleading with her.

Tyler opened the passenger door for Rosalie. 'Get in.'

'Wait!' She turned to the man called Joe. 'Are you sure Marc is—'

'Dead?' The man finished, a scowl creasing his bruised face. 'Yeah, pretty sure. And if he wasn't when we left, he will be by now.'

He was flying over Raventhorn, over the forest and the loch. As he glided down he saw a shape in the water – a small building, or what was left of it. He had to get inside. What he sought was there. He was so close, so close ...

The wind blew him away from the water and then he was falling and spinning down towards Raventhorn's cobblestone courtyard. He hit the ground, and it felt like his head exploded. A raven flew down from a tree branch and landed next to him. Its small, beady eyes stared at him, its feet made light tapping sounds as it hopped around him on the cobbles, and its beak poked at his head.

Marc groaned. What a weird dream. Only it felt so real. The pain in his skull felt too damned real too. As did the hard, bumpy, frozen surface under his body and the wet snow on his face.

He opened his eyes and blinked as snowflakes fell on and around him. It was dark. He must have been lying there for some time – long enough for the security lights to switch off.

Flinching against the pain, he sat up, lifted a hand to his head and touched his hair. It was matted with blood and there was a gash at the side of his head where McBride had hit him. The ground moved and swayed in front of him as he tried to get up, so much so that he only managed to kneel down. Closing his eyes, he waited for the dizziness to pass before trying again. The security lights came on when he stood up, and their raw glare made his headache a hundred times worse.

He needed help, and fast. He patted his jacket for his phone. Nothing. He looked around but couldn't see it in the courtyard either. He must have lost it during his scuffle with Tyler's associate. He would have to use the phone in the hall to call the police.

The kitchen door was open. He closed it behind him and went up to the hall, but when he lifted the phone receiver, all he got was silence. The line was dead.

'Hell.' He put the phone down. Where was Rosalie? His only hope was that Tyler was staying at the holiday lodges up at Geal Charn again. That was where he needed to go. He was heading back downstairs when there was the noise of a car outside.

Chapter Thirty

Despite the snow, Tyler drove fast down the mountain road. Far from being scared, Rosalie silently urged him to go faster as desperate thoughts churned inside her, filling her with almost unbearable pain. Marc was dead. He had been beaten up and had been left alone in the freezing night.

After what felt like an eternity, they reached Raventhorn at last.

'That must be Petersen's car.' Tyler slowed down as they drove past a Range Rover parked at the side of the lane just after the old bridge.

He drove into the courtyard and slammed on the brakes. The vehicle skidded and came to a bumpy halt. 'I can't see him. Where the bloody hell is he?' He stopped the car, flung the door open, and got out.

Rosalie hurried out after him, not daring to hope just yet. Marc was nowhere to be seen. In fact the only traces of his presence was an area of compacted snow stained with patches of bright red blood where the struggle with Joe had taken place, and where Marc had been hit on the head by Rupert and collapsed.

Relief surged inside her. Rupert and the others had got it wrong. Marc had survived the blow, and since his car was still parked on the lane, he must be in Raventhorn. Perhaps he had phoned the police or an ambulance and they were on their way.

That was what Tyler must be thinking too, judging by the determined look on his face when he kicked the kitchen door open and marched in. The kitchen was a mess, with papers, broken pots and plates littering the floor, cupboard doors swinging open and drawers pulled out. Tyler looked around, pulled a large kitchen knife from a drawer and strode towards her. Before she could slip away, he yanked her to him, and pressed the tip of the knife against her throat.

'All right, princess, now let's see how much your boyfriend loves you,' he whispered into her ear, manoeuvring her so that she faced the door leading to the staircase and he could use her as a shield.

'There's no way I'm going to let him blab to the cops about what happened here tonight, and let him implicate me. I need to finish the job Rupert botched. Call him.'

A cold, calm feeling descended upon her. She wasn't afraid of

Tyler. It meant nothing to him that they shared the same blood, and she knew that he would hurt her without a moment's hesitation if it helped his cause, but she didn't care. She wouldn't put Marc in any more danger.

'Call him yourself,' she said through clenched teeth.

Tyler kneed her in the back and pulled on her arm. Tears sprung from her eyes, she cried out but immediately bit her lip, hard.

'I said to call him,' he snarled between clenched teeth.

'And I say you can go to hell,' she replied, almost choking with pain and loathing.

He spun her around so that she now faced him, slipped one hand around her throat like a vice, and pushed her against one of the kitchen cabinets. Tilting her face up, he glared straight into her eyes.

'Let's get something clear. I give the orders, you obey. Got that? Now, if you don't want me to start knocking you about, I suggest you do as I say.'

A shadow moved near the kitchen doorway. Rosalie blinked, and suddenly Marc was standing just behind Tyler, holding Lorna's copper pan. He brought it down on Tyler's head with a loud bang. Tyler's eyes widened in shock. His hold on her slackened. He crumpled in on himself, and the knife he'd been holding slid onto the tiles.

Rosalie stared down at his unconscious form at her feet.

'Is he dead?'

'I don't know, and I don't care,' Marc answered in a harsh voice, still holding the copper pan. 'The scumbag was hurting you.'

She couldn't stop staring at Tyler. His face had turned deadly white, and he didn't appear to be breathing.

'Rosalie, please talk to me. Look at me.' Marc's voice became urgent.

She lifted her gaze up slowly and met his worried eyes. His face was bruised and smeared with blood. There was dried blood in his hair too, and his jacket was ripped at the armhole. He'd been hurt, but he was alive. It was as if all the trauma and the emotions of the past few hours were finally catching up with her.

'They said you were dead. I thought ...' Tears welled in her eyes, and she started shaking.

Marc put the pan on the kitchen table, stepped over Tyler's body and wrapped her into his arms. 'Shh … it's all right. It's over.' She buried her face against his chest, breathed in his scent, and listened to the thunder of his heartbeat.

'I was so worried about you.' He stroked her back, kissed her hair, her forehead, her tear-stained cheeks. She moulded herself to his body and for a short moment nothing else mattered but the sheer joy and relief of being in his arms.

His hand moved up to her shoulder and she couldn't repress a whimper of pain. He released her straight away. 'You're hurt.'

'It's my shoulder.' She smiled. 'You're going to have to fix it again.'

'This time, I think I'll let the doctors do it.' He let go of her, knelt down next to Tyler and felt the pulse at the side of his throat.

Tyler groaned but didn't wake up. Marc patted the pocket of his jacket and extracted a mobile. 'The lines are down and I lost my phone,' he explained. 'We'll use his mobile to call the police and an ambulance.' He gestured towards the unconscious man at his feet. 'Tyler needs seeing to.'

The blood drained from her face and she took a step back. 'You know his name?'

Marc nodded. His eyes softened, he took a deep breath and rose to his feet. 'Actually, it's not the only thing I know. Rosalie, there is something I must tell you … about him, and your mother. I'm sorry.'

So Marc knew everything! Shame burnt like acid inside her, and she feared she might be sick. 'I don't want to talk about it – about him,' she mumbled, stepping towards the door. 'I need to go … to the bathroom.'

'Rosalie—'

'Tell the police about the others, too – his two associates, and Rupert and Cheryl,' she added. 'They are all at the holiday lodge where they were staying the night of the accident.'

At the mention of Geoff's cousin, Marc's face hardened. He touched the wound on the side of his head. 'Rupert tried to kill me.'

'He also sabotaged the Porsche's brakes, because he was so desperate to inherit Raventhorn.'

'I suppose he was under the influence of his girlfriend, who by the way is also Jake Tyler's niece.'

She nodded. 'I know.' It was true that she was related to Cheryl too.

Upstairs in the bathroom, she splashed water on her face, and tried to calm her nerves. When she no longer felt like she was going to be sick, she went back downstairs to the kitchen.

She heard Tyler's raspy voice as soon as she reached the bottom of the stairs.

'I'll make it worth your while,' he was saying. 'I know you're loaded but I have contacts that could prove interesting for you.'

'Shut up,' Marc answered. 'Don't make things worse for yourself. The police are on their way.'

'I hope they lock him away forever,' Rosalie said as she walked into the kitchen. Tyler was sitting against the wall, with Marc standing in front of him.

'Tut, tut … that's not a very nice thing to say about your daddy, is it, princess?' Tyler looked at Marc. 'Now you know about me, son, perhaps I should tell you about Rosalie's mummy too so that you get the full family picture.'

'Stop it!' Rosalie hissed.

'Come on, princess,' he sniggered, 'you have to be honest in a relationship. You should tell your rich boyfriend that your mummy was a glamour model. A bloody good one, I must say, although I often had to give her something to loosen her up at first. She was quite partial to a few shots of vodka before a session. It made her more … compliant.'

'Enough,' Marc snapped. The man must have heard the steel in his voice because he snorted but didn't utter another word.

Marc cast a worried glance towards Rosalie. If only he could take her in his arms again, shelter her from the ugliness and the pain, and kiss away the shame and the hurt he could see in her eyes. But there was nothing he could do or say right now, not with Tyler watching and goading them.

'You should go back upstairs and have a rest while we wait for the police,' he told Rosalie.

She nodded, and went out of the kitchen again. As soon as he was sure she couldn't hear him, he stared hard at Tyler and said, 'Now listen, you scumbag. I'll make sure you are put away for the rest of your miserable life. It shouldn't be hard to prove that you were involved in Rosalie's accident in the forest, and that you asked your associates to make hoax calls to Rosalie's taxi company and wreck Duncan's cab.'

Tyler snorted. 'Not guilty on those accounts, mate. I wasn't involved in any prank calls, car chase or taxi vandalising.'

The man was lying, of course. 'There won't be any parole this time,' Marc carried on. 'And don't even think about getting in touch with Rosalie or sending one of your mates to make trouble for her when you're back inside, because from now on I'll be watching over her like a hawk.'

Muscles twitched at the side of Tyler's mouth.

'I won't let you hurt her ever again,' Marc added. 'You're finished.'

'We'll see about that, mate.' Tyler leaned up against the wall and closed his eyes. He looked deflated, vanquished, as if all his bravado had left him.

Turning his back on him, Marc walked to the window to look out for the police. His head wound pounded and made him feel dizzy. He turned the cold tap on, bent down and splashed water on his face. The cool water numbed the pain and revived him, so he splashed some more.

A bird crowed on the other side of the window. He opened his eyes, just in time to see Tyler's reflection as he stood behind him. The man was going to knock him out.

Instinct took over. Marc swung round, stepped aside to avoid Tyler's fist then lunged forward to grab hold of his collar.

'Haven't you had enough?' he growled as anger surged inside him, swamping any rational thought. He lifted Tyler off the floor and slammed him hard against the kitchen cupboard. Tyler went limp and slid to the floor, as floppy as a rag doll. He looked too weak to even blink. Marc glanced out of the window again. The raven had flown away. It had warned him just in time to dodge Tyler's blow.

It took another half an hour for a police car and an ambulance to pull up into the courtyard, sirens flashing and blazing in the night.

Tyler was checked by paramedics and interviewed by the police then bundled into an ambulance. Rosalie and Marc each gave a brief statement. Rosalie gave one of the police officers a blue metal box and a key, said something about a diary and a list of dates and names inside. Then they climbed in the back of the police car and were driven to the hospital in Inverness. During the journey Rosalie kept her eyes closed. She wasn't asleep because when he touched her hand, she snatched it away. Even though all he wanted was to take her in his arms and comfort her, he didn't insist, didn't even talk.

Once at the hospital, they were taken to two different treatment rooms. Marc's wound was cleaned and dressed, and he was told he needed to stay the night to make sure he wasn't suffering from concussion. When he enquired about Rosalie, he was told that she too would be spending the night at the hospital.

He was given a private room and a couple of painkillers, and just about managed to take his shoes off before collapsing on the bed, and falling asleep.

Chapter Thirty-One

'Thanks for coming.'

'That's the least Niall and I could do, after what happened. He's waiting in the truck.' Alice gave Rosalie a hug and stepped back to look at her. 'Poor Roz. You look like hell.'

Rosalie sighed. She was only too aware of the cuts and bruises on her forehead, and her stained anorak and jeans. She slipped her arm under Alice's and the two women walked out of the hospital.

'I'm fine, really. I didn't sleep much, that's all.'

She hadn't slept at all. It wasn't her aching shoulder that had kept her awake, nor the uncomfortable hospital bed, but memories from her early childhood that kept playing in her mind, like a broken film. She must have buried them deep inside her, and they had resurfaced, vivid and disjointed, after her being face-to-face with Tyler.

She could recall her mother's voice, hushed and scared, as she urged her to hide and make herself small; her cheeks wet with tears as she kissed her goodnight. The sobbing, the cries, and Tyler's cold, raspy voice … A few hazy, less scary, memories had come back too – of a small, red brick bungalow, perhaps her grandparents' house, with sunshine streaming through neat white net curtains, the smell of cakes baking, and the feel of a teddy bear she cuddled to fall asleep.

Alice stopped and stared at Rosalie. 'You're not fooling me, you know, and you don't have to be so brave. What happened last night was bloody awful. It's lucky both Marc and you made it without being seriously injured.' She frowned. 'Where is he, by the way, your knight in shining armour? We could give him a lift back to Raventhorn too.'

'He was discharged this morning. The nurse told me that he left with a very glamorous blonde woman. Kirsty, no doubt.' Rosalie let out a bitter laugh. 'She must be tending to his wounds at the Four Winds Hotel as we speak.' Heavens, how she hated the sound of her voice. She sounded like a sad, bitter and jealous woman.

She forced a smile. 'At least Geoff is getting better.'

'Does he know what happened?' Alice asked.

Rosalie nodded. 'I gave him the edited version.'

'It's wonderful that he has pulled through. You must be so relieved, so happy – I mean, under the circumstances. At least there's something to be happy about. What did he say … you know … about Tyler being your dad?'

'What do you think he said? He's sorry I had to find out about him, but he's glad the man is back in jail where he belongs.' Rosalie halted and cast a suspicious glance towards her friend.

'Hang on a minute. How do you know Tyler is my father?'

Alice had the grace to look embarrassed. She lifted her shoulders in a dismissive shrug then fiddled with the handle of her handbag. 'You know Eddie, the young policeman who's just been transferred from Inverness – the blond one who has breakfast at the café every morning. He kind of let it slip.'

'Did he now?'

'He mentioned the trouble at Raventhorn and at the holiday village at Geal Charn this morning, and I was understandably worried about you.' She bit her lip, and looked so sheepish Rosalie felt embarrassed for being so grumpy. Alice was her best friend, and she would have been the first person she told about Tyler anyway.

'Go on,' she said.

Alice sighed. 'I gave him an extra large coffee and a plate of scrambled eggs on the house, and he told me about Tyler.'

'Was there anybody else in the café?'

'The usual suspects, and Marion and Fergus who were having a pot of tea and a couple of toasted teacakes.'

'Did Marion hear what Eddie said?'

'I'm not sure.' Alice paused and pressed her hand to her mouth. 'Oh, Roz, I'm so sorry. If Marion heard him, then the whole of Irlwick knows that Tyler is your dad by now, and possibly the whole of Aberdeenshire too.'

Rosalie's heart sank. Soon everybody would know her father was a criminal and her mother had a shady past. She forced a smile. 'Let's look on the bright side. This way I won't have to explain the story time and time again, or write a family announcement for the *Gazette*.'

They resumed their walk across the car park.

'Tyler isn't exactly the father you had in mind, is he?' Alice asked.

'You can say that again.' How could she explain to her friend how tainted she felt by her connection to him, how much she hated herself for being his daughter, and for any trace of him there was inside her?

They arrived at Niall's pick-up truck. He climbed out, kissed her cheek, and held the passenger door for her and Alice. 'Sorry to hear about your ... hmm ... problems last night,' he said as he helped her climb in.

'Thanks.' Rosalie slid onto the bench. It was nice and warm inside the truck. She closed her eyes as soon as Niall started the engine, and dozed on and off all the way to Irlwick.

'Looks like someone's home,' Niall remarked as they approached Raventhorn.

'Really?' Rosalie opened her eyes and stared at the castle. The lights were on downstairs, and Marc's hire car was parked in the courtyard. So he was there.

She had been so sure Marc would be at the Four Winds Hotel with Kirsty that she hadn't prepared herself for a confrontation, and had no idea what she would say to him.

'Would you like us to stay?' Alice asked as Niall stopped in the courtyard.

'No, thanks. All I want is to go to my flat and sleep.'

Niall and Alice exchanged a glance.

'Actually, there was something I needed to tell you.' Niall coughed to clear his throat. He looked worried suddenly, and Alice gave him an encouraging nod. 'It's very awkward.' His face was pale and strained, and his fingers shook as he spread them on the steering wheel.

'Niall, you're scaring me. What's up with you?' Rosalie asked, but he only hung his head down and let out a deep sigh.

'What Niall is afraid to tell you,' Alice said then, 'is that he was the one who made the hoax calls.'

'What?' Shock made Rosalie's voice hoarse.

Niall closed his eyes. 'I'm so sorry, so ashamed. I don't know what came over me.'

'You mean *you* made me and Duncan drive around, wait in empty car parks and waste our time for nothing? But why?'

'Because I wanted your business to fail so you would close up shop and be with me. I'm so sorry, I wasn't thinking straight.'

Rosalie turned to Alice. 'And you knew about this?'

Alice shook her head. 'I only found out this morning. Niall told me after we heard about all the commotion here.' She pulled a face. 'He also told the police.'

'Now I understand why you were always turning up in your tow truck whenever I was stranded somewhere,' Rosalie said.

'I am sorry. I behaved like a total eejit. I know that.'

'Aye, you did.' She frowned, anger twisting her stomach in a knot. 'The threatening note on my windscreen the other day ... the one that said, "I am watching you." Was that you too?'

He sighed. 'No. That was Julia. She was annoyed when she saw you having lunch with Petersen. She only told me what she'd done today. She was afraid she would get in trouble with the police.'

Alice sighed in disbelief. 'I hope she does. Who would have thought your sister would be so nasty and want to scare Rosalie like that?'

'It's a lot to take in,' Rosalie said. 'Hang on a minute. What about Duncan's windscreen getting smashed in the Duke's car park? Did you do that too?'

He rubbed his face. 'No! That was that idiot Kian. I swear I had no idea he was going to do that.'

'What does Kian Armitage have to do with it?'

Alice reached out and put a calming hand on Rosalie's forearm. 'Apparently Kian was outside the Duke's that evening, completely drunk. He saw that the cab was empty, and decided to teach you a lesson.'

'A lesson? Why?'

'Because he's an Armitage and you're a McBride by association,' Niall said, 'and because I asked him to make a few prank calls so that Fergus or Fiona wouldn't recognise me, and he thought wrecking the cab would scare you more.'

'I see. Who else knew about this?'

'Stacey, his girlfriend. He asked her to make a fake call once.'

The so-called woman stuck in the car park at Loch Armathiel ...

Her heart grew heavy. 'I can't believe you did this to me, Niall, and you drew Kian and Stacey into this stupid scheme of yours.'

Niall hung his head down. 'Kian told me about Duncan's cab this morning. He told me something else too – and it's a lot more serious.'

For some reason, Rosalie already knew what Niall was about to say. 'He was the one chasing after me on the forest road in his father's car the night of the ceilidh, wasn't he? He probably wanted to teach me another lesson for spilling his beer all over him.'

Both Alice and Niall nodded. 'Stacey confessed everything to Kian's dad. She felt awful about lying about the so-called crash Kian made up to explain the dents and scratches on his father's four-by-four. His dad gave him a right good bollocking, then dragged him to the police station to tell the cops. After that he came to the garage to tell me everything and to grovel for me to keep him on.'

He looked at Rosalie, worry in his eyes. 'Now it's my turn to grovel. Do you think you can ever forgive me? Do you think we can still be friends?'

Rosalie swallowed hard. 'I'll have to think about it. For now, I just want to go home. Thanks for the lift.'

Alice let her out, pecked a kiss on her cheek, and Rosalie stood shivering in the courtyard to watch her friends leave. A cold wind blew her hair around her face, sneaked into her anorak. She felt as frozen inside as outside. The kitchen door creaked open behind her. She stiffened, and slowly turned round.

Marc stood in the doorway, projecting a large shadow on the snowy cobbles. He wore his green jumper and jeans. There was a small dressing on the side of his head, and cuts and bruises on his nose and cheekbones.

'I phoned the hospital,' he started, 'and they told me you were on your way. Please come in. It's freezing.'

She shook her head. 'No. I ... I want to go to my flat.'

He frowned and took a step in her direction. 'Rosalie. We need to talk.'

She heaved a deep sigh. She wasn't sure she could bear listening as he explained why he had changed his mind about everything he promised her, or told her their night together had been a mistake, and he wanted to go back to his life, his work, and his glamorous girlfriend.

So she took the coward's way out. 'I'm tired, and I want to be on my own.'

'Of course. I understand. Why don't you stay here tonight? I have made something to eat.' He smiled. 'I bought a chocolate cake too. Flo recommended a brand she said you'd like. I even got whipping cream to go with it.'

Surprise almost made her speechless. 'You saw Flo?' she asked at last.

He nodded. 'I popped over this morning after being discharged. I was one day late for her supermarket trip, so she had run out of crackers and Battenberg cake.'

Anger now tightened inside her. Why was he being so nice? What was he playing at?

'Do you really think chocolate cake and cream would make me forget you're a liar and a coward who sends his girlfriend to do his dirty work?'

She took a deep breath. 'I understand now why your secretary always said you were too busy to take my calls. You didn't have the guts to tell me you'd changed your mind about Love Taxis and the bus company. Well, you may regret sleeping with me,' her voice hitched in her throat, 'but believe me, I wish it hadn't happened either. You're not the man I thought you were.'

She wasn't sure but in the glare of the security lights, he seemed to have become paler. She wasn't feeling any better at all, but desperately sad and horrible and mean.

'Let me walk you up to your flat and make sure you're all right,' he said in a quiet voice. 'It's the least I can do.'

'The least you can do is leave me alone when I ask you to,' she snapped, as she desperately tried to hold back the tears.

She walked to the entrance of her flat, trying to pull out her keys from the pocket of her jeans, but her hand shook too much, and her vision was blurred with tears. She heard footsteps behind her, then felt his warmth against her back. His hand touched her shoulder lightly and she tensed.

'Give me your key. I'll unlock the door for you.'

It was quicker to give in than to argue so she handed him the key. He opened the door. 'If you don't want to talk tonight, then we should talk tomorrow, but it will have to be very early because I have a plane to catch.' He looked down, holding her captive in his serious grey gaze.

Her chest tightened. So he was leaving already. He probably would have left tonight if his damned good manners hadn't nagged at him to make sure she was all right.

'That won't be necessary,' she said. 'We have nothing to talk about.'

'We have plenty to talk about, starting with what happened last night.' This time his voice was sharp and steely.

She started to go up the stairs but turned round. 'Actually, you are right. Let's talk about last night. I'm sorry you got mixed up in my family's sordid affairs. Sorry you had to deal with my thug of a father. In fact, I am more sorry than you'll ever know – and more ashamed than you'll ever know too.'

'What do you have to be ashamed of?'

She swallowed hard. 'I would have thought it was obvious. My father is a criminal.'

'I see.' He sounded infuriatingly calm. 'And what has it got to do with you?'

'He's my father. It has everything to do with me.'

He shook his head. 'Rosalie, your father has done despicable things, that's true, but you do not have to feel ashamed or guilty because of him.'

'How can you say that?' she cried out, her voice choked with emotion. 'I am his daughter. I have his genes, his blood. He is part of me.'

'He always was. The only difference now is that you know who he is – what he is. You are still the same Rosalie, the kind and loyal Rosalie who cares for the people she loves, who would do anything to help out her friends and family. Please don't let Tyler define you.'

He let out a deep sigh. 'I hope you sleep well. If you want to talk, come over in the morning. If you don't ...' He shrugged. 'Then I'll see you when I come back.'

There was something final as he spoke the words, as he closed the door behind him, leaving her alone on the dimly lit staircase.

She was up early the following morning, early enough to watch the sunrise turn the cloudless sky into liquid fire. It had become so cold during the night that thick icicles had formed and now shot down from the eaves like giant ice-lollies.

She made a cup of tea, nibbled on a piece of toast and got dressed. She was brushing her hair when the sound of an engine made her rush to the window, just in time to see Marc drive away in his rental car and disappear down the snowy lane. Where was he going? London, Paris, or some other city where business meetings awaited him?

He said he would be back, she wished he wouldn't. It would be far easier if he stayed away and entrusted Kirsty or another member of his staff with selling up Raventhorn, and she never saw him again. At least then she might forget the sound of his voice, the stormy grey of his eyes, and the feel of his arms around her. This way the raw pain ripping her apart might fade with time.

She slumped on the sofa, cuddled a cushion to her chest and spent the morning crying and feeling sorry for herself. It was the sound of Marion's car backfiring as it bumped up the lane that forced her to go out. She draped her woolly cardigan over her shoulders and went over to the castle. It was time she confronted Irlwick's chief gossip. Perhaps if Marion knew the brutal truth about her mother and Tyler, she would agree to keep certain details to herself and her mother's reputation would be safe.

Marion was in the kitchen pulling her boots off and slipping her feet into her slippers, when she walked in. A frown creased her forehead when she saw her. 'What are you doing up, pet? You should be in bed, resting.'

'I need to talk to you. It's important.'

Marion nodded and pulled out a chair. 'All right, but sit yourself down first. I'll put the kettle on and make us some tea.'

It took over half an hour and two cups of tea for Rosalie to tell Marion her mother's story.

'Poor pet.' Marion patted Rosalie's hand. 'You're afraid I'll open my big mouth and blether to everybody about her, aren't you? Don't you worry. I can keep a secret when I have to. I'll never betray your mum.'

She looked around the kitchen. 'Now, where's Petersen? I want to thank him personally for making my Fergus a very happy man yesterday.'

'What do you mean?'

Marion shook her bright orange hair and beamed a smile. 'I suppose I can tell you.'

'Tell me what?'

Marion laughed. 'Petersen came over yesterday and told us about that minibus company he's setting up with you. He wants Fergus and

Fiona to work in the office. He even asked Fiona to design the logo. He said it will be called the Love Bus in homage to Love Taxis. And it's going to be pink too! He didn't want us to tell anyone before he spoke to you last night. It was hard to keep my mouth shut but I did it, so you see, I can keep secrets when I have to.'

Rosalie felt the blood drain from her face. Was that what Marc wanted to talk about last night when she'd brushed him off? But why then had Kirsty said that he'd changed his mind about the bus company?

'I don't understand. Are you sure he said it was definitely going ahead?'

'Of course, I'm sure.' Marion tutted. 'I'm not likely to get something that important wrong, am I? I must confess that we were a bit cross with you at first, young lady, for not telling us that Petersen owned both this place and Love Taxis in the first place, but he said we shouldn't be too harsh on you because you had a lot on your plate.'

'Oh. Did he say anything else?'

'Only that it would take a few months to get the paperwork sorted and the company up and running, and Love Taxis will carry on serving the community in the meantime. Of course, you'll need to hire a couple of drivers, since Duncan is still in Edinburgh looking after his mum and you're poorly. Petersen said he would be too busy from now on to do any more driving.'

'Oh,' Rosalie said again.

'There's something else.' Marion couldn't keep another smile off her face. 'He's going to help Angus set up his brewery. Isn't that grand?'

She got up and tied her apron behind her back. 'Anyhow, it's time I started work. This place won't clean itself, especially after the mess that Tyler and his cronies made.'

Rosalie nodded absent-mindedly. It was almost too much to take in. Marc was setting up the bus company after all, and he had even decided to help Angus with his microbrewery.

Marion came back into the kitchen holding a can of dusting spray and a cloth and angled her chin towards the window. 'It looks like you have visitors.'

Rosalie glanced out of the window to see a MacKay taxi pull up in the courtyard. Kirsty stepped out, elegant as always in her purple coat, her straight blonde hair smooth and shiny in the pale winter sunlight.

'I'll tell her to sling her hook, shall I?' Marion scowled. 'You're not well enough to deal with that snooty madam.'

'Thank you, Marion, but you can let her in.' Rosalie took a deep breath as Kirsty walked in and cast a surprised look in her direction.

'You're up,' she said.

Rosalie forced a smile. 'I'm not that ill.'

Kirsty arched her perfect eyebrows. 'According to Marc, you're at death's door and your every whim should be indulged.'

'She does need a rest, so you can't stay long,' Marion interrupted, waving her dusting cloth as if to get rid of annoying midges. 'What is it you want?'

Kirsty unbuttoned her coat and sat down opposite Rosalie. 'Believe me, I don't really want to be here but Marc made me.'

'Made you?' Rosalie asked, a little distracted by Marion's energetic dusting of the dresser.

Kirsty's cheeks coloured. 'He asked me to come here and apologise for giving you the impression we were romantically involved. It's not true. We were never lovers, and there were never any plans of us living together, even if we had both moved to the States. I made it all up.'

'I knew it!' Marion put the dusting can down and curled her fists on her hips. 'You were jealous of Roz, weren't you?'

The colour on Kirsty's cheeks deepened.

'What about that photo on the cover of *Newsweek* magazine?' Rosalie asked. 'He was holding you ever so tightly.'

Kirsty sighed. 'I pretended to trip and clung to him, and he was too polite to make a fuss.' She shook her hair and sighed. 'Listen, I'm sorry, all right? I always had a thing for him, always thought we were well matched and should be together. Obviously, I was wrong.'

She rose to her feet. 'There are a few other things I have to tell you as well. It's about Raventhorn. It really doesn't make any business sense whatsoever, but Marc told me this morning that he meant for you to keep living here. He's sending his lawyers instructions to gift the place back to McBride.'

Rosalie's heart did a little flip. 'He's going to give Raventhorn back to Geoff?'

'Yes, and you should hear from his lawyers in the next few days.

Now, I'll leave you to your gloomy castle and terrible weather. The airport has reopened so I can fly back to London, and civilisation.'

'Wait!' Rosalie stood in front of Kirsty. 'Where is Marc? He said he was going away for a few days. Did he go back to London too?'

'No. He went to Denmark.'

Chapter Thirty-Two

'Denmark? What for?'

'He wants to scatter his father's ashes on the beach on the family farm.' Kirsty arched her eyebrows. 'I never thought Marc was the sentimental type. His father's death must have shaken him more than I realised.'

Rosalie bit her lip, and tears welled in her eyes. She'd been so busy trying to avoid a conversation with Marc the night before that she hadn't even told him she was sorry for his loss, or asked about his father's funeral in Hong Kong. How heartless of her.

Kirsty was still talking and Rosalie tried to concentrate on what she was saying. 'Anyway, he won't be coming back – not for a while at least. He said he would go straight to Paris from Denmark, and would liaise by phone and email about the brewery and the bus company.'

A fist crushed Rosalie's heart, tighter and tighter, as Kirsty's words rang in her ears, and she leant against the table for support.

Kirsty looped her handbag around her shoulder. 'There's one last thing. It was my fault you couldn't talk to Marc when you phoned the London offices.'

'What?'

Kirsty looked sheepish. 'I had instructed his secretary to screen his calls and discard any coming from you. I told her you were stalking him.'

'I wasn't!' Rosalie cried out, indignant.

'Look, I said I was sorry, all right? I had no idea he'd get so mad when he found out. I have never seen him look so angry before – except perhaps when he learnt how his father and I had handled a very unfortunate case a few months ago.'

'Are you talking about Van Bernd by any chance?'

Kirsty looked surprised. 'You know about that? Marc was most annoyed to read what a journalist wrote about him. Personally, I can't understand what all the fuss was about – I mean when you're in business, you have to learn to take the bad with the good – but Marc changed after that. He had countless arguments with his father, and now he behaves as if he wants to turn the company into some kind of charity.' She shook her head. 'He is also trying to save other companies against all business sense.'

Rosalie's spirits sank even lower. 'Fitzpatrick ...'

'That's one of them. Marc has invested vast sums of money to help the man save his company, and it caused a massive rift between him and his father. He is even talking about selling up parts of the company. He's changed so much, he seems to have lost his drive and become ... soft.' Kirsty pulled a face, as if she couldn't think of a worse insult.

Rosalie lifted a shaky hand to her throat. What had she done? Marc was doing everything, and more, she'd ever dreamed of, and she had accused him of being cold and callous. If only she could take her harsh words back. He had called her kind and loyal, but she'd been anything but kind and loyal towards him.

In fact she'd always been prepared to think the worst about him. It had never crossed her mind that Kirsty could be lying about his plans or their relationship, or that the article in the magazine could misrepresent the truth. How could she have been so stubborn, so obtuse, so prejudiced?

Outside, the taxi beeped, and Kirsty glanced at the window. 'I have to go or I'll miss my plane.' Kirsty picked up her bag and with a toss of her hair, walked out of the kitchen.

'You have to go to him, lass,' Marion said.

Rosalie nodded. Marion was right. She had to apologise for saying all those mean and hurtful things the night before. She had to tell him how wrong she'd been about him being cold and heartless, and how grateful she was that he was helping Geoff, Lorna and all her friends.

But above all, she couldn't stand the idea of him being on his own when he was scattering his father's ashes on his grandfather's farm at Hantsholm. With tears burning her eyes, she hurried to the library, fired up the computer and searched travel sites.

Fifteen minutes later, she was forced to accept that her only option was to fly, since direct ferry services between the UK and Denmark had been discontinued, and driving through Holland and Germany would take too long.

What should she do? She hated the idea of flying, and had vowed as a child never to set foot on a plane. As far as she was concerned, no exotic holiday, no urgent business had ever been worth the risk. Until now.

Her finger hovered over the keyboard. A warning flashed on the screen that there were only a few seats left on a flight from Edinburgh to Aalborg the following day. She swallowed hard, pushed back the fear, and clicked. After entering her credit card details, she hired a car to travel from Aalborg airport to Hanstholm where the Petersen farm was located, then went back to her flat to pack.

Packing didn't take long. She threw a T-shirt, a jumper, a pair of black corduroy jeans and some underwear into a holdall, squeezed in a few toiletries, and retrieved her passport. She then called the hospital to talk to Geoff. She explained briefly about Marc, he gave her directions to the farm from the airport, and told her the exact address was in a file in the library. A quick glance at her watch told her it was time to leave for the station or she'd miss the Edinburgh train.

Marion gave her a lift to Aviemore.

'Bring him back, lass,' Marion said, a smile creasing her face. 'Tell him to come home.'

The train was packed. Everybody it seemed was going to Edinburgh to do some Christmas shopping. It was several years since she'd been there with Geoff. Her mother was supposed to come with them but she had changed her mind at the last minute, claiming a migraine. Rosalie had been annoyed with her for spoiling their weekend away. Now of course, she understood why her mother rarely left Irlwick and why she shied away from busy places. She must have been terrified of bumping into anyone who might recognise her.

Zipping her anorak up against the cold, she left Waverley Station and stood on the railway bridge to gaze at the giant Ferris wheel and the Christmas market overlooked by the ominous castle perching on a craggy rock.

Twinkling lights may have turned Edinburgh into a fairy-tale town, but there was no joy in her heart as she walked past an old-fashioned carousel, listened to the children's laughter and shrieks of joy rising above the nostalgic organ music, and watched as their parents smiled and waved, and when it started snowing she wasn't sure if it was melted flakes or tears that ran down her face.

She found a chemist shop still open and bought a box of extra strong travel sickness pills then left the festive crowds behind to walk to the

B&B she had booked online. Once in her small bedroom, she made a cup of tea, nibbled at the shortbread biscuits from the hospitality tray, and switched the television on. None of the programmes could hold her attention and she soon walked to the bow window, drew the curtain open and stared at Edinburgh's night sky. All she could see however was Marc – the line of his mouth when he smiled, the shadows dancing in his grey eyes.

She loved him. She loved him so much it hurt, and she yearned to rest her cheek against his chest and listen to his heartbeat.

She only hoped it wasn't too late to tell him.

'Ladies and gentlemen, welcome on board this Lufthansa flight. We hope you will have a pleasant flight and ask that you now switch off all electronic devices for take-off.'

Rosalie's sweaty fingers gripped the armrests more tightly and she closed her eyes. *Please let it be fast, and let everything be okay*, she repeated over and over again. She had dutifully swallowed the travel sickness pill as soon as she'd got up and now hoped for a miracle. If only she could fall asleep now and wake up in Aalborg – having missed the whole ordeal.

She may not have fallen asleep but the flight was mercifully short, and after a moment of heart-stopping panic when the plane took off, she spent most of the time with her eyes tightly shut, taking deep breaths and trying to not to think about being stuck in what was little more than a metal tin high up in the sky. She even managed to drink a cup of tea and munch on a couple of biscuits.

It was early afternoon when she landed at Aalborg. The staff at the car hire counter gave her a road map and directions for the address Geoff had given her. Negotiating the traffic and finding her way whilst driving on the wrong side of the road demanded all her attention, but she soon left the town towards the coast. And towards Marc.

Chapter Thirty-Three

The small wooden house nestled between the sand dunes. With its pointed roof and walls painted a light blue, it looked like a fairy tale cottage – an abandoned fairy tale cottage, by the looks of it. Yet this was where Marc was staying, the man who lived at the Petersen farm with his young family had explained in broken English when she'd visited earlier. Not wishing to impose on his tenants, Marc had rented a holiday cabin nearby.

Rosalie climbed out of her rental car. Shivering in the bitter wind, she walked to the front door to check she had the right number and knocked. Only silence answered.

Now what? Daylight was fading fast. Should she try and find Marc? Should she sit in her car, or drive back to the nearest town a couple of miles down the road, find a hotel and try again in the morning?

Turning away from the cottage, she took in the bleak winter landscape, the huge clouds churning and swirling in the darkening sky, the dunes covered in coarse brown grass that undulated in the wind, and the steel grey line beyond – the North Sea.

It looked like a long walk to the beach, but she started on the narrow path anyway. Her feet sank into the sand, she lost her footing a few times, and had to stop to catch her breath, but at last she reached the end of the lane and caught her first sweeping, uninterrupted view of the beach and the sea.

Several fishing boats had been pulled up on the golden sand. Their masts clanged and rattled in the wind. Waves climbed hungrily onto the beach, leaving white froth behind as they retreated. She narrowed her eyes to peer into the distance but there was no sign of Marc.

Where was he? How naive of her to think that she would find him. Perhaps he had already left.

Unsure of what to do next, she stood on the dune until her face was almost numb with cold. She was about to turn round and go back to the car when somebody walking at the far end of the beach caught her attention. A man, hands in his coat pockets, was striding in her direction. Hope bubbled inside her, making her heart beat faster. Even though he was too far for her to see his face, she knew it was Marc.

She started running down the sand dune, the wind whipping her hair around her face, pushing her forward, and giving her wings.

He stopped and stared at the woman. It was getting dark and she was only a tiny figure in the distance but he caught a glimpse of her pink anorak, of long, curly brown hair. Could it be ...? He shook his head. No, surely not. He was imagining things.

Rosalie didn't know where he was, for a start. He had instructed Kirsty not to tell anybody he was coming here, and even if she had found out, Rosalie was too afraid of flying to travel to Denmark. More importantly, she had made it very plain what she thought of him. She hated him, despised him, didn't want anything to do with him, and he had decided to grant her wish by staying away from Raventhorn.

The woman was still running, and every step she took made his pulse beat more erratically. If it wasn't Rosalie, then it was someone who damned well looked like her. He stood still, not daring to hope.

And when he realised it was indeed her, his body felt too frozen to move.

'I'm so glad I found you.'

Rosalie stopped a few paces away from him. Her cheeks were red, her hair wild, and her soft brown eyes sparkled in the dimming light. She had never looked more beautiful.

He took his hands out of his pockets and let them fall by his sides when all he wanted to do was to touch her, take her in his arms, bury his face in her hair and get drunk on her sweet, delicious, fruity scent.

'Rosalie. What are you doing here?' His voice sounded clipped and cold.

'I wanted to speak to you. I'm so sorry for getting everything wrong.' Breathless, she lifted her hand to push her hair away from her face. 'Marion and Kirsty explained everything. They told me about you setting up Love Bus, and helping Angus with the brewery.' She smiled. 'And most of all, about your signing Raventhorn over to Geoff. I can't believe I misjudged you so much. I wanted to thank you and tell you I was sorry, and very grateful.'

Disappointment crushed his chest, and tightened his throat. So she had only come out of loyalty for her friends. He swallowed hard.

'Don't worry about it. It's no big deal.'

She lifted her hand to his arm. Her touch was warm and soft, almost tender. 'Oh, but it is. I said so many hurtful things you didn't deserve. It's wonderful what you're doing for us all. Geoff will be so happy to be able to stay at Raventhorn. And Lorna too.'

How he wanted to kiss her, crush her lips under his, hold her tightly against him. He remembered only too well how she had felt under him, how soft and silky her skin was, and how wild her sweet, intoxicating kisses had driven him. Their night together would stay with him forever. He had to remember that Rosalie didn't feel the same way, that she'd said it had been a mistake.

He took a step back. 'How did you get here?'

She laughed. 'I flew! Can you believe it? I who always said I would never set foot on a plane.'

He couldn't help but smile. 'Really? And how was it?'

'It wasn't half as bad as I'd feared.'

She moved close to him again. It was torture, to be so close and not be able to hold her – to know she'd never be his again. He looked at the darkening sky. 'It's getting dark. We should go back to the cottage. We'll talk there.'

She nodded and he led the way, setting off at a fast pace in the direction of the cottage.

'Marc, wait,' she called as he started climbing the sand dune. 'I can't go as fast as you.'

'Sorry. Here, take my hand.' It was so cold he was reluctant to let it go when they got to the top of the dune. She must be freezing, and exhausted too after her journey – not to mention she'd only just come out of hospital, having been beaten and abducted by her madman of a father.

When they reached the cottage, he pulled his key out of his pocket, pushed the door open and switched on the lights.

'What a lovely place,' she said as she walked in and looked at the pine-clad walls of the open-plan lounge and kitchen, the deep blue velvet sofa and matching curtains and soft furnishing, and the wood burning stove he had left on before going for a walk.

'It is nice indeed,' he agreed, although he had hardly paid attention to his surroundings since he'd arrived. Finding the cabin had been a stroke of luck but he could have stayed anywhere, as long as it was close to the farm. When he had introduced himself to the family who rented the farm, they had invited him to stay with them, but he hadn't wanted to impose his black mood onto them. What's more, the farm was their home, for now at least.

He shrugged off his coat and draped it over the back of a chair before going to the kitchen area to fill the kettle.

'I'll make us a hot drink. Would you like some tea?'

'Yes, please.' Rosalie seemed about to add something, then bit her lip.

'It won't take long. Please make yourself comfortable.' Did he have to sound so stiff and formal? He could almost see Cédric shake his head and hear him snigger that he'd turned into an iceman all over again.

The silence between them became increasingly strained as he got two cups out of the cupboard and threw a tea bag into a teapot. Rosalie took her anorak off, and he noticed that she was wearing a black jumper with her black cords and boots. It wasn't like her to be dressed in sombre colours from top to toe.

'What's with the black clothes?' he asked.

'I didn't think pink would be appropriate under the circumstances.'

He arched his eyebrows. 'The circumstances?'

'Kirsty told me about your father, and what you came here for. I am sorry. It must have been very hard for you to be on your own at a time like this.'

He closed his eyes for a moment. It had been lonely indeed on that empty, weather-beaten beach that very morning, with the sea roaring in his ears and sadness almost choking him as he said his final goodbyes to the man he had admired more than any other, the man he had so completely misjudged – his father.

'It's kind of you to care,' he said, but once again his tone was cool, almost indifferent. He couldn't help it. It seemed he was reverting back to what he did best – distancing himself from people and feelings. Rosalie was only being kind and thoughtful. She'd be the same with anybody. That was the way she was. What's more, it was obvious she now felt obligated to him – so much so she had braved her fear of flying to thank him in person. Well, he didn't want her thanks, her gratitude or her pity. And he wanted even less her feeling indebted to him.

He handed her a cup of tea and they sat down on the sofa.

285

Putting his own cup down, he leaned forward and rested his elbows on his knees. 'Listen, Rosalie, I appreciate you coming all the way to thank me in person, but it was completely unnecessary. I don't deserve your thanks. I'm doing this for myself and the company, not for you, Angus or McBride, or anyone else in Irwick. Setting up the bus company and the brewery makes good business sense and will turn out to be good advertising for us.' It was a lie of course. He was doing it for her. Only for her.

She heaved a sigh. The light went out of her eyes, as if she was disappointed. His stratagem was working, so why did he feel so annoyed?

Her hand shook as she lifted the cup to her lips. She drank a sip of tea then said, 'Kirsty mentioned you might be selling up your company.'

At least he didn't have to lie about that. 'That's right. I have just accepted an offer from an American firm who've been interested in a merger with us for a long time. I'm selling them all our overseas operations, including the Paris branch, and will only keep our London office.'

The decision had been surprisingly easy to take. In fact, he had realised he'd been mentally ready to sell up for weeks. He just needed the incentive to do so.

'I thought you lived in Paris, and the only reason you came to London was to settle your father's business.'

He shrugged. 'Paris … London … It doesn't really matter where I live. I'm going back to Paris at the end of the week to show the American team around. I suspect I have a busy few months ahead of me, but don't worry, I won't forget about Irlwick, or Raventhorn.' *Or you*, he finished silently.

'I'll delegate one of my best men to set up the bus company and the brewery, and you'll receive all the help you need.'

He took a deep breath. 'As for Raventhorn … well, I have no intention of living there. It would take a long time to sell and I don't want to be lumbered with it. McBride might as well have it back.'

He hoped his dismissive tone would convince her, because once again, he was lying. Raventhorn was the only place he'd felt at home for many years, and he had considered living there permanently, but it was meaningless without Rosalie by his side. After what she'd told him on

286

her return from the hospital, the look of utter dislike she'd directed towards him, he knew there could be only one thing to do – give it back to its rightful owner so that Lorna and Rosalie could stay there. He had been kidding himself to think he could ever belong.

He glanced at the window and the darkening skies and rose to his feet. 'I'll take you to a hotel now. Thorup Strand isn't a big place but we should be able to find somewhere decent for you to spend the night.'

She put her unfinished cup of tea down and got up too. 'There's no need. I'm going straight back to the airport.'

He scowled at her. 'It's completely out of the question. I don't want you to drive alone at night somewhere you don't know, in a country of which you don't even speak the language. You could get lost, have an accident ...'

She snatched her anorak from the sofa. 'I won't get lost, and it doesn't matter what you want. I've been a fool to come here. It was a mistake, a terrible mistake. I thought ... I hoped ... I've been stupid.'

She turned away. She made a strange, strangled sound. Her shoulders were shaking. Was she crying?

He didn't move as she grabbed her handbag, made a dash for the front door, and opened it onto the cold, blustery gale.

The cold breeze jerked him awake from his torpor.

'Rosalie, wait!' He caught up with her in a couple of strides and pushed the front door shut again. 'What mistake?'

She swirled round to face him and looked up. Her eyes shone with tears, her cheeks were wet. She shook her head. 'It's nothing.'

'You're upset, so it clearly is something.'

Her lips quivered as she took a deep breath. 'All I wanted was to be with you. Right, are you happy now?'

He stood still. Not daring to breathe. Not daring to hope. Even his heart felt like it had stopped. 'You said you came to thank me for Raventhorn, the brewery, and the Love Bus company.'

'That too, but I wanted to be here, with you, after you scattered your father's ashes. I thought you might need a friend.' She shook her head and whispered. 'I see now I was wrong. You don't need anybody, and me even less.' She let out a bitter laugh. 'After all who am I but the daughter of a thug?'

She tilted her face towards him, and even though she was crying there was so much light in her eyes it took his breath away. Nobody had ever looked at him like that. With so much warmth. So much … love.

The truth hit him like a blow to the chest. He'd been the stupid one. He hadn't understood anything at all! Rosalie loved him. She'd only pushed him away at Raventhorn because she was hurt and ashamed after meeting her father. She'd believed Kirsty's lies, and thought he had betrayed her.

He lifted his finger to catch a tear as it rolled down her cheek. 'It's not a friend I need,' he said in a low voice. 'It's you. Only you.'

She shivered under his touch. He wrapped his arms tightly around her waist and pulled her against him. Her hands came up to rest on his shoulders, and it felt like she was melting in his arms.

Sliding a hand to the back of her neck, he bent down to kiss her. It was the sweetest kiss he'd ever given, the sweetest kiss he'd ever received. She tasted of the sea, she smelled of the wind and her own sweet, deliciously feminine scent. Rosalie's fingers traced slow patterns at the back of his neck, giving him a jolt of desire. His need for her grew stronger, overwhelming, obscuring any conscious thought.

He pulled her closer, kissed her harder. Suddenly it wasn't a lover's gentle, tender kiss but the kiss of a man staking his claim, taking possession. 'I want you.'

The words came out in a harsh whisper as he kissed the side of her mouth, the fragrant skin of her throat. She threw her head back, her fingers tangled in his hair and she arched towards him in silent surrender.

He needed more. He needed everything. And he needed it now. Feverish, he lifted her jumper, the T-shirt she wore underneath, and touched her bare skin before kissing her mouth again, and again. His hands glided over her back, the sides of her waist, moved to cup her breasts and stroke her through her bra's thin fabric. Her breathing shallow, her heartbeat erratic, she moaned softly as their bodies moved and sought closer contact. He couldn't get enough of kissing her, of touching her. It was torture. It was heaven.

Her clothes were in the way. Impatient, he pulled her sweater up and over her head and threw it on the floor. Her T-shirt soon followed. His throat went dry and his heartbeat increased as he took in her creamy white skin, and the tips of her breasts straining against her bra. She clung to him, stroked the back of his neck, sending electric jolts all over his body as he slid the straps off her shoulders and pulled the bra down. He kissed and touched, teased and aroused with his fingers, his lips, his tongue.

Soon it wasn't enough. Breathing hard, he tore himself from her, and looked down, an unspoken question in his eyes. 'Rosalie.'

'Yes, yes,' she answered in a whisper, her eyes dark. 'Kiss me, hold me, make love to me. Please.'

His heart skipped a beat. 'Is that another of your Happy Baby songs?' He tried to laugh, but his voice was hoarse and his body painfully hard. With a barely repressed growl, he lifted her into his arms and marched across the living room. 'There's no magic bed here, no Crimson Room. And no ghosts.'

'There is no magic bed, and no ghosts, they're just stories,' she replied, her fingers still caressing his neck.

'I'm not so sure about that.' How could he tell her that once or twice he'd had the crazy thought that Isobel had something to do with him falling in lust, and in love with Rosalie – that she'd somehow pushed them together?

'The sofa is fine,' Rosalie added in a breathless voice.

So the sofa it was. The way he was feeling, he doubted whether he could reach the bedroom anyway. He put her down on the blue cushions and she crossed her arms on her bare chest with an endearing modesty that made his heart ache. He couldn't stop gazing at her. Her hair formed a halo of dark curls around her face, a deep pink coloured her cheeks and her mouth was red and full. But it was her eyes that held him, as always. Her deep, beautiful brown eyes. Right now they were dark and stormy, and incredibly arousing.

He kicked his shoes off, dragged his sweater over his head and lowered himself on top of her, almost groaning with pleasure at the contact of her naked skin, at the scent of her body, the soft embrace of her arms around his neck. She was the woman he dreamt of, the woman he craved, the woman he would love for the rest of his life … and he hadn't even told her.

'I love you,' he said in a deep, low voice, before kissing her and pulling the rest of their clothes off.

And when her body cradled him, he pushed inside her, harder and faster until she arched and cried out and their worlds became one.

Chapter Thirty-Four

Raventhorn, end of April

'Lorna, they're here at last! Come and have a look!'

Rosalie swung the front door open and ran down the steps just as three pink minibuses drove up the lane and parked in front of Raventhorn.

'I can't believe it! They're beautiful.' She was so excited she almost skipped around the vehicles.

She'd seen them in the workshop in Dundee before, of course, but today was different. Today was her Love Buses' first day on the road.

She waved at the drivers. Duncan waved back, the others – a middle-aged woman called Aisla, and Duncan's nephew Hamish – cheered and beeped in return. The sound effects made her smile. It was the jingle of her favourite radio station. In a stroke of genius, Marc had approached Happy Baby Radio to ask if they were interested in sponsoring their community bus project. Their answer had been enthusiastic. The radio station had even agreed to sponsor more buses for neighbouring villages, which, like Irlwick, were in dire need of public transport.

'So, what do you think, boss?' Duncan asked, leaning out of the window and waving his cap.

'The buses look wonderful and you're all very smart,' Rosalie replied, bursting with pride as she took in the drivers' dark purple uniform, and the heart logo Fiona had designed. The young woman had also designed the company stationery, posters and all the promotional material.

'I can't believe that from today Love Bus is a reality,' Rosalie remarked when Lorna joined her and the buses tooted again as they left on their respective routes to take their first paying customers.

'You've done well, sweetie,' Lorna said with a smile. 'Who would have thought a few months ago that your taxi operation would lead to this?'

'It's all thanks to Marc. I couldn't have done it without him.'

Lorna shook her head. 'Of course you could have. He may have come up with the investment, but the original idea was yours – all yours.' She looked around. 'Where is he, anyway, that gorgeous husband of yours?'

Rosalie smiled. 'At the loch, with Geoff and the team of divers. They've been there since dawn, ready to try again.'

'They are either very brave ... or completely mad.'

'No, they're determined to find the chest, and they think they know where to look this time. Geoff never imagined Harald's chest might be in the ruined hunting lodge in the loch. It was Marc who suggested looking there. He said he got the idea after he thought he saw a woman in the loch.' She shuddered as she recalled how scared she had been when she'd rescued him from Bran Loch's icy waters.

'Geoff says the woman was Isobel,' Lorna remarked. 'He says she was always appearing in Corby Woods, and around Bran Loch and Armathiel, and enticing men into the water because she wanted them to retrieve Harald's treasure so that her darling husband could find peace at last.'

Rosalie shrugged. 'Whether it's one of Geoff's fantasies or not, I must say I'm excited about the divers fishing the chest out of the loch.'

'I wonder if we'll see Isobel again after today, or if she'll vanish forever,' Lorna said in a dreamy voice. She shook her head. 'I'll prepare flasks of tea and coffee, scones and bacon sandwiches for the men. Can you take them down for me?'

'Of course.'

An hour later Rosalie fetched the basket from the kitchen and made her way to Loch Bran. She could hear the noise of conversations, the clanking of equipment being winched and lowered into the water long before she reached the loch's shores.

'Breakfast is ready!' she announced as she walked onto the pebbly beach.

Half a dozen men, some dressed in jeans and sweaters, others in wetsuits, turned to look at her. Standing head and shoulders above the others, and with the early morning spring sunshine warming his dark blond hair, was the man who made her heart beat faster and her pulse race – the man who made her feel like the luckiest, the most cherished, woman in the world. Her husband.

She still had moments when she couldn't quite believe she was married to Marc, and there were mornings when she woke up next to him in the big bed in the Crimson Room and wondered if he wasn't real and it had all been a wonderful dream.

Whenever that happened she would pick up her wedding album, flick through the pages and gaze at the photos. There were some of the vintage white Rolls Royce Geoff had borrowed from a friend to take her to Irlwick's kirk; of Marc holding her hand after the ceremony, a pink rose pinned on the lapel of his dark blue jacket, to match her flowing pale pink dress; of the magnificent buffet Alice had prepared for the reception at Raventhorn; of the guests dancing, laughing and pulling silly faces, their high spirits no doubt helped by the gallons of champagne, whisky and Angus's finest ale that had flowed freely until the small hours and the saxophone music played by Marc's friend Cédric, who had travelled from Paris with several of his musician friends. There were also photos of her honeymoon in Paris and on the French Riviera where she had got to know Marc's mother, and finally of the beautiful chateau near Bordeaux where they had visited Marc's other childhood friend from his days at boarding school, Luc Peyrac.

No, she thought as she watched Marc walk over from the loch shore, a happy smile on his lips. It wasn't a dream. It was real.

He bent down to kiss her and took the basket from her hands. 'They've located the chest at last. They're bringing it up in the next few minutes.'

'I can't believe that after all these years we're finally about to find out what Harald was carrying,' Geoff said, rubbing his hands together.

'Do you still think it was King Ragnar's raven banner?' Marc asked him.

'We'll soon find out, won't we?' Geoff grinned.

'Whatever it is, there will be no celebratory dram of whisky for you, and certainly no cigar!' Rosalie waved a warning finger at Geoff.

Although he had now recovered from his heart operation, he was still frail and Rosalie and Lorna kept a close eye on him.

'Not even a tiny little one?' he asked with a twinkle of excitement in his blue eyes.

She shook her head. 'No. You can have a cup of tea with a dash of rum and a slice of lemon because it's still a little chilly, that's all.'

'You're too hard on me, Rosalie,' he said with a sigh.

'They're coming out!' Marc walked to the edge of the water as four divers carried a box covered with mud and slime out of the loch.

They put it down on a plastic sheet laid out on the beach.

'I guess it's the moment of truth.' Geoff kneeled down and brushed some of the mud off the cover with a rag before selecting a tool to open the casket. 'I'm not sure how much will be left after so long in the loch or in what condition it'll be.'

Marc wrapped an arm around Rosalie's shoulders and together they stepped closer and bent down to look at the casket. Geoff slid a metal tool carefully along the groove between the casket's lid and its main body, then tried to prise the box open. The lid didn't budge.

'I'm going to need more muscle,' he said after several attempts. He turned round and gestured to Marc. 'Look at the pattern on the lid.'

'They're birds ... ravens.'

'Just like on Harald's shield,' Geoff said.

So this was another link between Marc's family and Harald, Rosalie thought. Marc had taken her on a tour of the Petersen farm one morning during their stay at the beach cottage. It hadn't taken long to find the runestone with the same design as Harald's shield. 'Geoff thinks this proves you are related to Isobel's husband,' Rosalie had told Marc. 'That's why he sold Raventhorn to your father, who he said was very interested in finding Harald's treasure.'

As they were walking back to the cottage Marc had declared that he owed it to his father to fund Geoff's research. True to his word, he had given Geoff carte blanche to hire a team of archaeologists as soon as he'd got out of hospital. He had even indicated that he might have an idea where to find the chest. It looked like he had been proven right, and now Harald's chest stood in front of them.

Marc pushed down on the wrench and the lid snapped open.

'Let me see.' Geoff bent down, pulled out a pair of gloves from his pocket, slapped them on and sifted delicately though the contents of the box.

'There's an awful lot of sediment,' he said. 'If the raven banner was ever here, it has degraded so much there's nothing left. We'll have to take the chest to the university research centre, of course. They'll be able to tell us more. Hang on, it looks like there's something here ...'

His face lit up as he brought the small object out of the box and rubbed the mud off it with a cloth. 'An amulet. Gold, I think.' He held out his hand to show Rosalie and Marc.

'What is it?' Rosalie asked, bending down to take a better look.

'It looks like a raven,' Marc answered.

That night, Rosalie couldn't sleep. Marc was working late, as usual. Even though he had sold off the largest part of Petersen Holdings and appointed Maguire executive manager now that Kirsty had moved to New York with the new firm, he still supervised, monitored and controlled most of the business, and since Geoff had moved into a small cottage on the estate after the wedding, he had turned the library into his own study.

She drew the curtains onto the clear night and stood at the window. The silver moon danced at the centre of the loch's glassy surface. Darker shadows from Corby Woods laced the edges of the water. Not a breath of wind stirred through the trees, not a sound could be heard outside. The night was silent and still. It was as if it was waiting for something.

And yet she felt restless, no doubt because of the excitement of finding the chest and the beautifully carved amulet. The chest had been sent to the university lab straight away but Geoff had decided to keep the amulet and display it in a glass cabinet in the tower room for now. He had been very pleased to get an email late in the afternoon letting him know that there were traces of fibres in the sediment consistent with the presence of a piece of textile. 'It was the raven banner, I'm sure of it!' he had exclaimed.

There was another reason for her unrest – the phone call from Marc's lawyer earlier that evening, announcing the death in prison of Jake Tyler, stabbed to death by an inmate – a Russian suspected to be on Anatoly Bazanov's payroll. The lawyer had explained that even though Bazanov was now on the run, he was powerful enough to take his revenge on Tyler for keeping a record of their past association in the diary. Rosalie's initial reaction – that overwhelming relief at never having to stare into Tyler's cold blue eyes or listen to his voice ever again – had been mingled by shame at being such a coward.

Tyler may be dead, but his actions – and her mother's past – would still come up during Rupert's trial later in the year, since Rupert had been charged with attempted murder and fraud.

Rosalie narrowed her eyes to stare at Loch Bran. Something was moving on the shore. A large black bird. As a piercing shriek resounded in the night, raising goosebumps all over her skin, a disturbing thought crossed her mind. What if Isobel's raven had just called?

The lights flickered, fizzed and popped, and everything went black. Marc put his pen down and got up from behind the desk. It was the first time in months that the lights had gone off. He would need to have a word about it with the electrician who had rewired Raventhorn. First, of course, he would find a torch and go down to the basement.

Somewhere on the ground floor, a door slammed followed by another one.

'Rosalie? Is that you?' he called.

There was no answer. Rosalie had gone to bed hours before and must be asleep by now. But if not Rosalie, then who was banging doors in the castle? Geoff didn't live here any longer, having given Raventhorn to Rosalie as a wedding present, and Lorna never came at night.

What if it was … *Isobel?*

He immediately dismissed the thought as ridiculous and made his way down the corridor in the pitch black.

'Marc! Where are you?' Rosalie called.

'Down here,' he replied. 'Don't worry, I'll fix the lights. Go back to bed.'

'I can't. Listen, it sounds crazy but there's something we need to do.' Rosalie's footsteps resounded down the stairs and a few seconds later she was next to him and put her hand on his arm.

'I took the amulet from the display cabinet. I think we have to take it to the loch.'

He could only make out her silhouette in the darkness. 'What are you talking about? It's the middle of the night.'

'It's important,' she insisted as she followed him down to the kitchen.

He opened a drawer, pulled out a torch and switched it on. 'I'm going to fix the lights and you're going back to bed.'

He saw then that she had slipped a jumper on top of her pyjamas and had trainers on her feet. Ignoring him, she unhooked the key from the rack and unlocked the door. 'No. I'm going out, whether you're coming or not.'

He couldn't leave her on her own. 'All right, then.'

She smiled at him, slipped her arm under his and hugged him tightly. He was tired, the air was cold and sharp, yet there was something magical about being out under the shiny stars in the middle of the night.

'Have you ever wondered about Isobel?' she asked suddenly, breaking the silence.

'Why should I think about her? She doesn't exist.'

That was a lie. He often thought about the hooded woman he'd seen in Corby Woods, on the ruined Armathiel tower, and in the loch. He had even wondered if she wasn't indeed behind Raventhorn's sudden power failures, which caused Rosalie to trip and fall into his arms, or the hot dreams that had tormented him for nights on end.

He shook his head. 'My love, I do understand your passion for mystery and romance, but believe me, there is no Isobel. She and her raven are just a fantasy.'

All was still near the loch. The air, the water, and the woods. Rosalie opened her hand and the amulet glinted in the silver moonlight. She stepped forward, put the amulet on the tree stump that stood on the pebbly beach.

'What are you doing?' he protested. 'You can't leave this here. It's a valuable antique.'

'Geoff will understand. If he is right, Isobel has been looking for Harald's treasure ever since he was shot dead by an arrow. There's nothing left of the raven banner but if she has the raven amulet, she might stop haunting the woods and the lochs.'

She pulled on his hand to drag him away. He shrugged, and followed her. He could always come back early the following morning to get the amulet and put it back in the display cabinet.

'There. They will both be at peace now. Let's go home,' she said, and a warm feeling spread inside him.

It still amazed him that he had found somewhere he could call home. And it amazed him even more that the woman he loved with frightening intensity loved him back.

'Yes, you are right. Let's go home.'

He turned to look at the loch one last time and the words died on his lips. On the loch shore stood a woman. Only it wasn't really a woman. It was a mist, a reflection, a cloud in the shape of a woman. It had to be! A raven flew down silently and hopped on the pebbly shore. Its beady eyes gleamed in the moonlight, and in its beak was the amulet.

* The End *

Thank You

Thank you so much for reading *Little Pink Taxi*. I loved writing Marc and Rosalie's story, and I hope you enjoyed spending some time with them and their friends in Raventhorn and the little Scottish village of Irlwick.

If you did enjoy the story, then I would be very grateful if you could take a few minutes to leave a review on Amazon, Goodreads or your reviewing platform of choice. It is a wonderful feeling for an author when readers let you know that they loved your story and your characters. Reviews are invaluable, not only to raise a book's profile, but also to encourage the author to keep writing, especially when self-doubt creeps in.

Love Marie
X

About the Author

Originally from Lyon in France, Marie now lives in Lancashire and writes historical and contemporary romance. Best-selling *Little Pink Taxi* was her debut romantic comedy novel with Choc Lit. *A Paris Fairy Tale* was published in July 2019, followed by *Bluebell's Christmas Magic* in November 2019 and bestselling romantic suspense *Escape to the Little Chateau* which was shortlisted for the 2021 RNA Jackie Collins Romantic Suspense Award. She also writes short stories for the bestselling Miss Moonshine anthologies, and is a member of the Romantic Novelists Association and the Society of Authors.

For more information on Marie visit:

www.twitter.com/MarieLaval1
www.facebook.com/marielavalauthor

More Choc Lit
from
Marie Laval

A Paris Fairy Tale

Is Paris the city of happily ever afters?

Workaholic art historian Aurora Black doesn't have time for fairy tales or Prince Charmings, even in the most romantic city in the world. She has recently been hired by a Parisian auction house for a job that could make or break her career. Unfortunately, daredevil journalist Cédric Castel seems intent on disrupting Aurora's routine.

As Aurora and Cédric embark on a journey across France, they get more than they bargained for as they find themselves battling rogue antiques dealers and personal demons, not to mention a growing attraction to each other.

But with the help of a fairy godmother or two, could they both find their happily ever afters?

Visit www.choc-lit.com for more details.

Bluebell's Christmas Magic

A flick of a feather duster and a sprinkle of Christmas magic ...

Cassie Bell is used to mess. Her cleaning business, Bluebell Cleaning, is well known in the Cumbrian village of Red Moss. However, now it's almost Christmas and Cassie has a slightly messier situation to deal with than she's used to.

She's been hired to help Stefan Lambert, an injured army helicopter pilot who's staying at the local Belthorn Manor whilst he recovers. Stefan resents Cassie's interference and is definitely not looking for Christmas cheer. But Cassie prides herself on sparkling surfaces – so, can she bring some festive sparkle to Stefan's life too?

Visit www.choc-lit.com for more details.

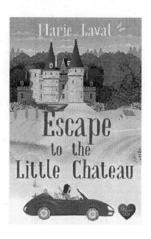

Escape to the Little Chateau

Will Amy's dreams of a Provençal escape come true?

There are many reasons Amy Carter is determined to make Bellefontaine, her farmhouse hotel in the French countryside, a success. Of course, there's the time and money she's put in to making it beautiful, but she also has something to prove – particularly to people like Fabien Coste.

Fabien is the owner of the nearby château, and he might just be the most arrogant, patronising man Amy has ever met ... unfortunately, he's also the most handsome.

But as rumours circulate in the local community and secrets about the old farmhouse begin to reveal themselves, Amy quickly sees the less idyllic side of life at Bellefontaine. Could Fabien be the man to help prevent her Provençal dream from turning into a nightmare?

Visit www.choc-lit.com for more details.

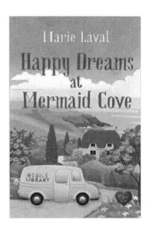

Happy Dreams at Mermaid Cove

From the big city to a little yellow mobile library on the Isle of Skye ...

When Jenna Palmer agrees to the new position of mobile librarian on the tiny Arrandale peninsular of the Isle of Skye, she knows she's signing up for difficult working conditions and mediocre wages. But Jenna needs to get away, and a little yellow mobile library called Buttercup could be her escape to happier dreams ...

However, whilst Jenna can get to grips with foggy island roads, local mermaid legends and even big purple monsters, she never expected to have to contend with a boss as grumpy as Daniel McGregor, or a young book lover as enthusiastic as his niece, Katrina.

Arrandale might represent Jenna's safe port in a storm, but could she and Buttercup also become a beacon of hope to Daniel, Katrina and the entire island community?

Visit www.choc-lit.com for more details.

Angel of the Lost Treasure
Linked to Queen of the Desert

An ancient secret hidden within a mother's song ...

When young widow, Marie-Ange Norton is invited to Beauregard in France by the mysterious Monsieur Malleval to collect an inheritance, she has no choice but to accept.

But when she embarks on the voyage with her fiery-tempered travelling companion Capitaine Hugo Saintclair, little does she know what waits for her across the sea in turbulent nineteenth-century France on the eve of Napoleon's return from exile. When she arrives, she is taken aback by Malleval's fascination with her family – seemingly inspired by his belief they are connected to a sacred relic he's read about in coded manuscripts by the Knights Templar.

As it becomes clear that Malleval's obsession has driven him to madness, Marie-Ange is horrified to realise she is more the man's prisoner than his guest. Not only that, but Hugo is the only person who might be able to help her, and he could represent a different kind of danger ...

Visit www.choc-lit.com for more details.

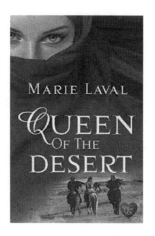

Queen of the Desert
Linked to Angel of the Lost Treasure

Sometimes the most precious treasures exist in the most barren and inhospitable of places ...

Harriet Montague is definitely too much of a gentlewoman to be frequenting the backstreet taverns of Algiers. But her father has been kidnapped whilst on an expedition to the tomb of an ancient desert queen, and she's on a mission to find the only person who could save him.

It's just unfortunate that Lucas Saintclair, the man Harriet hopes will rescue her father from scoundrels, is the biggest scoundrel of the lot. With a bribe in the form of a legendary pirate treasure map, securing his services is the easiest part – now Harriet must endure a treacherous journey through the desert accompanied by Saintclair's band of ruffians.

But on the long, hot Saharan nights, is it any wonder that her heart begins to thaw towards her guide – especially when she realises Lucas's roguish façade conceals something she could never have expected?

Visit www.choc-lit.com for more details.

Introducing Choc Lit

We are an award winning independent publisher creating a delicious selection of fiction.
Quality stories with a romance at the heart.
See our selection here:
www.choc-lit.com
We would love to hear how you enjoyed *Little Pink Taxi*. Please leave a review on the eBook store where you purchased this novel or visit **www.choc-lit.com** and give your feedback.

Choc Lit novels are selected by genuine readers like yourself. We only publish stories our Tasting Panel want to see in print. Our reviews and awards speak for themselves.

**Could you be a Star Selector
and join our Tasting Panel?**
Would you like to play a role in choosing which novels we decide to publish? Do you enjoy reading women's fiction? Then you could be perfect for our Tasting Panel.
Visit here for more details:
www.choc-lit.com/join-the-choc-lit-tasting-panel

Keep in touch:
Sign up for our newsletter for all the latest news and offers:
www.spread.choc-lit.com.

Follow us on:
Twitter: **@ChocLituk**
Facebook: **Choc Lit**
Instagram: **ChocLituk**

Where heroes are like chocolate – irresistible!

Printed in Great Britain
by Amazon

35362747R00175